Then it struck Pita. She'd had to tip her head back to look at Yao. He should have been shorter than that. And some of the things he said had been odd. And the body language had been all wrong.

Pita glanced nervously at the man beside her. This wasn't her friend Yao.

She didn't want to find out who it really was. Ducking out from under his hand, she bolted for the top of the stairs, back toward the main entrance of the KKRU building. But before she'd taken two steps, the imposter barked out a sentence in a foreign, lilting language. Suddenly Pita was running in midair. She struggled wildly, trying to make contact with the ground. But the stairs were a good half meter under her feet. She twisted about—just in time to see the man who'd been posing as Yao shed his skin in a shimmering transformation. Clothes, hair, features—all blurred and changed. The man was suddenly thinner, darker. With a shock Pita recognized the elf who'd tried to cast a spell upon her earlier. The mage! Like a fool, she'd fallen into his trap. Pita cried out, but even as she did, a bolt of yellow streaked from the elf's fingers toward her, enveloping her. Pita's eyes closed and she fell forward into darkness. . . .

SHADOWRUN

THE LUCIFER DECK

Lisa Smedman

A ROC BOOK

ROC
Published by the Penguin Group
Penguin Books USA Inc., 375 Hudson Street,
New York, New York 10014, U.S.A.
Penguin Books Ltd, 27 Wrights Lane,
London W8 5TZ, England
Penguin Books Australia Ltd,
Ringwood, Victoria, Australia
Penguin Books Canada Ltd, 10 Alcorn Avenue,
Toronto, Ontario, Canada M4V 3B2
Penguin Books (N.Z.) Ltd, 182-190 Wairau Road,
Auckland 10, New Zealand

Penguin Books Ltd, Registered Offices:
Harmondsworth, Middlesex, England

First published by Roc, an imprint of Dutton Signet,
a division of Penguin Books USA Inc.

First Printing, January, 1997
10 9 8 7 6 5 4 3 2

Series Editor: Donna Ippolito
Cover: Carl Gallian

 REGISTERED TRADEMARK—MARCA REGISTRADA

SHADOWRUN, FASA, and the distinctive SHADOWRUN and FASA logos are
registered trademarks of the FASA Corporation, 1100 W. Cermak, Suite B305,
Chicago, IL 60608.

Printed in the United States of America

Many thanks to the members of the B.C. Science
Fiction Assn. writers workshop, whose advice
and careful critiquing helped make
this book possible.

1

"Pita! Hoi, chummer, have you made the patch?"

Pita lay on her back, screwdriver clamped between her oversized teeth. The service shaft was narrow, just wide enough to accommodate her broad shoulders. She'd had to strip off her jacket and worm her way in, her arms stretched out ahead of her. Now she shivered in the cold.

Working by the light of a cheap Brightlight rip-off with a rapidly depleting power cell, she pried open the protective plastic covering the trideo cables. Feeling along one of them, she located the splitter that branched the cable off to individual apartments. Then she smiled as her blunt finger found a free port.

"Hoi, Pita!" One of the other kids kicked her feet, the only part of her that remained outside the service shaft. "Is this going to take all night?"

"Yeah, yeah. Nearly there," she growled back. She popped one end of the cable feed into the port and then plugged the other end into Chen's electrode net. "I gotta test it, first."

The trode net was the poor person's version of a datajack—a means of translating raw electronic data into a multi-sensory experience without the need for expensive cybernetic implants. She snugged the headset's electrodes around her temples, closed her eyes, and broke into a wide grin as an image sparkled to life behind her closed eyelids. The upper-right corner was a mess of white static, probably due to the worn cladding of the fiber-optic cable she'd used to patch in. She should have boosted a new cable from the local Tridio Shack outlet, but for now, this dumpster-diver's special would have to do. At least the rest of the image was sharp.

She'd tapped into an infomercial for the Yamaha Rapier. The sleek, wasplike body of the motorcycle burst out of a shower of chrome confetti and screamed past on a strobelit highway that looped across the flame-filled sky. "Ride the wind. Feel the fire. The '54 Rapier. Just ten thousand nuyen."

Pita snorted and winked to change channels. Ten thousand nuyen? Not in ten of her lifetimes.

She skipped over a nostalgia rock channel and then past *Name That Logo*, a game show in which children from the Aztechnology arcology competed with each other for expensive simulator sets. The first station catered to sludge-minds who'd been born before the millennium and the game show was kid stuff. At seventeen, Pita was too old for that drek. She curled her lip as she caught a few seconds of a rerun of a speech by Governor Schultz, in which he promised to clean up Seattle's streets. Didn't she know that some people had to boost the odd package of Soygrits, just to get by?

She flipped past a Salish-language station and devoted a few seconds to an advertorial by the Church of Sorcerology. "Is your child among the one per cent of the population with natural magical ability?" an overly enthusiastic announcer asked. "In this Awakened world of 2054, can you really afford to let your child's magical abilities slumber? Our free stress test can reveal your child's hidden talents. Just call our office at—" Pita changed channels.

Her attention was caught by a local newscast. A snoop who looked vaguely Native American was jamming on about another brain-bashing by the local chapter of Humanis Policlub. The trid zoomed in on an ork, a little younger than Pita, whose head had been laid open like a smashed fruit. Then it panned down to the globular red spillage on the boy's shoulder and the letters scrawled on his chest: "One meta-freak down. Half a billion to go."

Pita tore the 'trode rig away from her temples and fought to keep from heaving. Simsense made everything seem so real. So close. She could practically reach out and touch the spilled brains, could smell the blood that had soaked his shirt. The bashing had taken place just a few kilometers from here, in Seattle's downtown core. Like the boy who had died, Pita was an ork too. What happened to him could have happened to her.

The aural trode was still in contact with her scalp. A tinny voice squawked in her right ear as she held the goggles in her hand: "KKRU Trideo. The station that puts 'U' in the picture."

Pita thumbed the headset off and called back over her shoulder. "Hoi, Chen. I've got a patch! Now all we gotta do is scan for the broadcast. What channel do you think they'll tap into this time?" Funny. It was awfully quiet out there. Then she noticed the flashing blue light.

Something wrapped tightly around one ankle. Before Pita could even shout in alarm, she was hauled roughly out of the service shaft. The fiber-optic cable pulled taut, then popped from the port. Then she was out on the sidewalk, her elbows scraped and hurting like drek, staring up into the barrel of an automatic rifle. The Lone Star cop behind it didn't look happy. Behind him, a blue light flashed in regular circles on the roof of a patrol car. Lone Star was the private corporation hired to provide Seattle with police services.

Pita's three friends had assumed the position against the apartment block's wall and were being patted down none too gently by a second Lone Star officer, this one female. Pita glanced down at her chest where the red dot of the rifle's sighting laser was targeted and groaned. They were in some serious drek now.

"What's that in your hands, kid?" the cop behind the rifle asked. "A stolen simsense unit?" His chromed cyber eye whirred softly as he scanned her face.

Chen, the oldest of Pita's three friends, turned his head away from the wall. "It's not stolen," he gritted through oversized teeth. "My brother gave it to me so I could watch his broadcasts. He's a—"

The cop behind Chen kicked savagely at his ankle and Chen collapsed, gasping in pain.

"Nobody asked you, porkie," the cop hissed. "Keep talking, and you're only going to get iced. Now get back into line."

Stun-stick in hand, the Star watched as Chen climbed painfully back to his feet. Even though he was just seventeen, Chen was twice the size of the cop. Unlike Pita, who had only goblinized two years before, Chen had been born an ork, and had the broad shoulders and huge hands to prove it. Yet he also had the laser-straight black hair, flat face and eye folds of his Asian ancestors. Aside from his bulk and jutting canines, he looked almost human. Pita, on the other hand, had a face as coarse and ugly as any true-born ork. No wonder the cop glared at her. She tried in vain to close her lips over her snaggled teeth.

The cop above her plucked the 'trode rig from Pita's grasp. He turned it over, inspecting it. "Frag it, Doyle, this is old tech. Nobody in their right mind would boost it. The kid probably lifted the unit out of a trash 'pacter. You really want to waste time inputting a report for this crud?"

The female officer stepped back from Chen and the two smaller orks, still keeping her stun stick aimed at Chen's back. Then she shook her head. "Not really. Trash it."

The cop standing beside Pita dropped the headset on the cement, raised his booted foot, and slammed it down hard. Metal and plastic splintered and circuits crunched, leaving a shattered mess. After wiping the heel of his boot against the pavement, the cop stepped back. The thin red line of his weapon's sighting laser winked out. "Get up, boy."

Pita cringed. Was she really so ugly that they couldn't tell she was a girl? She felt even worse when she saw the look on Chen's face. His eyes were locked on the broken goggles. Behind him, the two younger orks, Shaz and Mohan, looked stunned. Like Pita, they'd never seen Chen cry before.

Pita rose to her feet, shaking, as the cops backed into

the shadow of their patrol car. The first cop still held his weapon ready, but it was no longer trained on them. While the female officer clicked her teeth, activating her radio headware to call building maintenance, he jerked his head to one side. "Scatter," he told the orks.

"Disappear."

They did.

Twelve blocks later, puffing from their run, Pita and her friends slowed. Chen had been running with a peculiar hop-step, and now he settled into a limp.

"Fragging goons," he panted, surreptitiously wiping the last of the tears from his cheeks.

Shaz and Mohan walked a pace behind him. They were brothers, twelve and thirteen years old. They'd only been on the streets a year, and looked to Chen, with his six years of city smarts, for leadership. They had shaved their heads, thinking it would make them look tougher, and wore matching black T-shirts emblazoned with the grinning face of the ork rocker and go-gang leader who fronted Meta Madness. The group's logo was stitched across the T-shirts in silver wire.

"Yao gave me that headset," Chen muttered. "He said I wouldn't be able to talk to him once he went underground, but that I could use it to watch his broadcasts. Now I won't even be able to see him on trideo."

"I know." Pita untied her black synth-leather jacket from around her waist and tugged it on over her sleeveless flannel shirt. Her threadbare sneaks, cheap like everything else that came out of the Confederated American States, scuffed the sidewalk. Knobby knees poked out of the holes in her jeans as she walked. "At least you know he cares about you. My sister never even . . ."

Chen jerked to a halt. He turned toward Pita. "I'm sorry." Wrapping his massive arms around her shoulders, he hugged her close. She felt Shaz and Mohan touch her back with gentle fingers.

Bitterness gnawed at her with sharp teeth as her mind flew back to when she'd first begun to goblinize. She'd hidden it from her family for a week, mumbling into her hand to conceal her expanding canines and wearing baggy clothes to hide her sudden growth. Then her sister had caught her in the bathroom, shaving the curly brown hair that had started to sprout from her shoulders. The next day, Pita came home from school to find the front door locked and her clothes jumbled into foamboard boxes on the lawn. Her old clothes. They'd saved the good ones for her sister.

She'd wound up in downtown Seattle without a cred-stick. Like so many kids before her, she decided to sell the only thing she had. Herself. She hadn't been pre-pared for the jeers, the mocking laughter. Fleeing down an alley, she'd run head-first into Chen, knocking him flat on his ass on a broken bottle. Later, she'd discov-ered the blood on the seat of his pants. And found out why he gave her the nickname Pita. From that day on she answered only to it, instead of to Patti, the name her parents had given her.

Now he tipped her head back and kissed her cheek. "Hey, there, Pain In The Ass. Null perspiration. We still got each other, don't we? That material drek is just stuff, eh?"

"Just stuff," Mohan echoed.

Beside him, Shaz was making a low, throaty grumble. "Fragging goons," he growled, his voice cracking. "Why can't they leave us alone?"

Just up the street, a patrol car was rounding the corner. Its blue light washed the buildings in rapid sweeps, chasing the shadows from the streets. A voice crackled out over a loudspeaker. "This is Lone Star Security. Freeze."

"Leave us alone!" Shaz shouted. Suddenly stooping, he scooped up a broken piece of concrete and hurled it at the patrol car. It bounced harmlessly off the armor plating with a dull thunk. The car braked to a screech-ing halt, and the front port slid open. The dark tube of a gun barrel poked through.

"Frag it!" Pita yelled. "Run!"

Chen was still turning to look at the car when the first of the shots ripped the night. Pita had barely begun to run when she heard the wet meaty sound of bullets hitting flesh. Chen grunted in pain.

"Run!" Shaz screamed.

Behind her, Pita heard another burst of gunfire. Mohan groaned, and then Shaz began to scream. "Mohan, get up! Get up, frag you! Get—"

The automatic weapon opened up a third time, just as Pita reached the corner. A spray of concrete dusted her jacket as she rounded it. Gulping back sobs, she pounded down the block. Somewhere behind her, she heard an engine rev and the squeal of tires. Lone Star Security was going to make sure there weren't any witnesses.

Pita rounded another corner, feet skidding to find purchase on the pitted sidewalk. The blue flash of the patrol car's lights washed her shoulder as she leaped into the shadows. Feet pounding, eyes blurry with tears, she gulped in great lungfuls of air and ran as hard as she could. Around another corner. Over a parked car and across an intersection. Down a side street. And at last into an alley. Spotting a rusted fire escape ladder she leaped, caught the bottom rung. The ladder creaked in a slow descent and she scrambled up it, hand over hand. She could hear the patrol car getting closer, coming down the side street.

With a shrieking groan, the ladder gave way. Suddenly Pita found herself tumbling. She grabbed for a handhold, missed—and fell into an open dumpster. Squishy bags of garbage broke her fall and a rank smell filled her nostrils. The ladder clattered to the ground beside it. She was just about to scramble out when she saw a blue flicker on the dumpster's open lid. Deciding to stay put, she eased bags of garbage on top of her, burrowing deeper into the pile.

A bright light swept across the alley, searching its shadows like a sniffing dog. Pita heard the thud of a car door, the footsteps of an approaching cop. She crouched rigid as death, trying not to breathe. *Please*, she begged whatever fates would listen. *Don't let him find me. Don't let him see me.* Her ragged breathing seemed to echo loud inside the dumpster, giving her away. She heard the footsteps approach, saw a flashlight beam linger on the open lid of the dumpster. She closed her eyes, focusing every effort of her will on becoming motionless, on becoming invisible. It was too late now to move, to worry about whether the trash covered her completely. She heard the faint rasp of the cop's gloved hand on the lip of the dumpster, saw a flash of light sweep across her closed eyelids. Any second now, the cop would point his gun and . . .

No. She forced the image out of her mind. *He doesn't see me,* she chanted, over and over like a mantra. *He doesn't see me.*

The flashlight beam swept away, leaving her in darkness. Pita heard footsteps departing and the slam of a car door, then the soft purr of the patrol car's engine as it motored slowly up the street. Relief flooded over her in a cold, shivering rush. She wasn't sure who to thank for protecting her, but someone or something must have been listening.

At last she allowed herself to cry. Shaz, Mohan, Chen. She hadn't seen them go down, but what she'd heard behind her as she ran from the cops hadn't sounded good. Instead of trying to help them, she'd run away. Turned her back on her friends and bolted. Her stomach clenched with guilt. Gnawing her lip until she tasted blood, Pita at last heaved herself out of the dumpster and jogged cautiously back in the direction of her friends.

2

Carla leaned over the shoulder of Wayne, the on-line editor, watching as the letters on the trideo monitor did a slow reveal: "H . . . U . . . M . . ." Gradually they spelled out Humanis Policlub, then turned from black to silver and oozed bright drops of red. Behind them, a man's face resolved itself. His forehead was puckered into an angry frown, and his white teeth gleamed in a feral smile against his dark skin. His hair was neatly clipped, his face clean-shaven.

"Special rights for metahumans?" The man's nose flared. "I'd sooner give special rights to a ghoul. They're animals. Subhuman. Oh, I know, some say that metahumanity was always part of the gene pool. But that's nonsense. It's bad magic at work. These people have impure thought processes. That's why they goblinize when they hit puberty."

Wayne shook his head and keyed in an edit command. "This guy's argument isn't even logical. What about the kids who are born meta? Babies with 'impure thoughts'? Gimme a break."

Behind him, Carla laughed. "The public doesn't want logic," she answered. "Just infotainment."

The screen dissolved to a close-up of Carla's face. The on-screen image asked a question: "And what does the Humanis Policlub advocate as the solution to the 'problem' of metahumans? More brain-bashings?"

Wayne's fingers flicked across the keyboard, pulling in a series of one-second clips of some of the recent bash victims. Then he froze the screen.

Carla studied it a moment. "Toss in the 'bash back' quote from the Orc Rights Committee piece we aired yesterday, and wrap the piece up with a five-second clip of the Los Angeles Meta Madness concert. The part where the lead singer leans into the lens and spits on it, then screams, 'Frag the securi-goons. Madness must rule.' That ought to stir something up."

Wayne looked uneasily over his shoulder. "You sure you want to do that?"

Carla smiled. "The only way I'll ever get noticed by the majors is if I get down 'n' dirty and prove I can muckrake with the best of them."

As her editor worked, she watched her image on the second monitor. Long black hair pulled back in a single braid, dark hungry eyes. The right eye tracked a fraction of a second faster than the left; hidden behind its iris was a miniaturized cyberoptic camera. Subdermal fiber-optic cables one-tenth the diameter of a human hair carried the images it recorded to a data display link implanted behind her right ear, next to an audio recorder. A datajack just below it had allowed her to download the images that Wayne was manipulating. The shots of herself, repeating the questions she'd asked earlier, had been mixed in later.

Two years after her surgery, Carla was still getting used to her new face. Wider cheekbones, a slightly flared nose, and melanin boosting had shaped her into a passable replica of an Indian. The Native American Broadcasting System actively denied any racial bias in its hiring practices, but one look at its anchors told the story. Someday soon, Carla hoped to leave KKRU's nuyen-pinching behind and move up to NABS. Their producer had promised her a slot if she could demonstrate to him that she had what it took to "play hardball with the big boys." By that, he'd meant the ability to do tough, investigative pieces—the kind that probed deep into the dark underbelly of the corporate beast. "Show me something worthy of NABS, and I'll give serious consideration to your application," he'd said.

Carla was determined to do just that. And soon. Her exclusive interview with the leader of the local Humanis Policlub chapter was a good start. But it would take a bigger story than that to prove herself.

On the trideo screen, the Humanis Policlub leader was droning on. "We do not advocate violence." He favored the camera with a sickly smile. "Just segregation. Metahumans belong with their own kind. They're not happy in the general society. Those of us of pure stock make them feel inferior. And we don't want them mixing with us. Can you imagine one of those rabid, hulking orks, dating your daughter?" His mouth curled as if he'd eaten a spoonful of warm drek. "Or your son? Do you really want a goblinized grandchild?"

"And cut," Carla said, stabbing a finger against the on-screen menu. "Add a clip of those three ork kids that were bashed the other night, and fade with some Meta Madness music. Then patch in my usual sign-off and the station call letters and it's a wrap."

Stretching, she looked around the editing booth. Someone was tapping on the glass window. Opening the door beside it, Carla stepped out into the studio. "Yes?"

Masaki, one of the other reporters, jerked a thumb at the monitors that lined one end of the newsroom. One of the screens showed a view of the front entrance of the KKRU building. A young ork sat on one of the synthleather lobby chairs, hands clenching the fabric of his jeans. The kid's eyes darted nervously around the room.

"Some ork kid claims to have a hot story. Won't talk to anyone but Carla Harris, 'ace snoop' for KKRU Trideo News."

Carla stifled a yawn. It had been a long shift, with three hours' overtime. "Did he say what it was about?"

"She." Masaki shrugged. He was overweight, and spoke with a wheezy voice. A graying mustache and beard framed his soft mouth, but his cheeks were clean-shaven. "The kid muttered something about your series on Humanis Policlub. When I pushed for more, she froze up. Hard to tell if she's got anything worth saying. But there might be something there."

Carla snorted. "Trying to steal my story, eh, Masaki?"

He grinned at her. "Can't blame a snoop for trying."

Carla walked down the hall toward the lobby. Pausing before the reception area's tinted door, she put her cybereye in record mode. The kid was probably just another streeter, vying for her fifteen seconds of fame. But it didn't hurt to shoot a little trid, just in case.

"Hi, kid." Carla crossed the room with smooth, graceful strides, intending to settle on the chair beside the ork. But halfway across she caught the odor that clung to the kid. Had the girl been sleeping in a trash heap? Wrinkling her nose, Carla chose a chair a couple of meters away. Her cybereye whirred as it telephotoed in on a tight head shot, then automatically focused.

The girl visibly started at the greeting. Synthleather creaked as she leaned forward, resting on the very edge of her seat. The toes of her sneakers were poised on the polished tiles of the floor as if she were a sprinter preparing to run. Carla leaned forward in her best reassuring pose. "You got a story for me, kid?"

The ork wet her lips and glanced up at the videocam that monitored the lobby. "Not here," she whispered.

"Before I'll let you in the studio, you're gonna have to convince me you've got something," Carla prompted.

While the ork chewed her lip, trying to decide whether or not to talk, Carla let her camera pan the girl. It was hard to tell how old these ork kids were. They bulked up quicker than normal children. Carla guessed the girl was in her mid-teens. A street waif, by the look of her torn clothes. And by the smell of her. Carla half rose, as if tired of waiting.

"Wait!" The girl cracked her knuckles with nervous twists of her hands. Carla groaned inwardly. If the interview really cooked, she'd have to edit the noise out later.

"That story you did, on the three orks that died." The girl's lip quivered for a moment as she sucked in a deep breath. "Those were my friends."

"Sorry to hear that, Miz—"

"Pa . . . Pita." The girl answered.

"No last name?"

Pita shook her head.

"And you want to make a comment on their deaths?" The girl nodded.

"Sorry," Carla answered. "Old news. They died two nights ago. We gave it a thirty-second spot. Quite a long piece, considering the fact that it was the tenth Humanis Policlub bashing this year. Only the fact that their blood was used to paint the slogans made it newsworthy at all."

The girl's face suddenly paled. Carla sighed and hoped the kid wasn't going to heave on the floor. Maybe she shouldn't have been so blunt. But then, news was a hard-ass business.

Carla nearly missed the girl's whisper as she walked back to the door. Only the amplified hearing mod in her right ear picked it up.

"Humanis Policlub didn't kill my friends. Lone Star Security did."

"What?" Carla spun around, cursing herself for not getting it on trideo. "You got proof of that, kid?"

The ork met Carla's eyes for a fleeting second, then dropped her gaze back to the floor. "I saw the whole thing. They were shot from a Lone Star patrol car. The cops tried to scrag me, too, but I ran away. Later I came back and saw . . . and saw . . ."

Tears spilled down the girl's cheeks. Carla crouched low, giving her cybercam a better angle. She did a slow zoom until the girl's face filled the eye's field of view, let it linger there for a full three seconds, then pulled back to frame a head-and-shoulders shot.

"My friends were already dead, but the cops were cutting the bodies with machetes," Pita whispered. "Then they used their blood to paint the slogans on the walls."

"The autopsy didn't find any bullet fragments in the bodies," Carla pointed out. "The pathologist said the wounds were consistent with an attack by edged weapons. I trust my sources. If there'd been anything unusual, I'd have heard about it."

"But there must have been bullet holes in the buildings where it happened." The girl looked up hopefully. "That would prove—"

"It proves nothing, kid." Carla resisted the urge to shake her head. She kept the eyecam locked on the girl, waiting for any reaction. "Columbia's a rough part of Seattle. Every building in it has its share of scars, many of them carved out by Lone Star guns."

"One of the cops had a cyber hand. If you could find him, you could—"

"Cybernetic enhancements are pretty common among cops," Carla countered. "There must be dozens of officers with cyberhands."

"I know it was cybernetic, because it gleamed like chrome," Pita continued. "I couldn't see the cop's face, but I could see that."

"A chrome cyberhand?" Carla asked. "It sounds like you got that one out of a comic vid. What you saw was probably an interface on the cop's glove that caught and reflected the light."

The girl winced, then stared up at Carla with angry eyes. "I'm not making this up."

"I never said you were, kid."

Carla sighed and deactivated her cybercam. "You tell a very passionate story, Pita, but the Star could refute every word you've told me. You've got no concrete proof to back you up. No firm details. And without proof, I haven't got a news story."

The ork girl dropped her eyes, her shoulders hunching in a defensive slump. Carla keyed her security code and opened the door that led back to the studio. She paused on the threshold, debating whether to offer the kid a few words of reassurance. She'd seen the bodies after the Policlub was through with them. If those were really the girl's friends . . .

But when Carla turned back again, the lobby was empty.

3

Pita sat in an alley in the shadow of a rotted-out chesterfield. She'd tried sleeping on it the night before, but the
springs had dug into her back. Now she leaned against
its padded arm, ignoring the musty smell of moldy
fabric. She took a bite of a Sweetnut Puff and washed it
down with some steaming soykaf. The doughy pastry
made her teeth ache, so she tossed it aside. Then she
dug inside her pocket.

The alley was only faintly illuminated by the sodium
light up the street. Tilting her hand to catch its dim
yellow glow, Pita looked at the capsules that lay on her
palm. Three pale white ovals that promised an end to the
flip-flops that wrenched her stomach and the nightmares
that plagued her sleep. They'd cost her plenty—an
unpleasant favor for the off-duty DocWagon attendant
she'd met at the local bar. She grimaced, still feeling his
sloppy kisses on her shoulders and neck. It hadn't been
anything like what she'd had with Chen . . .

Blinking away the sudden sting in her eyes, Pita
tossed the capsules into her mouth and took a gulp of
her soykaf. It was still hot enough to burn her lips, but
she drank it anyway, not wanting the capsules to get
stuck in her throat. Then she waited.

She heard a rustling noise somewhere to her left and
turned her head. A cat with a matted coat and torn ears
emerged from a recessed doorway and began to nibble
at the piece of Sweetnut Puff she'd tossed. It paused as
it sensed her movement, then turned to stare at her. Its
eyes were twin red moons, reflections of the streetlights at the end of the alley. Pita felt suddenly uneasy,
as if the cat were looking into her soul. Somehow, the

cat shared the hunger that burned inside her. Then the animal turned and scuttled back to cover, favoring one leg in an ambling limp.

A wave of warm fuzziness washed over Pita. The Mindease capsules were kicking in. Her hand drifted out in a gesture of goodwill to the cat, willing it to return and share the bounty she'd offered. Her head felt like a balloon attached to a string, floating high above her body. Something hot flowed over her other hand, trickled down her arm to her elbow. The soykaf. It must have been burning her skin. Pita laughed, and raised the cup to her lips to take a drink. The dark liquid sloshed out over her chin. Her wide grin made it impossible to shape her lips around the cup, so she dropped it and watched the kaf splash in slo-mo across the cement.

The bang of a metal door brought her head around. She frowned, peering deeper into the alley. The office buildings in this part of town had been closed for hours. Lights still burned in some of the upper stories, but only for the benefit of the cleaning crews. Were they coming out into the alley to empty the trash? Pita hunched down in the shadow of the chesterfield and giggled. This was just like playing Hide and Search, the virtual reality game she'd enjoyed so much as a kid. She even felt like a computer icon, all thin and transparent.

A man staggered up the three steps leading to street level. He emerged from the doorway clutching his shirtfront, gasping as if he couldn't catch his breath. Even though the drug blurred her vision somewhat, Pita's low-light sensitivity allowed her to pick out details. The man was sweating profusely; the underarms of his expensive-looking suit jacket were heavily stained. His tie had been jerked loose and sweat plastered his dark hair to his head and trickled down his neck.

The man took one staggering step, two, then collapsed on the cement in front of Pita. He landed facefirst with a solid smack. When he turned his head, she could see blood trickling from his nose. His mouth gaped open wide and his eyes rolled back in his head. A strange burning smell rose from him.

The Mindease stripped all of her fears from Pita's conscious mind, burying them deep in the back of her brain. She sat forward, intrigued. Giggling, she reached out a finger and poked the man's cheek. It was hotter than her soykaf had been.

A dim red light appeared in his mouth and nose. Pita knelt forward, lowering her head to the cool cement to peer closer. The smell of burning meat filled her nostrils. Then a steady rush of smoke began pouring out of the man's mouth and nose. Sweat steamed off his body.

"Mega wiz," she whispered, wondering if it was only some crazy effect of the Mindease. Then her street instincts took over. She flipped the man over and patted down his suit pockets. The way he was dressed, this guy had to be a corporate executive, his pockets full of goodies.

The first suit pocket held a smog filter and a melted Growliebar. Pita tossed them aside. The next held a folded hardcopy printout and an optical memory chip, which she palmed. It just might have a simsense game on it. The only other thing the guy had on him was a credstick. But even if it had a million nuyen on it, she wouldn't be able to access a single credit of it. To do that, you had to give a thumbprint, retinal scan, or voice sample. And Pita didn't have the technical knowhow to fake any of that stuff. She was just about to throw the credstick away when she spotted the magnetic keystrip on the side of the stick. Maybe, just maybe, it opened a locked door with something worth boosting on the other side. She slipped the credstick into her pocket.

The man was flopping now like someone hooked up to an electric current and his skin was nearly too hot to touch. And something else weird was happening. White light was now pouring out of his mouth and nostrils, the beams straight as lasers. His movements jerked the light around in jittering arcs. As it did, Pita glimpsed a flash of gold around the man's neck. It was a gold chain, hung with a tiny pendant shaped like an angel with outstretched wings. She reached for it.

"Ouch!" One of the light beams brushed her arm. Even through the dulling effects of the Mindease, she felt it burn. A bright red line now creased the inside of her wrist. She jerked her arm back, afraid the burning light would catch it again, but the man had already stopped flopping and lay still, his head to one side. The beams now focused on the wall beside her, slowly charring the cement. Still giggling, Pita experimentally held the hardcopy she'd pulled from his pocket in the path of the beam and watched it burst into flame.

Suddenly, the light beams slid away from the man's head. They merged into a single ray of light that ricocheted off one wall and did a zigzag across the alley, bouncing back and forth from one tinted window to the next. The night was filled with strobing light as the light alternately broke apart into a scattering of laser-thin beams, each a different color, then melded again into a solid white flash that left Pita blinking. It was weirdly beautiful, and at the same time terrifying in its intensity. At last seeming to find its way out of the alley, the light shot up into the darkened sky like a reversed shooting star. Then the sky lit up with a flash of sheet lightning. Pita waited for the thunderclap, but none came.

The smell of burned meat was overwhelming. Pita couldn't help but gag when she saw that the skin around the man's lips and nostrils had blackened and was beginning to flake away. She glanced down at his wrist and saw a DocWagon wristband. A winking light indicated that it had been activated.

Drek! The meatwagon could be here any second!

The artificial calm of the drug dampened her fear. She wanted to curl up and sleep. But instead she willed herself to rise to her feet. The last thing she needed was to be questioned about a corpse—especially one whose pockets she'd just rifled.

It took Pita a moment to orient herself. The Mindease was making her fuzzy, making it hard to think. With one hand on the wall, she staggered out of the alley. Dimly, she registered a man across the street, fiddling with a trideo camera. A tiny red light glowed above its lens. Pita smiled and waved at it, remembering how the cat's eyes had glowed red with reflected light.

The man's head jerked up. He flattened against the wall, looking wary, tucking the trideo camera in against his body. Then he relaxed as Pita staggered past him.

"Fragging druggie," he whispered under his breath.

Lulled by the Mindease, Pita let his comment slide away like oil down a gutter.

"Hey, Carla! Got a minute?"

Masaki grabbed Carla's arm, jerking her to a halt in mid-stride. Angrily, she turned on him.

"No, I don't have a minute, Masaki," she snapped. "In just thirty minutes I'm doing an interview at the Chrysler Pacific showroom. It's going to take me twenty-three minutes to get there—longer, if traffic is bad. I'm already cutting it fine." Tucking the coil of cable she carried under one arm, she used her free hand to pry Masaki's fingers away.

"Spare me thirty seconds," Masaki insisted. "I want to show you a trideo clip I shot last night."

"Jack off, Masaki. I don't have time to give you any editing tips."

"Twenty seconds! That's all it will take!"

Carla turned and strode away down the hall. Masaki trotted after her, speaking as rapidly as he could and wheezing with every word.

"I went out last night to shoot an interview. I had a tip from a junior exec at Mitsuhama Computer Technologies. He wanted to tell me about some top-secret project the corporation's research and development lab was working on. Some radical new tech that he thought the public should know about. He was going to spill his guts, give me an exclusive. He promised the story would be the biggest one of my career. He was going to give me both hardcopy and a datachip with the project specs on it."

Carla snorted. "Yeah, right. So why didn't your source take it to the majors?"

"He owed me a favor. Before signing on with Mitsuhama as a wage mage, he owned a thaumaturgical supply shop down on Madison Street. I did a puff piece on the store that brought in a lot of business." Masaki sighed. "He was murdered last night before I could conduct the interview. Burned to death."

"So?" A murder was hardly unusual, considering Mitsuhama's rumored yakuza connections.

"He was burned from the inside out."

Despite herself, Carla was intrigued. "How? Magic?"

"Maybe." Masaki shrugged. "But if so, it's something I haven't seen before, in all my twenty-eight years as a snoop. And I've seen some pretty weird things through the lens of my portacam, believe me."

"And the hardcopy and datachip he was going to give you?"

"The hardcopy was nothing but ashes by the time I got there. And the chip was gone."

Carla pushed the door open and focused in on her headclock. According to the glowing red numbers that appeared in the bottom right-hand corner of her field of vision, she had just twenty-six minutes to make it to her interview. "If you really had the goods on a hush-hush Mitsuhama research project, you'd have a big story—not to mention a tiger by the tail. But it sounds like you've got nothing, now that your source is dead and your proof has vanished. So why are you pestering me?" She jogged across the parking lot to her Americar XL, slid in behind its padded leather steering wheel, and voice-activated the ignition. She revved the engine and watched the seconds scroll by over her right eye. She'd give Masaki his thirty seconds.

He leaned in through the car's open door, talking rapidly. "I was mucking about with my portacam just before I went to meet my source. I didn't realize it was on. But it's a good thing it was. There was a witness to the murder. Remember that ork kid who wanted to talk to you two days ago about the Humanis Policlub? I think it was her. She even waved at the camera. And guess what was in her hand?"

"The datachip," Carla whispered. She smiled, realizing that Masaki had just handed her, on a silver platter, the story that would get her a slot at NABS. She laughed to herself. Had Masaki been a little smarter, a little more cutthroat, he'd have asked her for the name and address of the kid without revealing the reason he wanted it. Oh, well—his loss and her gain.

Carla cut the engine of her car. "Forget the Chrysler story," she told Masaki. "It's nothing more than a trideo op for the corporate execs. One of the junior reporters can cover it. We've got a real story to follow."

4

"Hey, mister!" Pita held out her hand. "Spare me something for a burger?"

She stood in the shelter of an awning on Broadway Street, watching the people hurrying past. With the light drizzle of rain falling, there was little foot traffic on the sidewalks. On a sunny afternoon, this trendy street would be packed with shoppers. But today the sidewalk soykaf stands were empty, their plastic chairs and tables beaded with water. Rather than venturing out into the elements, the shoppers were sticking to the connecting network of tunnels and skywalks that laced the city's downtown shopping core.

Normally, Pita would have been panhandling there. But after her run-in with Lone Star, she didn't want to face anyone in uniform. Even the mallplex security guards gave her the shivers.

Rain pattered on the awning overhead as Pita tried to catch the eye of the few people venturing out onto the sidewalks. Most stared straight ahead, doing their best to act like they didn't see her. A few pretended to be consulting their watches or electronic address pads. Others—particularly the humans—glared at her with open contempt, freezing the words in her mouth.

After nearly an hour of this, Pita was about to give up. The cashier in the trendy clothing shop whose awning Pita was sheltering under was beginning to get more serious in her efforts to wave her away. But just as Pita was turning to leave, an elderly woman in a shabby coat, her fingers curled with arthritis, pressed a crumpled bill into her hand.

"Jesus loves you," the woman said, her eyes bright. "Are you ready to accept Him into your heart?"

Pita glanced at the paper money. It was an old UCAS dollar bill. Not even enough for a basic burger at McHugh's. "At the moment I'm more interested in accepting some food into my stomach," she answered. "But thanks for the . . ."

Pita's eye fell on a man across the street. He was a dark-skinned elf with copper-colored dreadlocks that had flexible glo-tubes braided into them. A baggy jumpsuit, patterned with rainbow slashes, hung loosely on his gaunt frame. In one hand he held what looked like a small glass sphere. The fingers of his other hand brushed over it lightly, as if feeling its smooth texture. He seemed completely focused on the sphere, oblivious to the falling rain. Then he looked up and his eyes locked on Pita.

The elderly woman stepped closer to Pita, cutting off her view of the elf. "Do you believe in God?" she asked. "Have you heard—"

A faint yellow glow washed about the woman's head like a halo. For a moment, Pita almost thought she was witnessing some sort of religious miracle. But then the woman staggered, blinking heavily. With a sigh, she collapsed onto the sidewalk.

Pita could see the elf again. He stood rigid, one hand extended. Then his other hand shoved the sphere into his pocket in a gesture of frustration. With a heart-wrenching shock, Pita realized that the elf was a mage, and that the spell he had just cast had been intended for her. She saw movement up the street. Two burly humans in suits had broken into a rapid jog and were heading her way.

The mage touched his fingers to his eyelids in what Pita guessed was some new spellcasting gesture. She didn't wait to see what would come next, but plunged headlong through the front door of the nearest shop.

She could see her two pursuers through the windows, on the sidewalk outside. One was heavyset, the other slender. Both were Asian. As the shop clerks shouted protests, Pita hauled herself back to her feet, tipping over a rack of expensive jackets. She didn't think she'd been hit by a spell, but there was no time to wonder about either that or why people were suddenly after her. The two men were at the door.

Bolting for the back of the shop, Pita swept her arms right and left, knocking over other racks of clothing. One of the men chasing her tripped, landing in a tangle of dresses and hangers. The other leaped the rack like a hurdle, pulling something from his suit jacket. A bright spark crackled just above Pita's shoulder and she smelled the tang of ozone. The taser wire had just missed her.

As Pita skidded around the corner of the counter that separated the front of the store from its stock room, one of the clerks hit a PANICBUTTON near the credstick scanner. A shrill siren filled the air. Pita bolted through the stock room toward its back door. It was held open with a wedge of plastic. Through the crack, Pita could see a store clerk, cigarette in hand. He was just reaching for the door, a puzzled expression on his face.

Pita slammed into the door, kicking away the plastic wedge. Before the startled clerk could react, she spun and pushed the door shut behind her. Electronic locks clicked into place. Until the siren was deactivated, the door would be sealed. But there was no time to heave a sigh of relief. The two men were temporarily stalled, but sooner or later the dreadlocked mage would figure out she was in the alley at the back of the store. From inside the stock room, someone pounded on the door Pita had just run through.

The shop clerk, a moon-faced boy in his teens, watched Pita fearfully. "I don't have any credit on me," he said, backing slowly away into the rain. "My credstick's inside the shop."

Pita ignored him. Her heart was pounding. Which way to run? She stood in a narrow service lane between two buildings. At either end of the block it opened onto wider streets. Cars slid along these, their tires making hissing sounds on the wet pavement. At one end, traffic stopped for a light. Pita saw the distinctive markings of a Lone Star cruiser. That decided her. She turned and sprinted for the other end of the alley.

Pita ran easily now, in long, loping strides. Fear sharpened her senses and gave her a burst of speed. Soon she'd put several blocks between herself and the store. She slowed to a rapid walk, glancing nervously behind her.

Who was chasing her, and why? Were the two men in suits off-duty cops, coming back to button up the only witness to their crime? Neither of them looked anything like the male Star who'd confronted Chen, Shaz, and Mohan the night they'd been caught patching in to the apartment's trideo feed. But it could have been a different pair of cops who'd gunned her friends down. The dark, uniformed shapes Pita had seen bending over the bodies of her friends had their backs to her. All she could tell was that they were human. She had no idea what they looked like.

And who was that dark-skinned elf with his magic globes and who knew what else trying to hit her with spells? Why would he do that? Was he with the Star? From the way that woman had gone down she knew he had to be a mage. Pita hoped his aim wasn't any better next time.

She glanced again over her shoulder, wiping her cheek with the back of her hand. Her eyes were stinging, but she told herself it was rain on her face, not tears. Why couldn't the cops just leave her alone? Were they so afraid she'd tell someone what really happened that night? Fat chance of anyone believing her. The reporter at KKRU hadn't. Nobody else would, either. Except . . .

Except Chen's brother Yao. His crew would broadcast the story in a millisecond. They would give a lot of air time to a story about Lone Star Security trying to disguise the killing of an ork as the work of Humanis Policlub. Yao would see to it that his brother's murderers were put in the spotlight.

But only if Pita could find him. Yao and his friends were pirate broadcasters, always on the move. It was hard enough for Chen to find his brother on trideo, let alone in person. The pirates used a different frequency each time, hopping from one unused channel to another

or cutting in on a regular station while it was off the
air, ghosting over its test pattern. The few times they'd
broadcast live from a recognizable location, they'd
only stayed on the air for a minute or two. By the time
Chen and Pita hopped the monorail across town in an
effort to track Yao down, he was long gone. But that
only made sense. The *Orks First*! broadcasts were an
intense scan, literally slinging drek at the windows of
corporations that refused to implement affirmative-
action hiring programs, or cutting into legitimate station's newscasts and using graphics to distort the
images of anyone who made a disparaging comment
about the Underground. They slotted the networks off,
and more than one had probably sent out its corporate
security goons to deal with the problem. If the professionals couldn't track Yao down, what chance did a
lone street kid have? Still, she had to try. The best
place to start would be the Ork Underground.

Reaching Madison Street, Pita turned right and
headed down the hill, toward the overpass that crossed
the highway. Seattle's downtown lay on the other
side of the freeway. There, in the shadow of the Renraku Arcology, was one of the many entrances to the
Underground.

The orks had claimed the Underground years ago,
gradually renovating and expanding the network of tunnels that crisscrossed the city's waterfront. They'd
tossed out the dwarfs in the early 2020s, and had turned
the Underground into a city within a city, with its own
shopping malls, city hall, and security force. Lone Star
Security occasionally entered the Underground to make
a bust, but almost never patrolled there.

Pita gave herself a mental kick for not thinking of
going to the Underground sooner. Not only was it the
most likely place to find Yao; it was also the least likely
place for Lone Star to find her. She shrugged and
blamed it on the Mindease. She'd been doing entirely
too much of the stuff since Chen died. This was the first
time in two days that she'd been completely straight.

Pita kept watching for Lone Star cruisers, mindful
of the possibility that the mage might still be on her

trail. He could be following her in an unmarked cruiser, even now. The thought made her quicken her steps. She turned up the collar of her jacket and ducked her head down into it, hoping that it hid her face from the passing cars.

She crossed the highway and angled down Madison. The Renraku Arcology loomed at the base of the street, a towering pyramid seven blocks wide and more than two hundred stories high. Its silver-green windows shimmered with light; the rain sliding off them filtered it into soft ripples. Behind that tinted glass, thousands of people lived and worked in a climate-controlled atmosphere. Seattle could be experiencing gale-force winds or chilling hail, but inside Renraku, everyone would be wearing shorts and sunglasses.

Pita hung a right and headed down First Avenue, turning her back on the arcology. The buildings along First were modern, but at street level they'd been designed to look like the historic structures they had replaced. The shopfront glass was bullet-proof, but was hand-lettered and framed in dark-grained plastic that was indistinguishable from real wood. The street was lined with brass-trimmed street lights and paved with cobblestones. Cars passing over them made a rumbling sound. This was an area of taverns, restaurants, and shops that sold tourist trideos and T-shirts.

One of the largest of the area's restaurants served as an entrance to the Underground. Pita pushed through the doors of the Seattle Utilities Building and caught an escalator to the basement. As she descended into the Big Rhino Restaurant, the noise level grew. This was a huge eatery, filled with long dining-hall tables crowded with patrons. The vast majority were orks, although a sprinkling of humans and dwarfs were squashed in among the larger patrons. Waitresses hurried back and forth with steins of draft beer or plates heaped with RealMeat and fries. Blue smoke curled around the ceiling fixtures in flagrant disregard of Seattle's no-smoking bylaw.

The rich smell of the gravy-smothered RealMeat made Pita's stomach growl. She wound her way between the tables, inhaling the savory smell. At the same time, her lip curled with disgust. The restaurant was filled with orks of every size and description, all of them chewing noisily and shouting at one another. They stuffed too much into their gaping mouths at once, they picked their teeth with splinters of bone, they slurped their beer noisily and then belched when the stein was empty. Pita knew that some of the behavior was natural, some of it exaggerated. It was bad enough they were orks. Why did they have to flaunt it?

She winced. That was her father talking. He'd never liked metahumans. Any of them. The elves were "pointy-eared pricks," dwarfs were "foot stools," and trolls were "horn heads" with the intelligence of a brick. Orks . . .

Orks were what Pita was now. But she didn't have to like it.

She hurried through a second hall where most of the patrons were male. She tried not to look at the half-clothed woman who leered at the customers from behind a tall brass pole. The stripper had huge breasts, but it was hard to tell where they stopped and her bulging chest muscles began. Her face was painted in a horrible parody of a human woman; the dark eyeshadow gave her face even more of a greenish tinge, and the jutting canines ruined the effect of her lipstick. Even so, the men hooted and whistled, bellying up to the stage to wave in the hope of catching the stripper's eye.

Someone pinched Pita as she went by. Still hyped up from the encounter with the off-duty cops, she yelped and spun around, one fist raised. The pinching fingers belonged to a troll, so huge that his eyes were level with Pita's even though he was sitting down.

"You got a nice ass, girl," he said. "How about you sit it down here, on my lap."

"Frag off," Pita snapped back. She was trying to sound tough, but her voice was close to cracking.

"Ooh," said a man next to the troll. "I don't think she likes you, Ralph. But don't worry if this one gets away. She's not much to look at anyhow."

Pita hurried away, her cheeks burning. She found the

door at the back of the restaurant that led into an underground passage. It was about half as wide as a city street, and was fronted by shops and offices on either side. The walls were cobbled together from a mix of brick, concrete, and plastiform, while rusted metal pillars held up the ceiling. A grid of overhead lights, pocked with burned-out tubes, cast a pattern of shadows. The floor underfoot was heavy-duty linoleum, scuffed by the passage of many feet and littered with drifts of plastic cups and paper wrappers that smelled of day-old food. Orks of every description walked back and forth along it, pausing to look into barred windows or bustling in and out of doorways. A handful wore double-breasted business suits or dresses and pumps, but most were wearing cheap, ill-fitting clothes that had been intended for human proportions. Mothers dragged complaining children along by the hand, while teens in baggy stretch pants and MetalMesh shirts lounged against pillars or rattled past on gyro boards. Some of the orks rode scooters or electric bicycles, weaving their way between those on foot. The effect was a strange cross between an enclosed shopping mall and a rundown city street.

Pita walked slowly along the corridor, wondering which way to go. Unlike a megamall or an arcology, the Underground had no directory, no color-coded strip lights in the floor to follow. The narrow streets didn't even run in straight lines. They zigzagged this way and that around the support pillars, disappearing around corners and then reappearing again. The shops seemed to be wedged in wherever they would fit.

Two orks wearing gray jumpsuits and leather holsters with oversize pistols walked boldly down the center of the corridor, scanning the people who streamed past. Occasionally one grabbed someone by the shoulder, dragging the pedestrian over to him. Crumpled dollar bills would change hands, and then the pedestrian would be given a rough shove and sent on his way.

Pita ducked behind one of the supporting pillars and kept it between herself and the two uniformed men until they had passed. These were the "security guards"

who served as the semi-official police force for the
Underground. They were little more than goons who
shook down the inhabitants of the Underground for
protection fees. They were also the reason why Pita
and her street chummers never ventured into the Underground much. If you couldn't pay the fee for the "protection" offered by the uniformed guards, you could
always work off your fee as a press-ganged member of
one of the maintenance crews who did all of the hard,
dirty, and dangerous work of expanding and repairing
the Underground's ever-growing maze of tunnels. It
didn't sound like much fun.

An electronics shop seemed the most likely place to
start her search for Yao. The first three Pita tried didn't
produce any results. None of them had heard of Yao—
or was willing to admit that they'd sold equipment to
Orks First! Exhausted and hungry, Pita was about to
give up. She had decided to find a fast food outlet and
do some scrap snacking—eating the soggy fries and
burger crusts that patrons had left behind—when she
spotted an electronics shop. It was tucked into the bend
of a street, its merchandise displayed behind barred
windows. A flickering holo of a trideo camera floated
above the door, slowly rotating. A closed-circuit trideo
set in the window broadcast the passing shoppers. The
view panned back and forth, as if the holo-camera was
doing the recording. It would have been a neat trick if
the trideo set's tracking hadn't been so bad. The picture was smeared with static.

Pita rapped on the door of the shop, then waited for
the clerk to buzz her in. It was a tiny store, just a
couple of meters wide and deep. The shelves on either
side were lined with home entertainment equipment,
most of it second-hand. Large yellow price tags hung
from each item. The center of the store was taken up
with bins of off-the-rack electronics: fiber-optic cables,
datachips, mini-amps, and interface plugs. Glass counters held cheap knock-offs of designer watches and
electronic toys, made in some Third World sweat-shop.

The shopkeeper was a female dwarf who sat on a tall
stool behind one of the counters. She was hunched over

a cyberdeck, her short legs dangling. Half of her head was shaved, revealing multiple datajacks. A cable stretched from one of the jacks to the deck. On the other side of her head, her hair hung down in a thick braid. Her fingernails were covered in a thin layer of polished metal, making light clicking noises as she drummed them against the counter. Her eyes were unfocused at first, but then she blinked and looked up at Pita.

"Can I help you?" she asked, gently tugging the jack from the slot above her ear.

Pita started to shake her head. What would a dwarf clerk from a crummy little shop like this know about ork trideo pirates? But she'd come this far. Might as well ask.

"I'm looking for someone," Pita said. "Yao Wah. Yao is the first name. He's a pirate who shoots trideo for *Orks First!* I thought you might know him. He's my friend's brother and I need to tell him someth—"

The dwarf's eyes narrowed. "What makes you think I know this Yao?"

Pita shrugged. "I don't know. I thought maybe he came in here to buy equipment."

The dwarf stared at her impassively.

"Guess I was wrong," Pita said, reaching for the door.

"I know him."

"You do?" Pita turned around quickly.

"Yeah. He's a class-A slot," the dwarf said, wrinkling her nose. "Stiffed me for a signal booster. Owes me five thousand nuyen. But is the fragger going to pay me? I doubt it. He'd rather deal with his own kind."

Pita waited, sizing up the dwarf. "Do you know where I can find Yao?"

"You could try posting a message on the Matrix. *Orks First!* runs a bulletin board on the Seattle network."

"I don't even have enough nuyen to use the public telecom," Pita said. "Besides, I need to see him in person."

"You need to meet the meat," the dwarf said. "Why?"

"Something's happened to his brother. I need to tell Yao about it, face to face."

"This brother's important to him? You think Yao would answer if I posted something about the kid?"

Pita nodded. "Tell him it's a message about Little Pork Dumpling. Then he'll know it's for real. He used to call his brother that because he was so fat when he was little."

"Right. Wait one." The dwarf slotted the jack back into her head and closed her eyes. After a second or two she opened them again. "It's done. A friend of his is passing the message along."

"That's great!" Pita said. "When can I meet him? And where?"

"Right here," the dwarf answered. "But not until he pays his bill, plus interest for the three months it's overdue. And don't get any ideas about going off to find him yourself. The door's locked and armed. If Yao wants the meet, he'll come. We'll see if his 'little pork dumpling' is worth five thousand nuyen to him."

5

Yao was shorter than he looked on trideo. He was about Pita's height, but had broader shoulders and a thicker neck. He looked like an older version of Chen, with the same straight black hair and Asian eyecast. He wore his hair "high and tight"—shaved over the ears and spiky on top. It was starting to gray a little, although he was still probably only in his mid-twenties. Life on the streets had given his eyes a hard, wary look. But he was good-looking, for an ork. His jaw was narrow and his nose straight. He wore jeans torn off at the knee and a black leather vest over a loose-fitting sweatshirt— probably to deliberately contrast with the carefully groomed reporters of the legitimate news stations.

Yao sat on the other side of a small plastic table, watching Pita scarf down her second plate of noodles. There was no way to tell whether he had anything so fancy as an cybereye cam, but there a datajack showed in his temple and a mini-radio was clipped to one ear-lobe. When Pita asked what it was, he told her it was a Lone Star scanner and decryption unit. "Keeps me one step ahead of the cops," he explained, one arm draped across the back of the bench. She noticed he always kept one eye on the doorway, where his friend Anwar lounged.

The second pirate wore jeans, a muscle shirt, and cowboy boots. He leaned against a wall next to the door, one arm cradling a bulky trideo camera whose size gave it away as being more than two decades out of date—nearly an antique. He grinned at Yao and gave him a thumbs-up sign indicating that none of the Underground's security goons were in sight.

Pita finished her noodles and drained the last of her soda. She toyed nervously with one of her chopsticks until Yao gently touched her wrist. The back of his hand was covered with a mass of spiky black hairs; he didn't shave his hands to look more human the way some orks did. "Well?" he asked. "Are you going to tell me something about Chen? Or do you want to soak me for another plate of noodles first?"

The chopstick in Pita's hands snapped in two. "He's dead," she blurted.

"Yes."

Pita looked up. "You knew?"

Yao shook his head. On his trideo broadcasts, he was animated and expressive, but now his face was strangely still. Only a faint wince of his eyes betrayed what he must be feeling. "I didn't know. But I could guess. I can read people. I can see that Chen meant a lot to you."

Pita stared at the tabletop. Its edge was scarred with cigarette burns. The brown stains reminded her of the dried blood she'd found on her jacket the morning after Chen had . . . After the cops had . . .

Tears dripped onto the bright yellow plastic. Yao reached across the table and lifted Pita's chin with one massive hand. "What happened? How did he die? Was it a fight? An overdose? How?"

"The Star," Pita answered. She had to swallow before she could go on. "They shot him. And two of his friends, Shaz and Mohan. We were hanging out, trying to boost a trideo feed to catch one of your broadcasts. Lone Star stopped us and—"

"And Chen pulled a weapon. Stupid fragger. You'd think he'd know better."

"No!" Pita protested. "It wasn't like that at all. At first all the Stars did was smash the 'trode rig you gave him. But later, they came back in their patrol car. Shaz threw a rock at them, and they opened fire on us. But none of us had a weapon. Not in our hands. Mohan had a knife, but it was still in his pocket. The cops never even got out of their car or gave us a warning. They shot before we even had time to run."

"But you escaped."

Guilt washed over Pita like ice water. "Yes," she muttered, looking down at the tabletop once more. "But I came back, later, to see if the others were all right. That's when I saw the cops cutting them up. And writing the Humanis slogans on the wall."

"Humanis Policlub?" Chen leaned forward, a hard glitter in his eyes. "You mean fragging *cops* belong to that drek-eating hate club?" A muscle worked in his jaw. "Well, it figures. Orks represent sixteen percent of Seattle's population, but nearly fifty per cent of the prison population is ork. Not only are we arrested and thrown in jail more often, we're also under-represented as cops. Only one fragging per cent of the Lone Star cops patrolling Seattle are ork. Nearly eighty per cent are human. Those figures have been documented by the Ork Rights Committee. And their numbers don't lie. Prejudice against metahumans runs long and deep in the Star. Chief Loudon's going to have a lot to answer for the day the coalition takes over the city. And that day is coming—soon."

Pita was impressed by all the facts Yao had at his fingertips. He was informed. He was determined.

He stopped talking as the waitress came to clear the table. She was a pretty girl—human—a little older than Pita. But Yao looked at her with open contempt. "Wait until we're finished eating, drekhead," he snapped at her.

Pita pushed her bowl away. "I'm done," she said quickly. But the waitress had already scrambled away.

Yao stood up, motioning his friend forward. He took the trideo camera from him, then spoke quietly to him. Anwar grinned, then loped out of the restaurant.

"I want you to take me to the spot where it happened," Yao told Pita. "I'll interview you there, on location, while Anwar monitors the uplink. We're using a portable dish to go live. Save your story until we get there. That way it'll sound less rehearsed. When I give you the sign, you start from the beginning and don't leave anything out." He smiled grimly as he motioned for Pita to follow. "This could be just the story we need to spark the uprising."

"Uprising?" Pita echoed, trotting along behind Yao. He walked quickly, threading his way through the crowded corridors. She had to hurry to keep up.

"Look around you," Yao said, lowering his voice. "The overcrowding, the condition of these tunnels. You don't think we orks are going to be penned up in the Underground forever, do you? The day isn't far off when we'll rise up into the city and push the weaker races aside. When we'll take what's rightfully ours and pay the fraggers back for what happened in '39. The Night of Rage is going to look tame compared to what's coming."

"My parents told me about the Night of Rage," Pita said. "I was only two, but Mom used to tell a funny story about how Dad made us hide in the basement, then sat at the top of the stairs with his shotgun to protect us. It wasn't until the next morning that he realized he'd forgotten to load the gun. When I was little, I didn't understand what could have sent him into such a panic. But now I realize he was afraid of the—"

Pita stopped herself. She'd been about to say, "of the metahumans." Thinking back on it now, she wondered at her father's extreme reaction. Seattle's metahumans had responded with violence to the city's attempt to forcibly relocate them outside of its boundaries, but that violence had been tightly focused. Their rage—and the burnings, lootings, and attacks it sparked—was triggered by a series of explosions in the warehouses being used to hold the deportees. A militant wing of the Humanis Policlub was rumored to be behind the bombings. Pita knew her father sympathized with the Humanis Policlub, but now she wondered just how deep those sympathies ran. Was her father a member of the racist group, and thus a potential target for the metahuman retaliation?

"Yeah, the Metroplex Guard were even worse than Lone Star," Yao said, interrupting her thoughts. He glanced at Pita. "You weren't at the warehouses? Then your family hadn't been rounded up yet by the Guard when the trouble began."

"Uh, no." Pita realized that Yao assumed her entire family was ork. Given the arrogant, hostile tone he'd used when speaking to the waitress in the noodle bar, she was afraid to tell him she'd once been a member of the "weaker races" herself.

"You were lucky, then," Yao continued. "My father died when the first explosion hit the waterfront. My mother was never the same afterward. She tried to reverse the confiscation order on our house, but the city appealed every court decision, and eventually our money ran out. After that, she didn't have the strength to do much but sit and cry.

"Governor Schultz glosses over the whole thing now, and talks about our current 'racial harmony.' She seems to think the Night of Rage could never happen again." Yao's smile tightened. "Well, she's soon going to find out just how wrong she is. When your interview hits the air, the sparks will fly."

6

The street kids were clustered near the base of the Space Needle, listening to a simsense deck, and it looked to Carla like a Sony Beautiful Dreamer. Two of the teenagers were simming the music directly, via datajacks slotted into their temples. They jerked in time with the music, eyes focused on some distant point as the deck pumped sights, sounds, and other sensory input directly into their brains. The rest of the kids heard only the music that blared from the speakers. Some lounged about, smoking, too chill to acknowledge the driving staccato beat. Others danced, arms flailing, occasionally knocking foreheads together like wild rams. One of the kids—a troll dressed in black leather pants and a Japanese kimono hacked off at the waist—even had the curling horns necessary to complete the picture. Overhead, the night sky was a solid black, devoid of stars.

Carla shouted over the din from the speakers. "Do any of you know an ork girl named Pita? She came looking for me at my office the other day, but left before I had a chance to really talk with her. The last bunch of kids I talked to told me she hangs somewhere down here, at Seattle Center. Have any of you seen her? This is what she looks like." She held out a playback imager. Its flatscreen showed a still of Pita sitting in the KKRU lobby.

The teenagers stared at the imager, their eyes a mixture of boredom and suspicion. "You her social worker?" one asked. By the way his nose flared as he looked up and down Carla's expensive Armanté jacket, he wasn't impressed with her corporate image. Maybe she should have dressed down before trying to interview street kids. But the Armanté was bullet-proof as well as stylish.

"I'm not a social worker," Carla answered. "I'm a reporter. Carla Harris of KKRU Trideo News. Pita had a story for me. A story we're willing to get behind. Be sure to tell her that if you see her."

The troll stopped dancing and ambled over to stand behind Carla. He loomed over her like a building, throwing her into shadow. She resisted the urge to back away, even though he reeked of sweat. *Never let a dog see that you're afraid of him,* she thought. *It only encourages him to bite.*

"Unless you got some credit to spend right here, lady, you'd better just frag off," he grumbled.

Across the parking lot, a car horn beeped twice. That would be Masaki. He had cut the tint on the windows of his car, and was gesturing frantically inside it.

Carla met the troll's eyes and smiled. "I'd love to stay and chat," she told him. "But my father doesn't like it when I stay out late, and he's quite particular about which boys I talk to. That's him in the car over there. Perhaps you'd like to meet him?"

Carla almost hoped the troll would call her bluff and say yes. If Masaki saw the huge brute shambling toward his car, he'd wet himself. He'd been working the lifestyles beat too long, and had gone soft. He'd rather spend the evening behind the multiple locks of his apartment door than chasing down stories. Carla had practically dragged him out tonight. She would have gone on her own, except that Masaki knew more about the background to the piece, including the background of the mage who'd wanted to spill the beans on Mitsuhama's special project. But the way Masaki was acting, she wasn't sure if her fellow so-called "reporter" still deserved a byline on the story.

The troll shifted his kimono slightly so that Carla got a good look at the Streetline Special pistol tucked into the top of his pants. She knew better than to flinch.

"You got *cojones* coming out here at night, lady," he said grudgingly at last.

Carla smiled sweetly at him. "Ovaries, actually." Behind her, Masaki honked the horn twice more. "Remember," she told the other kids as she turned to go, "if you see Pita, tell her Carla Harris of KKRU Trideo is looking for her." She handed the kid her business card.

Carla strode across the parking lot and wrenched open the car door. She and Masaki had been trying all that afternoon and evening to find Pita, but none of the street kids would admit to seeing the girl. She'd disappeared into thin air—and taken the Mitsuhama datachip with her. Their producer had given Carla and Masaki one day to dig up some proof that there really was a story. So far, all they had were dead ends. And now Masaki was acting like an idiot, honking the horn like a frightened kid. He even had the engine running, as if fearing that a fast getaway would be imminent.

"What the hell are you doing?" Carla asked Masaki angrily. "Trying to wake up all of Seattle? If you weren't such a timid—"

Masaki didn't wait for the insult. "Look at this!" he said, pointing urgently to the compact trid built into the dash of his car. "I was channel surfing and stumbled across this pirate broadcast. Looks like they've found Pita for us."

Carla climbed hurriedly into the car, thumbing the volume key beside the tiny trideo screen. Pita's voice crackled from the speaker and her image wavered. At first Carla thought it was just the trideo unit acting up, but then she saw the channel display. The broadcast was coming in on Channel 115—a channel that should have been carrying nothing but a blank blue field. This was clearly a pirate broadcast, fed illegally through a cable booster into a "dead" channel. The pirates were probably transmitting via remote feed to avoid getting caught, should their input be traced. The resulting distortion had caused the color to shift; Pita's face was distinctly green. But her voice was coming through, loud and clear, despite the occasional pop of static.

"This is where it happened," she said in a quavering voice. "This is where my friends were killed."

The camera pulled back from Pita, revealing the wall behind her. The words that had been painted in the orks' blood were faint but still legible, thanks to an overhang that protected them from the rain that had been falling steadily throughout the day: "Human Power!", "Goblin Scum Must Die!" and "Keep Our Human Family Pure!"

Carla jabbed a finger at the screen. "That's Rainier Avenue South, the spot where those three orks were killed by Humanis Policlub. I shot trid there a couple of days ago. If this is a live broadcast, that's where Pita is right now."

"It's live all right," Masaki said, wheezing with excitement. "But the pirate would be a fool to broadcast from an identifiable location. Lone Star would be all over him before he'd even finished his intro.

"See this faint blue line?" He traced Pita's outline with a finger. "The kid's image has been inserted over a shot of the corner where the kids were killed. The pirate is shooting with two portacams, one slaved to the other. He's using a mixer to paste the two images together."

"So how do we find him?" Carla asked.

"The portacams can't be more than a few hundred meters apart," he said. "He's got to be within a block or two of that corner or else the signal would suffer too much distortion and the images wouldn't match up. And he must be shooting outside to capture traffic noise. We'll find him." Masaki put the car into gear and punched the accelerator. "Now what was that name you wanted to call me? A timid what?"

"Shh!" Carla hissed. "I'm trying to listen to this. Has the kid said anything about the dead mage?"

"Not yet." Masaki rounded a corner, tires squealing. "It's been nothing but intro so far. After introducing Pita, the reporter went into this rambling spiel about the coming revolution and injustice against the meta-races. Usual bulldrek. About what you'd expect from amateur propagandists like *Orks First*! They're eating up the kid's story with a fork and—"

"Quiet!" Carla leaned closer to the tiny screen. The

camera was back on the ork girl, locked in a closeup that showed the tears at the corners of her eyes. Carla made sure the machine was set on record, for review later in case she missed anything.

"We were stopped outside an apartment a few blocks from here," Pita began, gesturing up the street, "by two Lone Star cops. There were four of us. Me, Chen Wah . . ." She paused, blinking furiously. "And two younger orks, Shaz and Mohan Gill. The cops took our simsense headset and . . ."

Carla glanced up as the car came to a halt. They were stopping for a yellow light. Cross traffic was light. "Let's move, Masaki!" she said impatiently. "The pirate is going to wrap this story and disappear."

"This intersection is monitored!" Masaki protested. "I don't want to risk getting a tick—"

Carla grabbed the wheel, slid across the seat, and punched her foot down on top of Masaki's, depressing the accelerator. Masaki gasped in fear as the car leaped across the intersection, narrowly missing the oncoming traffic. Horns blared, but then they were through and racing along Rainier. Masaki glared at Carla as she released the wheel, then drove on, grinding his teeth. Carla was pleased to see that they were at last making some decent speed.

She returned her attention to the trideo screen. The pirate reporter was standing beside Pita, one arm draped protectively over her shoulders. He was talking earnestly into the camera, his eyes glittering with intensity.

"Most of us have gone through what Pita has just described," he was saying. "Lone Star seizes our property without warrant, stops and questions us without due cause, and talks to us in the most derogatory way they can think of. We live our lives in the Underground, afraid to venture onto the streets of our own city, shut out from the homes we once owned. Governor Schultz and Lone Star Chief Loudon have promised to 'clean up' Seattle. They pretend they're talking about street crime. But anyone who remembers the events of 2039 will read between the lines and realize that the 'housecleaning' these humans are talking about is far more serious than the round-up that triggered the Night of Rage. We at *Orks First*! are about to bring you the true story of the links between our city's 'security' force and the policlub that was notorious for—"

"We're close now!" Masaki called out. "They've got to be around here somewhere." He weaved around another vehicle, cut off a truck, and pulled back into the curb lane.

The pirate's voice was lost in a roar of static. The trideo screen had gone blue.

"Damn!" Carla thumped the dash above the trideo set. "We've lost the transmission."

"Doesn't matter," Masaki wheezed, slowing the car. "There they are!"

Carla looked up. The ork girl was perhaps a block away, standing near the curb. Her body posture was hunched, frozen. She looked like a frightened animal, caught in the glare of headlights and uncertain which way to run. The pirate reporter lay at her feet, tangled in his tripod as if he had tripped over it. He was struggling to raise himself to a sitting position, to point something black he held in his hand. At first, Carla thought it was a portacam. But then she recognized the streamlined shape of a pistol. She was just powering down her window when shots coughed out from across the street. The ork reporter sagged to the ground, then went still.

"That's gunfire!" Masaki said, slamming on the brakes. Around them, other drivers were also reacting, some accelerating away as quickly as possible, others spinning in tight fishtail turns. Two cars slammed together with a dull crunch and the scraping squeal of torn metal in the intersection ahead.

As their car skidded to a stop, Carla peered around Masaki. On the opposite side of the street, a man was tucking a pistol into a holster under his arm. A smaller man sprinted out into traffic, heading for the ork girl.

Cursing the power window for its slowness, Carla stuck her head out the opening. "Pita!" she cried. "This way!"

The girl hesitated no more than a millisecond, then sprinted for the car. The man chasing her changed direction, angling across the street to intercept her. A car narrowly missed him, honking furiously. But he was gaining on the girl.

Masaki had thrown their car into reverse. It jerked backward, wheels spinning.

"What are you doing?" Carla screamed. "Wait for the girl!"

Masaki was wheezing heavily, obviously scared. His pudgy hands were white on the steering wheel. He shook his head, eyes wide. "That guy's got a gun! Close the window before he shoots!"

Instead, Carla cracked the car door. The force of the backward acceleration made it slam open. She leaned out, reaching for Pita, who by now was running alongside the vehicle. One hand on the door, the other on the wrist of the ork girl, Carla yanked. At the same time, Pita jumped, knocking Carla back into the car.

The man chasing Pita, a willowy Asian fellow, was barely a few steps behind her. His face was set in a determined grimace. Something snaked out from the gun he held in his hand, licking against Carla's wrist with a hot electric snap. A wave of pain coursed through her as her body convulsed. For a moment or two, the world spun. Or perhaps it was the car. They were whipping around in a tight backward turn, leaving the man with the taser behind. The corner of the open car door caught his shirt, tearing it open and spinning him around. Then the car was rocketing forward, away from the spot where the pirate reporter had been gunned down. Something heavy was in Carla's lap— the ork girl, she remembered fuzzily. The car door thudded shut. Then the kid clambered into the back seat.

Carla shook her head to clear it. Her right wrist was on fire; looking down she saw a bright white circle on the back of it. She blinked, testing the focus on her cybereye. The response time of the miniature camera inside it was a fraction of a second too slow, but the unit appeared to be undamaged. She hoped it had caught a good, clean shot of her assailant. If this story panned out, she could probably use it.

Beside her, Masaki was cursing steadily, sweat rolling down his temples. His moustache and goatee framed white lips. He was at last ignoring the speeding limit, running lights and driving with terrified determination.

The ork girl sat in the back seat, pounding a fist against the upholstery. "Fragging cops!" Her voice held an edge of hysteria. "Fragging, fragging bastards!"

"Did you see that guy's shoulders?" Masaki asked in a low voice, his eyes darting to the rear-view mirror. "They were covered with tattoos. Those weren't cops. They were yakuza. I hope to drek they didn't get my license bar code, or we're all dead."

"Yakuza? But what would they want with me?" The girl twisted around to glance fearfully out the rear window. "They killed Yao, didn't they? They must have been aiming at me."

Carla turned her anger on Masaki. "You're not helping!" she told him. "And slow down. There's no one following us."

She turned to the girl, who now sat with her arms wrapped around her chest, hunched into herself. Carla took a moment to compose herself, then spoke in a soothing voice. "Everything's all right now, Pita. We'll take you back to the station. The building has a tight security system; you'll be safe there."

Carla took a breath, brushing her hair back into place with one hand. Her heart was still beating rapidly, but whether it was from fear or excitement, she couldn't tell.

Things were falling into place now. Somehow, Mitsuhama must have found out that the ork girl had acquired the datachip containing the specs of the research project and had sent its goons out after her—apparently the rumors that someone at MCT Seattle had connections with the local yakuza were accurate. The yaks had panicked when they saw her being interviewed by a reporter, and had geeked the guy—while he was on-air, yet. It was stupid and brutal, just the sort of thing you'd expect from gangsters. But it meant that the datachip was a top-priority item. Something worth killing for.

Wetting her lips, Carla did her best not to seem too anxious. "Those men were chasing you because of something you found, Pita. Something you picked up in an alley from a man who had burned to death. An optical memory chip like those used in cyberdecks. Do you still have it?"

Carla scarcely dared the breathe. If the kid had tossed the memory chip away . . .

"What if I did?" Pita asked defensively. "The guy was already dead. It's not like I stole it or anything."

"That doesn't matter to those men back there," Carla said soothingly. "They want the chip back, and they won't stop chasing you until they get it."

"Then I'll give it back to them." The kid reached for the window button. "Right now."

"No!" Carla fought to control her voice. So the kid did have the chip, after all. Now she'd just have to talk her into handing it over.

"Even if they get the chip back, they'll want to make sure the information it contains doesn't get out," Carla told the girl. "You've had the chip for twenty-four hours. Even if the information on the chip is encoded, that's plenty of time for an experienced decker to decrypt it. You're just a kid, without any connections, but those goons don't know that. They've got to assume you've read the data it contains. And that means—"

Masaki cut her off. "Stop it, Carla!" he said. "You're scaring her. You're scaring me, too."

"I was going to say," Carla said, an icy tone in her voice, "that it means we've got to air our story on Mitsuhama as soon as possible. Once the technical data on the chip is public knowledge, there'll be no need for the corporation to try to keep us quiet."

"Oh." Masaki was still driving quickly, but not recklessly. They were only a few blocks from the KKRU building. It was late, but Carla was keyed up with the excitement of the chase. This story was going to be a big one; she could feel it in her bones. After all, Mitsuhama had killed the mage to make sure word of their top-secret project didn't get out, and had burned the hard copy printout he'd been about to give Masaki. Funny, though, them overlooking the chip.

She reached out a hand. "Give me the chip, and I'll make sure the story airs. Then you'll be off the hook with the yakuza."

The kid rummaged in the pocket of her jacket. She pulled out a tiny bronze disk. But when Carla reached for it, the kid yanked her hand back. "I want you to promise me something, first," she said.

"What?"

"That you'll do the story on my friends," the girl continued. "About how the cops killed them."

"Sure, kid," Carla promised smoothly. "Just as soon as the Mitsuhama story airs. That's the important thing right now. Getting those goons off your back."

The kid studied Carla for a long moment, then grudgingly agreed. "O.K.," she said, dropping the data-chip into Carla's hand.

"Now," Carla said, "tell us everything that happened the night you found the dead man."

7

When they reached the station, Carla immediately popped the datachip into a deck. Masaki fretted about encryption devices and self-wipe programs, but as it turned out, the chip wasn't even encoded with a password.

As the two reporters hunched over the display, Pita could tell from their perplexed expressions that they didn't understand what they were seeing. The screen was filled with a series of weird diagrams and symbols and long blocks of text. Whatever was on the chip apparently had something to do with magic because she heard Carla and Masaki muttering stuff about "hermetic circles," "astral space," and "multi-something conjuring." They at last concluded that it must be a spell formula of some sort.

By the time they gave up on trying to figure it out themselves, it was morning. Rather than going home to sleep, the two decided to visit a mage friend of Carla's. Pita, despite the fact that exhaustion threatened to overwhelm her at any moment, decided to tag along. She was already coming to realize that the reporters were more interested in the datachip than in her. But they'd saved her ass once, and she felt safer with them than in an office full of strangers. Besides, she was curious about the chip.

Their destination was an odd little shop on Denny Way, tucked into the middle of a block of buildings that looked as if they'd been built in the previous century. There was no sign out front, no indication of what type of store it might be. The large window in the front was entirely covered with intricate designs, done in gold leaf. Pita wondered if they were magical wards of some sort.

As Carla knocked, Pita peered in through the glass. The interior of the shop was dark, but she could see that it was filled with untidy stacks of hardcopy texts bound in boxy coverings. These were books—the old-fashioned, difficult-to-use data storage units that had been so popular in the last century. Pita couldn't see the attraction of them, and wondered how a place like this could make any money. She'd take a Pocketpad graphic novel over one of these dusty antiques any day.

The door opened suddenly, and the brass bell above it tinkled. Carla stepped inside, then motioned Masaki and Pita to follow. As Pita closed the door behind them, a small white cat leaped down from one of the stacks of books and wove itself, purring, around her ankles. She reached down to scratch its head, looking around the shop. There was no sign of the proprietor.

"Hello. Welcome to Inner Secrets Thaumaturgical Textbooks. Aziz Fader at your service."

The voice came from somewhere just ahead. Pita jerked back as a human shape suddenly appeared a step or two in front of her. One minute there had been nothing but empty air in front of her; the next, some guy was standing there. It gave her the weirds to think he'd been there all along, watching her invisibly. Masaki was equally startled, but Carla just smiled. "Hello, Aziz. Long time no scan."

The shopkeeper was a tall man with jet-black hair combed straight back from his high forehead. He was human, but thin enough to be an elf. His nose had a slight hook to it, and his eyes were so dark it was hard to tell where the iris ended and the pupil began. He wore a flowing, one-piece garment with an ankle-length hem and wide sleeves, and held his hands in front of him, fingers laced together.

His eyes were locked on Carla. They took in every centimeter of the reporter, from her neatly braided hair and high cheekbones, to her tailored suit, to her stylish, expensive leather pumps. "I like the new face," he commented, one eyebrow arched. He barely glanced at

Masaki, with his rumpled shirt and uncombed graying hair, or at Pita, who still wore her torn jeans and cheap synthleather jacket.

Masaki cleared his throat. "We've come to—"

"I know why you're here, Carla," Aziz said, still addressing the female reporter. "I did a minor mind probe before I let you in. A little protective measure. I hope you don't mind."

"Not at all," Carla said smoothly. "Let's get right to it then, shall we?"

Carla handed him the chip.

The shopkeeper waved them to a large wooden desk in the back of the store. A telecom unit sat on one corner. The rest of its surface was covered with a jumble of books, loose papers, and datachips. Aziz pushed these aside, revealing an ancient data display with a fold-up screen and a battered-looking keyboard. It didn't even have a pickup for voice recognition, let alone a jack for a datacord. The shopkeeper must have a jones for old-fashioned stuff.

Aziz seated himself at the desk and powered up the datadeck. Carla and Masaki pulled up chairs on either side of him, and Pita, left without a seat, perched on a stack of books.

"Get down from there!" Aziz barked. "Those are valuable!"

Pita leaped to her feet, but the mage had already turned his attention to the flickering screen in front of him. He scrolled through the text, muttering to himself. Pita flipped him the finger behind his back.

"It's a conjuring spell, all right, but not one I'm familiar with," Aziz said. "Definitely hermetic, and definitely related to the summoning of a spirit. But the diagram for the hermetic circle isn't like any I've seen before. Usually it encloses a square pattern representing the four elemental energies. This one omits the square entirely, and instead places a pentagram at the middle of the circle. The first four symbols at each of the lower points I recognize—they're the standard glyphs for the elements of fire, water, air, and earth. But I'm not familiar with this fifth one, here at the top of the pentagram. It's almost reminiscent of a yang symbol. Hmm . . ."

Pita was bored by the shopkeeper's ramblings. If she stood here any longer she'd fall asleep on her feet. She ambled over to pat the cat. It was wedged into a space between books and shelf, licking its paw and affecting complete boredom and disdain. As Pita reached up and stroked it under the chin, the cat broke into a rumbling purr. Now that it was at a level where she could see its face, Pita noticed the animal's unusual eyes. One was a vivid yellow, the other a soft sky blue.

The cat shifted, rolling over so that Pita could scratch its belly. It used its rear paws to push itself along the books, and as it did so one was dislodged. Pita instinctively picked it up, intending to put it back into place. But then she looked around at the shelves on which books were stacked every which way, wedged into any available space. She was tempted to just drop the thing back on the floor, but the picture on the cover, done in brilliant primary colors and outlined in gold, caught her eye. It showed a beautiful woman reclining on the ground with her arms straight out in front of her, palms flat against the sandy soil, staring forward intently. Just above and behind her, framing her body with its own, was the shadowy outline of a cat whose eyes were twin dots of gold. To either side of the woman were strange sculptures of a creature with a cat's body and a human head. The statues looked vaguely familiar, and after a moment Pita remembered where she'd seen them before—in one of her history vids. They'd had a weird name: finks, or spinks, or something like that.

"You recommend this book, huh?" Pita jokingly asked the cat. It *mrrrowed* softly in response.

Slowly, Pita sounded out the book's title: *Way of the Cat: The Shamanistic Tradition from Ancient Egypt to Current Day*. It didn't sound very exciting. But flipping through the pages, Pita saw that it was full of beautiful pictures like the one on the cover. The book wasn't anything like the visual aids she'd been used to at school, with their animated graphics and icon-prompted info blips. With a vis-aid, all you had to do was touch the icon and a voice would explain what you were looking at. In comparison, these old-fashioned books were way tougher, full of long passages of printed text that looked like heavy gray blocks. It would be a real yawn having to sound out all the words yourself just to see what the pictures were about.

One of the illustrations on an inside page caught Pita's eye. It showed a woman wearing a cat-shaped headdress and standing in a building whose walls were covered in strange symbols. Around her feet sat dozens of cats of every description, looking up at her with a mixture of awe and intense loyalty. What appealed most to Pita was the woman's air of self-confidence and pride. Her eyes conveyed a clear message—this was one chummer you didn't want to mess with.

Instinctively, Pita touched one of the cats as she would a vis-aid icon. Then she sighed and shook her head. Lips moving, she sounded out the words beneath the picture: "Bastet, cat goddess of ancient Egypt."

Pita flipped to the front of the book, looking for instructions, and found something there called a Table of Contents. It seemed to be a kind of static menu, like the kind they put at the beginning of text-based computer files. The menu was organized into blocks called chapters, each with a title and a brief bit of text that was like a dialogue box underneath. Pita read through a few of them. There were chapters on the ancient rituals used to worship this Bastet, on something called mummification, on the jaguar priests of ancient Aztlan, and on the lion kings of Africa. But the chapter title that really intrigued her was one called: "The Way of the Cat: Empathy and Mind Control." She liked the sound of that. Mind control. Cats had a way of getting people to do what they wanted. Pita wouldn't mind being able to do that, too.

She turned her back to the others, then slipped the book into an inner pocket of her jacket. Quietly, she zipped her jacket shut. The cat watched her, its head tilted inquisitively to one side.

"You won't tell, will you?" Pita whispered to it.

It purred and closed its eyes.

When Pita returned to the others, Aziz was leaning back from the display, stroking his chin. Suddenly he jumped to his feet. Pita was worried that he might have been mind-reading again, that he'd monitored her thoughts when she boosted his book. But he ignored her and strode over to a messy pile of papers on the floor. Rummaging through them, he withdrew a book bound in cracked red leather.

"Here it is," he said, returning to his seat. "Remember what I was saying before, about the pentagram? The five-pointed pattern reminds me of the writings of the fourth-century Chinese alchemist Ko Hung." Aziz leafed through the book as he talked. "He postulated not four elements, but five: water, fire, earth, wood, and metal. His spell formulas are nonsense—no hermetic formula that omits the elemental energy of air stands a chance of working properly. It's simply too unbalanced. And despite extensive research, no 'fifth element' has ever been found. It's simply an impossibility.

"But what if the *Pao P'u Tzu* was misconstrued? Chinese alchemists used a lot of code words—they called mercury 'dragon' and lead 'tiger.' It's possible that the names of the elements were coded, too.

"Now this passage here"—Aziz tapped a page with his finger—"refers to the fourth element as 'firewood.' It's usually translated simply as 'wood.' I've always thought that wood was a curious choice as an element, but what if the original translation was 'burning wood'? When wood burns it produces smoke—not just particles of soot but also various gases. Ko Hung might have used 'burning wood' as a metaphor for 'air.' That would make more sense."

Aziz rapidly turned pages, then found the passage he wanted. "Here, Ko Hung refers to the supposed fifth element as 'bright-shining metal.' The translators always simplified this to 'metal,' but what if they missed the point?"

He looked up at the two reporters. Carla was leaning forward, lips parted, waiting for the punchline. Masaki's forehead was crumpled into a frown. He blinked slowly, as if he were on the verge of falling asleep.

Aziz had his back to Pita, but his rigid posture spoke volumes about his excitement.

"What if," he said slowly, "Ko Hung was not referring to a fifth element, but to a form of energy? And what if the text indicated not the metal itself, but its shiny surface? The proper translation would not be 'metal' but would instead be 'shining' or—"

"Light," Carla answered.

"Exactly." Aziz tapped the circle-and-pentagram graphic on the display screen. "So what we have here is some experimental spell that's apparently trying to summon a spirit whose physical manifestation is composed not of the usual four elemental energies, but of light." He stopped, eyebrows furrowed. "Of course, that just isn't possible. . . ."

"But it fits with the kid's eyewitness account," Carla said. "She said she saw light pouring out of the mage just before he died."

Pita shuddered at the memory of the brilliant white light and burning flesh.

Aziz turned to face her. "You were the one who saw this spirit?" he asked. His eyes bored into hers. Pita was unable to look away. She felt unseen fingers sifting through her mind and tried angrily to push them away. Then the mage sighed, as if suddenly very tired. "Yes, I see."

"What?" Carla asked sharply.

"The man in the alley that Masaki was going to interview. He claimed to know all about this spell. If he was the one who was going to spill it to the media, he must have been involved in the research—he probably helped design the spell. Be that as it may, it does sound like this was the spirit that killed him."

"But why would it do that?" Masaki asked.

Aziz shrugged. "Once a spirit has been conjured, the mage has to be able to control it. If the spirit's will proves stronger, it can resist being bound. Sometimes the struggle drains the mage to the point of unconsciousness, and the spirit escapes. An uncontrolled spirit is dangerous—and violent. It quite often tries to kill the mage who summoned it.

"Now here's the curious thing," Aziz added, scrolling to the end of the text. "According to this note at the bottom, addressed to you, Masaki, your contact was going to post this spell on Magicknet as soon as your story had run. Looks like your mage friend *wanted* other mages to try casting the spell themselves. But that would be suicide for most magicians. Not only is this spirit of a type I've never heard of before, it's extremely powerful. You can tell by the number of hours specified for the ritual."

Carla sat, thinking, tapping a manicured finger against her chin. "So maybe Mitsuhama didn't kill the mage," she mused. "Maybe he was stupid enough to try conjuring a spirit that was too powerful for him. You're lucky you weren't there when the spirit broke free, Masaki. It might have killed you, too."

Masaki paled and licked dry lips.

"It didn't kill me," Pita observed.

Carla shrugged the comment off. "You were just lucky, I guess."

"I don't get it," Masaki said, sitting up in his chair. "That chip was supposed to hold the specs of a research project Mitsuhama was working on. Where's the profit in summoning a spirit composed of light?"

"Like I said, I don't know how it's possible, but it would make a deadly weapon," Aziz observed. "Given the energy that would be bound up in the spirit, its light could blind, burn, or irradiate a person instantly. Imagine an assassin that could travel at 300,000 kilometers per second—at the speed of light. You'd quite literally never see it coming.

"*If* such a thing were possible," Aziz repeated, arching an eyebrow.

"But it's gone now, right?" Masaki asked.

"Possibly," Aziz answered. "A spirit that has escaped its summoner usually flees back from whence it came. But sometimes it hangs around in the physical world, for reasons known only to itself. The technical term for an uncontrolled being like this is 'free spirit.' Some of these spirits are playful and protective, but others are extremely dangerous. Lethal, even. And the only way to summon one is to learn its true name."

Masaki glanced uneasily at the window. Outside, sunlight was shining through a break in the clouds. It slanted into the shop, painting scrollwork shadows on the floor. "Could such a spirit get through your window, Aziz?"

The mage shrugged. "This shop is protected by every kind of magical ward I know how to create. The walls, floor, and ceiling are all—" His comment was cut short by the buzz of the telecom. An icon on its screen flashed, signaling that the incoming call contained a visual feed. Aziz reached over to answer the call.

Pita glanced down at the datacord that ran down from the telecom unit out to a jack in the wall. "Could the spirit get in through a fiber-optic cable?" she asked.

Masaki's eyes widened. "Damn!" he wheezed, diving for the cable. He yanked it from the wall, leaving a frayed stub hanging from the metal jack.

"What did you do that for?" Aziz snapped. "The spirit doesn't know who you are, much less that you're here." He glared at Masaki. "But assuming the spirit did somehow want to attack you, it would have done it out there, in the street. You'd be dead already. What are you going to do—hole up in my shop for the rest of your life without even a bloody trideo feed?"

Masaki glanced nervously around, then shot Pita a pained look. She made a face at him. All she'd done was ask a question, one that had seemed perfectly logical at the time. It wasn't like she'd told him to panic or anything.

"Excuse me, but I'd like to shoot some trideo," Carla reminded them. "That is, if we're all calm enough to handle it," she added sarcastically.

The mage grudgingly broke off the glare he'd been giving Masaki.

Carla smiled sweetly at him. "Now if you'll just face me, Aziz, I'd like to shoot a little trid while you explain the significance of the spell that's on the chip. Keep it short and put it in lay terms so our viewing audience will understand."

Aziz popped the datachip from the deck and turned to face Carla. When she reached for it, he pulled his hand back. "How about I keep this for awhile as payment for services rendered?" he asked. "I want to study the spell. I've never seen anything quite like it. The formula is highly theoretical, real cutting-edge stuff. The spirit it supposedly summons doesn't fit any of the known categories of hermetic magic. I'd like to know more about it."

When Carla started to protest, he waved a finger at her. "If I know you, Carla, you've already got a copy of this stashed away somewhere. And don't worry that I'll spill the beans before the story airs. Living with a reporter taught me all about confidentiality and not revealing my sources. Nobody's going to scoop you on this one."

Carla studied Aziz a moment, then nodded briefly. "All right," she replied. "If you think you can dredge up more information on this, go ahead and try. But be careful. And don't try casting that spell yourself. I don't want to see you wind up like Masaki's friend, burned to death from the inside out."

Aziz nodded solemnly, and drew a cross pattern over his heart. But Pita caught the greedy gleam in his eye. Carla might be a smart lady, but she was a sucker for a handsome face. Pita wouldn't trust this guy as far as she could heave him.

8

Carla rubbed her temples with her fingertips. The night without sleep had drained her; only the double-strength kaffetamine pills she'd taken were keeping her awake now. She resisted the urge to catnap in the back seat of the taxi, and decided instead to review the file footage from the interview Masaki had conducted, five years ago, with the mage who'd died in the alley. She jacked into her playback imager, then slotted a datachip into the handheld unit. Focusing on one of the icons that appeared in her cybereye's field of view, she initiated the playback.

The story was a standard puff piece, describing the opening of a new thaumaturgical supply store. The owner was Farazad Samji, a young entrepreneur from India who was trained in the hermetic tradition. The store specialized in talismonger's supplies from the Far East—rare herbs, vials of water from the Ganges, raw silk cocoons, polished gemstones, and cobra skins. But its main draw had been glazed bricks inscribed with cuneiforms. They were said to have come from a ziggurat of ancient Babylon. Whether or not this was a legitimate claim, the bricks had proved a popular item with mages who wanted to build their own alchemical kilns. A single brick was said to be enough to increase the magical potency of a kiln by a factor of ten.

Farazad Samji was an affable man with dark hair and a square jaw. Despite the exotic nature of his shop, he dressed conservatively, in a double-zip suit and solid-tone pants. He was keen about his craft, earnest and bright. Although he came from a rural background, he had interesting ideas on the modern technological applications of magic. Carla could see why Mitsuhama had offered him a job in their R&D division.

Although the puff piece had been no more than a minute long, the unedited trideo footage ran over half an hour. Carla muted the video portion, and, while half-listening to the audio, ran over in her mind what KKRU's researchers had learned about the mage thus far. Farazad was married to a woman named Ravinder and had two young children—Jasmine, age seven, and Bal, a boy of three. He lived in a tony condominium in North Beach, an upper-class section of Seattle that overlooked the ocean. He had a solid credit history with only moderate debts, no criminal convictions, and he rarely traveled. He was in every respect a good corporate citizen, devoted to his family. He was said by his neighbors to be a respectable, religious man who sometimes even led the prayers at his temple. Hardly the sort of person you'd expect to find dead in an alley.

Farazad had sold his store and joined Mitsuhama three years ago, back when the company was aggressively hiring for its magical research division. The advertised starting salary for the position had been 120,000 nuyen—twice Carla's current wage. What Farazad's salary had been when he died was anybody's guess; the IRS databanks certainly weren't telling. But given the value of his home and the small balance outstanding on his mortgage, it must have been plenty.

Carla looked out the window at the passing traffic. As far as she could tell, there weren't any vehicles following her. But if the Mitsuhama goons were on her trail, a taxi was the safest place to be. Not only was the vehicle bulletproof, but it was also warded against magical attack.

The driver, a heavyset man with a round face and wearing a black beret decorated with a Celtic pin, caught Carla's eye in the mirror. "Weird weather we been having lately, eh? You see that lighting flash last night?" His voice crackled through the speaker that was set into the plexiglass partition that separated the front and back seats.

"No." Carla answered. "I was inside all night, working."

"Well, it was tremendous," the driver continued. "It lit up the whole sky. I've never seen—"

His commentary was cut off by the beep of Carla's cel phone. "Excuse me," she said. "I've got a call. It may be personal. You mind turning off the intercom?"

"Sure thing," the driver answered. He touched an icon on his dashboard, cutting the com, then reached into a pouch that lay on the seat beside him. He pulled a chocolate from it and popped it into his mouth, then munched happily, staring straight ahead at the road.

Carla thumbed the talk button of her cel phone. "Yes?"

"Hi, Carla. It's me."

Carla recognized the voice of Frances, one of the deckers at KKRU.

"Yes?"

"Our subject just accepted a delivery of flowers," Frances answered. "She's home, all right."

"Did you get a digital sample?" Carla asked.

"You bet." Frances sounded smug. "I'm going to work on it right now."

"Perfect. And thanks."

Carla thumbed the phone's Off button and smiled. She was taking a risk, coming to the Samji house unannounced. But although it was possible to do a pickup straight off the telecom line during a phone interview, face-to-face interviews always looked best on trid. Of course, when Carla confronted her, Mrs. Samji might just shut the door in her face. On the other hand, she might open up and tell Carla everything she knew about her husband's work. All Carla had to do was find a subject that would get her talking. Children, maybe. Carla could always pretend that she had children the same age as the Samji kids. Or pets, perhaps. People always warmed up when you asked them questions about something they loved. It was then just a matter of easing them around to the more difficult questions. Like why her husband wanted to divulge corporate secrets. And whether Mitsuhama might have killed him because of it.

Carla gazed out the window, reviewing what she knew about the mage's employers. The Mitsuhama corporation specialized in computer technologies such as neural interfaces and guidance systems for autonomous robotic vehicles. It also did a substantial business in defense contracts, particularly smart guns and computer-controlled targeting systems.

From its headquarters in Kyoto, Mitsuhama Computer Technologies had expanded rapidly in the few years since its founding and now was truly multi-national. Its multiple branches and divisions encompassed the globe, and its net worth was said to rival the GNP of a moderately sized nation like the Confederated American States. MCT North America had hundreds of offices, labs, and manufacturing plants in the continent's various nations. In Seattle alone the corporation had a set of posh executive offices, a factory that produced data processors, and two separate R&D labs—one devoted to cybernetics, the other to pure magic research. Heading them all up was Tamatsu Sakura, vice-president of MCT's UCAS division.

Once she had a better grasp on her story, Carla would try to arrange an interview with Mr. Sakura. The job at hand, however, was to establish—on the record—the links between the Mitsuhama Corporation and the spell formula Farazad had intended to hand over to Masaki. Carla could speculate all she liked about the possible applications of a spell to conjure the ultimate stealth weapon. But what she had so far—a formula on an unmarked datachip that could have originated anywhere—was hardly conclusive evidence. If only the mage had lived long enough to be interviewed by Masaki, the uses to which the corp had intended to put the new spell could have been documented on trideo.

Pita would provide an eyewitness account of how the mage had died, but once again, that wouldn't prove anything. It merely implied that a mage—who just happened to work for Mitsuhama—had died at the hands of a weird spirit, probably one that he had conjured up using the spell on the chip. The fellow hadn't even had the courtesy to die outside the Mitsuhama offices. Instead, he'd been found in an alley behind the brokerage firm where his wife used to work. It was hardly the incriminating tie-in to Mitsuhama that they needed.

Carla drummed her fingers on her lap, hoping Masaki wasn't so bagged that he'd blow the interview with Pita. It was to be a straightforward take, a head-and-shoulders shot of the kid repeating her account of what she'd seen in the alley that night. They would run it as a picture-in-picture over the trideo that Masaki had shot when he found the dead mage. The trid was underexposed and jumpy; Masaki had only captured a ten-second clip before a DocWagon arrived on the scene. Rather than answer their questions, he'd scuttled away. But Wayne could probably enhance the image and use pixel splicing to stretch the clip into half a minute or more. If the story went to air tonight, Carla would use the interview she was about to shoot with Farazad's wife. Then tomorrow she'd chase down Mitsuhama Seattle management for a reaction. She'd probably get a "no comment" or a denial, but if she barged into the corporate offices during a live feed, the story would wrap with a bang.

If only Masaki had arrived at the alley a few seconds earlier, he might have gotten a shot of the mage's death. Now that would have been some take, to hear the kid describe it. In hindsight, it was a wonder Masaki had set foot outside at night to meet with the mage in the first place. Maybe there was some reporter left in him yet.

If so, it certainly didn't show in his interview with the young Farazad. Restoring the video and watching the unedited footage, Carla was amazed at all the loose ends Masaki didn't pick up on. If it had been her doing the interview, she'd have quizzed the shop owner about the bricks, which had a distinctively modern-looking glaze. And there, when Farazad called himself a "parsee," she'd have asked what that was. It was probably some obscure Indian caste, but Carla wouldn't have just let it slide the way Masaki did.

She focused on the icon that switched off the playback imager, then pulled her Encyclopedia Cybernetica datapad from her purse. Pressing the icon for a dictionary-format keyword search, she spoke the word "parsee" into the unit. A second or two later, text scrolled across its microscreen.

Parsis. Literal translation: "People of Persia." A name given to Zoroastrians who emigrated to India in the 7th century A.D.

Carla looked out the window. They had nearly reached the Samji home. She tried again, this time keying the unit for full encyclopedia mode.

"Zoroastrian."

Zoroastrian. A follower of Zoroastrianism, a mono-theistic religion founded approximately four to nine thousand years ago by the Persian philosopher Zara-thustra. Traditionally, both lay membership and member-ship in its priesthood were hereditary; the religion did not accept outside worshippers, nor did it admit children whose parents were not both members of the faith. In 2047, the religion had fewer than 20,000 practitioners, most of them in the Indian city of Bombay.

The scroll of words paused for a moment as the screen showed a graphic of a flame, burning in a silver chalice. It slowly dissolved into another graphic: a human figure with outstretched wings, which the ency-clopedia identified as a *farohar*, or angel.

With the increase in inter-faith marriages, it was thought that the Zoroastrian faith would die out in another generation or two. But in 2048, the religion opened its doors to outsiders and the first conversions were sanctified. Today, the membership is slowly increasing, but it remains to be seen if this relatively obscure faith will survive into the next century.

The Zoroastrian god, Ahura Mazda, is worshipped in a temple that contains an eternal flame that repre—

Carla shut off the encyclopedia as the taxi came to a stop outside a brick wall fronted by a heavy, wrought-iron gate. The wall completely encircled a number of ultramodern condominium units designed to look like terraced pueblos of adobe brick. The dun-colored condos looked strangely out of place against the gray Seattle sky.

A security guard in a neat beige uniform leaned over and tapped on the window next to Carla. She powered it down and handed the woman her press card. "I have an appointment to do an interview with Mrs. Samji, in unit number five."

The guard slid the card through a hand-held scanner, then stepped inside her booth. She would be calling Mrs. Samji, confirming the appointment. Carla waited, hoping that Frances had done her job. If all went well, the guard's call would be subtly re-routed to the station's telecom unit, where a sampled image of Mrs. Samji—copied from the telecom call she'd just answered, and hastily remixed—would give permission for Carla to be admitted. It was a classic reporter's trick, highly effective, albeit illegal. And it worked. The guard stepped out of the booth, handed Carla her press card, and waved the taxi inside the wall.

As the taxi pulled up in front of the Samji residence, Carla inserted her KKRU expense-account credstick into a scanner and keyed in a tip. Payment accepted, the driver unlocked the doors. Carla asked him to pull into a nearby visitor parking stall and wait for her. If the Mitsuhama goons showed up, she wanted a safe haven close at hand. She realized that the interview with Mrs. Samji might take some time. But with the overtime Carla was putting into this story, the station could bloody well pay to keep the meter running.

Carla stepped out of the taxi, smoothed her skirt, and climbed the three steps to the front door. A message board in the door scrolled a greeting and warning in one: "Welcome to the Samji residence. These premises protected by a watcher spirit."

Despite the rustic Western look of the condo, the door was solid enough, made of heavy wood that had been carved with ornate designs. Carla suspected that these were magical wards capable of blocking unwanted astral intruders. There was no maglock; just a thumbprint scanner, set into the middle of the door. It would be an easy security system to fool, but the high walls and guarded gate of the complex provided most of the protection. For visitors, there was a com unit set into the faux adobe brickwork beside the door.

As Carla touched the pad, a woman's voice issued from a hidden speaker. "Who is calling, please?" The screen inside the unit remained blank.

The response had been too swift to be anything other than an automated answering program. But Carla activated the camera in her cybereye and made sure her audio pickup was working, just in case Mrs. Samji activated the com screen. As soon as Carla identified herself as a reporter, anything she recorded was fair game, and could be aired on the news.

"It's Carla Harris of KKRU Trideo News," she answered.

"I have no wish to talk to reporters." This time, the voice sounded live.

"It will only take a moment or two, Mrs. Samji."

"I have answered enough questions already," the voice continued. "Of course I recognized my husband's body, even though it was badly burned. I had to identify him for the officers. It was a terrible experience. I wish . . . Please leave me alone. You reporters ask such horrible questions." The woman sounded close to tears.

Carla frowned. Had Mrs. Samji already spoken to other reporters? As far as Carla knew, the other newsnets hadn't bothered to pursue the item. They were playing it as a straightforward crime story in a city where muggers used magic as often as they used muscle. As far as they were concerned, Farazad Samji was just another wealthy corporate exec who had wound up on the wrong end of an unusual form of fireball in a violent robbery attempt. Hardly a lead story, considering the nightly body count. But maybe someone was having a slow news day, and had decided to try for a reaction piece from the family. Worse luck, they'd slotted Mrs. Samji off. She wasn't likely to want to talk to anyone now. But if Carla could just get her to open the door, maybe she could fire off a question or two and get a reaction shot before the door was slammed in her face.

"I'm not here to ask ghoulish questions, Mrs. Samji," Carla said quickly. Searching for inspiration, she remembered the information she'd gleaned from the encyclopedia. "I work the religion beat. I understand that Mr. Samji was an important member of his temple. I want to do a profile on him . . . a simple obituary. I think the story could help to increase awareness of the Zoroastrian faith. I'm sure your husband would have liked to see an increase in membership in the temple, and this story just might—"

The screen beside the com pad flickered to life, framing Ravinder Samji's head and shoulders. Carla quickly focused her cybereye on the image.

Mrs. Samji proved to be a small woman with long black hair that was twisted up into a bun at the back of her neck. She wore a mauve jumpsuit that looked as if it were made out of raw silk, and gold earrings that glittered against her dark skin. Her eyes were bloodshot and puffy, as if she'd been crying. There were dark circles under them that she hadn't bothered to hide with makeup. Although she met Carla's gaze, she kept glancing down.

"Farazad would have liked a story on the temple," Mrs. Samji said softly. She gnawed at her lip with white teeth. "I do not have to talk about my husband's death?"

"Not if you don't want to," Carla answered. She kept her fingers crossed, hoping the com unit didn't have a lie detection spell built into it. At the home of a mage, anything was possible.

Mrs. Samji looked down at something off-screen again, hesitated, then nodded. "Very well."

Locks clicked and the door swung open.

Mrs. Samji stood just inside the door. Carla glanced down to see what she had been looking at. It turned out to be a hazy, doglike shape—a magical spirit of some sort. As the creature trotted out from behind the door, Carla could see that it had only partially manifested on the physical plane. It had a translucent, ghostly body about the size of a terrier, with a head like a Chinese lion.

"This must be the watcher that your message board

warned me about," Carla said. "Is it one of your husband's magical creations?"

"A watcher?" Mrs. Samji shifted uneasily. "Yes, I suppose it is. But it's one of Miyuki's creatures, not Farazad's. She left it here for me yesterday, as . . . protection for the children and myself. She said that people might try to take advantage of a woman whose husband had recently died. It's much more powerful than our usual—"

"That was kind of Miyuki," Carla said, smiling. "She must be a good friend."

A peculiar look crossed Mrs. Samji's face. "Yes. A good friend. Of my husband." The comment seemed to be directed as much at the lion-headed dog as it was at Carla.

Carla filed that away for future use. Clearly Mrs. Samji didn't like this Miyuki—whoever she was. Yet she'd accepted a magical creature from her that made her nervous. Interesting.

"May I come in?" Carla asked. She braced a foot against the floor, in case Mrs. Samji changed her mind about the interview and tried to shut it suddenly.

"I suppose that would be possible," Mrs. Samji answered, glancing down again at the creature.

The lion-headed dog backed up, but kept Carla under its scrutiny. She thought she could see tiny drops of mist dripping from its bared fangs, but that might have just been her imagination. The creature, despite its small size, projected a palpable aura of menace.

Mrs. Samji ushered Carla into a living room furnished with two overstuffed leather couches and an expensive-looking trideo home entertainment unit that took up most of one corner. Children's toys were neatly lined up like soldiers on parade at one edge of the room. From the plush feel of the carpet, Carla suspected that it was real wool. The lion-headed dog followed them into the room, its feet leaving faint gray smudges on the white carpet. As Mrs. Samji settled onto one of the couches, it sat by her ankle. She glanced uneasily at it before beginning to talk. Carla thought she saw the creature's head move slightly, a bobbing motion something like a nod.

"Where is your camera?" Mrs. Samji asked.

Carla settled into the opposite couch. "I don't need one," she said. "This is an informal interview—more like a chat." While she spoke, she adjusted the zoom in her eyecam for a tight shot of Mrs. Samji's hands. The woman was twisting the rings on her fingers; the shot could be edited into Carla's story as evidence of a widow's grief. Noticing that a vase was slightly blocking the shot, Carla reached across the table between the two couches to shift it slightly. As soon as she sat back, Mrs. Samji leaned forward to slide the vase back into its original position. It was an instinctive action, the habitual act of someone who liked everything in its proper place. Exactly in place.

"You wanted to know about my husband's work with the temple?" Mrs. Samji asked.

"The temple, yes," Carla answered. "Please tell me about it." Having bluffed her way in here, she decided to let Mrs. Samji talk and see what came up. She would work in questions about Mitsuhama as the opportunity arose.

Zooming out again to capture a full-length shot of Mrs. Samji as she started to speak, Carla spotted a holo image of Farazad on a side table. She shifted along the couch until it appeared in her field of view, just over Mrs. Samji's shoulder. The holo of the mage, holding what Carla presumed was one of his infant children in his arms, would make a nice graphic element.

"Farazad often spoke at the *mabad*—at the temple," Mrs. Samji began. "His father was a *mubad*—a priest—and his grandfather before him. My husband could have claimed the title as well, but instead he chose to study magic. He regarded his studies as a religious practice, as a way of becoming closer to his god. He often spoke of this at the temple, and encouraged others to follow the hermetic tradition. He said that magic was a manifestation of the divine spark that exists within all—"

"Let me make sure I have your husband's history correct," Carla interrupted. "Instead of becoming a priest, Mr. Samji worked as a mage. For which company?"

"Mitsuhama Computer Technologies," Mrs. Samji answered, after a brief glance at the creature at her feet.

"He was employed there at the time of his death?" Carla asked.

Mrs. Samji's lips whitened slightly as she pressed them together. "Yes."

"Working in their magical research and development lab?"

The pause lasted longer this time. "Yes."

"What sort of work did he do for them?"

"What does it matter?" Mrs. Samji replied. "Farazad was planning on taking a leave of absence from Mitsuhama, and devoting himself to the temple."

"But if you could just tell me a little more about his work with Mitsu—"

"I thought you wanted to talk about the *temple*," Mrs. Samji said, frowning.

"Of course," Carla answered smoothly. "This is just background material—the usual sort of questions a reporter asks when doing an obit piece. Name, occupation, age, names of surviving family members, number of years spent with the corporation, the type of work he did for Mitsuhama, whether he was working on anything especially important when he died . . ."

"I thought you were a religious reporter." A hint of hostility had crept into Mrs. Samji's voice.

"I am," Carla said, backpedaling quickly. "I find Zoroastrianism one of the most interesting of the world's religions. I'd like to hear more about its history, and its founder, Zarathustra. Perhaps you could start by telling me more about him. And about the significance of the eternal flame that burns in your temple."

She seemed to have allayed Mrs. Samji's suspicions, at least for the moment. The woman picked up a framed flatscreen portrait of Zarathustra from the table beside her and held it out for Carla to look at. It showed a young man with a full brown beard and flowing hair, wearing a white robe and hat. His eyes looked earnestly up—to heaven, Carla supposed. Mrs. Samji began talking about the life of the prophet, explaining how he had aided the poor and extolled the virtues of morality and justice. Carla bided her time, waiting for another lead that would allow her to ask about Mitsuhama. In the meantime, she focused her cybereye on a point just over the woman's shoulder. A door in the wall behind her was partially open. Using her low-light boosters and image enhancers, Carla could see that it led to a study. A desk just inside it held a typical business work station. Everything in the room was neat and orderly, from the two pairs of men's slippers lined up with perpendicular precision against the wall to the precisely aligned row of family portraits on the shelf above the desk. The only exception to this rigid neatness was the work-station itself. An interface cable lay in an untidy heap on the floor, and empty plastic memory chip cases had spilled onto the chair. A cyberdeck lay wrong-side-up on the desk, its circuitry exposed. It looked as though the deck's central processing unit had recently been removed.

Carla rose and began walking toward the open door. "Is this your husband's study?" she asked. "Perhaps we should do the interview in here. It would help to give me a feel for his—"

"No!" Mrs. Samji leaped to her feet and grabbed Carla's arm. She yanked Carla back toward the couch, a frightened look in her eyes. "You can't go in there," she said. "It's a mess. I haven't had time to clean it since Miyuki . . . since Farazad died. He left it in a jumble."

Carla paused. The explanation just didn't scan. Mrs. Samji was a neat freak who went to the extreme of organizing her children's toys into neat rows. The sight of the messy den should have driven her nuts by now. Unless . . .

The lion-headed dog was focusing all of its attention on Carla. It had shifted away from Mrs. Samji's ankle, and stood directly in the path that Carla would have taken to the study. Suddenly, Carla realized what must really be going on. The desk was rifled because Mitsuhama had been here already, picking up any incriminating pieces of data that Farazad might have left behind. They must have had some inkling that he'd been ready to blow the whistle on their research project when he died, and had come to his home to make sure he hadn't left any files at his work station. And just in case Farazad had shared information about the new spell with his wife during pillow talk, they'd left the magical creature behind as a reminder to her to keep quiet.

No wonder Mrs. Samji was reluctant to talk. One word about her husband's work and she'd be lion-dog chow. The spirit creature might be only semi-corporeal, but Carla was sure it had a nasty bite. Or that its handlers did.

Mrs. Samji continued steering Carla toward the door. Clearly terrified, she was trying to end the interview. Carla tried to get her talking again. She focused upon the playback icon in her cybereye, keying an instant replay of the last ten seconds of data. "Uh, you were telling me about Zarathustra," she prompted. "You were starting to tell me the origin of his name . . ."

They had reached the door. Carla glanced behind her, saw that the lion-headed dog was close at her heels. Now that it was closer to her, Carla could feel the chilling cold that radiated from it.

"The word is Persian," Mrs. Samji answered. "In the ancient tongue, it translated as 'the golden light.' We conceive of Ahura Mazda as the source of all light, of all love. And thus his prophet shared this attribute. Now I really must insist that you leave. My husband's death has left me feeling very drained. We will continue this interview at another time." She held the front door open, motioning for Carla to leave.

"The source of all light," Carla mused. "How interesting." She turned to capture a good, clean image of Mrs. Samji. The lion-headed dog squatted behind the woman, its mane ruffed. Carla had no way of knowing if the creature would react to the question she was about to ask, but decided to take a chance. She stepped closer to Mrs. Samji, and framed her in a head-and-shoulders shot.

"Is that why your husband wanted to make public

the spell formula for summoning a spirit made of light?" she asked suddenly. "Did he really believe they were messengers sent by Ahura Mazda, your god? Did Mitsuhama murder your husband because of what his religious beliefs compelled him to do?"

Tears welled in Mrs. Samji's eyes. "Farazad was wrong," she cried. "If the creature had been a *farohar* it never would have—"

The lion-headed dog lunged forward. It was amazingly fast—quicker than Carla expected. She gasped and leaped backward, expecting to feel its cold fangs lock on her throat. But instead it thudded against the door, knocking it shut.

"Drek!" Carla pounded a fist against the door. She'd almost had it in the can. And what was going on in there? Carla stabbed at the com unit on the wall. "Mrs. Samji! Are you in there? Are you all right?"

"Please," Mrs. Samji said through the speaker. "I have my children's welfare to consider. The interview is over. If you do not go, I will call security to remove you."

Carla felt a rush of relief. The woman was unharmed! Then the reporter's instincts took over. "Mrs. Samji! Can you make a statement on the record? Can you confirm that the spirit that killed your husband was conjured as part of a Mitsuhama research project?"

"The Samji family thanks you for stopping by," an automated voice replied. "Unfortunately, we are not receiving visitors at this time. Please call again."

The pills Carla had taken earlier were starting to wear off. She blinked, trying to fight off a sudden rush of exhaustion. She'd been so close to confirming the link between the spell on the memory chip and Mitsuhama. If only the lion-headed dog hadn't . . .

Then it struck her. The doglike spirit had acted in a sophisticated manner. What if it had been providing a direct, telepathic feed to Mitsuhama? The corporation certainly had the resources to have someone on the scene immediately, possibly even the corporate goons who'd tried to gun down Pita last night. And given the knowledge that Carla had just displayed about the contents of the datachip, they might be ready to take measures to keep her quiet. Measures like those they'd taken against the pirate reporter. Measures that could kill both the story—and Carla.

Carla sprinted for her taxi. This story was getting hot. It was time to get back to the station and its nice, bullet- and spell-proof glass.

9

Pita rolled over in her sleep. She knew she was dreaming, but was unable to shake the terrifying images from her mind. She was being chased by people whose tattooed skins were made of thick dabs of water-soluble paint. They followed her through the rain, their skins melting from their bodies, revealing skeletons beneath. The click-click of their bony feet was growing closer, closer . . .

"Hey, kid, wake up."

A hand shook Pita's shoulder. She awoke instantly, her heart pounding.

Wayne, from the editing department, looked down at her. He was a red-haired man in his thirties with a slight pot belly. Tucked under one arm was a miniature decks whose flatscreen displayed a freeze-framed image of an oil rig going up in flames. Wayne smiled and jerked a thumb at the door. "There's someone at the front desk asking for you, kid."

"There is?" Pita was immediately wary. "Who?" She swung her legs over the edge of the plastifoam cot that was tucked into a storeroom just off the newsroom. Through the partially open door, Pita could hear the buzz of voices and the sound samples that were being mixed in the studio.

"Some guy with goofy-looking hair. He wouldn't tell the receptionist his name. All he would say was to tell you he wants to talk to you about 'little pork dumpling.' "

Pita jumped to her feet. "Yao's here?" Her street-wise skepticism warred with hope and relief. "But I thought he was dead."

"Doesn't look like it to me." Wayne pushed the door open. "Come and see for yourself. I've got the guy's image on the monitor that's patched into the surveillance camera in the lobby. Maybe you should scan it, just in case."

Pita followed Wayne into the studio. It was laid out in an open plan, with glass-doored editing booths along one wall, work stations at the center of the room, and banks of telecom equipment and computer terminals. An entire wall was devoted to hundreds of flat-screen monitors. Each displayed a different trideo channel. On several of the monitors, large letters that spelled out the word "RECORDING" were flashing.

"Which monitor?" Pita asked.

Just as Wayne was about to answer, his wrist began to beep. He glanced at the watch implanted into his skin. "Uh, oh. Thirty minutes to air. I'd better get back if I'm going to finish editing the interview Masaki did with you." He pointed toward the left-hand side of the bank of monitors. "It's the one just over there. Between the satellite feeds and the foreign language channels."

One of the reporters called out urgently from across the room. "Hey, Wayne! You added that take to the Quetzalcoatl story yet? We're running out of time!"

"It's nearly done!" Wayne shouted, then hurried away.

Pita glanced at the monitors, but their sheer number overwhelmed her. She didn't see any that seemed to be showing the lobby. Besides, did it really matter? Only Yao knew about the "Little Pork Dumpling" code. It had to be him.

Pita hurried down the corridor that led to the lobby, but paused before opening the door, just to make sure. Looking through its tinted glass, she peered out past the reception desk. An ork in frayed jeans and a loose synthleather jacket was standing in the lobby, his back to the door leading to the street. He held one arm tucked against his chest and his shoulders were hunched, as if he were in pain. When he crossed over to one of the chairs and sat down, Pita recognized him at once by his narrow jaw and the wary look in his eyes. It was Yao, all right. Alive. For the first time in days, she smiled.

Somehow, Yao had escaped from the corporate goons. Pita was intensely curious to find out how he'd managed to survive the hail of bullets that had cut him down. But she was also reluctant to face him. She'd abandoned him on the street after he'd been shot. Just like she'd run off when Chen was gunned down. It would be easier just to hide in the newsroom, to let the receptionist send Yao away. But he'd promised to do a story on what Lone Star had done to Chen and the others. Unlike Carla and Masaki, he would surely keep his word. His own brother had died, after all. Pita should keep her end of the bargain and finish the interview. Assuming Yao still wanted to.

She opened the door and stepped out to the receptionist's desk. Yao immediately looked up and flashed her a smile. "I thought I'd find you here," he said. "Are you all right?"

"I'm sorry I ran away, Yao. I thought you were—"

He waved a hand in a dismissive gesture. "It wasn't anything a bulletproof vest couldn't stop. I'm just bruised is all."

"But I saw blood on your—"

"One bullet did hit my arm." He shrugged it gently. "So who was that woman in the car?"

"Her name's Carla. She's a reporter here."

"How do you know her?"

Pita scuffed at the floor with the toe of one sneaker. "Uh, I asked her to do a story on how the cops killed Chen." She glanced briefly at Yao to see if he was angry. "I would've come to you first, but I didn't know where you were. So I went to Carla, instead. But she wasn't interested. She didn't seem to give a frag about Chen."

"So how come she showed up when I was interviewing you?"

Pita shrugged. "I guess she changed her mind. She says she'll do the story now."

"I see," Yao said with a sneer. "So you were going to give my story to the competition."

Pita looked up. "I thought you were dead. Yao. I didn't know what else to—"

"Forget it." He stood awkwardly, shoulders still

hunched. "Now then, are you ready to finish our interview?"

Pita chewed her lip. "I don't think I should leave the station. Masaki doesn't think I'd be safe on the streets. He says those guys who shot you were yakuza."

"We won't be on the streets," Yao reassured her. "I've got a room at a hotel, just down the block. We'll finish the interview there. I'll walk you back here afterward if you like." He gestured at the door that led to the newsroom. "You got all your stuff? Need to get anything before we leave?"

"What you see is what I got," Pita answered. "Not much. So how did you know where to find me?"

"I got the bar code of the car, and had a friend of mine deck into the vehicle registry databanks to find out who the owner was. Imagine my surprise when I found out it belonged to Jun."

"Who?'

"Jun Masaki. The reporter who was driving the car. I helped him out with a news story once before I started working with *Orks First*! But he probably wouldn't remember me."

"Oh," Pita said. "Everyone calls him by his last name, around here."

Yao pushed the door open. "Anyhow, I knew that Masaki was a reporter for KKRU. I figured that he might have brought you back to the station." He held the door open for her. "And I was right."

Pita hesitated. "I should tell him where I'm going."

"Why?" Yao asked. "You'll be back soon enough. He won't even miss you."

Pita sighed. Yao was probably right. Masaki had been working furiously ever since they'd returned from Aziz's shop, and the lack of sleep had made him irritable. He'd practically bitten her head off during the interview, snapping at her for mumbling and for playing with the junk in her jeans pockets. He said the rattling noise spoiled the audio, and told her to empty her pockets. Grumpy old fragger.

"O.K.," Pita told Yao. "As long as we're back in half an hour." She wanted to be back at the station in time for the six o'clock news to make sure Masaki kept his promise and blanked out her face to hide her identity. Those corp goons knew what she looked like by now. But there was still a chance those Lone Star fraggers didn't.

She followed Yao outside. "Hey," she said, noticing his ear, "you lost your scanner."

"Yeah. Come on."

He led her down the steps, one hand resting protectively on Pita's shoulder. As she descended them, something nagged at her. Something she couldn't quite put her finger on.

Then it hit her. She'd had to tip her head back to look at Yao's ear. He should have been shorter than that. And some of the things he said had been odd. As far as Pita could remember from things Chen had told about his brother, Yao had never worked as a real reporter. He'd only done pirate trideo broadcasts. And the body language had been all wrong. Yao kept a careful watch on doors; he didn't stand with his back to them, the way he had just now in the lobby.

Pita glanced nervously at the man beside her.

This wasn't Yao.

She didn't want to find out who it really was. Ducking out from under his hand, she bolted for the top of the stairs, back toward the main entrance of the KKRU building. But before she'd taken two steps, the man behind her barked out a sentence in a foreign, lilting language. Suddenly Pita was running in mid-air. She struggled wildly, trying to make contact with the ground. But the stairs were a good half-meter under her feet. She twisted about—just in time to see the man who'd been posing as Yao shed his skin in a shimmering transformation. Clothes, hair, features—all blurred and changed. The man was suddenly thinner, darker. With a shock, Pita recognized the dreadlocked elf who'd tried to cast a spell upon her earlier. The mage! The one who'd led the goons to her! Like a fool, she'd fallen into his trap, despite the dream warning, despite Wayne's reminder that she should scan her visitor on the monitor first—where his true form would have been revealed. Now she was trapped, and he would kill her. Pita cried out, but even as she did, a bolt of yellow streaked from the elf's fingers toward her, enveloping her. Pita's eyes closed and she fell forward into darkness.

Pita woke up in a hotel room. She was lying on her side on a bed, her wrists tied tightly behind her back. Her eyes felt gummy and her breathing was slow and deep, despite her pounding heart. She found it difficult to think, to focus. It was like waking up from a dream that you didn't want to end—except this was a nightmare. With a start, she realized she was naked.

The two men staring at her were the same pair who'd been chasing her earlier. The heavy-set one was sitting on a chair near the bottom of the bed, feet propped up on the mattress. He regarded her with an utter lack of expression that Pita found frightening. His arms were folded across his chest, and the sleeves of his shirt had lifted a little so that Pita could see the dark blue tattoos extending from his arms onto his wrists. *Yakuza,* she thought, all hope fleeing at the thought.

The slender man was standing, leaning back against a table with his hands on the edge of it. One hand moved, clicking the rings on his fingers against the wood. The tip of his little finger was missing. As Pita groaned, he said something in Japanese to the other man, who grunted in reply. Then he leaned toward Pita.

"You took something that didn't belong to you," he said in perfect, unaccented English. "A small bronze disk about so big." He held his thumb and forefinger about three centimeters apart. "A datachip. We want it back."

"I don't know what you're talking about," Pita said.

The slap across her cheek took her completely by surprise. The man had moved as fast as a striking snake. Pita's head bounced off the bed with the force of the blow, and tears welled in her eyes. Her cheek stung.

The man leaned back against the table once more. His eyes ranged up and down Pita's naked body. She suddenly felt horribly vulnerable.

"We can do anything we like with you," the slender man said. "Anything at all." He let the words hang in the air for a moment. "And don't try to scream for help. We'll kill you if you do."

The larger man shifted in his chair. Pita looked fearfully at him, blinking back her tears.

"We know you take chip," he said in a low voice that was devoid of all emotion. "Chip not in pockets of dead man. DocWagon not take; cops not take. Mage do sensing, say you take. But chip not in your clothes. You tell us where chip is."

Pita gnawed at her lip to stop herself from sobbing. "What if I tell you?" she asked. "Will you let me go?"

The slender man's lips curved in a smile that did not reach his eyes. "Of course."

Pita knew she was trapped. There was no way out of this; the best she could do was buy herself a little time. "I thought the chip was a simsense game," she said. "I tried it in my digideck, but it didn't work. All that came up were these weird diagrams. They looked like something maybe a mage would use. I thought maybe I could sell it for a few nuyen, so I took it to a shop on Denny Way. The guy there gave me ten nuyen for it."

The larger man lifted his feet from the bed and sat up. "What is name of man?" he asked.

Pita tried to shrug, to look as casual as possible, but her bound wrists prevented any motion. "I only know his first name: Aziz."

"And the name of the shop?" the slender man asked.

"The Secret something-or-other," Pita answered.

The slender man glanced at his companion and said something in Japanese. Then he turned for the door.

"Wait," Pita said. "I kept my part of the deal. I told you where the chip was. Let me go!"

"Not until we get that chip back."

"But you could at least untie me and let me get dressed," she pleaded. She gave a meaningful look at the larger man, who was plainly intent on staying behind to watch her. "Even with my hands free, I'm not going to get past him."

"You may dress," he said after a moment's consideration. "I'm sure that Tomoyuki is tired of looking at you. But afterward you will have to be tied up again. And if I find that you have lied to me about that chip, you will die. There will be no second chances."

10

The blare of the telecom's alarm snapped Carla awake. She groaned and wiped the sleep out of her eyes, then sat up and looked around her apartment. She'd slept in her clothes after kicking off her shoes and neatly folding her jacket over a chair. She'd only intended to take a quick nap, but she'd set the alarm for six p.m. just in case she slept too long. Now the logo and call letters of KKRU Trideo News scrolled across the screen as the newscast began.

The camera zoomed in toward Rita Lambrecht and Tim Lang, tonight's celebrity news anchors. Carla winced. Rita was a ditsy elf who smiled even when reciting the night's body count, and Tim was a dwarf wrestling champion who'd been chosen for his rugged good looks and deep baritone voice. It looked like Rita would give the lead-in to the top story. Carla hoped she didn't muff her lines.

Amazingly, the lead story wasn't on the dead mage. Instead, it was about a group of rebels who'd blown up an oil refinery in the Yucatán; killing 127 technicians in the explosion. A grim-faced Aztlan spokesman promised "swift and thorough" retribution for the attack. The footage that accompanied the piece was gruesome and graphic, but Carla still didn't think the story deserved the three minutes KKRU had given it.

Nor was the dead mage mentioned anywhere in the international slot. Carla fumed through the first seven minutes of the newscast, debating whether or not to call the station. But then the local news segment began to roll, and Tim "Tiny Terror" Lang began to read the first story.

"In local news, a Seattle resident whose body was found in an alley two nights ago appears not to have been the victim of the thief who has been dubbed the 'Magical Mugger.' Instead he apparently died at the hands of a new form of magical spirit that may still be at large on the streets of our city. Here, with an eye-witness report, is Jun Masaki."

Carla sat on the edge of her seat, waiting for the report. She had to wait for the end of a ten-second infomercial between the lead-in and the news clip. Annoying, but these commercials were what kept KKRU on the air. Indirectly, they paid her salary.

The piece opened with a shot that superimposed a framed image of Pita over the footage Masaki had shot in the alley. When she pointed at the ground, describing what she'd seen, the ork girl seemed to be gesturing at the body itself, then at the mirror-like windows from which the rays of light had bounced like a ricochet. As she spoke, white rays seemed to emerge from the body while the words GRAPHIC SIMULATION scrolled across the bottom of the screen. It was a standard editing technique; the dotted lines didn't look enough like beams of light to arouse complaints of news fabrication, while the frame around Pita told the viewers that her take was a super-imposed shot. The take ended with Pita describing how the dying man had dropped a datachip he'd been holding, and how she had picked it up. Funny, how she called it a "personal chip." Masaki should have called her on that one. It might weaken the Mitsuhama connection.

Carla was also irritated to see that Masaki had used a "Jane Doe" face to digitally mask the girl's features. But the kid was speaking well, giving a vivid descrip-tion of what she had seen.

The take dissolved into a split-screen pairing, the left half of the screen showing Aziz seated amid the clutter of his shop, while the right showed Mrs.

Samji. Wayne had done a seamless job of editing; the two seemed to bounce comments off one another, livening up an otherwise boring "talking heads" take.

Aziz: "The spell on this chip is unknown in the hermetic tradition."

Mrs. Samji: "My husband followed the Zoroastrian faith."

Aziz: "It's a formula for conjuring a spirit."

Mrs. Samji: "Farazad regarded magic as a religious practice. He often used it in his sermons."

Aziz: "The formula seems to summon a spirit I am unfamiliar with."

Mrs. Samji: "We Zoroastrians conceive of God as light."

Aziz: "The uniqueness of the ritual seems to indicate the spirit manifests as a blinding light."

Mrs. Samji: "Farazad was wrong . . . to . . . call on . . . the creature."

Carla caught the slight tonal shifts that indicated Wayne's splicing of the last comment. But it was extremely subtle, something the average viewer would never notice. The story would be getting to the point any second now, by revealing the Mitsuhama connection. She leaned forward expectantly as the right screen did a fast cut to an interview with the medical examiner who'd examined the body. The doctor reiterated that the mage had died of massive internal trauma due to heat—"cooked alive from the inside out," as she so eloquently put it. She also speculated that the burns were assumed to be magical in nature, since there had been no evidence of fire in the immediate vicinity.

The frame containing the image of the medical examiner did a flickering dissolve, as if it were being consumed by fire. Carla smiled and gave it the thumbs-up. "Nice touch, Wayne," she said to herself.

But her smile soon evaporated. There was one last clip from the Aziz interview, in which the mage speculated that the powerful spirit might have been conjured by Farazad and then somehow escaped from his control to become a free spirit—a magical wanderer. The story did a quick cut to a meteorologist, who noted that sheet lightning—a rare occurrence over Seattle—had been spotted over the city skyline in the past two nights. Then Carla and Masaki appeared for a quick voice-over byline.

And that was it. The story ended with a dissolve back to the studio.

"Well, well," Tiny Terror commented. "A dangerous new spirit on the loose in Seattle. That's not something to make light of."

His co-anchor laughed brightly at his pun. "Keep an eye on the sky tonight, folks. In other news . . ."

"What?" Carla leaped to her feet. "That's it?" She snatched up the telecom remote and furiously stabbed the icon that would fast-dial the station. After a second or two, the screen displayed the image of Gil Greer, producer of the six o'clock newscast. He was human, but large enough to be taken for a troll in the wrong light. His shoulders strained the fabric of his suit, and he usually ambled about the office like a large, untamed bear, scratching his back on door frames and glowering at the reporters. He frowned out at Carla from the telecom screen. A single word was all that was required; this was a line reserved for use by KKRU reporters only: "What?"

"The story on the dead mage—Farazad Samji," Carla said. "What's the idea of running it as a metro piece?"

"The death is two days old," Greer answered. "The only thing that made the story fresh was the free-spirit-as-cause-of-death angle. You're lucky your boy-friend is such a looker and that the story had a tie-in with the weather update, or we wouldn't have run it at all."

Carla stopped short of protesting that it had been more than three years since anyone could have called Aziz her "boyfriend." Instead she kept her professional cool. "But where's the Mitsuhama angle? This is a story about a corp dabbling in a dangerous new magi-

cal technology—not about unusual fragging weather
patterns!"

"What Mitsuhama angle?" Greer grumbled.

"Didn't Masaki tell you?" Carla asked, dumbfounded. "The chip from the pocket of the dead mage.
The spell. It's a Mitsuhama project."

"I didn't see any footage showing that connection."

"Farazad Samji worked for Mitsuhama's research
lab," Carla explained. "The day before he died, he contacted Masaki, telling him he'd turn over the specs on a
top-secret research project the corp was developing.
He was on his way to meet with Masaki on the night
the died!"

"I guess Masaki didn't think his own testimony was
enough to establish a link. Without outside confirmation and hard evidence, we haven't got a story."

Carla was dumbfounded. She couldn't believe Masaki had given up so easily. A story about the contents
of the chip that deliberately did *not* mention Mitsuhama probably made him think he was safe. He
could curl up in his cozy little world of feature pieces
and the big bad corporation and its goons would go
away. The sad part was, he was probably wrong.

"We've still got a story," Carla argued. "A good one.
About a corp that's experimenting with dangerous new
magical tech."

"No, we don't," Greer countered. "At least not until
I see some evidence that directly links this crazy spirit
thing to Mitsuhama." He sounded irritable; his patience
was obviously wearing thin. Still, Carla wasn't one to
give up a story without a good fight.

"We could have at least worded tonight's piece to
imply that—"

"You don't take on the big boys without documenta-
tion," Greer cut her off. "You don't even drop hints.
Not when Mitsuhama's legal department has a bigger
budget than our entire news network."

"Give me one more day," Carla pleaded. "I know I
can get something. If I follow up the angle that—"

Greer was glancing at something to one side, only
giving Carla part of his attention. "We're on the air,"

he reminded her. "I haven't got time for an extended debate on the merits of this supposed story."

"One more day!" Carla insisted.

"All right," Greer at last agreed. "But if you don't come with anything new, I spike the story."

11

Pita edged around the bed to the spot where her clothes lay in an untidy heap. The big yakuza stood by the door, arms folded across his chest. The look in his eye warned her not to try anything. Pita had never seen such an empty, merciless expression. She knew, deep in her gut, that this man could kill her with as little remorse as if he were swatting a mosquito.

Turning her back to him, she pulled on her underwear and jeans, then yanked her shirt over her head. She wrinkled her nose at how filthy her clothes were. It was warm in the room, but she put on her jacket anyway. If she got a chance to run . . .

The yakuza loomed over her, a police-style plasticuff strip in his hand. Pita rubbed her chaffed wrists. The plastic had been cinched tight, and had bitten into them. Deep red creases encircled her wrists. Her hands still tingled.

"Please," she said. "You don't need to tie me up. I won't try anything. I promise. When your friend comes back you'll see I told you the truth. You won't need to . . ." She couldn't bring herself to say the rest: to kill me.

The book Pita had stolen from Aziz's store was lying on the floor. She bent to pick it up. The yakuza had obviously searched it, perhaps thinking the disk was hidden inside. The spine of the book was bent and the cover had come loose.

The yakuza shoved her onto the bed and grabbed one wrist in his huge hand. "You stay quiet. No talking."

"Wait!" Pita said. "Couldn't you tie my ankles this time instead? Your friend's going to be a while; the magic shop is probably already closed. If you untied my wrists I could look at the pictures in this book to pass the time. That way I won't bother you by talking or anything. I'll keep quiet. And I still won't be able to escape, with my ankles tied together."

The yakuza grunted, then grabbed Pita's ankles and cinched the plasticuff strip firmly around them. He sat down again in the chair at the end of the bed. "You look at pictures," he said, still watching her impassively. "Keeping quiet."

Pita caught sight of her soiled face in a mirror behind the yakuza and reflexively wiped at the dirty smudges with the back of her hand. She'd been dirty and sweaty and smelly plenty of times before, but this time it seemed to get in her way somehow. But then she turned to the book, fumbling it open to the picture of Bastet, the woman whose expression of confidence had so appealed to her. On the next page was a picture of the same woman in a different pose, this time with her fingers curled into clawlike hooks. Her eyes were closed, but the eyes in the cat headdress she was wearing stared out from the page with glittering intensity. Pita scanned the block of text on the accompanying page and saw the words that had previously caught her eye: thought control. Tentatively, she touched a finger to the illustration, feeling the raised bumps of the golden eyes on the cat headdress, then running her finger down to the woman's clawlike hands. Without consciously meaning to do so, Pita flexed her fingers, curling her hand into the same shape.

She tried to read the text, but the yakuza who sat only a few steps away kept distracting her by his ominous presence. She didn't dare look around the room for a means of escape; his eyes followed her every move. Even when he lit a cigarette, he stared at her through the curling blue smoke. Unable to concentrate, she closed her eyes, trying to block him out.

She ignored the sound of his chair creaking, instead concentrating on the soft hum of the heating unit in the corner. It had a stutter to it, and the rasping of the fan made it sound as if the heater were breathing. The noise was almost like a cat's purr. It was soothing, somehow, and as Pita focused upon it, she felt her own breath slowing, synchronizing with it.

Although she'd had difficulty with some of the words, Pita had managed to read one section of the text, a passage describing how ancient shamans had controlled their fellow humans by emulating the patience and determination of the cat. She touched her finger to the illustration now, feeling the raised gilt that had been used to outline Bastet's headdress. Pita suddenly wished the headdress was a computer icon that would trigger the reassuring voice of the woman.

Without warning, a thought came unbidden to Pita's mind, the image of a house cat that desperately wanted to go outside, but who could not because of a closed door. In her mind, Pita saw the cat sitting and staring at the door, completely focused upon it, as if compelling its owner to come and open it. She saw a hand reaching for the doorknob. The purring of the heating unit grew louder and louder as the hand grasped the knob, began to turn it . . .

The image dissolved as Pita heard footsteps outside the door. Her eyes sprang open. Was the first yakuza coming back? Were they going to kill her now? Her mouth went dry, and a cold, sinking feeling settled in her stomach. Should she run—or hop, rather—to the door and make a break for it? She glanced at the yakuza seated at the end of the bed. He sat up a little, as if expecting her to make a move. Pita gnawed at her lip and winced with indecision. What should she do?

The footsteps continued on down the hall, past the door of her hotel room. Somewhere outside, Pita heard a door open and close. Then silence.

The yakuza settled back into his chair.

Pita stared at the door of the hotel room, the door that led to freedom, to escape. She focused on the doorknob, imagining it turning, imagining herself passing out through the door. So sharp was her imagination that she could visualize every detail. She curled her hand into a clawlike shape, imagined long sharp hooks digging into the back of the yakuza's head.

Tugged by their grip, he would stand up, turn the knob, and swing the door open wide. Pita would hop through it and be off down the corridor outside. Instead of chasing after her, the yakuza would quietly close the door, sit back down in his seat, and . . .

The yakuza gave a small groan and shook his head, as if troubled by a headache. The hand holding his cigarette hung at his side, ignored. The other hand gripped the arm of the chair. Its knuckles were white. Instead of his usual inexpressive look, the man was frowning, blinking rapidly. Then suddenly, his face went utterly blank. His jaw dropped open, and he swung his head over to focus with staring eyes upon the door.

"Open it," Pita whispered, "Please. Open it."

The yakuza lurched to his feet and crossed the short distance to the door with slow, wooden steps. He reached for the doorknob, his hand slipping off it twice before he finally got a grip. Then slowly, it turned. He pulled open the door, stopping as it bumped against his foot.

For the space of a heartbeat or two, Pita was too amazed to react. Then she realized what she had done. Just like the woman in the picture, she had controlled another human, had placed silent commands directly into his mind. But there was no time to stop and wonder at it, now. She swung off the bed and hopped as quickly as she could to the door. Avoiding the large yakuza, she slipped around him and out into the hallway of the hotel. With a series of ungainly hops, she made her way to the elevator. Slapping the call button with one hand, she turned fearfully back to look at the room she'd just vacated. The door swung slowly shut, locking with a soft click.

"Now sit down," Pita whispered. She imagined she was staring through the door. She visualized the yakuza taking a seat and resuming his watch over the now-empty bed. She imagined herself still lying upon it, quietly looking at her book.

The elevator doors hissed open. Pita, who had been leaning on them, fell headlong into the elevator.

Thankfully it was empty. Glancing at the numbers above the door, she saw she was on the sixth floor. When an automated voice asked for her destination, she ordered the elevator to the bottom parking level. Hopefully that would give her enough time.

She tugged her jacket down to protect her hand, then smashed her fist into the glass panel that covered the emergency stop button. Grabbing a shard of glass from the floor, she began to saw at the plasticuffs around her ankles. The plasticuffs were tough enough that even a troll couldn't snap them by brute strength alone. But if they were cut sideways, against the grain . . .

The elevator slid to a stop at the lobby. Pita sawed frantically with the shard as the doors began to open. All she needed now was to meet the smaller yakuza, who even now might be on his way back from the magic shop. Just as the doors slid open, the last strand of the plasticuffs parted. Pita struggled to her feet, but all she saw was an empty lobby. Whoever had punched the button must have taken the second elevator, which was just closing with a soft *ping*.

Laughing with relief, Pita sprinted for a side exit. She was free! She burst through the door and ran out into the familiar cover of darkened streets.

12

Carla slid her magkey into the slot and waited for the voice-recognition system to cue her sample phrase. A series of red lights flashed across the keypad, but the system was being unbelievably sluggish. Five full seconds had elapsed, and still the voice prompt hadn't activated.

Carla waited, tapping her foot. She was tired and just wanted to get inside her apartment. She'd fix herself a double martini, power up the bubble tub, and try to forget about the day's frustrations.

She'd pounded the pavement all morning and afternoon trying to crack the Mitsuhama story. But every attempt to get an interview with corporate vice president John Chang had failed. The director of the Mitsuhama Seattle Hermetic Research Lab had also refused to meet with her, as had the lab's project manager. None of the clerical employees whom she'd been able to corner was willing to talk, and nobody would provide her with the names of the mages who worked at the lab. Carla had finally been able to interview Mitsuhama's public relations officer, but the woman had been pleasantly uncooperative. No, Mitsuhama was not prepared to reveal details of the projects currently underway at the lab—certainly not until adequate patents and spell formula copyrights were in place. And to the "best of her knowledge," Mitsuhama was not currently experimenting with any spells similar to the one Carla described.

Yeah, right.

Carla pulled her magkey out of her purse and pushed it into the slot a second time. At last the system responded: "Please provide voice sample."

"I'm tired, I'm hungry, and my feet hurt," Carla said. "Now let me inside my apartment, you stupid machine."

The lights on the pad cycled to green. "Voice sample accepted. Alarm system is . . . off."

Carla pushed open the door. She stepped inside, peeling off her jacket and adjusting the apartment's lighting and temperature controls. Then she stopped. Something was wrong. The cushions on her couch were lying on the floor, and the doors of the cabinet beside it were open. One end of the throw rug in the living room was folded back, and it looked as if a drawer in the telecom cabinet had been tipped upside down, scattering its contents.

"Damn," Carla whispered. Letting the door close silently behind her, she pulled a narcoject pistol from her purse. The weapon was small enough to fit in a pocket, and could be carried anywhere since its plastic parts wouldn't trigger security alarms. Carla raised it to chest level and flicked the safety off. If the burglar was still in her apartment . . .

She didn't hear anything except the ticking of her kitchen clock and the low hum of the telecom unit in the living room. The unit's screen art was on, feeding into the speakers a low-frequency noise that mimicked the tonal harmonies of a Gregorian chant.

Quietly, Carla slipped around the corner, pistol at the ready. The living room was empty. So were the kitchen, bathroom, and bedroom. The burglars must have fled, but just to make sure, Carla checked in the closets and under the bed. Nothing.

Lowering her pistol, she began to take inventory. They'd obviously found her personal electronics, but had left them tossed on the floor. That was curious, because the laptop and digital camera were worth a lot of money and were easy to pawn. They should have been the first things grabbed.

Nor had the intruders stolen any of her jewelry, even though they'd dumped the clothing drawer in which it had been hidden all over the bed. They'd also dumped out the jar of coins in the corner, but hadn't taken any. The intruders had also gone through the kitchen cupboards—and the fridge, Carla noticed, when she reached inside it for a cold drink. She was thankful they hadn't dumped all the food on the floor.

She pulled a gin cooler from the fridge and sat at the kitchen table, surveying her jumbled possessions. Calling Lone Star would be pointless; the cops would merely take a brief look around, make a few notes on their datapads, and leave again. Break-ins were so common these days that sometimes the police didn't respond until a day or two later. By that time the victims had usually become frustrated and already cleaned up the mess.

The more Carla thought about it, the less certain she was that robbery had been the motive for this break-in. The intruders had overlooked just about every valuable in the place. Oh, sure, they'd taken all her simsense games and a few of her computer chips as well—the kind of thing kids usually went for. But these hadn't been kids. They were professionals. They'd gotten past her voice recognition system—and it was a good one, not likely to be fooled even by a digital recording—as well as the motion detectors and sensor unit in the hallway. To get that far and not be detected, the intruders had to be good. And motivated.

Carla suddenly realized what they must have been after. If she hadn't been so tired, she'd have guessed it right away. While she'd been out knocking on Mitsuhama's doors, the corporation had come to her. She hurried into the bedroom and picked up from the floor the jacket she'd worn yesterday. She slid a hand into its pockets. Empty. The intruders hadn't gotten what they'd originally been looking for, but they'd taken the next best thing. The chip onto which Carla had copied the spell was gone.

It didn't matter that much. Aziz still had the original, and she could always get it back from him. And the cops had a copy; they'd demanded one as soon as they saw the story. In the meantime, the intruders had probably been fooled into thinking they'd gotten the original. One datachip looked much the same as any other, and the one Carla had used for the copy was bronze, just like the original. Since it contained the spell formula the intruders were looking for, they probably wouldn't be back. They'd taken all her other memory chips, too, even though all they had to do was pop them into the telecom unit to see what was on them. But perhaps they'd wanted to be in and out quickly.

It was annoying to lose the other chips. The simsense games had been expensive, and the home trideo she'd shot of her niece couldn't be replaced. As for the rest of the chips, they were all blank except . . .

"Oh, drek," Carla moaned, closing her eyes. "Not my personal stuff."

But they'd found it. The drawer where Carla hid her "private" recordings had been overturned. The chips she'd stuffed into the back of it, behind her neatly folded sweaters, were gone.

She sat on the bed, looking up at the ceiling—at the spot where decorative, tinted glass blocks hid the lens of a holocamera. The closed-circuit camera was automatically activated every time anyone came into the bedroom. Carla used it to record her romantic encounters, then later would replay and savor her favorite moments. She wasn't sure if it was the reporter in her, compelling her to record her affairs, or some weird sexual kink. But it didn't matter now. Somewhere, somebody was no doubt having a good laugh at her expense, titillating themselves by watching her private recordings. Or perhaps the chips were already on their way to a porn shop. Or perhaps to a rival trideo station for broadcast on the evening news.

Carla groaned and threw her head into her hands. How could she have been such an idiot? She should have erased those chips long ago, or disconnected the holo camera before the intruders . . .

The intruders! The camera would have recorded them! Carla dragged a chair over to the spot beneath the hidden camera and clambered onto it. Reaching up, she swung aside the false front of the glass block. She hit the power-off key for the camera, then popped the chip out of it. Carrying it to the living room, she slotted the chip into her home editing equipment and hit the

Play icon. She had to skip around a little bit; the first track she viewed showed her sitting on the bed, staring up at the camera, while the next one she jumped to was of a romantic evening from three weeks ago. But at last she found the right track. She watched, leaning forward for a good look at the screen as the first of the intruders entered the bedroom.

The camera was looking down on the room, and thus it caught the top of the man's head and shoulders from an overhead angle. But by using the logic-rotation system built into the holo unit, Carla could fill in the rest, patching together a composite from the images the camera captured as the intruder moved around the room.

He was human—a Native American—perhaps in his mid-twenties. His hair was crewed to sharp points, and he had a black bird tattooed across the back of his right hand. His left hand was gleaming chrome. He wore jeans, a brown leather jacket with fringed sleeves, and heavy black boots. He had paused only briefly to scan the room, then moved immediately to the dresser and began methodically opening and dumping its drawers.

After a minute or two, a voice called from another room. Carla paused the recording, skipped back a few seconds, then boosted and sharpened the sound.

"Found anything, Raven?"

The crew-cut intruder sorted through the clothes on the floor, picking out datachips. "Yeah," he answered. "But there's more than one. Any idea what color it was?"

"It looked bronze in the broadcast," the other voice instructed. "But grab anything you can find. They might have used another chip for the story, just to be cute."

"Do you really think this is worth it, Kent?" Raven called back. "The reporters might have lied about what was on the chip. We may not find anything here to interest Ren—"

"Don't be such a fragging pessimist," the off-screen voice said. "Of course the spell is valuable. And even if it's not, what do you care? I'm paying you well enough, aren't I?" The voice grew louder as a figure moved into the camera's field of view. Once again,

Carla let the recording run, selecting pieces to edit together into a composite image.

The second man was a pale-skinned elf with thinning blond hair tied back into a scraggly ponytail. He looked to be in his late thirties, and wore baggy trousers, a white shirt, and a black opera-style rain cloak. A fiber-optic cable with a universal port hung out of one pocket, and his hands were sheathed in surgical gloves—probably to avoid leaving fingerprints.

He bent over to fish out a datachip that had fallen under the dresser. Carla, watching the screen, winced as he slipped it into a pocket. She hoped it wasn't the recording of the guy who'd wanted to . . .

Raven was talking again. "So let me get this straight. The mage hired you to extract him so that his bosses wouldn't geek his family after he spilled the beans on their hush-hush research project. He was gonna ask the newsies to make the interview look like a tape they'd gotten from his kidnappers, right? So how come he got himself scragged?"

The elf leaned against the door frame. His eyes scanned the room warily. "You sure you disconnected the security system?" he asked.

Carla held her breath, hoping they wouldn't stop talking.

The first man glanced up, a smug expression on his face. "I'm sure. Ain't that why you hired me, chummer? For that—and to crawl around on the floor, searching for chips so you wouldn't get your nice clothes dirty?"

The elf gave him a thin smile. "You want to know why he got geeked? Use your wetware. It's simple. Obviously Mitsuhama learned what their golden boy was up to and decided to shut him up. But in doing so they let the genie out of the bottle. Now everyone knows the secret—even if they don't know whose secret it is. That was sloppy of them, overlooking the datachip in his pocket."

From inside the closet, the other man made *tsk tsking* sounds. "Silly fraggers," he said in a mocking voice. "Rule number one: always check the pockets." He stepped out of the closet, one hand rifling the pockets of a pair of Carla's pants. He tossed them playfully at the elf, then began rummaging through the other garments.

"So you didn't do the hit?" Raven asked. "I thought you said you sold out Mister Mage."

"Not to Mitsuhama, I didn't. And now my employer is getting nervous. He wants to see some results for his down payment."

"You're sure the guy who was geeked in the alley was your boy? He might have figured your double cross and hired some other runners to fake his death."

"I'm sure it was him," the elf answered. "His wife confirmed it when I called her the next morning."

"Just like that?"

The elf chuckled. "I told her I was a reporter."

Carla, watching, nodded to herself. No wonder Mrs. Samji had felt pestered with "horrible questions." These two looked as if they would be anything but subtle.

On-screen, the elf nodded to himself. "We can still turn a profit on this one if we can find the chip. My 'Mister Johnson' would probably like that even better than a potentially uncooperative mage. A datachip doesn't take as long to give up its secrets."

The first man closed the closet door. "That's it," he said. "Nothing else in this room to search."

The elf consulted his watch. "We've been here twenty minutes," he said. "We'd better get going if we're going to make our second stop." He stepped out of the bedroom.

"Are we going to the shop?" Raven asked, following him.

"Too late for that," the elf answered. "Last night it—"

The recording ended abruptly as the Native American stepped out of the bedroom. The screen flickered, then showed Carla entering the room, narcoject pistol in hand.

She hit the screen's Pause icon, then skipped back to review the last few seconds. A time code in one corner of the screen showed the hour, minute, and second that the recording had been laid down. It had ended precisely at 2:16 p.m.—more than five hours ago. The two intruders could be anywhere by now.

Carla jumped when her phone beeped. She pulled it from her pocket, flipped it open, and saw Masaki's face on the tiny screen. He looked wild-eyed and nervous. A trickle of sweat ran down his temple. He wiped it away, then broke into a hurried rush of words as Carla activated the visual pickup.

"Thank god you're all right, Carla," he wheezed.

"What's wrong, Masaki?"

"While we were at work today, someone broke into my apartment and turned it upside down. As soon as I saw the mess I shut the door and called the cops. I had them go in first. I'm not taking any chances, after the yaku—" He glanced warily around as if expecting the yakuza to leap out at him from a corner at any moment, then wet his lips. "—after our run-in with those goons on the street the other night. They must be looking for the chip. You'd better not go back to your apartment. If they find you there alone—"

"I'm sitting alone in my apartment right now, Masaki," Carla said. She smiled at his shocked expression. "And thanks for the warning, but it's too late. My place has been trashed, too. And probably by the same people."

"Have you called the cops?" Masaki asked.

"Oh, come on, Masaki. You must know how useless that would be."

"I guess so," Masaki agreed. Then he shot her an accusing look. "I thought you said those goons wouldn't come after us if we aired the piece."

"It wasn't them," Carla said. "It was runners."

"Who?"

"Shadowrunners," Carla explained. "They saw our story and came after the chip, hoping to steal it and sell the spell formula. They were originally hired to fake a kidnapping of Farazad. He told them he wanted a cover for an unauthorized leave of absence, but the extraction was probably designed to prevent Mitsuhama from taking revenge on him after he went public about their research project. Farazad had planned to disappear the morning after his interview with you. But it looks like the runners he hired got greedy and were planning to sell him to the highest bidder."

Masaki gave Carla an incredulous look. "How do you know all this?"

Carla nearly told Masaki of the recording made by her hidden camera. But then she paused. Masaki liked to gossip; if Carla told him she had a camera in her bedroom, the story would be all over the newsroom before Carla had poured her morning soykaf. And she wasn't sure she wanted to say, over an uncoded frequency, that she had good, clean images of two professional shadowrunners on file. Given the right scanners, anyone could listen in on a cel phone conversation.

"I have my sources," Carla said, winking.

"You say they wanted to sell Farazad? Who to?"

Carla thought back over the conversation her camera had captured. What had the shadowrunner named Raven said? He'd started to say a name—something like "ren." Carla had thought it to be a man's name. Renny. Or Reynolds, perhaps. But now she realized what it had to be. "Ren" wasn't a who, but a what. A corporation.

"Renraku," she whispered.

Masaki caught the whisper. "Renraku Computer Systems? That fits. They're Mitsuhama's chief rival. They'd naturally want to know what the competition was up to."

"And now they do," Carla answered. "The runners got what they came here for."

Masaki frowned, then realized what her comment meant. "You mean they got your copy of the spe—"

"Masaki!" Carla said abruptly. "I think we'd better save this chatter for tomorrow morning in the newsroom."

Masaki's eyes widened. "Oh. Right." He tried to feign a casual air. "Well, good night, then. See you tomorrow."

The screen of Carla's cel phone went blank.

13

Pita sat in a corner of the main branch of the Seattle library, wedged into a space between two stacks of archaic twentieth-century books. She'd run here after escaping from the Yakuza at the hotel, and hadn't set foot outside since. The library offered everything a street kid needed—warmth, shelter from the rain, washrooms to clean up in, free entertainment, and the cafeteria had plenty of vending machines that offered Growliebars, soykaf, and nutrisoy snacks. Best of all, the library was open twenty-four hours a day. The only trick was in avoiding the security guards, who would turf out anyone they caught sleeping.

The secret was to keep moving from one area of the building to the next. Pretend you were scanning a chip at one of the data displays in the reading room, and had fallen asleep because it was boring. Then catch a nap in one of the viewing booths on the second floor. Then off to the children's department, where animated holos played continuously. The volume was a little intense, but the padded benches were soft. Then over to the reference department, where you could use an old piece of datacord to make it appear you were jacked into one of the municipal decks. If you could sleep sitting up, it was easy to look as if you had merely closed your eyes to eliminate noncybernetic input.

But the best place to crash was in the tiny, cramped section that contained old-fashioned hardcopy—books. The aisles were narrow and cluttered, and hardly anybody could be bothered with the cumbersome task of turning pages and manually scanning each one. The data display units, with their instantaneous keyword searches, animated holo graphics, and automated download systems were vastly more popular.

By moving from one area of the library to the next, Pita had been able to catch a few quick, brief naps. When morning broke and her stomach began to rumble, she jimmied one of the vending machines and grabbed a Growliebar and a kaf, then returned to the hardcopy section. She pulled the paperback she'd stolen from Aziz's shop out of her pocket and began to look through it. The colorful illustrations called to her somehow, and she couldn't stop looking at them. They aroused in her a curiosity that the vis-aids at school never had. Driven by a yearning to know more about these fascinating images, she forced herself to read the accompanying text.

Most of it was pretty complicated and difficult to understand. But Pita was able to glean a few of the basic concepts. According to the book, everything—people, plants, stones—even the book she held in her hands existed both in the physical world and in astral space. But there were some things whose true form could only be seen in astral space—totem animals, for example. Like the one called Cat.

The human shaman who followed Cat could do the same thing. And it was the totem that did the choosing, not the other way around. It wasn't just a matter of getting someone to give you magical training, or of building a "medicine lodge"—whatever that was. You could do all that drek, and still not become a shaman. Not until Cat called you.

Pita smiled at that one. It sounded pretty silly. She imagined a cat calling to her, just as her old neighbors had called their pet cat home at supper time. Instead of, "Here kitty, kitty, kitty! Come and get your dinner!" it would be, "Heeere Pita! Come and get your magic!"

Tired of reading, Pita set the book down and sat with her chin on her knees, thinking. A lot of strange drek had happened to her over the past couple of days. First there'd been the dream she'd had in the studio that had warned her about the disguise the elf mage would use to lure her out of the news station. She should have paid more attention to that. And then there was

the weird trance that Pita had been able to put on the
yakuza guard, back at the hotel room. Did that mean
she had some kind of magical talent? She hoped so.
Because that would also mean she wasn't just another
gutterpunk—some ugly ork girl that didn't amount to
anything. She was magic. She was special.

Pita's mouth broke into a wide grin as she thought
about the possibilities. Just wait until she met up with
those kids from her old school who'd called her "porkie."
She'd show them.

She heard footsteps, and looked up. A security guard—
the same one who'd rousted her earlier from another
corner of the library—rounded one of the stacks. Spotting
her, he stopped, then pointed a finger at her.

"All right, kid, this is your last chance," he said.
"This is a library, not a hotel for street trash. You've
been here for hours, and now it's time to go. Shift your
sorry ass out of here."

Pita smiled smugly at him. Staring hard at the man,
she visualized him turning around, walking away. She
curled her hand into a claw. "Go," she whispered.
"Leave me alone."

Nothing happened. Pita's heart began to beat more
rapidly. The power that had infused her earlier had
deserted her. She was alone again. Just a powerless
kid, about to be turfed back out on the street, out into
the open where the yakuza could find her.

She looked wildly around, preparing to make a break
for it. But she couldn't focus clearly. Something had
happened to her vision. The shelves around her had
gone all shimmering and fuzzy, and the books on them
were translucent. The guard had a weird glow sur-
rounding him, an ugly purple and green smudge that
she instinctively recognized as his anger.

Pita had a wild image of her eyes gone round and
small, with pupils that were slitted, like a cat's. She
imagined her ears flattened back against her head in
fear. Was she going crazy? Was this a Mindease flash-
back? Or was this some new sort of magical power
manifesting itself? If so, it wasn't helping any. She felt
so dizzy she didn't trust herself to move.

The guard's hand fastened around her collar. He yanked Pita to her feet. All at once, the world snapped back into focus as her vision returned to normal.

"I said move!"

"But my book . . ." Pita twisted around to see where it had gone. The book had fallen to the floor.

"You planning on taking out a book, kid? You got a library card?"

"I don't need one," Pita protested. "That book is mine. I brought it in with me."

"Sure, kid." He picked up her book and reached up to place it on the shelf.

Pita grabbed his arm. "It is mine," she insisted, wrenching the book out of his hand. She flipped open the torn cover. "Look. There's no library code."

"That does it." The guard was really slotted off now. "Out!" Grabbing Pita by the collar of her jacket, he hustled her through the library and out the door. She twisted, she protested, but the guard was as oblivious to her complaints as he had been to her silent mental commands. She was pushed out the revolving doors and onto the sidewalk.

Pita stood outside the library, shivering in the cold night air. She stuffed her book into a pocket, then slammed her fist against a pole that was holding up an awning. She was rewarded with a shower of water that doused her hair. From inside the building, through the glass of the revolving door, the guard watched to make sure she would leave. Pita tried again to penetrate his thoughts, to make him turn away, but even though she concentrated so hard that her head hurt, nothing happened. It seemed her magical talents appeared only when they felt like it. She couldn't call upon them at will. And that was fragging useless. Unless . . .

Pita flipped the finger at the guard, then trudged away up the street. If she went back to Aziz's shop, maybe the mage could put her in touch with a shaman who could help her. At the very least, she needed someone to explain what had just happened to her, to assure her that she wasn't going crazy after all. Aziz would probably still be slotted off at her for telling the yakuza that he had the Mitsuhama datachip. But if she explained that they'd forced her to tell them, that they'd have killed her if she didn't, he'd probably understand. She was just a kid, after all. Not a powerful mage like him. And knowing that sly fragger, he'd probably have made a dozen copies of the chip by now. He'd have handed the yaks the original chip, befuddled them with a spell, and sent them on their way.

For now, Pita didn't worry about how she would persuade Aziz to help her. She might have to flatback for him, or trade him some favor. But one way or another, she was determined to satisfy the curiosity that her strange experiences had awakened in her.

Pita stood in the rain, guilt washing over her. Across the street, where Aziz's shop had been, was an empty, blackened ruin. The stores on either side were intact, but the space between them was a darkened concrete shell, the interior filled with soggy piles of charred books and fallen ceiling tiles. Rain streaked across the broken shards of glass that still hung in the place where the front window had been, smearing soot across the ornate scrollwork. The smell of scorched wood, wet paper, and melted plastic hung in the air like a shroud.

People walking along the sidewalk in front of the store seemed oblivious to its demise. They hurried along the sidewalk, chins tucked against the evening rain. The burned-out shop was empty, devoid of life. Pita wondered if Aziz had died in there, and if the inferno had been triggered by the spirit somehow slipping in through a crack in his magical defenses. But perhaps he'd had some warning, and was able to escape.

A flash of white amid the charred remains of the shop caught Pita's eye. Something was moving in there, in among the ruined books. Pita pulled back into the shadow of a doorway, hoping it wasn't some spirit left by the yakuza mage to watch for her. But then the creature slipped out through the empty window, and Pita saw what it was. She breathed a sigh of relief, recognizing the shop's cat.

The cat was probably hungry and looking for its

master. Pita reached into her pocket, found the nutrisoy bar she'd boosted from the library vending machine. It was supposed to smell and taste like smoked beef. She wasn't sure if the artificial flavors could fool a cat, but it was worth a try.

Pita waited for a break in traffic, then slipped across the street. She crouched beside the broken window, unwrapped the bar, and held it out to the cat. The animal approached delicately, whiskers twitching as it sniffed the food. Then it started lapping at the salty coating with a pink tongue. Pita crumbled off a corner of the bar and dropped it on the ground. The cat ate it, then looked up plaintively at her with one yellow eye and one blue, and *mrrowed.*

Pita gave the cat more of the bar, then scratched it behind the ears while it ate. "That's it, kitty," she said. "You can't afford to be finicky when you're on the streets. You eat what you can get, and sleep where you can. I hope you have a dry place to curl up for the night."

The cat turned and trotted down the sidewalk. Curious to see where it was going, Pita followed it around the corner. The animal padded down the sidewalk for another half block, then turned into an alley. At first, Pita couldn't see where it had gone. But then she spotted the cat's tail disappearing through a broken window.

The window was at ground level and led to the basement of a department store. The glass was broken, and the mesh that had covered it was loose at one side. It would be a simple matter to yank it away, reach inside, and turn the latch.

Kneeling beside the window, Pita peered into a darkened room and a jumble of old junk. Mannequins lay on top of rigid foam boxes, display signs had been piled up in a corner, and an old sink fixture lay broken on the floor. A thick layer of dust covered everything; Pita could see the cat's footprints on several of the boxes. It was obvious that no one had entered the room in ages.

Pita glanced up the alley to make certain no one was passing by. Then she eased the mesh cover from the window. It squeaked a little, but soon she could reach inside. She shoved on the rusted latch, and the window opened. She slithered inside, feet first. Then she closed the window and reached between the shards of broken glass to pull the mesh back into place.

The room was quite dark; only a little light filtered in through the dirty glass of the broken alley window. Above, the store was silent, closed for the evening.

Satisfied that nobody would disturb her, Pita lay on her side behind some boxes, next to a heating vent. The cat leaped down beside her, then rubbed its head against her hand. Pita stroked it, then yawned. She hadn't slept that well the night before; the security guards at the library had kept her from taking more than a series of brief naps. This place was much better. Warm, dry, a little dusty, but a good place curl up. Here she could hole up for a while to hide from the yakuza. She cuddled the cat against her chest, pretending it was Chen. She hadn't felt this safe in . . .

She awoke from a fitful sleep to the sound of boards creaking overhead. Sunlight was streaming through the broken window and people were moving about in the store above. From somewhere down the hall came the sound of water gurgling in pipes.

Pita sat up and stretched. She was hungry, and still tired, and needed to go to the washroom. She stood, brushed the dust from her jeans, and made her way to the door. Opening it a crack, she peered out into the hallway. Like the room she'd slept in, the corridor was also piled with junk. Pita stepped between storage boxes and battered display signs, testing the doors as she went. Most of them were locked, including one at the end of a short flight of steps. Pressing her ear against it, she heard nothing. She decided it must lead to the store above. From the amount of dust on the landing, she doubted it had been opened in recent months.

Pita retraced her steps and found an unlocked door. She reached in and groped for a light pad. Palming on the light, she saw that this was a washroom. The fixtures were old and stained, but when she tried the taps she found that they still worked. She shut them off quickly; the running water made a hollow, groaning sound.in the pipes.

Pita smiled at her discovery. All she had to do to avoid detection was time her uses of the washroom to coincide with shoppers' visits to the bathroom in the store above. The water that rushed down through the connecting pipes would hide any noise.

In the meantime, she could stay here. There was a Growlie Gourmet and a Stuffer Shack just down the block. She ought to be able to boost a few snacks from the latter, and if she timed her visits to the dumpster behind the restaurant right, she'd be able to snag the kitchen scraps before they went bad. She wondered what time it was, and tried to remember when she'd last had a decent meal. She was pretty fragging hungry. And despite her sleep, she felt jangly and weird. She could tell herself over and over again that she was safe now, that she had found a place of refuge from the two goons who'd jumped her. But she still felt tense and on edge.

Something soft rubbed against Pita's ankles. She jumped, then realized it was only the cat. She picked it up and stroked its head, listening to its rumbling purr. If the cat had escaped the fire, perhaps Aziz had, too. And if he was still in the city, maybe he could help her, could put her in touch with a shaman who could tell her if she really did have any magical talent. Running the type of shop that he did, Aziz must have known plenty of people who practiced magic.

There was just one problem. Aside from the shop— which now lay in ruins—Pita had no idea where to find Aziz. He might be listed in the city directory, but she doubted if he'd just be sitting at home, waiting for the yakuza to come and get him. No, it was fragging hopeless. She'd never find him.

Pita heard footsteps in the alley outside, and ducked as she saw someone walking past the grimy window. It was someone in suit pants, someone with expensive shoes. A yakuza? Her heart thudded in her chest until the footsteps had faded into the general traffic noise.

She held the cat close against her, stroking it with one trembling hand. The animal gave a soft *mrrow* and rubbed its cheek against her chin in response. Pita closed her eyes and nuzzled against its soft fur. She'd wait until later to venture outside, until there weren't so many people on the streets. She'd just have to ignore the rumbling in her stomach and the dizzy feeling in her head. Her life was on the line here, and she didn't want to risk it for a fragging Growlie Bar.

14

Carla sat at one of the data terminals in the KKRU newsroom, scanning the files the computer had flagged for her. She'd set it to automatically download anything to do with Mitsuhama, and in just one day the file was already enormous. She tapped the icon at the bottom of the screen, rapidly flipping through the articles. It looked like nothing but noise—PR blurbs about corp executive appointments, announcements about the openings of new plants in Osaka and London, business articles analyzing MCT stock performance, a ridiculous "consumer bulletin" on a customer who claimed that his MCT neural interface was the cause of his marital problems, puff pieces on a new robotic mini-drone that the company had developed, a story about CEO Toshiro Mitsuhama taking tea with the crown prince of Japan . . .

Carla sighed. Going through all this drek made her eyes ache. Maybe she should limit the search to articles with a Seattle dateline.

She leaned back in her chair, glancing toward Greer's office. Officially, her Mitsuhama story was dead, spiked. But that didn't prevent her from trying, in her spare moments, to pick up a lead that would bring the story back on line again. She wasn't getting anywhere, however, with this passive search. Maybe it was time for her investigation to take a more active direction.

Officially, she was working today on a story about the Matrix. A number of system access nodes in the Seattle telecommunications grid had been experiencing problems over the past few days. Names were getting scrambled, passcodes and retinal scans weren't being recognized, and Matrix traffic had to be re-routed through alternative servers. Elsewhere in the Matrix, entire systems had shut down; one of the most recent casualties was the one serving the theological college at the University of Washington. The telecom providers were scrambling to assure their customers that all was well, that this was a minor, localized problem. But the systems experts Carla had contacted that morning were speculating that a powerful new virus was on the loose. The more nervous among them had drawn comparisons to the Crash of 2029, which had started in a similar fashion.

That had been a great interview, one destined to put the fear into deckers everywhere when it aired at six o'clock. But it was pure speculation. When you boiled it right down to the facts, the story didn't really have much bite to it. Who really cared if the datastores of an obscure university department were hopelessly corrupted? Carla had to admit that the eventual crash of the theology department's computer system made for some great puns about the virus being an "act of God." The deckers had even come up with a cute name for the virus: Holy Ghost. It had also struck the databanks of a televangelist network in Denver.

Carla had managed to inject some life into the story by including a take from the interview she'd done with a woman who seemed to draw the virus to her like a magnet. No matter which computer Luci Ferraro logged on from, the virus found her. She'd burned out her own telecom, six public terminals, and the one at the dental office where she worked as a receptionist. The interview had been great comic relief, especially Luci's comment that her son had locked her out of his room to prevent her from touching his hologame set. It gave the story just the edge it needed to become the lead piece in tonight's Metro news slot. It was just as well. The only other news item of note was yet another demand by the Ork Rights Committee to meet with the governor. That one was stale a week ago.

Carla wound her way through the busy newsroom, heading for the station's research department. It was a room next to the studio, removed from the noise and bustle, that contained a Formfit recliner and a fully equipped kitchen. A private washroom, off to one side, ensured that the researchers didn't need to waste precious seconds waiting for the restroom, like everyone else.

The three young deckers who made up this "department" were technically on call at all times for the reporters, but typically only one hung out here "in the meat," playing simsense games or writing utility programs to pass the time. The other two clocked in from remote work stations at home.

Today the decker on duty was Corwin Schofeld, a young ork barely out of his teens. In person he looked big, slow, and stupid. But Carla knew that, inside the Matrix, his persona was as quick and slippery as they came.

Corwin looked up as Carla entered the room. He was just preparing to jack in, and sat with his deck across his legs, a datacord snugged into his temple. "Hoi, there, Carla," he said with a big smile. "How's it scannin', snoop? Wus'up?"

Carla smiled at Corwin's streeter slang. She knew he'd grown up in Rosemount Beach, an upper-class suburb of Bellevue. The affected speech was as much a part of his image as his synthleather T-shirt, high-top sneakers, and torn denims. Normally she'd tease him about it. But today she couldn't be bothered.

"I want you to do a run for me, Corwin," she told him.

"Wiz." The ork nodded his head eagerly. "Jus' name your node."

"It's a tough one. Corporate research files. There'll definitely be ice. Maybe even black ice."

"Yeah? So?" He gave her a lazy, cocksure look. "What's the scan?"

Carla pulled up a chair beside the Formfit couch on which Corwin was sprawled. "Mitsuhama Corporation's magical research lab," she said. "It could be dangerous." She hoped Corwin was up to it. She didn't relish facing Greer with the news that one of his pet deckers had burned out station equipment on an unauthorized data snoop. The producer would chew her head off, then demote her to the sports-entertainment beat and make her cover the urban brawl matches, just to watch her squirm.

Corwin let out a long, slow whistle. "Mitsuhama, you say? Sure, it's a tough system. But I'm rezzed for it. What's the scan?"

"I'm looking for information on a high-level research project Mitsuhama's been working on," Carla explained. "I want you to deck into the project files, searching for anything connected to the words light, spirit, or the name Farazad Samji. The project was a current one, so hopefully you won't have to spend too long scanning through old records."

"Mitsuhama Computer Technologies, huh? This story you're working on got anything to do with their new deck hardware or ASIST interfaces? I heard from a decker in Kobe that MCT's developing a new co-processor that will exponentially boost the response time of a MPCP chip." Corwin had slipped out of street speech in his excitement.

"As far as I know, the research project has nothing to do with computers," Carla said, shaking her head. "If anything, it's probably connected with Mitsuhama's defense contracts."

"Oh." Corwin's hand hovered above the toggle that would power up the deck. "Black ice for sure, then. Well, it may scope out to be a high-rez jolt jump just the same. See you in a few millisecs."

"Wait." Carla laid a hand on Corwin's thick arm. "I'm coming along."

"Uh-uh," Corwin shook his head. "This cowboy rides alone."

Carla slotted one end of a datacord into the hitcher jack on Corwin's deck and twirled the other end in her hand. "Not if he wants this run authorized by a reporter, he doesn't."

"Black ice doesn't scare you?" Corwin asked. "It can fry your brain, you know."

Carla smiled. "It doesn't scare me. How about you? Are you sure you're not looking for an excuse not to make this run?"

Corwin gave her a long, level look. Then he returned her smile. "O.K., cowgirl. Jack in."

Carla jacked the other end of the cord into her temple and closed her eyes. The next instant she was inside a brilliant landscape of flickering neon colors, intricate grids, and floating, three-dimensional icons. Corwin's icon in the Matrix seemed to hover a meter away from her. It was a gray and white cartoon rabbit with white gloves, big floppy ears, and a mischievous expression. It turned and winked at Carla. "Wus'up, doc?"

Carla could only see portions of her own "body" as it appeared in the Matrix. When she held out a hand, it was a glowing, slightly blocky imitation of a human one. Her legs were tapering cylinders that ended in rounded stumps. Obviously Corwin hadn't put as much work into designing a persona program for his hitchers. Carla tried to speak, but found she didn't have a mouth. She would be an observer, only, on this run.

"Heeeere we go!" Corwin gleefully quipped.

His rabbit icon stretched out a hand along one of the bars of neon blue light that made up the grid that surrounded them. The arm lengthened like a rubber band, then snapped back to its original size. As it contracted, Carla found herself rushing through space, pulled along behind the rabbit like a balloon tied to a string. Grid patterns whizzed overhead impossibly fast as they raced through a landscape of shifting geometric forms. They changed direction several times as Corwin routed them through a confusing combination of local and regional telecommunications grids. It was a standard decker's tactic, designed to hide their point of origin.

They paused for a moment at the end of one of the tubelike lines, as the rabbit stabbed a finger at an icon shaped like a silver coin. Again they rushed through space, this time through a red field punctuated with a spangling of what looked like three-dimensional corporate logos that hung in the distance like stars. Ahead loomed a huge pagoda surrounded by halos of glowing light, apparently made out of coiled fiber-optic cables that bristled with datajacks. The stuff looked like barbed wire. They rushed toward the pagoda, then stopped abruptly at its base. The rabbit paused, brought its palms together in front of its chest, and did an elegant swan dive that carried it between two strands of wire.

Carla's perspective suddenly did a flip-flop. Now they were inside what looked like a reception area. Walls, floor, and ceiling were made of chrome. Behind a desk made of a slab of frosted glass, a robotic head hung in mid-air. Its eyes were whirling kaleidoscopes, its mouth a dark oval. Words scrolled across the front of the desk: YOU HAVE ENTERED THE MITSUHAMA COMPUTER TECHNOLOGIES SYSTEM. PLEASE ENTER IDENTIFICATION CODE.

The rabbit pulled a key out of its pocket and tossed it at the robotic head. The key slotted neatly into its mouth, turned, and the head dissolved in a sparkle of green light.

IDENTIFICATION CODE ACCEPTED, PROCEED.

The background changed color, becoming a soft green. The sound of rippling water surrounded them, and streaks of darker green seemed to be streaming past. It was as if they stood inside a vertical tube of gently flowing water. Around them, floating in a circle about waist-height, was a ring of icons. The rabbit considered for a millisecond, then reached out and firmly grasped one shaped like a microscope. The icon shimmered . . .

Suddenly, Carla couldn't focus properly. Everything around her began breaking apart, dissolving into a soft fuzz of broken squares. Back in the real world, she felt her fingertips start to tingle. And that frightened her. Black ice was designed to attack the decker himself, as well as his hardware. It would also attack his hitchers. But she'd been confident in Corwin's ability to avoid any intrusion countermeasures they encountered. It seemed she'd made a mistake—possibly a fatal one.

Slowly—too slowly—Carla felt her real-world hand start to drift up toward her head. It moved at a painfully sluggish rate, a millimeter at a time, while her mind was whirling. She had to jack out, had to . . .

The world refocused. The rabbit was holding up a forefinger. On its tip, a child's top spun furiously. It seemed to be creating a whirlpool in space that was gradually drawing together the polygons that had earlier been flying apart. At last it stopped. "Nasty," the rabbit commented to itself. Then it pulled another icon from the pocket at its hip. This one looked like a cluster of numbers, tangled together, each a different primary color. The rabbit threw it at the microscope.

The numbers danced for a moment in the air, then three of them settled onto the microscope icon, sticking to its sides. The other numbers dissolved. At the same instant, Carla had the perception that she was shrinking, moving with great speed. The eyepiece of the microscope loomed in front of her like a huge, round portal—and then they were through.

They floated in a velvety black space. Around them, bobbing gently, were a series of rectangular off-white squares. These were standard file icons—modeled after the old-fashioned pieces of folded cardboard once used to manually store hardcopy. The top of each was marked with a small color bar.

The rabbit pulled out a sewing needle. Its thread was a series of words: LIGHT. SPIRIT. FARAZAD. SAMJI. The rabbit threw the needle like a dart, then watched as it punched its way in and out of the files, piercing each one and drawing the word-thread through it. When it had finished, two smaller file icons hung on the thread between the words. Like the larger files, each was coded with a color bar. The rabbit pulled what looked like a highlighting stylus out of its seemingly bottomless pocket and drew the tip over the bar code of the first file. The blocks of color turned into letters: PROJECT PERSONNEL.

The rabbit looked at Carla. "Upload?" it asked.

Carla nodded.

The rabbit tucked the file into its pocket. Then it used the stylus on the second file. More words appeared: LUCIFER PROJECT.

"Uplo—?"

A sudden flash of white light obliterated everything. Carla had the sensation of tumbling crazily in space. There was nothing to grab on to, no reference points. The entire Matrix and all of its graphic constructs had been instantly obliterated. She spun wildly out of control, a knot of icy fear in her stomach. She was falling, drowning in a sea of featureless white, burning in an invisible white flame . . .

It ended as suddenly as it had begun. Carla was slumped over in her chair in the research department. Beside her, Corwin held the end of the datacord that he'd yanked out of the jack in her temple. His face was an ashen color, and had lost all of its usual cocky expression.

Both of them were breathing hard. For a moment, Carla was frightened that the intrusion countermeasure they'd run into had used a biofeedback loop to accelerate their heart rates out of control. She glanced up at the clock on the wall. Only ten seconds had elapsed since they'd entered the Matrix. It seemed like a lifetime.

"What the frag was *that*?" she asked. "Some kind of ice?"

Corwin shook his head. "I don't think so," he said. "It shut down everything in the sector—not just us."

"Do you think it was—"

"Jus' a sec," Corwin cut her off. "I gotta check something."

He jacked back into the deck and hunched over it, eyes unfocused. As the seconds ticked past, Carla saw his fingers tense once, then relax. Then his mouth dropped open and his breathing quickened. His eyes jerked back and forth rapidly, as if he were rapidly scanning text. Just as Carla was wondering if she should do something, he blinked and pulled the cable from his temple.

"Wow," he said.

"What?" Carla was bristling with impatience. "What is it?"

"Whatever wiped us wasn't ice," Corwin said thoughtfully. "It was more like a virus. I edged back into the Mitsuhama mainframe, just to scan what was rezzin' there. When I tried to access the research lab files again, guess what I found?"

Carla shrugged. She couldn't even guess.

"Nada. Zilch. Static. A whole lotta nothing. The

datastore for that sector is utterly clean, completely wiped. There wasn't a single graphics pixel, not a single byte of data. And none of the programs were functional. That system is toasted. Gonzo."

He paused. "Know what it reminded me of?" he asked.

Carla nodded. This time, she could guess. "The databanks at the U. of W's School of Theology?"

"Yup. Exactamundo. Same effect exactly."

"What about the files you uploaded?" Carla asked. "Did you manage to save them?"

Corwin tapped a button on his deck. With a soft whir, a datachip slid out of a slot in the side. "I got the personnel file," he answered. "But the second file was erased, along with the rest of the lab data. The deck didn't even have time to upload its name code."

Carla cursed silently to herself. She'd been so close. . . . But at least she had a tiny piece of the puzzle now. She had a personnel file that should contain the names of the mages who'd worked on the project with Farazad. The information in their dossiers might give her some leverage during the interviews she hoped to conduct with them. And she also had what had to be the name of the research project: Lucifer.

It was a curious name for what Carla had assumed was a weapons research project. Lucifer was a Latin word that translated as "bringer of light." It was also the name of the angel who was cast out of heaven and fell to earth in the form of lightning. That part certainly fit. According to the ork girl's description of the spirit, it had looked like lightning as it launched itself into the heavens away from the body of the wage mage. One big bright flash of light . . .

She suddenly realized that her previous assumptions had been all wrong. Mitsuhama hadn't been experimenting with spirits in order to use them as weapons. She'd let the fact that the spirit had killed the mage lull her into that crude conclusion. Instead, the research project had involved computers—Mitsuhama's chief industry—all along.

Carla could feel her heart pounding in her chest.

"Corwin," she asked softly. "Is it possible for a spirit to enter the Matrix?"

The ork shook his head. "No way. The Matrix is an artificial reality, nothing more than a series of computer-generated simsense impressions, while magic is inherently associated with living organisms. The two are completely incompatible; that's why mages have such trouble with simsense. Regardless of what it's actually made of, a spirit is a living creature And nothing living can enter the Matrix."

"I thought we just did."

"Nope. What we did was download sensory data from the Matrix directly into our brains, through these." He tapped the datajack in his temple while still watching the screen of the diagnostic unit. "We weren't actually 'inside' the Matrix—we just perceived it as if we were. We were actually downloading coded pulses of photons, which our datalinks translated into signals our brains could understand and interpret. Whenever I seemed to be manipulating an icon, I was actually executing a command, uploading the information that would do the job. My neural synapses fired, and the thought was translated by my datalink into a coded burst of light that activated the program in my deck." He paused, looked up for a moment at Carla. "You scan all that?"

"Uh-huh. But what if the spirit had a physical body that was composed of light?" Carla asked. "Couldn't it enter the Matrix like any other beam of light, through a fiber-optic cable?"

The decker paused for a second, then shrugged. "Maybe for a millisecond or two. It would just blast through at three hundred thousand klicks per second and be out again."

"What would it look like?"

"Like a flash of . . ." Corwin looked up, his eyes wide. "So that's what we saw," he whispered softly. "Mega cool." His deck lay ignored in his lap. He leaned forward, and the foam of the recliner squeaked slightly as it contoured itself to his new position.

"A creature composed of light would be one fragger

of a virus," he said, thinking out loud. "It wouldn't be affected by any intrusion countermeasures, since they're set up to attack the deck or the decker. It would be nearly impossible to detect, because it wouldn't interfere with the other data transmissions. Light doesn't interfere with itself unless the two beams are exactly in phase—that's why a fiber-optic cable can carry thousands of commands and transmissions simultaneously. One more pulse of light down the tube wouldn't affect it a bit. And it wouldn't hurt the hardware—at least, I don't think so. But there is one thing the spirit would do—it would sure mess up stored data."

His gestures grew more animated. "See, information is written on memory chips and hard drives by a beam of light, and read in the same manner. Individual pulses within the beam, as well as the light wave's pattern of crests and troughs, are all part of the information-carrying code. If a creature made of light suddenly surged through a data storage device, it would completely scramble the code that had been written previously. There'd be a whole new pattern laid down, none of it coherent. And that's what makes this spirit so perfect as a virus. There's no way to stop it from corrupting your data. Even if you installed a passcode system, any word or image you use is encoded as light. All the spirit would have to do is reconfigure itself to emulate the passcode, write-enable the datastore, and slide right in. Only a hardwired lock could stop it— and that involves completely locking the system away from the Matrix. It just isn't economically feasible to do that.

"You'd have to have some way of directing the spirit. Otherwise, it would wipe out every file it passed through along the way. Maybe if you got it to home in on a keyword . . ."

"That's it!" Carla said. "The spirit showed up in the research lab node of the Mitsuhama system as soon as we decrypted the name on the project file. It's also wiped datastores at a theology school and a televangelist network, and keeps attacking a woman by the name of Luci Ferraro each time she tries to access any computer or telecom unit that's linked to the Matrix. What do these four things have in common?" She smiled, pleased with herself for putting the pieces together and waiting for Corwin to do the same.

Corwin frowned, puzzled. Then he broke into a wide, snag-toothed grin. "The word Lucifer."

"There's your keyword," Carla concluded.

Corwin shook his head. "Doesn't make sense," he countered. "You say this spirit was developed at the Mitsuhama research lab. Why would they target their own facility?"

"As a test, maybe?"

Corwin snorted with laughter. "A test capable of wiping out their entire data-storage system? No way!"

"No, not a test," Carla agreed. Then the answer hit her. "The spirit is trying to wipe out the files on itself. In the process, it's erasing a lot of unrelated data—any file that contains the word Lucifer. But why does it feel the need to do that? It's already killed the man who conjured it and become a free spirit. Even if it was once under someone's control, nobody's controlling it now."

Corwin reached for his deck. "This is totally wacked. I'd better warn my chummers about—"

"Don't!" Carla grabbed the ork's hand. "Keep this to yourself, O.K.? At least until I've completed my story. That run you just did was on KKRU time, and as an employee of this station, you have to honor your confidentiality oath. Agreed?"

Corwin sighed heavily. "Yeah, I guess so."

"Good." She left him staring morosely at his deck and hurried back into the newsroom.

15

Pita sat in the basement room, stroking the white cat. She stared at the ray of sunlight that slanted through the broken window, trying to ignore the hunger that gnawed at her belly. She listened instead to the sounds of people moving through the store above her, to the traffic outside, to the purring of the cat in her lap. Without meaning to do so, she began to hum a ballad she'd heard on one of the muzak stations last week. She'd laughed at it when she first heard it; the song was some mushy thing, not a bit like the scream-rock she usually listened to. But humming it now somehow made her feel better.

She stroked the cat's soft fur, concentrating on its texture in an effort to focus her thoughts. She was beginning to feel light-headed, dizzy. As her mind drifted, her body felt thinner, less substantial. All that existed was the dust motes, the sunlight, the rumbling purr of the cat. Or was that the sound of her humming? The two had blended together in a gentle harmony.

Slowly, almost imperceptibly at first, the floor drifted away. Pita was floating, bobbing like a dust mote in the air. With a sense of wonder, she unfolded her legs from their crossed position and placed her feet on the floor. Through her legs, which had become translucent, she could see her body, still seated and leaning back against the wall. Her eyes had closed and her head hung to one side, mouth open. Her chest was still; it didn't look as though she was breathing.

Amazingly, the sight did not frighten her. It seemed natural, right. This detached perspective was better, somehow, than confronting her own face in a mirror.

From this angle, her wide face, jutting teeth, and broad shoulders seemed perfectly proportioned. She reached out to touch herself but overshot her mark, and her hand passed through the wall. Amazed, she drew it back. She could pass through man-made objects as if they were not there.

She looked down at her body once more. The cat, still curled in her lap, climbed out of its own body. Its ghostly form stepped delicately aside, extending each of its back legs in a spine-lengthening stretch. And then it began to change. It grew larger, sleeker, more supple. Its fur took on the pattern of a tabby cat, but with stripes the color of a rainbow. Its eyes began to glow, to turn into molten pools of gold. And its whiskers began to hum with a strange electric force. When the transformation was complete, it looked up at her and gave a faint, ghostly *mrrow*.

For the space of a few heartbeats, Pita was unable to speak. At last she was able to utter a single word: "Cat?"

The animal nodded. Then it turned and leaped gracefully onto a box, and from there to the window ledge.

Pita felt no fear—only a burning curiosity to see where this magical creature was going. She followed it, climbing up and through the wall as if it were not there. She had a brief moment of disorientation as her form flowed through the cement; she saw every grain, every particle. Then she was standing in the alley, beside Cat. The animal gave a quick backward glance, then trotted around a trash can and into another wall.

Pita followed, her mind bubbling with laughter as she explored her newfound perceptions. She could walk through walls, or across a busy street while cars zoomed through her ghostly form. She was jostled once, when a passenger in one of the cars made contact with her, and found that trees felt equally solid. But she could, if she chose, climb a flight of stairs, her feet never once touching them. Or she could wade chest-deep through a floor, as if it were made of water. The only things that presented a barrier to her were those that were alive—people, plants, and the earth itself.

And the things she could see! Magical energies

swirled and eddied about her like colored mists. In some
spots she could sense strong emotional residues—here,
in this intersection, someone had suffered great pain.
There, in that room, was a bright sunburst of joy. The
streets were alive with odd-looking, magical creatures.
Some were the size of mice, with multiple heads and
shimmering fur. They scuttled up the street or peeked
out of drain holes. Other presences were more natural—
and more alien. When Pita walked through a park, the
trees, grass, and earth pulsed with life, with emotion.

Drifting along a busy sidewalk, she could clearly see
the violet aura that clung to one of the men in the
crowd. Looking closely at him as she passed, she saw
his true form—not human at all, but a hideous, mis-
shapen beast with reptilian scales and cloven feet. It
exuded a miasma of hatred and anger. Pita circled
warily around the creature, but it seemed as oblivious
to her presence as any of the others she passed.

She followed Cat for some time. She had no idea what
streets they followed; she could see the signs, but the
words on them were meaningless symbols. Some were
tangled scribbles, others were asymmetrical patterns of
circles, triangles, and squares. She was able to roughly
gauge her progress by keeping an eye on the Renraku
and Aztechnology complexes. But although she could
pass through walls with ease, she could not see through
them. Much of the time, the buildings blocked her view.

Eventually Cat led her to an old, wood-frame building on the corner of a quiet residential street. It looked
as if it had once been a Stuffer Shack; the sign over the
front door was the right shape, even if Pita couldn't
read it. The windows were boarded up and the door
secured with a chain and padlock. At some point in the
past, a vehicle had collided with a corner of the building; large sheets of chipboard covered a gaping, splintered hole. Cat stopped in front of this boarded-up
wall, looked back at Pita, then disappeared inside.

Pita followed, and found herself inside a large room.
Dusty counters and broken display racks had been
pushed against the walls, clearing a space in the
middle. At the center of the room, Aziz lay sprawled

on his back, arms and legs spread wide. His dark hair fanned out in a halo around his head, and the loose sleeves of his robe made him look as if he had angel wings. At first Pita thought he was dead. But then she saw his mouth working. He was chanting. Although it looked as though he were shouting, all Pita could hear was a faint whisper. His words were incomprehensible gibberish.

The floor was ablaze with a pattern of glowing, magical lines. It looked as though a cherry-red circle had been painted on the floor with neon tubing. Inside the circle were five straight lines, each a different color, that formed the branches of a pentagram. In each point of the pentagram, a different symbol had been drawn. Aziz lay with his head in one of the points of the pentagram, his hands and feet on the other points. One of his hands clutched a lighted candle, the other, a lump of earth. A clear glass bowl near one of his feet held water, and an empty bowl was near his other foot. His head rested upon what looked like a jagged piece of window glass that had been placed flat on the floor. His eyes were focused on the ceiling; he showed no signs of realizing that Pita was there.

Pita heard a faint hiss and glanced down at Cat. Its multi-colored body was curved into an arch. Every one of its translucent hairs was on end, quivering. Its claws were extended, buried in the floor. It was staring— straight up—at a skylight in the ceiling.

Pita looked up. Now she, too, could see what had startled Cat. A spiral pattern was forming on the ceiling, swirling inward through the grimy glass to coalesce at the spot at which Aziz was staring. It was fantastically bright, as difficult to look at as the sun. In another second the brilliant light formed a tornado spout. It spiraled down, down, closer to Aziz. As it approached him, he chanted faster. A frightened look crept into his eyes. Face locked in a grimace, he screamed at the thing that had formed above his head. His face was awash with light. The candle in his right hand flared brilliantly, was consumed in one burst. The earth in his left hand turned to ash. Aziz screamed as blisters erupted on his face and hands, and turned his head aside, his eyes screwed shut. He seemed to be struggling, unable to move.

With an angry hiss, Cat turned and fled.

"Aziz!" Pita screamed. She flung up her arm to shield her eyes from the brilliant light. This was horrible. Aziz was dying, being burned alive by the same spirit creature that had killed the mage in the alley. Pita was terrified. Yet she could not run. It wasn't fear but guilt that held her fast. How many times in the past few days had she run out on someone, left them to die? Much as she disliked Aziz, she couldn't add his name to the list. Not after she'd been responsible for his store being torched. Besides, she wasn't really here—her body was back in the basement of the department store. Nothing could hurt her, right?

Praying that she was correct, Pita ran forward, her arm still raised to protect her eyes. She tried to leap across the glowing bar that formed the circle and crashed into an invisible wall. Stunned, she staggered back.

Pita heard a tearing, shuddering noise overhead, and looked up. The glowing spirit had drawn back, was spiraling against the ceiling once more. As Pita moved forward, it seemed to back away from her. Then it exploded outward with a brilliant flash, hurtling away through the skylight with impossible speed.

Aziz groaned, rolled over stiffly. He sat up slowly, blinking and holding his head. Squinting, he peered around the room. It didn't look as though his eyes were working properly. The pupils were mere pinpricks. But then his head turned, as if he had sensed Pita's presence. He crawled to his knees, fumbled toward her like a blind man. Then he stopped and held his palms to his temples. Pita saw a glow of magical energy coalescing about his head, centered on his eyes.

His mouth fell open. "Pita?" he gasped. "That was you? But what are you doing in astral space?"

Pita tried to answer, but found that she could not speak. Then she heard an echoing meow that called her mind elsewhere, and the walls of the convenience store started to waver. She felt a silent tug, somewhere behind her. Dimly, she sensed her body. It was weak, its heartbeat fluttery. She suddenly knew, with urgent certainty, that she had to return to it.

She turned and ran through the wall.

16

"Aziz! What happened to you? You look awful."

Carla hurried toward the mage. His clothes were smudged with dirt and had a sooty, campfire smell. His face and hands were bright red and covered with weeping blisters, as if he'd suffered a severe sunburn. His dark hair was mussed and looked as if it had been hacked off short, just above the forehead. And his face looked odd. After a moment, Carla figured out why. Both eyebrows and lashes were gone. He stood in the lobby of the news station, dripping water onto the floor. Outside, the morning sunshine had disappeared and rain was sprinkling down.

He looked past Carla at the door that led to the studio. His dark eyes were watery, blinking. "Where's the girl?" he asked.

"Who?" Carla's mind was still trying to process what she and the decker Corwin had just uncovered. She'd been in the middle of scanning the personnel file they'd downloaded, rapidly absorbing every bit of information she could about the three mages who'd worked with Farazad on the Lucifer Project.

"The ork girl," Aziz said. "Pita."

"I don't know. Masaki said she disappeared the night before last, around the time of the newscast. He was on the phone all day to the social services agencies and soup kitchens, but no one's seen her." She shrugged. "If you ask me, she probably got bored and went back to her street friends. Wayne said one of them stopped by just before she left." She shrugged. "Maybe she just got tired of the colored dishwater that passes for soykaf

around here. In any case, it's good riddance. I don't
think that kid had taken a bath in—"

"I need to find her," Aziz cut in. "It's important.
She's the key to—"

"Have you seen yourself in a mirror?" Carla asked
suddenly. "You're a mess. And those blisters look
painful." She keyed a code into the door behind her,
opened it, and motioned for Aziz to follow. "Come on
into the studio. There's a first aid kit in the lunch room;
I'll put something on your burns. What happened? Did
one of your spells backfire on you again?"

Aziz trudged after her down the hall. "Not exactly."

Carla spun on her heel, suddenly guessing the truth.
"Aziz! You didn't try casting the spell from the Mitsuhama lab, did you? The spell you said it would be
suicidal to try?"

"No." Aziz shook his head and winced slightly as his
facial skin tightened. "I tried something else. I wanted
to learn more about the nature of the spirit Farazad
Samji conjured. I thought it might be some new form
of elemental. If the writings of Ko Hung were correct, I
wondered if there was a fifth metaplane—one previously undiscovered. A metaplane of light. I figured that
if I could find this metaplane, I'd be able to learn more
about the spirit. And so I used a piece of window glass
from the alley where the spirit apparently went free as
a focal point for my meditation, and set out to find its
native plane."

"And did you succeed?" Carla asked. Despite her
concern for Aziz, her reporter's curiosity was aroused.

"No. As far as I can tell everything we've always
believed till now is true: no fifth metaplane exists.
Period. The spirit Farazad summoned isn't from a new
metaplane and it isn't an elemental. It's another form
of beast entirely. I'm not even sure that we should be
calling it a spirit, but it's the only word that fits. By all
the laws of magic, this creature shouldn't even exist."

He shrugged. "Whatever this astral entity really
is, my attempt at an astral quest attracted its attention.
Perhaps it thought I was trying to learn its true name,

and tried to stop me. Whatever the reason, the spirit was drawn to me. It, uh . . . attacked me."

"Attacked you!"

They were passing through the newsroom. A few of the reporters and editors raised their heads and stared curiously at them. She took Aziz firmly by the arm and steered him toward the lunch room. Thankfully, it was empty. Pushing Aziz inside, she closed the door. She pulled the first aid kit out of a drawer, found the tube of burn cream, and twisted the lid off. Aziz sank into a chair and sat with his hands a few centimeters short of his lap, as if afraid that letting them rest on anything would hurt. Carla gently dabbed the cream onto his burns with a fingertip. The sharp smell of the ointment filled the room. "Tell me what happened," she urged.

"The spirt came close enough to burn me," Aziz said. His dark eyes winced at the memory. "I thought I was finished—that I'd be cooked alive, like the fellow who died in the alley. But then I sensed someone trying to break my hermetic circle. The circle held, but the interruption disturbed the spirit somehow. It vanished—just like that." He started to snap his fingers, then winced at his burned skin.

"I must have passed out for a second or two. When I came to, I couldn't see anything. I thought . . ." He looked up at Carla, blinking his watery eyes. "I thought I'd been permanently blinded. But then I remembered my astral senses. I looked into astral space, and guess who I saw, standing just outside the circle?"

"Pita?" Carla asked as she gently applied the burn cream to his face. "You mean to tell me you had her along with you when you were working your magic?"

"Not intentionally," Aziz answered. "And not in the flesh. I tried to touch her, but couldn't. She'd projected herself into astral space."

"What?" Carla said incredulously. "How in the world could she manage to—"

"She's a raw magical talent, I guess," Aziz said with an envious sigh. "And powerful, too. I didn't do anything to drive the spirit away. I was toast—literally—

until Pita came along. She was the one who drove it away."

Carla sank into a chair beside Aziz. "Wow," she said at last. "That's a story in itself. There's more to that kid than meets the eye."

"That's right," Aziz said. "And that's why I want her with me the next time I try to find out more about this astral entity. She seems to have some sort of natural power over it. The thing fled as soon as she tried to penetrate my hermetic circle. She must have done something to banish it. I've got my suspicions about what it might have been, but it's too unbelievable to be true." He turned his hands over, flexed them slightly, and winced. Then he smiled at Carla. "That feels better. Thanks."

Carla shook her head. "You're crazy," she told him. "That spirit nearly killed you. What do you want to mess with it again for?"

"Why, Miss Carla"—Aziz arched an eyebrow—"if you keep talking like that, you're going to make me think you still care for me." He reached out for her cheek with fingers that smelled of burn cream.

Carla jerked her head away, sorry now that she'd revealed her feelings. Aziz was the same stupid slot he'd always been, putting his quest for magical knowledge ahead of his own safety. Ahead of her.

The mage lowered his hand and sighed. "If anyone should understand, it's you, Carla," he said. "This is a brand new form of spirit. Something that's never been seen before in the hermetic tradition. I've got to know more about it." He tried to catch her eye. "It's just like when you're onto a big story. You have to follow it through to the end. Well, it's the same with mages. Once we get our teeth into something we—"

Carla held up a hand. "I don't want to get into that old argument," she told him curtly. "I don't have the time right now. I've got a news story to pursue." She stood. "You can help me, if you like. But I don't want to have to worry about you getting killed mucking about with uncontrollable spirits. I'd rather know you were tucked inside your shop, safe behind its wards."

"That's the other thing," Aziz said slowly. "The shop. It's gone."

"Gone? You make it sound like it dematerialized or something."

"There was a fire. Two nights ago, while I was gathering the materials I needed to cast the spell. The store was completely gutted. All those books . . ." His face crumpled and Carla thought he was actually going to cry.

"My god," Carla said. "That fire on Denny Way. That was your shop? I was so busy putting the Matrix story together that I didn't pay any attention to the trideo feeds that night. I'm so sorry, Aziz. I know how much the shop meant to you."

"At least I had insurance," the mage said bitterly. "And a hardcopy printout of the Mitsuhama spell," he added, patting one bulging pocket. "The memory chip you gave me burned up in the fire."

"I don't think so," Carla said slowly. She screwed the top back onto the burn cream, then toyed with the tube, unwilling to look Aziz in the eye. "There was something I didn't tell you the morning we came to your shop. The girl who saw the mage die—Pita—was being chased by two yakuza when we caught up to her. They were after the chip. I didn't think they'd still be looking for it after our story on the spirit aired. It should have been too late by then for them to continue trying to plug the leak. But I guess I was wrong. Maybe they thought there was something on the chip that would link the spell to Mitsuhama. They probably saw the interview I did with you, broke into your store, and set the fire to cover their tracks once they had what they'd come for." She sighed. "I'm sorry, Aziz. Really. I didn't realize that this would happen."

"So Mitsuhama sent its goons after the chip, did they?" Aziz frowned, then winced as the movement pulled his skin. "And you haven't seen Pita for two days? That doesn't sound good."

"I thought you said you just saw her."

"In astral form, only," Aziz corrected. "Her physical body could have been anywhere. Even in the clutches of the yakuza. Maybe she came to me for help."

Carla felt a stab of guilt. Maybe she should have kept a closer eye on the kid. But she was a reporter, with a story to follow. Masaki was better at playing mother hen than she was. Let him fuss over the street urchin. "The kid's probably fine," she said in a deliberately reassuring tone. "Masaki has lots of contacts. He'll track her down sooner or later.

"But there is something I need your help with. I've learned the names of three mages who worked with Farazad on the development of the spell. If I can get one of them to agree to an interview, I can verify that the spirit was developed as part of a Mitsuhama research project. And maybe, in the process, I'll find out more about how to work the spell."

"What are the names of these mages?" Aziz asked, instantly hooked. "Maybe I know one of them. I've met a number of Seattle's mages, over the years, through the shop."

Carla recited the names she'd pulled from the personnel file: "Evelyn Belanger, Rolf Hosfeld, and Miyuki Kishi."

"Belanger. Hmm . . . Is she a big woman in her thirties, with dark hair and a soft voice?"

"I wouldn't know about the voice. But the dark hair fits with the picture in her personnel file. Do you know her?"

Aziz nodded. "She's a regular customer, although she hasn't been to the shop in months. She was always looking for rare books on botany and herbal lore. She's an avid gardener. And from the little she's told me about her garden, I gather that it's quite something. She moonlights by growing herbs and exotic plants for use in fetishes. I knew she was a wage mage, but never did ask what company she worked for. So it's Mitsuhama, huh? No wonder she has so much money to drop on antique books."

"Would she remember you?"

"Oh sure. I special-ordered material for her more than once."

"Would she find it odd if you paid her a visit?"

"Not if I said I'd finally found one of the books she's been looking for."

"And could you find one on short notice?" Carla asked. "And deliver it this afternoon? And at the same time, strike up a conversation about the conjuring spell that 'some reporter from KKRU' asked you to comment on?"

A sly grin stole across Aziz's face. "I've got a book at home that would be perfect," he said. "It's badly water-stained, and some of the pages are missing. I didn't think that it would sell, so I've been scanning some of the undamaged illustrations and selling them on-line. But perhaps our wage mage would like to own the original art. The book is old enough and rare enough to interest her—despite its condition."

"Perfect." Carla clapped Aziz on the back. "Let's go get it."

The ruse worked even better than Carla had hoped. Evelyn Belanger was at home when Aziz called. She said she was working and was quite busy. Carla could guess why; after the system crash at the research lab that morning, the mages would have rushed home to see what they could salvage from their own files. But after hearing that an extremely rare herbals book was available at a cut-rate price and that a second buyer was also interested and might purchase it if she didn't make up her mind quickly, Evelyn agreed to take a break and meet with Aziz later that afternoon.

Belanger lived in a modest wooden house, perhaps a century old, in Brier, a semi-rural section of Sno-homish. Much of the district had been gobbled up by agri-business, but the area still contained a scattering of half-hectare hobby farms. Evelyn's home was on one of those properties, but instead of a barn, her back-yard boasted a large, flower-filled garden.

When Aziz showed her the book, Evelyn Belanger invited him to join her for a cup of tea and readily agreed to his request for a tour of her garden. She obviously enjoyed showing it off. Carla, listening from the sidewalk while cloaked in an invisibilty spell Aziz was sustaining, slipped around the house and in through a side gate. She caught up to the two mages as they emerged through a door at the back of the house and tiptoed behind them, careful not to knock anything over or brush against anything that made noise.

Aziz, too, had cloaked himself with a spell. His was a simpler form of magic—a mask that hid the reddened blisters on his face and hands. No sense in giving the game away too early; Evenly Belanger would probably be able to take one look at his injuries and guess what he'd been up to.

The backyard was large and parklike. Paths of natural gravel wound their way between garden beds and raised boxes filled with a profusion of vegetation. There were leafy bushes, variegated vines drooping over the cedarwood slats of the raised plant beds, fragrant-smelling herbs, and daisies with wide, sun-yellow flowers. Clumps of chives thrust up between the other plants, their purple powder-puff blossoms lending a delicate scent to the air. Wind rustled a patch of bamboo in one corner of the garden, and water gurgled in a rock-lined pond whose surface was covered with white-flowered water lilies.

Belanger led Aziz to two benches arranged at right angles to one another near the center of the garden, sheltered by a gazebo. She placed the tea tray on a table that stood between them, then motioned her visitor to sit down.

Wary of the crunching noises her feet made on the gravel path, Carla stopped where she was, a few paces away from the benches. Behind her, rain pattered gently on the leaves.

Carla looked around cautiously. She didn't see any overt security—either technological or magical. Either Evelyn Belanger trusted her semi-rural neighborhood to be crime-free or she was confident she could protect herself with her magic.

Mitsuhama seemed to trust Belanger more than they had Mrs. Samji; there was no evidence of a watcher or paranormal guardian. The only animal present at the house was a calico cat that ran down the path to join

Belanger on the bench. The animal's whiskers twitched as it passed Carla and paused to sniff the air around her ankles. Fortunately Belanger didn't notice the animal's reaction.

Aziz sat on the bench and admired the garden, sipping chamomile tea and murmuring politely while Belanger described the various plants that grew around them. There was woad, the dye plant used by the ancient Celtic warriors to stain their bodies blue, and now popular with mages who specialized in combat spells. Mandrake, whose dark, forked root was used as a fetish in spells affecting the emotions—love spells, in particular. Pennyroyal, used in purification spells. And mistletoe and slippery elm, favored by both European druids and Native American shamans.

Belanger spoke lovingly about each plant, describing it in a gentle voice. She was a large woman, taller than Aziz and probably twice the weight of the rail-thin mage. She dressed in plain, earth-brown clothing. If she'd chosen, she could have been an imposing presence. But she had the soft features and quiet voice of a woman who took pleasure in sitting back and watching events unfold like the slow blossoming of a rose.

Aziz started to turn the conversation around to the events of the other night. As he did, Carla focused her eyecam and did a slow zoom on Evelyn Belanger. At the same time, she cupped a hand behind her ear so the pickup slaved into her eardrum would catch the soft voice of the wage mage. She boosted the gain a little and stepped up the filters, eliminating the faint patter of rain that came from the edge of the garden.

". . . see me on the trideo the other night?" Aziz was asking. "I was interviewed by a reporter from KKRU who wanted my opinion on a spell formula that was written on an datachip she'd been given. The chip was ah . . . found . . . in the pocket of a mage who worked for Mitsuhama. His name was Farazad Samji. The reporter let me keep the chip so I could study the spell, and I've been trying to figure out the formula ever since. I thought that, since you worked with the fellow who had the spell, you might be able to help me decipher . . ."

His voice trailed off as he noticed the way Belanger's eyes had narrowed. "What makes you think I can tell you anything about this spell?" she asked.

Aziz gave a deliberately casual shrug. "The file was tagged with the Mitsuhama logo," he lied. "So I assumed it was developed at your lab."

"Nice try," the wage mage said softly. She reached for the antique book Aziz had placed on the bench and pushed it back at him. "I was one of your regular customers, but I never did tell you where I worked. Who sent you here? The reporter?"

Carla cursed silently to herself as Aziz's usual suave manner deserted him. At least he had the sense not to look around to see if Carla had suddenly become visible. That would have been a complete giveaway.

"No one sent me," Aziz said, nervously licking his lips. "I just wanted to find out why Mitsuhama wanted the spell formula back so badly."

His voice grew hard. "Did the goons your corporation sent after the chip tell you what they did after they found it? No? Well, they burned down my shop. All of those books—gone in a puff of smoke. Books I'd spent years collecting. Valuable books. Rare magical tomes. Gone. Destroyed." He made a chopping gesture with his hand, then took a deep, shuddering breath. "Ignorant bastards," he said under his breath.

"I'm sorry to hear about your shop. I really liked it. All of your lovely books . . ." Evelyn Belanger's regret sounded genuine.

"I tried to learn more about the spell on the chip myself," Aziz said. "In doing so, I managed to attract the attention of the astral entity that killed Farazad—with disastrous results, as you can see." With a wave of his hand, he negated the spell that had been masking his blisters and red skin.

Belanger's eyes widened. Then her lips whitened as she pressed them together. "You were lucky to have survived. Farazad was the only one who was ever able to control that thing, and it killed him just the same. What made you think you could do better, now that it's a free spirit?"

"I used . . . Hey, wait a minute." Aziz sat up a little straighter, eyes glittering. "Farazad didn't just summon the spirit and then lose control of it? He actually had it bound beforehand? Then how was it able to kill him?"

Evelyn stared at Aziz. For a moment, Carla thought she wasn't going to answer, that she would simply ask Aziz to leave. But then she seemed to change her mind.

"Farazad said it wasn't right to keep the spirit captive," Evelyn answered. "Perhaps he was foolish enough to set it free."

Then she sighed. "Whatever the explanation is, the secret of how to control the thing died with him."

Carla frowned, uncertain what to think. If Evelyn was telling the truth—and seemed to be genuinely confiding in Aziz—none of the other mages who had worked on the Lucifer Project had been able to control the spirit once it was summoned. And this despite the fact that, according to their personnel files, they were more adept in the magical arts than Farazad had been. Somehow, only Farazad knew how to find the spirit, and he had held this critical piece of data back from his fellow researchers.

Refusing to keep the spirit bound and setting it free would have made sense, given Farazad's Zoroastrian faith. He'd honestly believed that the spirit was a messenger sent by his god. Enslaving a holy messenger just wasn't done; it was hardly something he'd want some other mage to do—even one of those involved in the spell's development. At the same time, Farazad was a hermetic researcher, a man every bit as meticulous as his wife. He must have kept some notes somewhere, describing the process he'd used to bind the spirit. Perhaps Mitsuhama had assumed that these notes were on the datachip Farazad had intended to hand over to Masaki during his interview. That would explain why the corp had been so keen on obtaining the chip. Someone at Mitsuhama must have had their hopes bitterly dashed when it was at last recovered.

Aziz watched the other mage carefully as he spoke. "I can't control the spirit that killed Farazad either," he said slowly.

Belanger's lips pressed together in a frustrated line. "But I know someone who can."

Belanger drew a sharp breath. "You do? Who?"

Instinctively, Carla made a chopping motion at her throat—the on-air sign for "cut," *Don't let the cat out of the bag, Aziz,* she thought furiously. *Don't tell them about Pita's magical abilities or they'll—*

Aziz waggled a blistered finger at the wage mage. "That's going to be my secret, for now," he said smugly. "If Mitsuhama wants the answer, they'll have to pay for it." He held up a hand to still Belanger's protest. "Not a lot of money, mind you. I'm not greedy. Just enough to put me back in business again, say, three hundred thousand nuyen or so. I'd like a new shop, one with a private thaumaturgical lab in back. I'm sure Mitsuhama can spare the nuyen. The corporation can draft a contract to bring me temporarily on board as a private thaumaturgical consultant, and make it all nice and legal. Just be sure to tell your bosses not to send their goons after me in the meantime. I'll be more willing to cooperate without their 'persuasion.' "

"How can I assure my superiors that you've actually got something to offer?"

Aziz tapped his burned cheek lightly. "I survived my encounter with the spirit, didn't I? That proves that I—and my colleague—have some degree of control over it. The knowledge of how to do that ought to be worth something."

"We'll see." Belanger tried to shrug casually, but the tension she must have been feeling was evident in the set of her shoulders. She rose to her feet. "Stay in touch. I'll let you know what the lab's director says."

Drek! Is that going to be it? Carla zoomed out for a head-to-toe shot of Evelyn Belanger escorting Aziz back through her garden. She still didn't have the documentary evidence she needed to complete her story. Belanger had more or less admitted that the Mitsuhama research lab was the source of the spell, but hadn't said anything direct enough to be used in a newscast. Aziz had been too greedy, and the other mage's replies to his questions too vague.

Carla was tempted to make her presence known, to confront Evelyn Belanger with what they knew so far, and go for a gut-level reaction shot. But then she stopped herself. Belanger wasn't the sort who could be startled into talking. Subtlety was the key here. But subtlety had failed.

Aziz and Belanger had reached the front gate. With a sigh, Carla stopped shooting trid and sneaked out along a side path. She hadn't gotten much, but perhaps she could use what she'd learned thus far. If she could arrange a meeting with one of the other two mages who'd worked on the project with Farazad, maybe she could entice one of them to talk. The interview would have to be set up quickly, before Aziz sold out the ork girl—if indeed that was what he had in mind. Carla didn't think her ex was that devious, but then she hadn't expected the curve he'd just thrown either. Was his offer to consult for Mitsuhama a spur-of-the-moment pitch, or had it been in his mind all the time?

Carla would have to ask him about that.

17

Pita picked her way through the crowd of chanting, clapping people. Hundreds of orks—perhaps even thousands—were seated in the street in front of the Metroplex Hall, refusing to move. They had come out to join the Ork Rights Committee demonstration. The thirty-story office block they sat in front of, at the corner of Fourth and Seneca, housed the city's council chambers, as well as the offices of the governor. It was closed for the evening; the elected officials and staff had gone home an hour ago. But that didn't stop the protesters from shouting up at its blank, tinted-glass walls.

For several weeks, the Ork Rights Committee had been trying to organize a meeting with Governor Shultz, to voice its concern over the lack of Lone Star response to the wave of recent ork-bashings by the Humanis Policlub. Earlier in the day, twelve ORC members had forced their way into the Governor's office and staged a sit-in. They'd been dragged out by Metroplex security guards and unceremoniously dumped on the sidewalk. Now ORC had mobilized their people in protest.

Pita had learned of the protest when she'd powered up an old trideo set she found in the basement of the building where she'd holed up last night. She had to keep the sound down low, and the screen had an annoying flicker. But she'd seen enough in the news stories about the protest to send a shiver of anger through her. No wonder the governor wasn't willing to do anything, she thought grimly, recalling the recent deaths of her chummers. The Lone Star cops themselves were doing the killing.

Although the story on the sit-in had been brief, it aired on a number of the trideo stations' six o'clock newscasts. The most strident reports had come from the *Orks First*! pirates, who had interrupted he newscasts, urging Seattle's ork population to "rise up out of the Underground and show Governor Schultz what you think about the way this city treats orks."

Pita felt compelled to join in the protest. To say something. She owed it to Chen, Shaz and Mohan—her dead chummers. She had to be there. She'd be safe enough—just another ork face in the crowd. If the goons were still looking for her, it was doubtful they'd be able to spot her. And, being human, they'd stand out like sore thumbs.

Orks of every description—and a smattering of trolls, as well—were firmly in place in front of Metroplex Hall. Even the slight drizzle of rain that had started to fall wasn't budging them. They completely filled the street in front of the building; at the edges, car horns honked angrily. Traffic had come to a standstill. A pair of cops tried urgently to sort out the snarl of vehicles, waving their arms and blowing whistles in futile gestures.

A woman holding a megaphone stood at the front entrance to Metroplex Hall. Pita recognized her as a member of the Ork Rights Committee. The woman was dwarfed by the statues of the Indian chief Seattle and Charles C. Lindstrom—first governor of Seattle Metroplex—but her amplified voice rang out as she led the crowd in a series of chants: "Orks unite! Demand your rights!" Behind her, Metroplex Hall security guards eyed the crowd through the triple-thick safety glass of the building's main doors. The woman changed to a different slogan: "One, two, three, four. We won't take it any more! Five, six, seven, eight. The cops don't come 'til it's too late!"

Pita gingerly stepped around seated orks, trying to make her way to the front, where the woman with the megaphone stood. The closer she got, the more tightly people were packed. She finally squeezed herself in a few meters from the front, and sat down between two burly men. The woman had begun a speech—Pita caught the words "priorities," "inadequate presence," and "Lone Star procedures." She waited for a break in the tirade, occasionally waving a hand and at the same time screwing up her courage. She hoped that the committee member would let her speak. She wanted to tell everyone how the Lone Star cops had gunned down her chummers. It would be even better than going on trid—here, the audience was live. Carla and Masaki at KKRU might have strung her along with false promises to do a news story on her friends. But these people—these orks—would listen. If only Pita could catch the woman's eye . . .

The speaker paused, startled, as something flew through the air a few meters away. A beer bottle smashed against the side of the building, painting the smoked glass wall with a trail of foamy liquid. She pointed her megaphone at the portion of the crowd from which the bottle had come. "Please!" she urged them. "This is meant to be a peaceful protest. Let's keep it that way! We don't want to give the police any excuse to—"

A few meters away from Pita, an ork leaped to his feet. He was in his twenties, with wild, uncombed hair, wearing a black leather trench coat studded with jagged bits of chrome. Waving his arms to get the crowd's attention, he used the pause in the speech to start a new chant: "Bash back!" *clap, clap* "Bash back!" *clap, clap* "Bash back!" He alternately thrust a fist in the air in time with the chant, then led the clapping that punctuated the simple phrase. As people jumped to their feet to join him in the new chant, the woman with the megaphone tried to get the crowd back on track. But more and more people were picking up the younger ork's angry chant, stamping their feet in time with it. At last Pita also clambered to her feet. It was either that or get stepped on.

Another bottle arced through the air. At one corner of the building, the crowd had moved forward until its front ranks were up against the building's glass wall. They pounded on it with fists, sticks, and bottles, a wild drumbeat of anger that drowned out even the chants and claps.

Behind Pita, there was a sudden jostling as the now-standing crowd surged to one side. She turned, stood on tiptoe, and tried to look out over the crowd. At one end of the street, Lone Star officers in full armor and helmets had materialized—as if out of thin air—and drawn up in a line across the street. Those in the front rank held stun batons, and were thumping them rhythmically on their shields. They advanced slowly on the assembly of orks, stepping in time with the thud of their batons. Behind them, other cops in riot gear held the oversized guns that were used to fire gel rounds. At least, Pita hoped they held gel rounds.

The sight of the gun-toting cops turned her stomach to ice. She let out a small whimper of fear. She had to get away. Now. Things were going to get ugly, and soon.

A Star drone zoomed around one corner of the Metroplex Hall. It flew low over the crowd of orks, broadcasting the same message over and over: "This is an illegal gathering. Please disperse. Return quietly to your homes. This is an illegal gathering . . ."

A wave of people swept up the steps that led to the building's front entrance, carrying Pita with it. The wave broke against the front doors, pushing Pita face-first into the hard, unforgiving glass. The woman who had been addressing the crowd from the step had disappeared in the rush forward, but a burly troll had grabbed her megaphone. "Open the doors!" he shouted through it. Hands poured on the locked doors. "Let us in!" Inside the building, the Metroplex Hall security guards backed away from the door and looked at each other with uncertain glances.

Pita fought her way down the steps to the street. The bulk of the crowd was moving now, hurrying away from the advancing line of riot officers. But then an armored Star vehicle rumbled into their path. It rolled to a stop in the intersection, oblivious of the people who were scattering away from it in every direction.

Hatches opened, and Pita heard dull thumps as canisters were fired out. The canisters exploded against the pavement with a loud crack and immediately began to release hissing clouds of white vapor. Pita caught a whiff of it and blinked rapidly as her eyes began to sting. Tear gas.

There were screams and angry shouts as the orks realized they were hemmed in, with the line of riot cops on one side and the armored vehicle on the other. More bottles arced through the air, breaking against the armored vehicle that now blocked the intersection. Other, braver orks had wrapped T-shirts around their faces and were picking up the tear gas canisters and hurling them into the ranks of the riot cops. It was a futile gesture; the cops were masked as well as armored. From behind the cops with shields came the crack of gunfire as the second rank of cops aimed and fired gel-rounds into the crowd. People screamed, clasped suddenly bruised flesh, and jostled against each other.

The sight of the Star using their weapons terrified Pita. Tears were pouring down her face—either from the whiff of gas she'd inhaled or from simple fear. She fought to reach the edge of the crowd, to escape. Bodies jostled her from every side; hands grabbed at her or pushed her this way and that. Someone yanked her jacket, choking her. Someone else tripped over the curb, crashed into her, and nearly knocked her down. What had once been an organized, peaceful protest now was a maddened mob. Everyone—including Pita—had only one thought: escape. And none of them knew which way to run.

Pita balled her fists in frustration and sobbed. It was stupid of her to have joined the protest, to have thought that her presence would matter. She never should have come here. What good had it done? None. All the protest had done was give the cops an excuse to vent their prejudices against the "porkies." To put them back in their place. To drive them back Underground, where they belonged.

A space cleared around Pita for a moment, allowing

her to catch her breath. An ork boy, perhaps six or seven years old, was hunched on the ground, clasping a bloodied knee and trying not to cry. Pita turned to help him, then froze as the front rank of riot officers charged forward at a trot, batons raised. From somewhere behind Pita, a teenager with bright purple feathers woven into his hair ran forward, gesturing at the cops. An invisible force slammed into the shields of two officers, knocking them sprawling on their butts. Then one of the cops behind them aimed her gun, fired. Purple feathers and blood exploded as the gel round caught the teenager in the eye, shattering his skull.

Pita clenched her fists. "You fragging bastards!" she screamed, heedless of the line of shields bearing down on her. "Why can't you just leave us al—"

She barely glimpsed the stun baton that cracked against her skull. Static exploded in her brain, and suddenly the pavement rushed up toward her. She slammed into the street and felt hands flipping her over roughly. As she lay blinking, cheek to the rain-damp pavement, dazzled by the spots that swam before her eyes, her arms were yanked back. Something tight cinched around her wrists. She saw boots, the cuffs of Kevlar pants—and then the cops were past her, waving their stun batons and running up the street. She lay on the pavement, fighting to control her heaving stomach. The dead boy lay only a meter or two away, his head leaking blood.

As her head slowly cleared, Pita realized how much trouble she was in. She was busted. And by the same fragging goon squad whose members had flatlined Chen. She closed her eyes and cried.

18

Carla stood just outside the line of yellow plastic ribbon that marked off the crime scene, straining for a better look. Inside the Lone Star barrier, two cruisers sat with lights flashing, illuminating the night with swaths of blue and red. Overhead, a surveillance drone took aerial pictures of the street, while on the sidewalk below it, plainclothes detectives bent over three bodies that had been covered with clear plastic sheeting to protect them from the drizzling rain. Other plainclothes officers combed the street, collecting shell casings and placing them in evidence bags.

The shooting had taken place in front of Underworld 93, a nightclub in Puyallup, a district of Seattle that was heavily controlled by organized crime. Two burly men in expensive suits—probably members of a local crime family—stood off to one side, observing the cops. Given the way things worked here, they'd probably get the details of the investigation before Lone Star did.

A few young bar patrons, dressed in trendy clothes, stood in a knot in the nightclub's doorway, answering questions and pointing up the sidewalk to where the bodies lay. Music boomed out through the open door.

Despite her enhancements, Carla was unable to make out the features of the victims. Rain beaded on the clear plastic that shielded them, blurring their profiles. Smears of red obscured the rest. There was blood—lots of it—on the cement. There hadn't been time for the rain to wash it away.

Carla lowered her umbrella, ducked under the crime tape, and approached the Lone Star officer who was keeping an eye on the handful of people who'd gathered in the street to watch the police at work. Given the area, he was probably on the take and wouldn't be averse to a cash "incentive" to let her know what had gone down here tonight.

As Carla approached, he immediately turned to confront her, one hand on the stun baton that hung from his belt. "Excuse me, miss. Officers only. Please step back behind the . . ." As his voice trailed off, his head tipped to one side. With a gloved hand, he reached up and flipped open the tinted visor of his helmet. "Carla?"

Carla smiled as she recognized the face. Corporal Enzo Samartino. What luck! She'd done an interview with him a few months ago, when the Men of Lone Star pin-up calendar was released. The officers who'd posed for it had gotten into some hot water, despite the fact that the calendar was a fundraiser for the children's wing of Seattle General Hospital. It seemed that Lone Star's top brass didn't like the idea of their officers appearing in nothing but cap and boots. Or maybe it was the creative uses to which some of the models put the Lone Star badge that had slotted the brass off. In any case, Enzo had provided Carla with some of the story's best quotes. And he'd been the best-looking of the bunch. She shifted her umbrella back to get a good look at his thick, dark moustache and long-lashed eyes.

"Enzo. Good to see you again! What's a good-looking fellow like you doing in a place like this?"

Enzo returned her smile and touched a finger to the visor of his helmet. "Just my job, ma'am."

Carla laughed. "Me too."

"Shouldn't you be downtown with all the other reporters? Sounds like the orks are really mixing it up with our City Center detachment, outside Metroplex Hall."

Carla shook her head. "Not me. I'm the day shift. I'm officially off." She tipped her head toward the spot where the detectives were working. "I heard about this shooting over the scanner in my car as I was driving home. Given the neighborhood, I thought it was just another driveby. But then I heard the description of one of the casualties. Native American, left hand cybered and chromed, right hand tattooed with a black bird . . ."

Enzo jerked a gloved thumb over his shoulder at one of the corpses. "That's him. You know the guy? We're still trying to get an ID on him. He wasn't local. And all he was carrying was a generic credstick."

Carla glanced at the figure that lay in a contorted heap on the ground. From the way the plastic sheeting dipped, it didn't look as if there was much left of the fellow's head. "He's a shadowrunner who goes by the name of Raven. Runs with an elf with blond hair—a Caucasian male about thirty or so. But I don't know his name."

"We wondered who that was. The sergeant had him pegged as a passerby who got caught in the crossfire. So he was involved too, huh? Doesn't really matter much, now. We sent him off by ambulance, but he was DOA at the hospital. He won't be answering any questions." Enzo frowned. "Those two weren't friends of yours, were they?"

"Hardly. Just sources, that's all." She winked. "I only consort with those on the right side of the law."

Enzo refused to be sidetracked. "So why the interest in them?"

"I'm just out ambulance chasing," Carla answered. "Even though I'm off work, old habits die hard. Anywhere there are dead shadowrunners, there's a story. What can you tell me about what happened here?"

Enzo chewed his moustache, then glanced back at the plainclothes detectives. "Is this an official interview? I can't release names until the next of kin are notified. I shouldn't even be talking to you. If the Homicide sergeant finds out I let anything slip . . ." He eyed the woman who was directing the plainclothes officers, then glanced even more nervously at the two gangsters in suits.

Carla could see that she was about to lose the slight edge she'd gained. If she didn't convince Enzo to talk in the next few seconds, he would shoo her back behind the tape, and she'd have to wait until the morning's press conference to find out what had happened here tonight. If, that was, the local ganglords allowed any press release at all. The shooting might have no connection at all with the shadowrunners' visit to her apartment. Or it might be a vital link in the chain that would lead to her cracking open the Mitsuhama story.

"Tell you what," she said, deactivating her cybereye. "We'll keep this strictly off the record. I won't use your name, or record your image or voice, and I promise to sit on any names you give me until they're officially released. I won't pester the relatives of the victims, and I'll give you whatever information I dig up that might help the Lone Star investigation." She favored him with her most winning smile. "If the sergeant asks what you were talking to me about, you can tell her you were finally getting around to asking me out on a second date. Deal?"

She was amused to see the big cop was blushing.

"All right," he said grudgingly. "I can give you a little, but you'll have to talk to the detectives—on the record— to get the full story. All I know is that the runner you said was named Raven tried to force Victim Number One to take a walk with him. Victim Number Two intervened to keep his girlfriend from being dragged away. Somebody started shooting, someone else started tossing mana bolts around, and a few minutes later, all three were dead. Or all four, I should say, since the blond elf also seems to have been involved in this."

"The names and occupations of the two victims?" Carla prompted.

"Victim One—a female human by the name of Miyuki Kishi—is a corporate executive. Victim Two— Akira Hirota—is a Japanese citizen who shares a Puyallup address with Victim One. Judging by his tattoos, he's a real bad boy. A local yakuza. He and the suit make an odd combination, by anyone's account. But as they say, love is blind."

Enzo shrugged. "If you ask me, this thing looks like a lover's spat that turned ugly. Except, of course, that shadowrunners and a corp exec were involved. That could add up to an extraction attempt.

"Now it's your turn, Carla. You can't tell me you

just happened to show up here on your way home. You live in Renton. You got an inside scoop on this one?"

Carla forced herself to keep her face expressionless. Miyuki Kishi! She was one of the wage mages who'd worked with Farazad Samji on the Lucifer Project. Not only that, but Carla had been on her way to pay her a surprise visit when she heard about the shooting on her scanner. She'd tried arranging an interview with Rolf Hosfeld, the other Mitsuhama wage mage, and hadn't been able to get past his apartment's security. And now her only other interview possibility was dead. Drek. It just wasn't her night. Or Miyuki's, either.

Presumably, Miyuki had remained loyal to Mitsuhama. By placing the lion-headed dog at the Samji home, she'd been trying to prevent the leak of the corp's research project. And so it was highly doubtful that she'd arranged for her own extraction, as Farazad had. Even if that was the case, she'd have been a fool to arrange an extraction on a night that her yakuza boyfriend was tagging along with her. Which meant the attempted kidnapping had taken her by surprise. It was a genuine extraction.

Interesting, that it was carried out by the same two shadowrunners who'd planned to sell Farazad out to the Renraku Corporation. Presumably the runners had already sold Renraku a copy of the spell for conjuring the spirit by now—the copy they'd gotten from Carla's apartment yesterday afternoon. A copy that was useless without Farazad's knowledge of how to control the spirit once it was summoned.

Assuming Renraku was the "Mr. Johnson" behind this job, the corporation would have been slotted off at purchasing this incomplete package. Its execs would have demanded that the runners supply them with the missing piece of the puzzle; and the shadowrunners would naturally have assumed that one of the other mages who worked with Farazad would have the key. Too bad for them that the wage mage and her boyfriend had proved such a tough target. Still, the runners had known they were going up against a mage—even if they didn't realize that a yakuza would be coming along for the ride. The money must have been good indeed.

Enzo was waiting for Carla's reply.

"It certainly looks like an extraction attempt," she answered. "The runners were probably after Miyuki Kishi because she works at Mitsuhama Computer Technologies research and development lab. She'd be a valuable target, with her knowledge of Mitsuhama's research projects."

Enzo's eyes narrowed. "How did you know where she worked? I didn't tell you that."

Carla's heart sank as the cop laid a hand on her arm and half turned toward the detectives. "I think I should call the sergeant in on this one," he said. "You know three out of four victims—hardly a coincidence, if you ask me."

"I don't know Miyuki personally," Carla told him hurriedly. "I've never even met the woman. I only recognized her name because of the story I did on an associate of hers—a Mitsuhama employee by the name of Farazad Samji, who died four nights ago. I was going to interview Farazad's co-workers for the story that KKRU did on his death. Miyuki was one of those who worked with Farazad at the research lab."

Enzo turned back to listen to her. He'd released her arm, but was keeping a close watch on her, as if worried she'd bolt away. "How did this co-worker die?"

"He apparently summoned up a kind of spirit. I don't know how or why, but apparently it killed him. The spell Farazad used was recorded on a datachip, which an eyewitness to his death found in his pocket."

"I remember now," Enzo said. "The exec who died in the alley. I saw your story on it. So what's the link? Why do you think what went down tonight was an attempted extraction?"

"The two runners who died tonight ah . . . contacted me . . . the day after our story on Farazad aired," Carla said. She decided to blend truth with fiction. "They tried to talk us into turning over our copy of the spell formula, presumably so they could sell it to someone else. There's a chance the spell was developed in the Mitsuhama lab, and that another corporation would pay big nuyen for it. But KKRU refused to deal with them.

"Raven and his elf pal seemed to want that spell formula pretty bad," Carla continued. "Maybe they thought they could get it out of Miyuki. When you come right down to it, my conclusion that this was a corporate extraction is just a guess, really."

Enzo stared at her in silence. She couldn't tell if he was buying her story.

"Listen," she added. "I'll give you something if you agree not to ask where I got it—and not to tell your sergeant who your source was. Something that could help Homicide crack tonight's case. If I give it to you, will you let me walk away without having to answer any more questions?"

Enzo folded his arms, considered a moment, then nodded. "All right," he said at last. "But it better pan out. I know where to find you if it doesn't."

"It will." Carla took a deep breath, then plunged on. It wouldn't hurt to have the cops do a little investigative work for her. It just might shake something loose. "I have it from a reliable source that the two dead shadowrunners were working for Renraku. Assuming this corporation has other shadowrunners on tap—and in this city, where runners are easy to come by, that's a given—there may be an attempt to extract another Mitsuhama wage mage. There are two more who worked in the lab with Farazad and Miyuki. Their names are Evelyn Belanger and Rolf Hosfeld."

Enzo's eyes widened. "You're saying they could get hit next." He reached for the portable radio at his hip. "I'd better call this in. Mitsuhama may want to contract for extra security for those two."

Carla lifted the crime tape and prepared to duck back under it. "Promise you'll keep my name out of it?" she asked. She shot a meaningful look at the two burly men in suits. "Since one of your victims is yakuza, there's bound to be a little heat on this one. And I don't want the yaks breathing down my neck. I don't think it would be healthy."

"All right," Enzo answered. "As long as you keep quiet about me giving you the names of the victims." He glanced at the two yaks. "For the same reason."

"It's a deal. And we're still on for that after-hours interview. Call me in a day or two, O.K.?" Carla blew him a kiss and hurried back to her car.

19

Pita watched through the grimy, wire-enforced window of the Lone Star transport van as the vehicle backed up against a building with gray concrete walls and a large, metal-plated door. She swayed as the van bumped to a stop with its rear doors flush against the door in the building's wall. Slowly, with a loud squealing noise, the building's armored door slid up. Then heavy mechanical locks in the van's rear doors clicked. The doors popped open a crack, letting in a slant of flickering fluorescent light.

A speaker in the prisoner transport section of the van crackled to life. A pleasant, well-modulated female voice emerged from it. "You have arrived at the Lone Star pretrial containment facility in downtown Seattle. Please exit from the rear of the vehicle in a quiet and orderly fash—"

One of the dozen orks who shared the back of the van with Pita roared, drowning out the rest of the instructions. Rearing up from the bench seat that lined the wall, he aimed a booted foot at the speaker. The ork was extraordinarily flexible, able to keep his balance and kick high above his head, despite the fact that his hands were firmly cinched together behind his back. But his foot just bounced off the thick, perforated plexiglass that protected the speaker, leaving only a dirty smudge.

". . . will be admitted, one at a time, into the station's booking room, where you will be processed before moving on to detention cells. Please proceed now into the arrivals bay."

An ork in her twenties with a bioluminescent tattoo of a golden spiderweb decorating her bald head pushed the doors open with her shoulder and jumped out. "This is it, chummers. First floor: cyberware scans, retinal scans, blood tests, and DNA typing. A bargain at zero nuyen down, zero per month."

The others broke into tired laughter, then shuffled forward with heads slightly bent to avoid the van's low ceiling. One by one, they jumped down onto the cement floor of the tubelike arrivals bay. Pita, still a little woozy from the effects of the stun baton, stumbled. The woman with the bio-lum tattoo caught her and propped her up with a shoulder.

"You all right, kid?" the woman asked.

Pita nodded, not trusting her voice.

"Never been arrested before, huh?" the woman continued. "Well, don't try taking a poke at a cop when your cuffs come off or tossing magic around. If you do, they'll slap you into pulse cuffs or pull a magemask over your head."

As the last of the prisoners clambered out of the back of the van, a voice came from an overhead speaker. This time it was male, but equally mechanical. "The outer door is about to close. Please stay well clear of the yellow line." On the wall beside the door, a red light began to flash. A buzzer beeped softly in time with it. "The door will be closing in five, four, three, two, one . . ."

With the same ear-splitting squeak that it had given upon opening, the outer door slid down, sealing one end of the arrivals bay and hiding the back of the police van from view. Over the noise, the prisoners began to chant. "Hell, no, we won't go. Tell Lone Star to let us go! Hell no . . ."

Their voices reverberated in the enclosed space, echoing back and forth. The orks stamped their feet in time with the chant, increasing the noise volume further. After a moment, Pita joined in, thumping one heel on the floor. Even though it wouldn't get her out of here, shouting slogans with the other prisoners made her feel better. She felt protected by the small mob around her, defiant. It didn't matter that one of the prisoners was bleeding profusely from a gash on his cheek and another was hobbling along on what was probably a broken foot. If they stuck together, fought back against the cops . . .

Pita suddenly felt a low vibration, deep in her bones. All of a sudden her stomach felt as if it were being twisted by a pair of invisible hands. She doubled over, fighting the urge to be sick. She heard someone next to her heaving and then the pungent smell of vomit filled the air. Beside her, the woman with the bio-lum tattoo gritted something through clenched teeth: "Bastards. They're pumping in low-frequency noise." Then Pita lost her supper. Now she had to concentrate on her bowels, which felt as if they were full of ice water.

Mercifully, the vibrations stopped just before she lost control. The orks in the arrival bay straightened slowly, hands still clutching their stomachs. One or two were crying—either with fear or frustration—as they wiped vomit from their lips.

Pita spat on the floor, trying to get the taste of partially digested Growlie bars out of her mouth. The air in the tunnel was foul. She breathed as shallowly as she could; her stomach was still heaving. Given the fact that the floor had been clean when they entered the arrivals bay and now was slick with vomit, Pita's group must have been the first of those arrested at the demonstration to arrive here. Or perhaps they were just the most vocal. She decided to be as quiet and non-confrontational as possible. Maybe the cops wouldn't notice her.

The voice resumed its toneless instructions: "Please proceed, one at a time, into the inner airlock for processing. Please proceed, one at a time . . ."

This time, the orks moved silently forward. As the voice droned on they formed a line and shuffled, one by one, through a smaller door at the far end of the tunnel. The bald woman with the tattoo was just ahead of Pita. She offered Pita a big-toothed smile, then trotted into the airlock, head up, with a defiant step. With a soft sigh, the door closed behind her.

After a minute or two, it was Pita's turn. She stepped nervously into the tiny space between two airlock doors.

The door behind her slid shut, leaving her in complete darkness. She had the strong sense of eyes watching her, and felt a prickling sensation that raised the hairs on her arms. "Magic," she whispered to herself; she'd become familiar with the feel of it, after the attack by the dreadlocked mage. They were doing something to her. What? She gnawed her lip with an oversized canine and prayed that this was only a harmless magical scan of some sort. She didn't think they'd be able to detect her newly awakened magical abilities if she wasn't in contact with Cat, but she couldn't be sure.

Pita didn't want to think of the other possibilities—that the cops might be messing up her mind, sapping her life energies, or . . . She forced those fears from her mind and strained her eyes, trying to see. But the blackness was absolute; she couldn't even see the door that was a few centimeters in front of her. Why weren't the cops opening it? She blinked rapidly, fighting back tears. Should she call out? Had they forgotten about her? Should she kick on the door with her feet or would that only make the cops . . .

The door in front of her slid open. Dazzled by the sudden brilliance of bright lights, Pita was unable to focus her eyes. Hands seized her arms and shoulders, dragging her out of the airlock. As she stumbled forward she heard the buzz of many voices and the humming of electrical equipment. Then she was pushed into a chair. Something attached to the back of the chair she was sitting on snugged against the back of her neck—a clamp of some sort, by the cold feel of the metal. Pita swallowed hard, wondering what it was for.

At last her vision returned. She looked around and saw that she was inside one of several cubicles that lined the walls of a central room where armed and uniformed guards stood watch. The walls of the cubicles were made of plexiglass, once clear but now scuffed and dirty. Through them, Pita could see a few of the orks who'd been with her in the arrival bay. Each was undergoing a different test at the hands of uniformed officers. Before she had a chance to look for the woman with the web tattoo, two officers strode into the cubicle. Pita cringed away from them, crushing her handcuffed arms into the hard plastic of the chair on which she sat. But the two barely looked at her. One forced her head into the metal clamp on the back of the chair while the other pulled down a camera that was attached to the ceiling by an extendible arm.

"Look into the retinal scanner, please," one of the cops said in a bored voice. "And keep your eyes still, or it will take longer."

"Don't get cute and try to close your eyes," the other cop added.

The scan took only a moment. The camera emitted a faint hum, and a flash of red dazzled Pita's eyes. Then a baton-wielding cop hustled her to the next cubicle.

In rapid, orderly succession the cops took Pita's photograph, pricked her finger for a blood and DNA sample, snipped a lock of her hair for some other obscure test, and at last took her fingerprints with an electronic scanner that was pressed to each finger and thumb in turn while her hands were still cuffed behind her back. Presumably all of the testing equipment was on-line; the only person entering data into a computer was the female cop who asked her name, age, race—as if that wasn't fragging obvious—address, and next of kin. Pita was asked if she had taken any drugs and was warned once more of her rights. Then a bored-looking female cop wearing latex gloves frisked her, patting down her clothes. The cop removed everything from Pita's pockets: her book on shamanism, the few coins she'd boosted after some drek-stupid customer had left a tip on a street-side restaurant table earlier that day, the silver ring Chen had given her that now was too small for her fat ork fingers—even a half-eaten Growlie bar in its crumpled wrapper—and heat-sealed these meager possessions inside a plastic bag. Taking a black marker, she wrote on the front of it: "Patti Dewar, PID 500387378."

Pita locked her eyes on the plastic bag as it was set

aside. "When will I get my stuff back?" she asked in a trembling voice.

"No personal possessions are allowed in the detention cells," the cop answered in an irritated voice. "These items will be returned to you later, after your first court appearance. If you make bail, that is."

"But couldn't I just have my—"

"Move along, please." The cop was already looking at the next woman she'd be frisking. "Next!"

Glancing behind her at the plastic bag that held her stuff, Pita reluctantly let herself be directed to a door in a side wall. When it opened, she was met by two uniformed officers carrying stun batons. She moved in the direction they indicated, trotting quickly ahead to keep some distance between herself and the batons. She didn't like the way one cop kept his thumb posed over the charge button.

The corridor led to a row of cells. The first one held two scruffy-looking humans and a dozen female orks. The prisoners milled about, muttering angrily. They shouted catcalls at the cops herding Pita. The cops ignored them, turning Pita to face the barred door of the cells and applying something hot to the plasticuffs that encircled her wrists. She smelled burning plastic, and then her arms sprang apart as the cuffs released.

The cops motioned for the women inside the cell to move back, threatening to poke their stun batons through the bars at those who moved too slowly. Then they opened the door and shoved Pita inside. Before she could turn around, the cell door slammed shut behind her with a loud clang.

Pita scanned the other orks who shared the cell with her. Three of them had been with her in the Lone Star van and the arrivals bay. But she didn't see the woman who had helped her earlier. Despite the physical proximity of the other women, she felt completely alone. Her eyes began to sting and she blinked to hide her tears. *Don't be such a slot-head, she told herself. You're in a detention center. Even if the cops who scragged Chen and the others do show up, they can't do anything to you while you're here.* Taking a deep breath, she looked around.

The cell was maybe ten meters wide and deep. It was rapidly filling up; the cops kept bringing in more ork women. More than one had a bloody scalp or white patches where a stun baton had grazed her. A few seemed to know each other, and were greeted with a fist in the air and an Ork Rights Committee slogan. These women shouted and spat at the cops who escorted other prisoners past the row of cells and laughed in the cops' faces when the cops called them "porkies." Other prisoners—particularly those who were better dressed—seemed as dazed and confused by their incarceration as Pita did.

Pita glanced from face to face, looking for someone who would befriend her. Then she heard a ringing noise as something metal struck the bars of the cell.

"Hey, you!" a male voice said. "The young one. Turn around and face the door of the cell!"

Pita glanced over her shoulder. On the other side of the door, looking in through the bars, stood a cop. He wore the padded leather jacket and heavy boots of a patrol officer, as well as a helmet. Its shaded visor hid his eyes completely, making him look even more threatening. Somewhere behind it, a red light blinked on briefly; he must have a cybereye. Light gleamed off the chromed letters on the upper-right side of his jacket: 709.

Pita turned away, moving slowly to the back of the cell. There were more than two dozen women inside it now. If she could just hide behind some of them, she might avoid the cop's gaze. Maybe—just maybe—he really was looking for someone else. But Pita didn't think so. She was the youngest one in the cell.

She started chanting the mantra that had saved her in the alley, the night she'd hidden in the dumpster. *Don't let him notice me. Don't let him see me.* But then the clang of metal on metal made her jump and broke her concentration.

"Hey, you!" the cop said, louder this time. "The girl

in the black jacket and torn jeans. Prisoner Number 500387378. I said turn around. Now!"

A clear space had suddenly formed around Pita. So much for the ORC slogans of solidarity. The "sisters" had abandoned her. Swallowing her fear, she turned to face the cop. She nearly fainted when she saw what he'd rapped on the bars with. His ungloved hand. It was made of articulated metal joints covered with gleaming chrome. She recognized the distinctive clicking and whirring noise it made as he extended a finger, pointing it at her. It had made the same noise as he wielded the machete that had carved up Chen and her other two chummers.

The flutter returned to her stomach. Pita was certain she was going to be sick again. She put out a hand, hoping one of the other prisoners would sense her plight and rush to her side to support her.

No one did.

"Is this yours?" the cop asked. In his other, meat hand, he held the book Pita had stolen from Aziz's shop.

Pita opened her mouth but was unable to speak. She managed only a slight nod. Her eyes were wide and round, locked on the cop's metal hand.

"Are you a shaman?"

"I—" Pita was unable to croak out any more. Her legs felt as if all the muscles in them had lost their elasticity. She was certain they would collapse under her at any moment.

"Where's your thaumaturgy license?" the cop asked. "If you're practicing magic within the city limits, you need a license."

Pita almost laughed with relief. Was that all the cop wanted? To enforce some stupid little bylaw? Maybe he hadn't recognized her, after all. The street where Chen and the others had been shot had been dimly lit. Perhaps the cops hadn't gotten a good look at her through the tinted windows of their patrol car.

The officer cocked a metallic finger at Pita. "Come with me. There's some special processing we've got to do."

Pita's hands began to tremble. Had the cop emphasized the word "special"? What did he mean by it? She didn't want to find out. She searched, desperately, for somewhere to hide.

But it was too late. The cop had already tucked the book under one arm and was opening the door of the cell.

20

The air wasn't cold. Even so, Pita was shivering. She sat on the plastifoam chair that smelled faintly of stale sweat, her hands nervously kneading the worn fabric of her jeans. The room was small and absolutely bare, with concrete walls and a single green metal door. There were no windows. The only light came from a single halogen bulb set into a recess in the ceiling.

The cop who'd pulled her from the detention cell—the same cop who'd killed Chen—walked around Pita in slow, predatory circles. He paused only once, to turn off the camera that was monitoring the room. He hadn't spoken since removing her from the cell, except to curtly direct her to this room. He'd flipped up the visor on his helmet, but what lay underneath was even worse: one cold blue eye and a cybernetic implant of glinting metal with a flat lens at the center of it.

Pita concentrated on looking at the ground, not wanting to look into that face again.

Suddenly, the cop was in her face. "Hey, porkie!" he shouted.

Pita jerked back, then tried to hide the trembling in her hands by clenching her fists around the folds in her jeans.

The cop chuckled, low and soft. He paced once more around Pita, then stood behind her, where she couldn't see him. But she could feel his eyes on her back.

"I asked you a question earlier," the cop said in a soft growl. "Are you a shaman, or not?"

"No," Pita whispered, not sure if she was lying. She wasn't formally trained, after all. "I'm just a kid." She tried to focus her mind, as she had earlier when controlling the yakuza's thoughts. But all she could picture was Chen's bloody corpse and the inhuman monster behind her leaning over it, hacking at it, dipping his cyberhand in the blood to smear a slogan on the wall . . .

"You don't look like a kid to me. You look awfully . . . developed . . . for the age you gave in Processing." He let the words hang in the air a moment.

Pita swallowed. What did he mean by that? She was big for her age—big for a human, that was, although not so big for an ork. But the human standing behind her was even taller than she was, and twice as muscular. And he had a cybernetic hand that could crush her skull like an egg.

"You didn't give an address." He said it hard and flat, like an accusation.

"I don't have one. But I used to live in Puyallup until . . ." *Until I goblinized*, she thought to herself. *Until my parents threw me out*.

"You're a Barrens brat, huh?" he guessed. But he was wrong. Pita and her family had lived on the other side of the tracks, in a neighborhood where metahumans weren't welcome.

The cop leaned closer; Pita could feel his breath on the back of her neck. "Well, you should have stayed in the Barrens. It's gutterpunks like you who cause all the problems downtown. Panhandling, breaking into shops, cluttering up the sidewalk by sleeping on it in your filthy blankets, spreading lice and disease . . . What are decent people supposed to do when they see you kids hanging about in gangs on the streets, selling drugs and sex? My girlfriend is afraid to go out at night because of trash like you. But oh, no—you porkies just keep breeding like rabbits. Spilling out of the Barrens in a never-ending wave of degeneracy. It's time somebody put a stop to it. Somebody with the guts to do what's right."

"Somebody like the Humanis Policlub?"

The words just slipped out. As soon as she said them, Pita cringed. She tensed her shoulders, waiting for his blow. But instead the cop paused—either to take a breath or to savor her fear—then started in on a new tack. "You and your precious committee want special rights, huh? And you think you're going to get them by blocking the streets and tossing trash at our government buildings? You aren't fit to sit in the gutter in front of Metroplex Hall, let alone walk in the front door and demand special treatment. Why don't you porkers stay in the Underground where you belong?"

Pita sat through the tirade, shoulders hunched. She didn't dare speak. Had she been human, none of this would be happening. She'd be safe at home, still attending high school, snug in her circle of friends. She hated being an ork—hated the way she looked. But not as much as this man did.

The cop strode around to face Pita and lifted her chin with the tip of his stun baton. He held the baton fully at arms' length, as if using it to shift a piece of foul-smelling trash. "So tell me, kid. How do you make a living on the streets? By selling yourself?" His eyes were no longer on her face, but were scanning her body.

Pita felt a tear trickle down her cheek. She hated this man for what he was doing to her, for how he made her feel. Cheap. And dirty. She had sold herself—but only twice, and only since Chen's death—for the drugs that had helped to ease her grief. Both times, it was to humans who looked at her much as the cop eyed her now, with equal mixtures of loathing and lust. Who wanted "something exotic." Not someone—some *thing*. But what could she tell this cop? That she kept herself alive by stealing? He was probably just looking for an excuse to hurt her. Either with his stun baton, or . . .

She jerked her head back, finally finding the courage to speak. "You wouldn't be doing this to me if I were human," she said in a quavering voice. "The woman in the processing room said I get to see a lawyer. Well, I want to see one. Now."

The cop laughed out loud. "The waiting list for public defenders is three weeks long," he said. "But I suppose you're talking about a real lawyer. How do you expect to pay for one, street trash?" His baton slid down her body. "With this?"

"I get to make a telecom call," Pita protested.

The cop rested the baton on his shoulder. "Yeah? Who to? You didn't list any next of kin. Maybe your pimp, huh?"

Pita thought about what Chen had told her. He'd been arrested once, for shoplifting. He'd done a year in a juvenile detention center. She hoped the rules were still the same. And that this cop would follow them. "I don't have to tell you that."

The cop was still holding the book on cat shamans in his flesh hand. He smacked Pita's face with it. "Don't get smart with me, porkie."

Pita rubbed her cheek. "I get one call," she said stubbornly. She cringed as he raised his hand. But this time, he shook the book in her face.

"You get nothing until I say so. You're a shaman, aren't you?"

One telecom call, Pita thought desperately. *Just let me make one call.* She couldn't think who she would call—who would possibly want to help her? Not her parents. Not the friends who'd deserted her when she began to goblinize. But if she could just get out of this room . . .

The cop waved the book at her. "We have a special processing procedure for shamans. It's called the mage-mask. It's a tight plastic hood, with nothing but a mouth tube for breathing. With it on your head, you won't be able to hear or see anything. And when the white-noise generator is turned on, you won't be able to think, either." He paused, and Pita could hear his cyberhand whirring as he tightened his grip on the handle of the stun baton. "I think it's just what you need."

Pita closed her eyes, shutting out the room. If she could just find an excuse to get out of here, into an area where there were other people, maybe she could call for help.

One phone call. One phone call. One phone call. She chanted it over and over in her mind, her lips whispering it silently. At the same time, she cast her thoughts out desperately, searching for Cat. *Please, Cat,* she cried. *Help me. Please.*

When the answer came, Pita nearly missed it. The touch was velvety soft, like a paw against her skin. A paw with claws sheathed.

As the invisible presence stroked her hand, an image came to Pita's mind. Of a hand slipping into a velvet glove. All at once, she knew what she had to do. She had to slide—soft as velvet—into the mind of her opponent. To become one with his thoughts. To guide him gently, instead of attacking him directly as she had the yakuza back at the hotel.

Cat purred, conveying pleasure that the message had been understood. The touch disappeared.

Pita forced her thoughts outward, toward the cop. She imagined herself flowing like a ghost, slipping gently into his mind through his ear. When his thoughts started to boil past her in an angry torrent, she nearly backed away, nearly broke contact. His mind was a seething cauldron of hatred, filled with his urge to hurt her, to humiliate her. There were memory pictures there, too—of the view from inside the Lone Star cruiser of a group of four teenaged orks on a darkened sidewalk. Of watching one of them—her friend Shaz—throw a chunk of concrete at the vehicle. Of the cop's partner—a man with the nickname Reno—smiling and squeezing the trigger that activated a machine gun built into the front of the cruiser. Of three orks falling, jerking like bloody puppets, while one ran off into the night. Of following the running ork, whose face merged in the cop's mind with the face of every other ork he'd ever seen, ever hated . . .

With a start, Pita realized that this cop had not, in fact, recognized her. She was just a young meta he'd picked out of the detention cell because she was smaller than the others and he thought he could bully her. He didn't believe she had any magical ability at all and didn't see her as a threat; he'd just used the cat shaman book as an excuse to bring her to this room. But the thoughts that swirled through his mind as he looked at her now—as she looked through his eyes at herself, cringing with eyes closed and mouth whispering as she sat on the plastifoam chair—made it clear that this wouldn't help her. He didn't care which ork he took out his misguided "vengeance" on. He only cared about making her too frightened to tell his fellow cops about it afterward.

Entering the cop's mind had taken only a second or two. Pita changed her whisper, molding it to his train of thought. *Let the kid make one telecom call*, she urged. *It'll look better that way. You can bring her back to the room later, in a few hours, when things cool down. It'll look less suspicious that way. But if you don't let her make the call, the guards in Detention will start to talk. They'll wonder why the kid was taken from the cell. And why you're not following procedure.*

Pita was still inside the cop's mind when she felt his lips begin to move. "One telecom call." He said it in time with her whisper.

"One call, and then back to the detention cell for you. We'll continue this interrogation later."

Pita rushed down the corridor toward the barred door that was all that stood between her and freedom. "Masaki!" she shouted. "You came!"

The reporter waved at her from the public waiting room. He was a most unlikely looking rescuer. His shirt was half untucked, and hung loosely over his chubby stomach. His wide cheeks were spotted with gray stubble, but even this wasn't enough to make him fit in with the tough-looking crowd of orks, scragged-out humans, and streeters who crowded the containment facility's waiting room. He looked old and soft, his face too open and friendly. If Pita had seen him on the street, she would have pegged him as an easy mark for panhandling. But right now, she looked upon him as her knight in fragging shining armor.

She waited impatiently for the Lone Star guard to key the code into a panel behind the door. When it opened, she ducked through it quickly, still afraid that some fragger would change his mind and order her back to the cell.

Masaki half lifted his arms, as if expecting a hug. But when Pita stopped a few steps away, he dropped his hands. She gave him a nervous grin. "Uh, thanks, Masaki."

The reporter nodded. He looked chill about posting her bail, but he'd probably want a more concrete thank you later. They all did. But for now, that didn't matter. Pita was happy to see a friendly face—any friendly face.

"You were lucky the holding facility was full. They were eager to clear out a few detainees," he said. "And lucky to have only been charged with a misdemeanor. If it had been anything more serious, they wouldn't have let me post bail. Certainly not on the night of your arrest, anyway."

"I know that." Pita couldn't keep the irritation out of her voice. Masaki sounded like he was lecturing her. Who did he think he was, anyway? Her fragging father?

"They said you could collect your stuff from the property office," he said. "It's down this way."

Pita followed him out of the waiting room and down a corridor. At the property office, the cops made her sign an electronic signature pad before they gave back the things they'd confiscated from her earlier. Pita heaved a sigh of relief, seeing that the book on shamanism was included among her possessions. Her final mental command to the cop who'd tormented her had taken root, after all. She opened the plastic bag and took out Chen's ring, the loose change, and the book, then dropped the bag on the floor. Let some drekhead cop clean it up.

"I'm parked in the visitors' lot," Masaki said. "Let's go."

Pita followed him outside, smiling as the door closed behind her. It was dark; it must have been close to one in the morning. The night air was cool and fresh; the light sprinkling of rain had washed much of the smog from it. Overhead, between the patchy clouds, a few stars sparkled.

Pita savored her freedom as they climbed the parkade stairs to Masaki's car. The feeling was overwhelming, better even than being on Mindease. Except, of course, for the small tickle of worry she still felt. How long until that cop—Number 709—caught up with her again? *It won't happen,* she told herself firmly. *He isn't looking for me. He'll find someone else to pick on.* But she couldn't be sure.

Masaki drove slowly, keeping exactly to the speed limit, despite the lack of traffic. Only after they had put several blocks between themselves and the containment facility did Pita think to ask where they were going.

"Back to my apartment," he answered. "You can spend the night there."

Pita gave him a sideways glance. "I already have a place to crash," she said carefully. "Just off Denny Way, near the highway. You could drop me there on your way home. Or I could walk if you don't want to—"

"I don't think so, Pita. You wouldn't be safe on the streets. You're better off with me. For the time being, at least."

"I wouldn't be on the streets. I'd be—"

A note of irritation crept into Masaki's voice. "Pita, I just paid five hundred nuyen to bail you out of that detention center. I think that gives me some say in where you're going to sleep tonight. Or don't you think so?"

Pita immediately fell silent. She stared out the window, suddenly very tired. She'd wanted to think that Masaki was a good guy, that she'd read him properly. Now she wasn't so sure. She hadn't been out of jail ten minutes, and already it was payback time.

The drive to Masaki's place took about fifteen minutes. He lived in a highrise complex in Bellevue. The entrance to the parkade was through a double-doored security gate that required the driver to provide two separate retinal scans before admission was granted, and the lobby of the apartment block itself was watched over by a live guard, rather than the usual remote cameras. Pita decided that the building was designed either for the very cautious city dweller—or the very paranoid.

The fellow gave Pita a long look as she trailed through the lobby after Masaki. Why was he staring at her? Didn't they allow orks in this building? Or was he just wondering what Masaki was doing, dragging in "street trash" in the early hours of the morning?

An elevator whisked them up to the twenty-fifth floor. Masaki led Pita down a corridor, carpeted with soft plush, to a door that bristled with yet more security features. He not only had to slide a magkey through the lock but also had to provide a voice sample and yet another retinal scan.

When the door was at last open, Pita reluctantly followed Masaki into the apartment. It was a little on the sloppy side—jackets that had been tossed on a coat rack had spilled onto the floor, and dirty dishes were piled in the sink—but it was a nice place, all right. Nicer than her parents' low-rent condo, and certainly nicer than the streets. It must have cost him some serious nuyen. The furniture was a bit sparse; this place probably ate up most of his salary.

Masaki tossed his jacket on the pile and palmed a sensor in the wall, illuminating the bathroom. Then he turned to Pita. "I thought you might like to take a shower before . . . That is, to clean up a little." He gave a lame shrug. "Not that you look dirty, but after being in jail, and everything, you probably want to freshen up. Ah . . . while I get the bed ready."

Pita tried to keep her lip from curling. She'd barely walked in the door, and already he was propositioning her. And he wanted her clean. Given his cautious nature, it was a wonder he hadn't asked her to take a test for VITAS too. "All right," she said, stepping into the bathroom. He didn't have to tell her to clean up—she couldn't wait. But she flipped him the finger after shutting the door anyway. She'd show him, all right. She'd take a shower. Not a long one—she didn't particularly enjoy getting wet any more. But she'd let the water run for a good long time.

Twenty minutes later, she cracked the bathroom door and peeked through the gap. Lying in the hallway outside was a pair of men's pajamas—sloppily folded, but clean. Pita snagged them with a hand, shut the door, and tried them on. She'd thought they'd be too big; Masaki had quite the pot belly on him, after all.

But they fit. And that only served to remind her of how large and ungainly she was.

She took a moment to comb her hair, not bothering to wipe the condensation from the mirror. Looking at the hazy reflection, she could imagine herself as she used to be. A big girl, yes. But with a narrow jaw, square white teeth, and without the pointed ears that poked out of her hair at odd angles. The only good part about her transformation had been the fact that her breasts had grown along with the rest of her. From the neck down—if you discounted the overly long arms and extra hair—she had the body of a grown woman rather than that of a teenage girl. Chen had always told her how beautiful she looked. But he was an ork, born and raised. How would he know what a real woman should look like?

Drek. There she went again, running Chen down. Running herself down. Pita silently chastised herself for what she'd been thinking. Real woman—hmph. Human, she meant. That was her father talking. She'd spent too many years listening to the hate that spewed from his mouth.

Wiping the mirror clean, she took a good long look at herself, trying to imagine what Masaki saw in her. Then she sighed. "Time to pay your dues, girl. All five hundred nuyen of them."

Masaki was in the apartment's living room, staring out of a floor-to-ceiling window. The view was of Lake Washington. Across the lake were the lights of downtown. It was easy to pick out the distinctive pyramid shape of the Aztechnology Pyramid and the towering Renraku Arcology.

Masaki had changed into pajamas, and as Pita entered the room, was yawning widely. Noticing her reflection in the window, he turned and cleared his throat.

"That was a long shower," he said.

Pita was immediately on the defensive. "Are you worried it will run up your fragging electric bill?" she asked. "I'll pay you back. For that, and the bail, too."

Masaki laughed. "Don't worry," he said. "The hot water is included in the rent. You can use all you want."

Pita glanced down the hall, bracing herself for what was to come. "Which one's the bedroom?" she asked sullenly.

"Last door on the left. If you need anything, don't be afraid to wake me up. I'm a light sleeper, anyway." He moved toward her, then gestured toward the couch. "You can sleep here. I've made up a bed for you."

Pita peered over the back of the couch. He was telling the truth. The couch was piled with blankets, and a pillow had been placed at one end of it.

Masaki touched a sensor in the wall, dimming the lights. "Well, good night. I'll see you in the morning."

He walked down the hall to his bedroom, shutting the door softly behind him. Pita shook her head in disbelief. Amazing. Masaki really was a nice guy, after all. Either that, or he found her so repulsive that . . .

She turned off the light, then burrowed into the blankets on the couch. Lying with her cheek on a pillow that smelled of fresh laundry soap, she stared out at the Seattle skyline. She liked the sensation of being above things, of looking down on the streets from a height. Of feeling clean, of curling into a tight little ball and snuggling down into blankets.

Sighing with contentment, she closed her eyes and fell almost immediately into a deep sleep.

Pita stared across the kitchen table at Masaki as he tossed two instant-breakfast packets into the microwave and set the timer. As they warmed up, he fished a carton of real milk out of the fridge. He sniffed it, made a face, then dumped the chunky white liquid down the sink. Turning to the cupboard, he pulled a packet of instant orange drink from the shelf and mixed up two glasses with water from the filtration unit.

"Not much of a cook, huh?" Pita observed. But she wasn't really complaining. Not with the rich smell of reconstituted eggs and RealMeat bacon wafting through the air, making her mouth water.

"I don't usually eat breakfast," Masaki explained. "I just grab a Poptoast and a cup of soykaf, and eat them on my way in to the station. But since I have company,

I thought I'd better get domestic and prepare a home-cooked breakfast."

Pita had to smile at that one. Home-cooked? Still, it would be a better meal than she'd had in weeks.

The microwave timer pinged. Masaki took the breakfast packets out of it, peeled off the plastic film that sealed the top of each, and set one on the table in front of Pita. He handed her a fork, then sat down to eat the other one while it was still steaming.

Pita ate until the edge was off her hunger. Then she paused, trying to phrase the question she wanted to ask. She at last decided to be blunt.

"How come you didn't try anything last night? Is it because I'm . . ." Pita was going to say ugly, but deliberately sought another word. ". . . because I'm an ork?"

Masaki chuckled and activated a holopic that was held to the fridge with a magnet. "See him?"

Pita nodded, looking at the three-dimensional image. It was of a middle-aged ork, a burly fellow with blond hair and a full, curling beard. "Yeah."

"That's a picture of my partner."

"Your what?"

"My boyfriend."

"Oh." Pita blushed. She'd been thinking of Masaki as a loser who didn't rate a permanent companion. Now she realized that she'd judged him by appearances, something she'd just accused him of doing to her. It was funny, thinking of someone his age having a "boyfriend."

She had one other question to ask.

"Carla's not going to do the story on how Lone Star killed my friends, is she?"

"No," Masaki admitted after a moment's silence. "She's not."

"Will you?"

Masaki sighed and laid his fork on the table. "No, Pita, I won't."

"Why not? Don't you believe me?"

"I do, actually," Masaki said. "I believe what you told me over the phone last night. About recognizing the cop who gunned down your friends. He probably is a member of the Humanis Policlub. But we don't stand a chance against Lone Star. You can't take on a big corporation like that—not even with KKRU to back you up. They're just too powerful. They'd find a way to spike the story before it even aired."

Pita's nostrils flared. "You're a coward," she told him.

Masaki kept his eyes on his breakfast. "Maybe." He stood up and cleared the empty breakfast packets from the table.

"It's useless trying to avenge your friends by taking a swing at Lone Star—even a verbal one," he told her. "That corporation would erase you faster than yesterday's data. The important thing now is to make sure that bad cop doesn't get his hands on you again."

"And what if he gets his hands on another ork kid?" Pita muttered. "Or on your boyfriend?"

Masaki ignored her and tossed the platters in the trash. "I'll try to arrange a spot for you in a group home in Portland; I've got a contact down there who owes me a favor and who can probably put your name at the top of the placement list. Until the visa application comes through, you can stay here."

"A group home?" Pita curled her lip. She wanted desperately to find a safe haven, but the thought of living in a city full of stuck-up elves and being bossed around by social workers repulsed her. Portland was part of the elven nation of Tir Tairngire, and she'd be even more aware of her physical size among that delicate and slender race. She'd rather stay in Seattle—right here, in Masaki's comfortable apartment. What did he want to do, get rid of her? He had a boyfriend; maybe he was worried she would cramp his style.

Masaki was still rambling on. ". . . and don't leave the apartment. You won't be able to get back in through the door, and the guard in the lobby won't let you back into the building if you don't have a passkey. But feel free to make yourself at home. Use the telecom unit as much as you like, but keep your net browsing confined to the local telecommunications grid and don't run up any long-distance charges."

Masaki picked up his magkey and scooped his jacket off the floor. "I've got some errands to run. I'll be back this afternoon. See you then, O. K.?"

Pita didn't acknowledge his goodbye or look up when the door closed. She was still burnt about the fact that he'd refused to do the story on Lone Star. If only Yao were still alive. He'd have run the story, then gleefully spat in the eye of any cop who tried to mess with him.

Pita went into the living room and powered up Masaki's telecom. It didn't take her long to find confirmation that Yao was indeed dead. On the Public Service Channel, she found a police bulletin, dated three days ago, that noted the shooting death of one ork, male, named Yao Wah. The cops speculated that it had been a mugging; Yao Wah was known to be a pirate broadcaster. It was thought that he'd been killed for his portacam; witnesses saw a troll carrying it away from the scene of the crime. The bulletin wound up with a short description of a suspect that would have matched ninety-nine percent of the trolls in Seattle. The bulletin made no mention of the real killers—the two yakuza who'd actually geeked Yao.

Pita stared at the telecom screen, tempted to dial Tokyo or Paris and chat for an hour or two with whoever answered the phone. She'd show that grumpy old fragger. Not run up any long distance calls, huh? She could bankrupt him in a single morning if she wanted to.

But she didn't want to. Despite his cowardice, Masaki had been kind to her. He'd been kind to her last night, without any ulterior motive she could think of. He'd let her have the run of this wiz apartment with the awesome view. He'd trusted her. And Pita hadn't been shown much trust. Not in the past two years of living on the streets. Shopkeepers stared at her, security guards watched her suspiciously every time she walked into a megamall, and pedestrians quickly stuck their hands in their pockets to make sure they still had their wallets when they passed her on the sidewalk. It felt good to have someone look at her without wariness and suspicion. It also felt so good to be clean and dry.

Pita switched on the trideo component, set it to the local broadcasts, and began flipping channels. She crossed to the couch, sank into it, and propped her feet up on the coffee table. She decided to enjoy the good life while she could. You never knew how long it would last.

21

Carla sat at a data display in the KKRU newsroom, scanning the stories that the Scan 'n' Sift program had selected. She'd broadened the scope of her search to include anything to do with Renraku Computer Systems. No telling what the cops had stirred up overnight.

She'd come downtown to the station's offices. She could have uploaded the information onto her home deck, but she liked the feel of being in the newsroom, even on a slow Saturday, her day off. She found it difficult to work without the hum of the studio's equipment, the overlapping chatter from the banks of the trideo monitors, and the ebb and flow of reporters' voices in the background. In the quiet of her apartment it was hard to work up the adrenaline needed to chase down a good story.

And this would be a good story; she had no doubt about it. The system errors and data corruptions had spread, and were hitting different parts of the Matrix all the time. The crashes were increasing in frequency. They were no longer limited to systems that could logically be expected to contain files that included the word Lucifer.

The spirit was infiltrating the Matrix with increasing frequency, and seemed to be drawn to it on some sort of preordained schedule. Judging by the timing of protocol problems, configuration discrepancy problems, and system crashes, it was making its presence known once every hour. According to Aziz, the spirit wouldn't like being inside the Matrix. In fact, it shouldn't even be possible for it to enter the Matrix at all. The rigid organization of a computer's light-encoding hardware would confine it, would twist it like a four-dimensional pretzel, then spit it out again. But like a moth to the flame, the spirit kept going back. It was in and out again in a mere nanosecond. But in that nanosecond, it could wreak a lot of damage.

So far only Carla, Masaki, and the young decker Corwin knew what the source of the "virus" really was. But it wouldn't be long before other reporters guessed, too. Carla ached to be first with the story. And to prove that Mitsuhama—the proud purveyor of the latest computer technology—was responsible.

"I said hi, Carla!"

Carla looked up as the voice finally registered as Masaki waving at her from the entrance to the newsroom. He crossed to his work station, still talking. "I didn't expect to see you in here on a Saturday. I thought you had the weekend off."

"I do," she told him. "I just came in here to scan the . . ."

She bent over the display as a Department of Vital Statistics report flashed across it. She read only a few lines before whooping with delight. "Got it!"

"Got what?" Masaki asked. He rummaged through a cardboard box that he'd rooted out from beneath the piles of hard copy and datachips that littered his work station.

"Another piece of the puzzle," Carla answered. "It's Renraku. It looks like they're experimenting with spirits and the Matrix too. And not doing too good a job of it, by the look of things."

Masaki bent over to peer at the monitor. Carla showed him the file the scanner program had tagged and downloaded. It was an obituary for one Gus Deighton, an employee of Renraku Seattle. He'd died suddenly yesterday evening at work. The obit contradicted itself, at one point noting that Deighton had died in a lab fire, but elsewhere attributing his death to "magical causes." It wound up with a tribute from his boss, Dr. Vanessa Cliber, and mentioned that Deighton had been employed for seventeen years in the corporation's Exploratory Sciences Division. He'd been just two months shy of retiring.

"I don't see the connection," Masaki said.

Carla gestured toward the graphic that accompanied the obit. It was a head-and-shoulders still of Augustus Deighton—a distinguished-looking elf with a high forehead, intense eyes, and a full head of hair.

"Exploratory Sciences is Renraku's magical research division," she explained. "And this woman—Dr. Cliber—is the director of computer operations for the whole of Renraku. Conclusion: the runners who broke into my apartment must have sold Renraku the incomplete spell. And now it's cost another mage his life."

Masaki was quicker on the uptake this time. "Does that mean there's another of these spirits loose in the Matrix?"

"I don't know," Carla said. She quickly scanned the rest of the Renraku-keyword files. "Assuming the spirit was conjured within the arcology and that it got away from its handlers, the closest entry point to the Matrix would have been through one of Renraku's system access nodes. But I haven't seen a single report of any Renraku system crashes. Of course, that doesn't mean anything; the corp would hush it up, and fast, if data was getting corrupted or parts of their system were shutting down. The last thing they need is a bunch of deckers storming the infamous black tower through some hole in the system."

Carla stared at the display, thinking out loud. "Aziz said that most spirits that escape from the mage who conjured them return to their place of origin—they vanish back into astral space. Perhaps one in a hundred remain on the physical plane as free spirits. But if we do have another spirit like 'Lucifer' on the loose, the Matrix won't be able to stand up to it. It'll be the Crash of 2029 all over again."

"So what are you going to do about it?" Masaki asked. "Air a sensationalistic story that will make everyone in Seattle afraid to touch their trideo sets and computers in case a spirit jumps out and burns them alive?"

"What do you think I am—some tabcast muckraker?"

Masaki gave an embarrassed shrug.

Carla was astonished that Masaki had such a low opinion of her. Yes, she wanted this to be a big story, one that would shake people up. But at the same time, she wanted it to be hard-hitting and accurate, rather than merely sensationalistic. It was the only way to make NABS sit up and take notice of her—and give her that interview they'd promised.

"I want to do a story that will force Mitsuhama to take responsibility for the mess it's created," she told Masaki. "A story that will warn Renraku off before one of their wage mages makes the same mistake Farazad did. A story that will *prevent* a repeat of the Crash of 2029."

She sat back, arms folded. What she'd just said had sounded good. She almost believed it herself. But deep down, she was willing to admit that the real rush would come from seeing her sign-off at the end of a really big story and knowing that her name would be a household word for days to come. All over the fragging world.

Masaki grunted, and resumed his rummaging through the box he held. "Yeah, well, the story is all yours, Carla. It became your story the night those yakuza shot at us."

"They weren't shooting at us. They were shooting at the kid."

"Just leave my byline out of it, O. K.?"

Carla shook her head. "Anything you say, snoop." She put an ironic emphasis on the last word. "Speaking of the ork girl, did you ever succeed in finding her? Or is she still out scuffing around the streets?"

"I found her," Masaki said. "In Lone Star's downtown containment facility. And it's a good thing I did, too. She was in a tough spot. That story she told you about patrol officers shooting her friends—the one we thought was so far-fetched. I think it's the truth."

"What if it is?" Carla asked. "There's nothing to go on."

"Yes, there is," Masaki countered. "She's got the badge number of one of the chromer cops who did it, plus the name of his partner. The one who pulled the trigger."

"Really?" Despite herself, Carla was intrigued. "This could be a hot one. I can hear the lead-in now: 'The Tarnished Star: Cop by Day, Humanis Policlub Basher by Night.' "

Carla could picture it, too. She still had the footage she'd shot of Pita that day she'd first come to the KKRU station. It would look great on trid. If the Mitsuhama story didn't pan out, Carla could still score a few points by doing the Lone Star piece. She looked at Masaki out of the corner of her eye. "Are you going to pursue the story?"

"I don't know." He paused, and Carla thought she saw a guilty look cross his face. "Maybe."

Drek. She'd have to move on this one as soon as the Mitsuhama piece aired. Otherwise Masaki would scoop it out from under her.

"So where's the kid now?" she asked. "Still in jail?"

"She's at my place. I just came down to the studio to grab the things she left here."

"Aziz is awfully keen to talk to her about . . ." Carla's eyes widened as she saw what Masaki had fished out of the box. A credstick. And embossed on the side of it, in gold, was a logo. A Mitsuhama Computer Technologies logo.

Carla snatched the credstick out of Masaki's hands. "Where did you get this?" she asked, her voice rising with excitement.

Masaki shrugged. "It's Pita's. While we were shooting her eyewitness take, she kept playing with the stuff in her pockets, making a rattling noise that her body mike picked up. I made her empty her pockets. The credstick was in them. Why? Is it stolen or something?"

Carla showed Masaki the logo, then turned the credstick so that he could see the magnetic keystrip down one side. "This is fragging unbelievable! This has been sitting here in our newsroom all this time, and you didn't notice. There's only one place the kid could have picked this credstick up—from Farazad's body. And there's only one door it could open. The Samji residence didn't have a magkey system—just a thumb-print scanner. And you don't put a corporate logo on a car key. So what's left?"

Masaki had followed her train of thought. "The place where Farazad worked. The Mitsuhama Research Center."

"Right." Carla jiggled the credstick in her hand. "Care to join me in shooting a little unauthorized trid at the Mitsuhama lab?" she asked teasingly. She knew Masaki wouldn't have the spine for it, but she couldn't resist. Just as she had expected, his face went pale.

"Are you crazy?" His wheeze was back. "Not only is that illegal—it's dangerous. Mitsuhama's security guards are rumored to be the toughest in the business, and their magical defenses are layers deep. You'll be killed!"

Carla tucked the credstick neatly into the pocket of her jacket. "Not if I have a good decker and a spirit backing me up," she answered with a smug smile.

"I think you're crazy," Masaki said.

"You're probably right," Carla answered. "But if you want to get ahead in this business, you have to be willing to take some chances."

22

Pita stared out the window of Masaki's apartment, watching the gray clouds that were scudding low over the city. It was still early in the afternoon, but already the sky was quite dark. The first few drops of rain left thin streaks on the heavy plate glass window.

After a moment of silent contemplation, she turned back to Aziz. The mage was sitting on the couch across from her, trying to look casual. But Pita had enough street smarts to read the tension and anticipation in his slightly parted lips and twitching fingers. What she had to say was vitally important to him. The only thing she couldn't figure out was why.

"How come you think it was me who banished the spirit?" Pita asked. "All I did was disturb your spell-casting when I tried to cross your magical circle."

Aziz looked annoyed. "I've already explained that to you once," he said tersely. "Your striking the hermetic circle was only part of it. It had to be that the spirit was affected by something you did or said."

He leaned forward, pointing a finger at her. "Think, now. Did you say any words that might have sounded like a name? Did you make any gestures or think any thoughts that—"

"I've already told you everything I can think of," Pita said. "I thought the spirit was going to kill you. I wanted to help. Cat led me to you. Maybe it—"

"That's old ground," Aziz said. "Your totem led you to me, nothing more. You said it had already fled the shop, which means it had nothing to do with driving the spirit away. It was of no consequence."

"Why didn't you go back and get your cat after the

shop burned down?" Pita asked coldly. "Wasn't it of any consequence to you, either?" Part of her anger was fueled by guilt. She hadn't seen Aziz's cat since last night—since just before she went downtown to join the sit-in. She hoped it was doing all right. That it hadn't been run over by a car or anything.

Aziz ignored her question. "If you could just tell me what you—"

"Listen," she said, cutting him off. "You're the mage. You've done this stuff for years. I'm just a kid who Cat helps out from time to time. I only let you into Masaki's apartment because I figured you wanted to thank me for saving your life. If I wanted to be cross-examined, I'd go back to fragging . . ." She swallowed, unable to complete the sentence, even though she'd begun it in jest. Not enough time had elapsed since her narrow escape from the jail and the cop who'd killed her friends.

"I am grateful that you saved my life," Aziz said tightly. "I already thanked you for that. And you're wrong about your magical abilities. You have a powerful talent—more powerful than you realize. I wish I . . ."

He made a dismissive gesture with one blistered hand. He didn't have to say the rest; Pita could see the envy in his eyes. And that made her pause. Maybe— just maybe—she really did have a unique and powerful talent. If she really had driven away the spirit— something Aziz himself, with all of his knowledge of the magical arts, hadn't been able to do—she had an edge. Something that made her special—something she could use to survive. Something that made her a better magician, in terms of her natural abilities, than the hermetic mage sitting across from her.

"Just humor me a little longer," Aziz said. "It's important."

"You promise you'll put me in touch with that shaman you told me about?" Pita asked. "The one who will teach me to use my power?"

"I already agreed to that."

"How am I going to get by in the meantime? I don't have a single nuyen."

Grimacing with frustration, Aziz plunged a hand into the breast pocket of his robe. He pulled out a credstick, rose to his feet, and stalked over to the telecom unit. "Do you have a bank account?" he asked.

Pita just laughed. "Who, me? You must be frizzed."

Aziz plugged the credstick into the slot. "What's your name?" he asked. "Not your street name—your real name."

She told him.

"Date of birth?"

"July 19, 2037."

Aziz keyed in a series of commands, muttering as he did. "Hmm. We'll use Masaki's apartment as your current address, and I'll say you're employed at my shop. That should do it . . ." He called her over and had her stand in front of the pickup camera, then told her to sit down again. After a moment or two, the printer scrolled out hard copy. He tore it from the unit and handed it to Pita with a flourish.

"What's this?" she asked.

"A statement from your bank account. Take a look."

Pita's mouth dropped open. If this was true, Aziz had just opened an account at the Salish Credit Union and deposited one thousand nuyen in it. In her name. When she looked up, he was smiling.

"Let's call that a deposit. There's more where that came from, as long as you promise to work with me. All right?"

Pita nodded mutely. This really was worth a lot to him. She wondered what his angle was—how he planned to capitalize on it. And whether the transaction was legitimate or just a drekking good con.

"O.K.," she said at last. "Ask me anything. What do you want to know?"

Aziz cleared a space in the living room, then cast a quick spell with a flick of his hand. A glowing green circle appeared on the carpet. Pita blinked, hoping Masaki wouldn't get slotted off at the mark Aziz had just made. But the carpet hadn't looked all that clean to begin with.

"Let's pretend that this is the hermetic circle I was

using when I was trying to find out if there really was a metaplane of light," he said, lying down on his back at the center of it and stretching out his arms and legs. "I'm here, in the middle of it. I want you to approach me at the same angle that you did, yesterday morning, when you were in astral space."

Pita did as she was told, positioning herself in a line with Aziz's right foot.

"Now run forward, the way you did before. Hold your body exactly as you did then, and try to make the same gestures."

Pita looked up at the ceiling, imagining the brilliant tornado of the spirit where the dusty light fixture hung. Then she held up her arm, as if shielding her eyes from it. "Aziz!" she shouted, feeling somewhat foolish. She ran forward and hopped over the green circle. She wondered whether or not she should mime falling over backward, but Aziz halted her before she could make up her mind.

"Stop right there!" He clambered to his feet and grabbed her right arm. He turned it over to inspect the underside of it.

"What's this mark?" he asked. "It looks like a burn. Did the spirit touch you?"

Pita turned her arm to look at the red line that was painted like a slash across the inside of her wrist. The mark had faded, but the burn itched where the hair was starting to grow back. "Oh, that," she said. "Yeah, it touched me. But not yesterday. This happened days ago."

Aziz's long, narrow fingers pinched tight around her forearm. "When?"

"The night the guy died in the alley. I was, uh . . . looking at him, and one of the beams of light coming out of his mouth touched my arm."

"Hmm." Aziz stared off into space, his eyebrows knitted together in a tense frown. For a moment, Pita was worried that he'd figured out she'd boosted stuff from the pockets of the dying mage, and that he'd call the cops on her. But his mind was apparently on other matters entirely.

"That was the night the spirit attacked Farazad," he

said, thinking out loud. "The night the spirit became free. Hmm . . ."

"Are you going to let go of my arm?"

"What?" Aziz glanced down. "Oh. Sorry."

Pita rubbed the spot his fingers had pinched. Then she looked again at the burn mark on her wrist. "You think this has something to do with it?"

"I do, indeed."

"You going to tell me, or what?"

Aziz gave her a coy look, as if deciding whether or not she could keep a secret. "Sure," he said. "Why not? I'm going to need your cooperation with this, anyway. There's no way around it."

He took a deep breath and began to lecture, sounding just like a high school teaching program: "When a spirit breaks the control of the mage who conjured it and escapes, it sometimes remains in the physical world rather than returning to astral space. The moment of its escape is the moment of its birth as a free spirit. It's also the moment the spirit attains its true name.

"A free spirit can be controlled by any magician—of either magical tradition—who knows this true name. The mage can use the true name to call, control, banish—or even destroy the free spirit. Or merely drive it away, as you did yesterday morning. The trouble is, finding out a free spirit's true name is usually an impossible task.

Pita frowned, completely lost. "I still don't see what all this has to do with the mark on my arm."

"I'm coming to that," Aziz answered. He ran a hand over his hair, smoothing it back. "According to hermetic theory, the true name is imposed upon the free spirit by the astral conditions in existence at the time and place of its birth. It's just possible that the spirit you saw was intoxicated by its newfound freedom and shouted its true name out loud as soon as it learned it."

"But I didn't hear anything. Not any 'true name,' anyhow."

Aziz took her arm—more gently, this time—and touched a forefinger to the burn. "Yes, you did," he said softly. "The spirit spoke in the only way it could—in pulses of photons. It inscribed the true name, there, in the cells of your skin."

Pita looked at her arm, uncertain whether to believe him or not. It sounded incredible—a magical spirit writing its name on her arm with a ray of light. But at the same time, it made sense. Somehow she had driven the spirit away. There'd been no one else in the room at the time except the helpless Aziz; Pita had to have been the one with the edge. The more she thought about it, the more her skin tingled. It was like suddenly waking up to find that someone had implanted a cybernetic device in your arm while you slept. Her wrist felt as if it were no longer entirely her own.

"I thought you said the magician had to understand the name," she said at last. "Well, I didn't understand it. I didn't even know about it."

"But it was there, just the same, when you entered astral space. You carried the name with you. And you used it—albeit without conscious volition—as a tool to drive the spirit away."

Pita thought about that a moment. "So, according to what you said, I can control this thing now? Can I make it do anything I want?" Visions of revenge danced in her head. She'd show that Lone Star fragger. She imagined the cop twitching on the ground, like a puppet with its strings cut while the spirit burned out his insides. It was a gruesome but satisfying image. One that brought a grim smile to her lips, exposing her curving canine teeth.

Aziz hurriedly dropped her hand. "Ah . . . yes. You do have the *potential* to control the spirit. But not without proper magical training. Control over a free spirit isn't automatic. Once you've learned the spirit's true name, you still have to best it in a test of wills. A battle that pits you against the magical force of the spirit." He gave her a grave, serious look. "And make no mistake, this is a powerful spirit. It's not one to be toyed with.

"Promise me, Pita, that you won't do anything rash.

That you won't try calling it or controlling it without my help."

Pita saw through him at once. The mage wanted to be part of this. He wanted to control the spirit himself, but he was going to need her to do it. He probably had his own revenge in mind—the yakuza who burned down his shop was a prime candidate.

Well, Pita would show him. If she was the one who could control the spirit, she'd be the one calling the shots. But not yet; she didn't fully trust her newly awakened magical talents. She sure as drek didn't want to wind up like the mage in the alley. Dominating a human mind was one thing. Dominating a magical creature of light was something else entirely. For the time being, it looked as though she was stuck with Aziz's "help."

"O.K.," she said. "Deal. As long as you don't make me call the spirit until I'm ready."

Aziz gave her a thin smile. "Deal."

23

Carla stepped out of the tour bus and looked up at the six skyscrapers that made up the Mitsuhama Computer Technologies complex. Setting the camera in her cybereye to wide angle, she began with a shot that included all six buildings. She would have liked to have filmed them earlier in the day—better lighting would have shown off the silver sheen on the plascrete walls and the gleaming black-tinted windows. But the skyscrapers were an impressive sight, even so. They would make a nice establishing shot to intro her story.

She zoomed in slowly on the public entrance to the central tower, gradually losing the manicured lawns and backdrop of Lake Washington, and focusing on the entrance to the Byte of the Future display. On either side of the automatic doorway, neatly groomed security guards watched the people flow in and out. In their peaked cloth caps and trim blue uniforms with the gold MCT logo on the breast pocket, the guards looked like bellhops at a glitzy hotel. They weren't carrying any weapons or sporting any obvious cyberware, but it was a given that they were in constant touch with the rest of their team via commlink. They could call for heavy-duty backup in an instant if the situation warranted it.

One of the guards smiled and nodded at the tourists, occasionally kneeling down to talk to a child. But his eyes constantly scanned the crowd, even when he was talking to someone right in front of him. He might appear to be relaxed, but Carla could see that he was alert and ready for trouble.

The second guard scrutinized the crowd with steely eyes, not even pretending to be friendly.

Carla let the camera in her cybereye continue to record as she followed the other tourists up the winding path that led from the bus loop to the complex itself. That way, she'd be able to prove to Greer, her producer, that she'd actually penetrated Mitsuhama's research lab. Assuming, that is, that she made it that far.

Instead of walking with her usual smooth reporter's stride—which would only give her away—Carla meandered along behind the others, gawking like a tourist. The resulting footage would be jumpy, but as long as she maintained continuity, Greer would be satisfied.

There were fifty-six people in the tour group Carla had joined, including herself. This was the second-to-last tour of the day—the 5 p.m. excursion.

As she approached the entrance, she resisted the urge to reach into her pocket, yet again, to double-check that the datachip Corwin had prepared was still there. The security guards would spot the nervous gesture instantly. They wouldn't know what it meant, and they probably wouldn't find it threatening. But their attention would be drawn to Carla just the same. And she wanted to remain as anonymous as possible. She'd disguised herself, just in case anybody recognized her from the KKRU newscasts. She'd styled her hair differently and tied a scarf over it. The heavy-framed fashion glasses she wore gave her eyes an entirely different look.

A few steps ahead of Carla, Corwin's girlfriend Nina and little brother Trevor ambled along with the other tourists. Trevor was just eight years old, but every bit as bright as his brother. And the girl, despite the fact that she was still in her early twenties, looked old enough for her role, especially in the clothes Carla had asked her to wear. Both had readily agreed to help out with this bit of subterfuge. The thought of doing something daring, just like his brother, had especially appealed to Trevor. His part would be a small one, entirely without risk. Carla just hoped that the kid had the brains and nerve to carry it off. He certainly had the acting ability; he'd appeared in ten commercials already as the token metahuman kid. He had a fetching smile, despite his oversize canines.

Trevor was pretending he didn't know Carla. As instructed, he walked beside Nina, making a point of smiling and talking to her. The other tourists would automatically assume she was his mother.

Carla followed the others into the building. They bunched up at a second set of heavy glass doors that blocked access to the lobby proper. This inner entrance was manned by two more security guards. One stood on this side of the doors, directing the visitors to an automated flatscan camera that took each person's picture, then spat out a laminated badge bearing the words VISITOR'S PASS and the date and time of the tour group's arrival. The other guard stood on the far side of the glass door, looking on with a bored expression as visitors who were leaving the building dropped their passes into a machine that automatically scanned and counted them. Eventually it would strip the digital photographs and dates from the badges so that they could be reused.

When it was her turn, Carla smiled for the camera, then attached the pass it spat out to the lapel of her jacket by its metal clip. She followed the others through the inner doors and into the lobby itself.

The lobby had a floor of silvered metal that was etched with black in a pattern that resembled the circuitry of an old-fashioned silicon chip. Banks of escalators at the back of the lobby led up to the second and third floors, which housed the Byte of the Future displays. Each had a balcony from which visitors could look down at the patterned lobby floor.

The other floors of the skyscraper—and the offices they contained—were accessed by entrances elsewhere in the building, rather than from this lobby. Mitsuhama encouraged the general public to view its displays, but took a dim view of them wandering through its office space.

As she stepped onto the escalator, Carla could hear Trevor, behind her now, talking excitedly to Nina about the new SimSea exhibit. She allowed herself a small sigh of relief. The kid was playing his part to the hilt, making sure everyone noticed that he and Nina were together, and frequently calling her "Mom."

Carla had been on this tour two years ago when doing an entertainment feature on a new series of games Mitsuhama had developed. It had been a fun piece; she'd strapped on the headset and was instantly transported into the cockpit of a fighter ship that was rocketing its way between the stars. They'd even gotten the feeling of zero-G right.

On that occasion, Carla had been an invited guest. This time, she would be a trespasser—no better than a shadowrunner. And Mitsuhama would be doing its best to evict her—by any means necessary.

The Byte of the Future display was tucked into a series of rooms that opened onto the second- and third-floor balconies. Dozens of adults and children moved back and forth from one display room to another, filling the air with their awed laughter. Behind the babble of voices, games beeped and chimed, automated announcements described the static displays, and robotic vehicles whirred and hummed.

The three Mitsuhama employees who'd been assigned to guide the 5 p.m. tour were waiting on the second floor. They did not wear formal uniforms, but all were garbed in corporate colors: blue slacks and a white shirt. Carla wore the same thing under her jacket.

Out of the three guides who would be leading the five o'clock tour, two were Asian. Mitsuhama might talk about being an equal-opportunity employer, but when you scanned the employee records—as Corwin had done earlier—the truth became clear. The corp showed a clear preference for hiring humans of Japanese descent.

As they split the tourists into three groups, Carla joined the group that would be led by a woman who was of approximately the same build as herself. Thanks to the cosmetic surgery that had given Carla's face a Native American appearance, she could pass for Japanese—or, at least, for a Eurasian of Japanese descent.

She'd be a close enough match for the picture on the woman's employee ID badge.

Carla kept to the back of the group as the hour-long tour began. The first stop was an exhibit of oversized, boxy computers from the late twentieth century. All of the machines were in working order, and each had an adaptor that allowed it to access the Matrix in a clunky, glacially slow fashion. The exhibit showed the gradual advances in the computer industry, and concluded with an exhibit of the latest direct neural interface technology—all of it, naturally, designed and built by Mitsuhama.

Pretending to examine one of these state-of-the-art computers, Carla fished the datachip out of her pocket and slotted it into one of the multi-ports at the back of the deck. The program on it had been hurriedly designed, that very afternoon, by Corwin. Precisely one hour after it was installed, it would write itself onto the virtual memory of this computer. It would then execute in the background, uploading itself to the display hall's central processing unit while it was running its batch maintenance programs. The system's operator might notice a slight stutter in the computer, but would probably pass it off as a hardware sequencing problem.

From there, the program would find its way onto the slave nodes that served the Byte of the Future display and would drop, without a trace, the name Lucifer. It would then be only a matter of time—hopefully no more than a few minutes, but certainly no more than an hour—before the spirit dove into the Matrix again and was drawn like an angry hornet to those nodes, corrupting the programs as it sought to eliminate the files containing its name. When that happened, the system that ran the display area would crash. Every computer-controlled display, lighting panel, and climate-control device in the Byte of the Future exhibit would shut down. And that would provide just the distraction Carla needed.

After exiting the display of antique computers, the group wound its way through a variety of exhibits:

autonomously guided vehicles currently being used in the Mars exploration program; war simulators used to train monotank drivers; simsense walk-throughs of CAD/CAM do-it-yourself architectural programs; animated-cartoon holograms that described the development of ASIST (emphasizing the minor role Mitsuhama had played in its development); and a gigantic, two-story-tall mockup of an optical data-storage and retrieval system. The kids loved that one; they got to slide through strobing tubes, pretending they were individual photons of light. By either bunching together or going singly, they could duplicate the pulses by which data was encoded and could trigger different sounds and holo images. Each group of children erased the data of the group who'd preceded them, writing their own combination.

Carla smiled. It was a bit prophetic, somehow.

The final stop on the tour was a large room that held a wide array of booths that displayed Mitsuhama's latest simsense games. Here, the members of the tour group were first warned that they had to meet back at the bus at six o'clock, sharp, then were turned loose to spend the last fifteen minutes of their tour playing with the interactive displays.

It was time for Carla to make her move. Winding her way through the people who crowded the room, she nodded at Nina and stepped into one of the simsense booths. It was a multi-user display; there were enough headsets for six people to interact with the program at once. Fortunately, no one else joined them in the booth.

Carla handed Nina her badge. "You remember what to do, don't you?"

The ork girl smiled. "Null perspiration, chummer. I just gotta drop it in the box."

Carla winced. Like her boyfriend, Nina had the habit of using street slang, despite her education. She took Nina's badge and slipped it into her pocket. "Good," she said. "Off you go, then."

As Nina stepped out of the booth, Carla focused on the digital display in the corner of her cybereye's field of view. It was nearly six o'clock. Time for her tour group to make its way back to the bus. And for Corwin's program to start doing its thing.

Trevor was watching her from a few meters away. As she passed him, Carla gave him the thumbs-up signal they'd previously agreed upon, then slipped him Nina's visitor pass. He smiled and winked at her, then waited while Nina headed for the escalators.

Carla took a deep breath to steady her nerves. This part was out of her hands.

She made her way to the balcony that looked down onto the lobby. She tensed as Nina approached the desk where they had come in. But the guard didn't even look at Nina as she dropped Carla's badge in the return slot, where a scanner automatically processed it. So far, so good.

Carla let a full minute pass after Nina had exited the building, then signaled to Trevor. He descended on the escalator, then rushed up to the guard who stood just inside the lobby. Carla couldn't hear what he was saying, but she knew the script; she'd written it. He was tearfully asking the bored-looking guard who manned the scanner if he'd seen his mother, whom he had lost at the end of the tour. As proof, Trevor showed the badge his mother had "dropped" during her ride down the photon slide.

The guard would probably remember that an ork woman had just left the building, and might even match that woman's face with the one on the badge. But because several other visitors had passed through the gate in the interim, he was unlikely to remember whether or not she had turned in a visitor's pass on the way out.

Trevor's act seemed to be working. The security guard pointed outside, took the two badges from him, and dropped them in the scanner. Trevor gave him a tearful smile, then jogged out the building after his "mother." As instructed, he didn't look back at Carla and give the game away. Later, when security did a count of the returned badges, they would assume that all fifty-six members of the 5 p.m. tour had exited the building.

Now Carla just had to wait for her distraction to hit. When it did, the building's security would get much tighter; the guards would immediately ensure that all visitors safely exited the Byte of the Future display. They'd be sure to retrieve a visitor pass from each person as he or she left the area, and to compare the number of passes collected with the number of visitors who entered the building that day. Assuming that none of the visitors actually did go missing when the spirit crashed the exhibit's computers, all of today's visitors would be carefully accounted for—probably within a matter of a few minutes. And by the time they were, Carla would be well on her way to the research lab.

She looked around for her tour group leader. The woman had gone back to the escalator to meet the six o'clock tour. As she assembled the group and gave them her memorized introduction, Carla followed discreetly behind, careful not to let the woman spot her. There was always a chance she'd recognize Carla as a member of the last group and would start wondering why this "tourist" had missed her bus. Or that she would notice Carla wasn't wearing a visitor's pass.

The six o'clock tour made it all the way to the photon slide before the spirit struck. The first sign that it had entered the Byte of the Future computer system was when the music and holograms in the transparent tube faltered to a halt. Next, the overhead lights began to flicker. In rapid succession, a number of displays blinked out. The ventilation system blasted out a jet of overheated air, then made a grinding noise as its rotors shut down, and the speakers began to hiss with static.

No more than a second or two after the whole chain of glitches began, the second- and third-floor display areas were plunged into darkness. As a babble of frightened voices filled the air, Carla made her move. She'd kept a careful watch on the tour guide, who now was shouting at her group to remain calm. Carla headed straight for the voice and deliberately jostled the woman in the dark. At the same time, she snatched the tour guide's employee badge. Given the mob of confused and frightened people the woman had to deal with, Carla doubted she'd miss the badge for some time. If she did discover it was gone, she would probably assume it had fallen off and was lying somewhere on the floor of the display area.

Carla shed her jacket and pinned on the employee badge. Then she made her way by feel to the photon tube-slide. It would be the fastest way to put some distance between herself and the tour guide. Just as she reached it, a handful of emergency lights—those powered by battery and thus independent of the main computer system—started to flicker to life. But these only dimly lit the area; there were still enough shadows—and enough confusion, among the milling visitors—for Carla to jump into the tube and escape unnoticed.

The slide down to the second floor took only a moment or two. Reaching the bottom, she clambered to her feet and headed toward an employees-only exit she'd noted earlier. A winking red light showed that the door's magkey was still functioning. It was a simple slide-through pad, operated by its own battery system. Carla aligned the magnetic strip on the employee badge, then slid it through the slot. When the light flashed green, she yanked the door open.

The corridor it led to was well illuminated; it must have been on a separate control system. Carla pulled the door shut behind her and hurried down the hallway. A security guard rushed toward her, heading for the door she'd just come through. Giving him her most earnest look, Carla jerked a thumb at the door behind her. "We've had a systems crash!" she shouted. "The power is down and we can't use the telecom system. I'm going to see if I can reboot the lights."

The guard grunted out a reply as he rushed past. "It fragging figures. Whenever there's a system glitch, it's on my shift." He obviously didn't yet realize the extent of the "glitch."

Carla slowed to a brisk walk as she rounded a corner. Unwilling to risk the elevator, in case the spirit had wiped its programming as well, she entered the first stairwell she found. She climbed eight flights, paused to catch her breath, then emerged onto the tenth floor, which housed a number of office units. Now it was just a matter of working her way to the building's outermost corridor and finding the skywalk that connected it to the next tower.

Aside from the few security guards who rushed past her, few of the employees on this floor seemed to realize the chaos that had broken out several stories below them. The corridors were filled with the usual hum of conversation and background office noise.

After a few minutes of searching, Carla found the skywalk that led to Tower C—the "Chrysanthemum Tower." This was the heart of the beast; unlike the other five skyscrapers, which rented space to a variety of different businesses, Tower C was occupied solely by Mitsuhama Computer Technologies. For this reason, it was under much tighter security than the rest of the office complex. Not only was there a gate and a monitor system at the point where the skywalk joined the tower, but a live guard as well.

The guard was a young fellow with sharp features and cratered skin. Japanese, judging by his surname. An oversized pistol hung in a holster at his hip. Carla had been prepared for that; she'd expected to have to bluff her way past an armed guard or two. But when she saw the retinal scanner that was built into the badge-recognition unit, her heart sank. There was no way she'd get past that.

In another moment, the guard would realize that she wasn't the woman whose name and scan code were on the badge. He'd demand to see some authentic ID, and would call his superiors to deal with the attempted intrusion. Things would be tense for a moment or two, but eventually, once somebody saw her press pass, they'd be forced to let her go. She was simply too well known, too public a figure, to rough up. The mythical "power of the press" would protect her. But it was still fragging disappointing to have come this far, only to have her plans fall apart.

Then Carla noted the way the guard was pacing back and forth in front of the gate. His manner suggested intense frustration. He reminded Carla of the security guard she'd encountered earlier in the hallway, and that guard's grumbled comments. And that gave her an idea.

The young guard waved her toward the gate. When he read her employee badge he showed immediate interest. "I hear there's some trouble in the display hall," he said eagerly. It was obvious he wished he could be seeing a little of that trouble himself.

She kept her eyes on the ground, trying to work up some tears. As she slid the employee badge through the scanner, she dug a manicured fingernail into her other palm, deliberately cutting the skin. That did it. Tears welled in her eyes.

"Hai," she said, giving the head bob that was the equivalent of an abbreviated bow. She'd decided to play the role of the demure, eyes-downcast Japanese woman to the hilt. She could do the accent perfectly, but she was taking a gamble, hoping he wouldn't switch to Japanese. With luck, he'd be a nishi or sanshi, with only a poor grasp of the language. She'd only remembered enough of her high-school Japanese to order sushi, recite her name, and count to ten.

"Two members of my tour group were seriously injured," she told the guard. "I have been called to give a personal report." She sighed heavily, and let a tear trickle down her cheek. "Everything always happens on my shift."

The guard nodded his sympathy and lifted the ret-scan unit from its cradle. Carla buried her face in her hands, pretending to be ashamed of her tears, and uttered a series of short, hiccuping sobs. "I never asked to be reassigned to the display hall. I should be in Accounting. That's what I'm trained for. And now I'll be fired!" She kept wiping tears from her eyes, deliberately getting her hands in he way of the scanner.

After one or two attempts to lift the ret-scan unit to Carla's eyes, the young guard gave up. "Go," he said to her at last. "Make your report. And good luck."

"Thank you."

Carla waited until she was around the corner to break into a wide grin. She was inside! She focused on the icon in her cybereye's field of view that would

activate the file containing the map Corwin had downloaded on his most recent run into the Mitsuhama
mainframe. The datalink to her cybereye let her read
information uploaded to it. Now all she had to do was
follow the map to the elevator that led down to the
research lab. And hope that everything was going
according to plan. Everything could still come unglued
if she ran into any more security roadblocks. Or if
Corwin ran into any ice. Or if the guard who'd just let
her slip through his post without a retinal scan learned
that an employee from the Byte of the Future exhibit
had lost her badge. Or if . . .

Carla shook her head, chiding herself for letting her
worries overtake her. The only thing now was to get as
far as she could. And to keep the camera in her
cybereye rolling. The chip she was using had plenty of
memory, but if need be she had plenty more to spare.

24

Carla walked down the hallway, trying not to stare at the security cameras. The thirtieth floor of the Chrysanthemum Tower was an area of plush carpets, dark wooden doors that looked as if they were made of ebony, and expensive bio-luminescent lighting panels. This was the floor occupied by MCT Seattle's middle management; gleaming chrome name plates, set in the middle of the polished black doors, bore the names of several of the people who'd been saying "no comment" to Carla recently. She resisted the urge to try any of the doors. The offices were sure to be well protected by sophisticated alarms and magic-activated intruder alert systems.

Since it was Saturday, only a few of the offices were occupied. The occasional office worker passed her in the hallway, but the normal hustle and buzz of a busy office complex was missing. Although Mitsuhama followed the Japanese tradition of expecting its employees to work copious amounts of overtime, few actually came in to work on a weekend in person; most put in the extra hours at home-based work stations.

According to the map in Carla's cybereye, the elevator that led to the research lab was just ahead, around a bend in the corridor. She stopped midway down the hall and pushed open the door to a washroom. As she'd suspected, the room was not monitored by camera—at least, no obvious monitors were in evidence. It was probably wired for sound, however, so she went through the motions of flushing the toilet and washing her hands in the sink.

Carla pulled out her cel phone, switched off its

visual pickup, and dialed a number. She heard a ring, a brief pause, and then another ring again as the call was routed through a series of telecommunications grids. If Mitsuhama security was monitoring this call by picking up its frequency from a remote scanner, they'd log it as being made from a rented cel phone to an auto body shop in Renton. In fact, the call was only being patched through that number—and from there, through telecommunications grids in Vancouver, Hong Kong, Seoul, and San Francisco—and back again to a Seattle residence, where the young decker Corwin answered the phone.

"Albert's Auto Body," he said. "Don't get bent; we'll fix that dent."

Despite her nervousness, Carla smiled. She used the rough code they'd prearranged. "Hello. I'm calling about the car I dropped off this morning. The Mitsubishi Runabout with the dented side panel. Has it been fixed yet?"

"It's fixed," Corwin answered. "And the paint job is perfect. You can't even see where we made the patch."

"That's wonderful," Carla answered brightly. "I won't be able to pick it up tonight; I've got a backlog of work to clear up. I have to be back at work in less than a minute. I'll stop around tomorrow morning, instead."

"Good luck clearing up that backlog. I hope you don't have to work too late. See you in the morning."

As she hung up the phone, Carla nodded. So far, so good. Corwin was inside Mitsuhama's computer system and had successfully cracked the node that controlled the security cameras on this floor. The "paint job" he was referring to was a direct feed of a digitized image of Evelyn Belanger. Using the trid that Carla had shot of the wage mage yesterday, he'd stripped away the background of the garden and used only the cropped image of Evelyn walking. Feeding this back into the security cameras, he used KKRU's sophisticated Movement Match graphics program to paint it over the image of Carla that the hallway monitors were picking up. If anything had gone wrong with the splice, he would have warned Carla just now. But everything was going perfectly. Anyone watching the security monitors would be unable to see the patch.

For her part, Carla had warned Corwin that she was less than a minute away from reaching the elevator that led to the research lab. Folding shut her cel phone, she tucked it in a pocket. Then she took a deep breath, braced herself, and stepped out into the corridor. She turned and headed for the elevator, keeping her hands by her sides, walking smoothly and not making any sudden or exaggerated gestures that the graphics program would have to compensate for.

Reaching the elevator, Carla stood so that the monitor cameras would be able to capture a clear shot of her as she pulled Farazad's credstick from her pocket and plugged the triangular tube of plastic into the key slot that called the elevator. It was essential that Corwin get a good look at her, that this be timed perfectly.

As the credstick clicked into place, a pleasantly modulated voice came from a speaker mounted just to the left of the elevator doors: "This elevator is for the use of authorized personnel only. Please provide a voice sample." It then repeated the instructions in Japanese.

This was the tricky part. Farazad's security clearance would have been purged, immediately following his death. But Evelyn Belanger's would still be on-line. And if Corwin was as whiz a decker as he claimed, he'd be able to squirt in a digital sample of Evelyn's voice, pair it with the lock combination encoded on the credstick, and effect a match.

Carla waited, tension knotting the muscles between her shoulder blades as the seconds ticked by. If anything had gone wrong at Corwin's end, an alarm would be sounding, somewhere deep in the bowels of the building. Mitsuhama security guards would be racing through the hallways, even now, with their guns drawn. . .

A soft chime sounded and a light above the elevator doors winked on. "Voice sample accepted," the automated system told her. "Please remove your keystrip. *Arigato.*"

Carla let out a long sigh of relief as the elevator doors opened. She hadn't heard it arrive—either it was very silent or it had already been waiting on this floor. She hoped for the latter—if the elevator had been on the floor that housed the research lab, that would have meant that someone had gotten off it there and not returned—there was only one exit from the research lab, as far as Carla had been able to determine.

She stepped into the elevator, turning slowly so the Movement Match program could patch in a clear, non-jerky image of Evelyn for the benefit of the monitor inside the elevator. The security camera was mounted just above the door, beside the digital display that gave a readout of the floor the elevator had stopped at. There were only two floors listed: the thirtieth—and "L" for Lab. There were no icons to press to select a floor.

The doors slid shut and the elevator automatically began its descent to the research facility, which was located deep underground, in the foundations of the building. Carla knew enough about magic to understand why this odd location had been chosen— the natural earth that surrounded and enclosed the research lab protected it from unwanted astral intruders. There were probably magical sensors in the elevator shaft, as well.

The elevator descended quickly, producing a fluttering lurch in Carla's stomach. She'd loved riding in high-speed elevators as a kid, and still enjoyed the partial sensation of free-fall that they produced. Now that feeling was overlaid with another, stronger emotion— excitement. She was in! She had penetrated Mitsuhama security—with Corwin's help, of course—and was about to shoot some trid of the very lab that had given birth to the spirit that was ravaging the Matrix. She was doing what few shadowrunners would have dared— penetrating a secret research lab. And enjoying every moment of it, despite the danger.

The elevator glided to a stop. Carla braced herself, prepared to be confronted by a room full of researchers who would demand to know what the frag she was doing in their lab. She set her eye camera for autofocus and got ready to brazen it out as best she could. She'd keep the camera running, identify herself as a reporter, then fire off questions in as authoritative a tone as she could manage and hope for some good reaction shots.

But when the doors slid open, they revealed a darkened lab. The only illumination came from above and behind Carla, in the ceiling of the elevator itself. It painted Carla's shadow in a dark puddle, just inside the large room, and only partially illuminated the large, open space that lay beyond it. Stale-smelling air wafted in through the elevator doors; it was clear that the lab's climate-control systems weren't working. They'd probably shut down yesterday morning when the spirit wiped the lab's data files and scrambled the computer's programming.

An icon of a double-headed arrow appeared on the wall of the elevator, next to the door. Next to it were the words: HOLD DOOR and a Japanese character that probably meant the same thing. Carla hit it, then stepped out of the comforting light of the elevator and into the shadow-filled room. As she'd hoped, the elevator doors remained open behind her. They probably wouldn't close again until the elevator was summoned from upstairs. If they did, Carla would know that trouble was on its way.

She activated the low-light compensator in her cybereye. Able to distinguish shape from shadow now, she did a slow pan of the dimly illuminated room. She didn't bother with a voice-over; she'd splice that in later. The room was utterly silent; all she could hear was the sound of her own breathing. Even the background hiss of air conditioning was missing.

She was on her own now. With the computer systems in this area disabled, Corwin wouldn't be able to monitor her. Instead of hanging around in the Matrix while she searched the place, risking an attack by ice with each second that ticked by, he would, at this very moment, be making the last few "adjustments" to the computer system that operated the building's security cameras. Then he'd jack out.

The area held a number of work stations, separated from one another by chest-high sound baffles. Each station contained a chair, data terminal, and various personal effects—soykaf mugs, desktop holographs of family members, brightly colored plastic knickknacks, flatprint photos attached with sticky gum to the sound baffles, and various hermetic fetishes, including an ornate gold amulet and chunk of raw crystal. Carla walked around the room with a smooth, practiced gait, pausing to zoom in now and again on a particular work station. Beside one of the data terminals was a blown-glass vase filled with fresh flowers whose delicate scent filled the air. Carla guessed that this must be Evelyn Belanger's work station. At another station, personal effects were neatly piled in a large plastic container. On top lay a holograph of Mrs. Samji. This must have been Farazad's.

Carla took a moment to riffle through it, but found nothing of interest. The plastic container held only a soykaf mug, family holos, and other personal effects. She opened the drawers of the work station, checking them one by one. A light stylus rattled around in one drawer, and a few magnetic clips and a tiny triangle of torn hardcopy were stuck to the back of another. But otherwise they were empty.

The research lab's data terminals and computers were state-of-the-art—Mitsuhama models, naturally. And all had been partially disassembled. Data chips had been yanked out, drives had been exposed, and diagnostic tools were scattered around. Some frantic salvage work had been done here after the lab's computer system had crashed. Carla wondered if they'd been able to save any files.

Some technician had jury-rigged an independent lighting system for the lab—cables snaked from a compact fuel cell unit to the lighting fixtures overhead. Carla considered powering up the lights, but instead picked up a flashlight that lay on the floor beside the power unit. Judging by the silence and stillness, there wasn't anyone else in the lab. But just in case someone was working in a back room, she'd wait until she'd checked the place out before announcing her presence with a blaze of light.

Carla was in full investigative mode now. Gone were her earlier fears of the dangers Mitsuhama's security systems might pose. She felt only a rising excitement at having finally achieved her goal. Now all that was left was to shoot as much trid as possible—and hopefully to find something that would make all of her efforts to get here worthwhile.

There was a door in each of the room's side walls and one in the rear. Carla opened the door to her left and shone the flashlight inside. A washroom. She crossed to the other side of the room and tried the second door. It was a simple lunch room, with table, uncomfortable looking metal chairs, a soykaf brewer, microwave, and sink. A half-eaten bag lunch still sat on the table; a wrinkled apple and wilted-looking sandwich lay on a plate.

The door at the back of the room had a sophisticated-looking maglock but was open a crack, due to the electrical cable that snaked through it and into the hallway beyond. There were doors on either side of the hallway, all but one of them held open by the electrical cable that had been run throughout the lab. All of these rooms were dark and silent. The one door that was closed bore a warning in both black letters and Japanese characters: EMERGENCY EXIT ONLY. WARNING. ALARM WILL SOUND. Carla wondered if the alarm was still working. If not—and if this door did lead up to the surface—this would make a good escape route if somebody surprised her in the lab.

The most interesting door was the one at the far end of the hall. It looked as though it had been lined with a layer of fuzzy green carpet. Set into the center of the door, at eye level, was a heavy glass window a couple of centimeters thick. The scrollwork etched into the glass reminded Carla of the wards on the windows of Aziz's shop.

The "carpet" that covered the door was in fact a

dense coating of moss. Carla scratched a little of it off with the tip of a manicured fingernail. The door underneath was made of what looked like tightly pressed wood fiber into which the moss was rooted. Carla puzzled over that a moment, but then realized she was looking at something that mages called a "living wall." The moss formed a natural, organic barrier through which astral creatures could not pass.

She couldn't see much through the window; the thick glass distorted the beam of her flashlight. But at least she was able to satisfy herself that nothing was moving inside the room. Even so, she felt a shiver of trepidation as she reached for the doorknob. Was the moss designed to keep something out—or to keep something in?

She swung the door open, propped it with one foot, and shone her flashlight into the room.

Paydirt! The room was completely empty—just bare plascrete walls, ceiling, and floor. But on that floor, painted in jet-black lines that glittered as if the paint had been mixed with tiny shards of crushed glass, was a circle containing a pentagram. Carla recognized it at once from the diagram on the memory chip. It was the hermetic circle used in conjuring the spirit.

She shot a ten-second take from the doorway, just to make sure she captured it on film. Then she turned and headed back for the room with the power source. This was too good a shot to pass up. She had to have some light. In a matter of minutes, she had powdered up the fuel cell. A steady hum filled the air, and the lights overhead flickered to life.

Hurrying back to the room with the hermetic circle on the floor, Carla did a wide-angle take of the entire room, then walked a slow, graceful circle, panning the painted floor from all angles. Then she dragged in a chair, climbed on top of it, and did an overhead shot.

"Perfect," she whispered to herself, pleased with her find. "Now let's see what other goodies the researchers left behind."

The first door she opened led to a storeroom that was crammed with magical fetishes and thaumaturgical supplies in neatly labeled containers. These didn't add anything to Carla's knowledge of the story, but the clutter of unusual items would be a great visual. She could get Wayne to superimpose a shot of herself over them later, introducing what she'd found in the lab.

The second door led to a board room whose walls were lined with erasable white message boards. All had been wiped clean. But at the center of the room was a long table with inset datapads. These were nearly buried by piles of hardcopy. The entire surface of the table was covered with papers, many of them wrinkled as if they'd been crumpled up into a ball and then smoothed flat again. Waste baskets lay empty on the floor, as if their contents had been dumped onto the table. Much of the hardcopy looked like garbage; there were paper food wrappers and even a few rats' nests of paper that had already gone through a document-shredding machine.

Carla rubbed her hands together, delighted with her find. It was obvious what had happened. Faced with the loss of their computerized files, the researchers had made a desperate search through their waste baskets, hoping to salvage some of the data on their research projects. They'd had half of yesterday and all of today to do the job, and by now had either found what they were looking for or had at last given up. But they hadn't bothered to clean up after themselves. And there was just a chance that a dedicated snoop could find enough for a story in what they'd left behind.

Carla pulled up a chair, sat down, and started going through the hardcopy printout.

An hour and a half later, she gave up her search. She'd skimmed all of the intact papers and found nothing. The shredded documents could have been pieced together with a computer matching program, but that would require hours of scanning time and equipment she didn't have. Her earlier optimism had faded. She realized now that Mitsuhama wouldn't be sloppy. The corporation wouldn't have stopped at merely shredding incriminating documents. Anything good would probably be ash by now.

Carla leaned back in the chair, stretching. She'd been through every scrap of paper in this room, but still had the nagging feeling she'd overlooked something. Getting up from the table, she walked back to the room that held the work stations. She paused, lost in thought, in front of the one where Farazad had sat. Compulsively, she tugged open the drawers once more, even though she already knew that they were empty. As she opened the last drawer, her eye fell on the magnetic clip that was stuck to the bottom of the metal drawer. It was a child's toy, a Mighty Mites face that smiled when Carla touched it. Beside it was a torn piece of hardcopy.

Carla leaned closer. The scrap of paper hadn't moved when her hand brushed against it. It wasn't just a tiny scrap—instead it was the corner of a larger piece of paper that had slid inside the crack where the back and bottom of the drawer met. Only the corner of it could be seen. Carla tried to move it with a finger, but found it was stuck. Instead she yanked out the drawer, turned it over, and pulled the hardcopy from it.

She let out a long, slow whistle as she read the crumpled paper she held in her hands. It was a memo, dated eight days ago—three days before Farazad Samji's death. It was addressed to the lab's director, Ambrose Wilks, and was signed with a wavering scrawl by the wage mage himself.

To: Director Wilks

Re: "Lucifer Deck" (Farohad) Project

As per your direct instructions, I have summoned and bound the farohad. Despite my formal protests to the board of directors, and against the dictates of my conscience and religion, I have performed the tests you have required.

If anything, the results of these tests prove that the farohad is unsuitable for the project you propose. It is true that the light effects the farohad produces can enter the Matrix, although the extreme measures we go through to tap this energy seems to border on torture. By all indications, it would seem that, as suspected, magical entities cannot stand the pure technology construct of the Matrix.

While I can force the farohad to allow me to tap its energies, and through trial and error we have been able to transfer that concentration of light into the Matrix, I am unable to control it once the energy is in the Matrix. Please note this because it explains why we cannot control the effects in the Matrix. The speed at which the light moves is beyond our capacities and the capabilities of the best deckers we have. The spirit's lack of cooperation makes training the farohad impossible. Our best brains alone cannot match the speed and short-lived usefulness of these bursts of pure light.

By its very nature, a creature composed of light must flow—it must remain in an active state. The farohad cannot "sit around" and wait for instructions. Nor can it remain within the Matrix for more than a nanosecond or two, at most. As a living spirit, it would completely lose its integrity if we tap too much of its elemental power, especially using so many technological systems. At any moment, the creature could dissolve and disappear.

It is thus impossible for the farohad to perform the function you wish it to. In theory, it should simulate the functions of a Matrix gopher program—one with unlimited access to data. It could bypass any intrusion countermeasures, seek out a keyword, reconfigure a portion of its body to exactly duplicate the data that contains this keyword, and return again to a computer to write that copied data on an optical memory chip or datastore. In theory. Obviously, in hindsight, this does not and cannot work. We did not foresee the inherent difficulties in forcing a magical creature into a pure technological construct. Even when we have tapped its energies, we have absolutely no control over the light. It will erase a memory chip or datastore instead of penetrating and copying the information. Without the human mind to understand the technology, we have set loose something, again in theory, that can destroy the Matrix.

I cannot in good conscience continue to subject the

farohad to this torture, only to prove what we already know—magical entities cannot exist in the Matrix and that light travels faster than the human mind. I believe that with the data we have learned we may be able to use the farohad's energy in the Matrix to create know-bots that function in a similar way—knowbots at least would be fully under our command. And from what I understand, our Software Division is very interested in what we have learned. If you approve this, I would be able to release the farohad. I cannot permit the farohad to die in captivity. I intend that it should be free—free to return to the paradise that is its natural habitat.

I have already outlined my opposition, on religious grounds, to the direction in which the Mitsuhama Seattle lab has taken my research. While I realize that my moral arguments cannot persuade you, I hope that the practical problems I have outlined above will do so. This project must be discontinued.

I cannot, in good conscience, continue this work. I hereby request a leave of absence, effective immediately, and a release from my contract with Mitsuhama.

Farazad Samji.

Automatically, Carla framed the memo with her cybereye, did an overall shot, then went to macro-focus and scanned the lines one by one so that they could be assembled later into a scrolling graphic. But even as she performed these mechanical functions, her mind was reeling. She'd jumped to the wrong conclusions not once, but twice. Mitsuhama hadn't developed the spirit for use as a new form of para-biological weapon. They hadn't even intended to use it as a virus—although it could certainly be put to that purpose, as Carla had done earlier in the Byte of the Future display. The corporation had instead been after the holy grail of magicians and deckers alike—an "interface" device that used magic as a bridge to the Matrix. They'd intended to use the spirit as an organic, magically based computer—as hardware and software in one. As a program that could ignore ice, enter any system freely, and use its own body to copy any data it found, no matter how much encryption was used to protect it. Had it worked, it would have been the ultimate stealth program and ultra-high-speed master persona control program, rolled into one.

Except that no mage or decker could control it.

And now its energy was running amok in the Matrix, randomly wiping data and crashing systems in an effort to get back at the man who had conjured it and forced it to enter the Matrix in the first place. The man who had presumably set it free, only to have the spirit turn on him and burn the life from him.

Carla stared at the project name: Lucifer Deck. Farazad Samji certainly considered the spirit to be an angel—a farohad. His boss had probably dreamed up the word Lucifer, putting a Christian spin on the concept. Lucifer, the "bringer of light," the shining angel who later fell from heaven in the form of lightning and became Satan, lord of darkness. The name choice was both ironic and appropriate. The spirit—Lucifer—was indeed the fallen son; instead of serving Mitsuhama, it now was trying to destroy the corporation's kingdom— the Matrix. It was, in every respect, as unruly and antagonistic an angel as the original Lucifer had been.

Carla folded the paper and slipped it into a pocket. That was it. She had what she needed. Her incursion was a wrap. But she'd been trained to be thorough, and so she peeked into the only other room she had yet to explore—a private office. Judging by its comfortable, overstuffed chair and plush carpet, it must belong to the lab's director. If so, the work station it contained just might contain some other, vital piece of information that Carla could weave into her story.

The data terminal here, like those in the front room, had been taken apart and its central processing unit removed. Carla wasn't going to get anything from it. And the rest of the room didn't hold anything of interest; there was no enticing hardcopy lying about. She was just about to leave when she noticed an electronic daytimer that had fallen onto the carpeted floor, under the workstation itself. It was a micro-thin model, no more than a few centimeters long. Picking it up, she thumbed the button that activated it.

The tiny liquid-crystal screen on the top of the data-pad came to life, revealing a name and title in an ornate gold font: Ambrose Wilks. Director MCT Seattle.

Curious to see what the daytimer contained, Carla paged through its entries, starting with a date three weeks ago. To her mounting disappointment, she saw that all of the entries were personal appointments and self-reminders: *Pick up Valerie after school. Lunch with Yuki, 2 p.m. Retirement present for Sabrina.* No wonder the datapad had no log-in code. It didn't contain anything incriminating at all. Still, she continued doggedly on through the entries, right up to today's date. And then gasped when she saw the name listed there: *Meeting with Aziz Fader, 6 p.m. Alabaster Maiden Nightclub.*

Blast that man! Carla had asked Aziz, after their visit to Evelyn Belanger's home yesterday, about his offer to sell Mitsuhama the information it needed to control the spirit. He told her that he was just sending out feelers to see if the corporation was interested—that it would be a day or two, at least, before he'd learned enough about Pita's magical abilities to make a serious sales pitch. He promised Carla he wouldn't begin negotiating with the corporation until after she'd put her story to bed. But he'd been lying. He'd gone ahead and set up this meeting with the director of the research laboratory without even asking if it would slot up her story.

Had Aziz already sold out Pita, turning over this "key" to the spell formula to Mitsuhama for a large chunk of nuyen? More to the point, had he sold out Carla? Was he telling Mitsuhama, even now, how far she'd gotten with her story on their research project?

Carla was furious. She glanced at her watch. It was already nine o'clock; Aziz would probably be home from the meeting with Ambrose Wilks by now. He wouldn't have stayed to party at the nightclub, even though it was a Saturday night. When Aziz was hot on the trail of a new magical formula, he was as much of a workaholic as Carla. He'd rush right home and pick up where he left off—and would probably work through the night.

Carla pulled out her cel phone and started to dial Aziz's number. But then she realized what she was doing, and thumbed the Off button. The confrontation would have to wait until she was out of this place. The thing to do now was get back to the station and file the footage she'd just shot.

Still angry, Carla headed for the main room and shut off the fuel cell. She stood for a moment or two in the silence, debating which exit to take. The door marked "emergency" probably led straight to the surface. It would be the quickest way out. But she didn't know what she'd find there. The carefully landscaped grounds were probably patrolled by security guards and bristling with hidden sensors. The smarter thing to do would be to go back the way she came. She still had the employee ID badge, after all. It wasn't that late yet. She could just say she'd been putting in a little overtime, and stroll right out the front doors. But she had to check on something, first.

She used her cel phone again, this time calling a different number. Corwin answered on the first ring.

"Albert's Auto Body. Wha's'up?"

"I was just calling back about the Runabout. It looks like I'll be able to pick it up tonight; I've finished work now. Can I come right over? Is anyone in the shop?"

"Just a minute. I'll have to check."

After a few seconds, Corwin was back. His voice held a note of self-satisfaction. "You sure can, ma'am. The shop is empty, but I'll be here."

"All right. Thanks. Bye."

She hung up with a satisfied smile. At least this part was going according to plan. Once again, Corwin had come through for her. Worried that the Movement Match program would be discovered if he left it in Mitsuhama's computer system for any length of time, he'd wiped it as soon as Carla stepped out of the elevator. In its place, he'd rigged a simpler and less detectable "glitch." He'd altered the programming of both the camera in the elevator and the side corridor on the thirtieth floor that led to it so that they were being fed a continuous loop of previously recorded data. According to the information provided by these cameras, both the elevator and corridor were now "empty"—and would remain that way, even when Carla passed through them. Carla would be invisible until she exited the elevator and turned the corner into the main hallway on the thirtieth floor. With luck, any security guards watching the monitors would assume that she had come out of a nearby office. She'd even mime closing a door behind her, to complete the illusion. With luck, they'd assume that Evelyn Belanger was still down in the lab.

At that point, it would only be a matter of getting out of the building itself. If something went wrong—if it came down to a serious confrontation with the security guards on the way out, she would give up the pretense, say who she really was, and rely upon her reputation—and KKRU's pull—to get her out in one piece.

Carla stepped into the elevator and hit the icon that would take her to the thirtieth floor. When the doors sighed open, she strode out, anger at Aziz still bubbling inside of her. She'd show that . . .

She saw something move, and came to an abrupt halt. No more than five meters ahead of her, passing through the T-junction where this side corridor met the main hallway, was a gigantic, coal-black dog. It padded along the corridor, its claws making faint clicking noises. Twin jets of searing blue flame puffed from its nostrils as it breathed. It stood a meter high at the shoulder, on powerful, muscular legs. As Carla stood, frozen in place, it turned to look down the corridor at her with eyes that were like glowing pits of fire. Flattening its ears, it bared gleaming white teeth. It stood its ground blocking the corridor and staring at Carla with eyes that burned with merciless, fiery intensity.

For a heartbeat or two Carla stood, afraid to move. Then slowly, she backed away from the creature. She took one step, two—and found the closed elevator doors a hard and unyielding wall against her back. This corridor was a short one, with no other exits—a dead end. There wasn't even an emergency stairway. She was trapped with a magical creature that might attack her at any moment. And she didn't have the first idea what to do.

The cel phone was still in her hand. Carla considered her options, then slid a finger over to the redial icon and tapped it twice. As the phone automatically dialed Aziz's number, Carla activated its video pickup. Mitsuhama might be monitoring the call, but if they were, the worst that could happen would be that they would find her sooner, rather than later. Before the hideous black dog tore her to shreds.

As the call went through, the tiny screen on the cell phone came to life. It showed Aziz hunched over a book, reading. He was busy scanning text with an electronic stylus and spoke without looking up. "Yes? Do we have a deal?" Then he did a double take as he saw Carla's face on the screen of his telecom. "Oh, it's you, Carla. Sorry. What do you want?"

Carla bit back her anger and spoke as softly as she could. "I'm in trouble, Aziz, and I need your help."

"What's wrong?"

With a trembling hand, Carla turned the cel phone slightly so that its visual pickup took in the slavering dog that had begun to slowly advance toward her.

"Holy drek!" Aziz exclaimed. "That's a hell hound. Don't make any sudden moves, Carla. It'll tear you apart."

Thanks, Aziz, Carla thought. *Just what I needed to hear.*

Aziz paused, then peered at his telecom screen. "Where are you, Carla? You aren't calling me from the . . ." His eyes widened. "You're there now, aren't you?"

"What should I do, Aziz?"

Aziz gave her a worried frown. "It must be part of the building's security system, Carla," he continued. "Just hold still. Its handler will be along as soon as he sees you on the monitor, to call it off. If you don't make any threatening moves in the meantime, you'll be fine until he arrives."

For a second or two, Carla was reassured. The hell hound had paused in its advance. It stood about a meter away from her now—still in a crouched position, ready for instant action—but for the moment seemingly content to stand and watch her. Even from this distance, Carla could feel the heat of its fiery breath. She didn't want it to get any closer. She'd do what Aziz said—hold still until the animal's handler came.

Then Carla groaned. "Its handler won't be able to see me unless he has a telepathic link to the animal, Aziz," she said in a whisper, moving her lips as little as possible. "The security cameras in this area have had their data re-rezzed. Unless someone is monitoring this cel phone frequency, nobody knows I'm here."

"You're in an office complex. Somebody will eventually come. Just wait where you are."

Yeah, right. Wait until someone noticed that the hell hound was no longer on the monitors, and came looking for it. She might get out of here alive, but she'd lose her story. The Mitsuhama's security guards would discover the hardcopy in her pocket and realize immediately what she'd been up to. They'd probably be bright enough to scan for a cybereye, and when they found it, they'd take her chip with all of her eye-camera's data on it. And that would be the end of her story.

There had to be another way out. Aziz hadn't been any help at all. But perhaps if she . . .

Looking at the hell hound, Carla saw that it had stayed its advance. Slowly, a millimeter at a time, she raised her free hand toward the pocket of her jacket. If she could ease Farazad's credstick from her pocket, maybe she could get the elevator doors to open again, with Corwin's help. She'd go back through the lab, take the emergency exit this time.

"I'm going to hang up now, Aziz. I have to call someone."

"Be careful how you enter the numbers, Carla. The

hell hound might think your cel phone is a weapon. It will be trained to attack anyone who . . ."

Carla had stopped listening to him. Her fingers touched the fabric of her jacket. Now it was just a matter of sliding her hand into her pocket and—

With a lunge, the hell hound launched itself at her. Instinctively, Carla screamed and flung up her hands. The animal smashed into her, knocking her back against the elevator doors. Then she was down on the floor with the creature on top of her. Its baleful, glowing eyes stared into hers, and its claws dug painfully into her skin through the fabric of her clothes. The blue flames from its nostrils flared and ebbed, flared and ebbed, washing her face with waves of heat. It stood poised on top of her, mouth open, white teeth gleaming. Even as Carla's natural eye filled with tears, she focused the trideo camera in her cybereye for a tight shot of the hell hound's face. If she was going to die, she was going to die shooting trid. Her last shot would be a dramatic one. Even as her mind whirled with fear, a tiny part of it was writing the lead-in to the piece: "This astonishing footage was shot by KKRU reporter Carla Harris just seconds before her death . . ."

Aziz's voice shrilled from the cel phone, which had fallen to the floor somewhere behind her. "Carla! What's happened? Are you . . . alive?"

Carla choked out a sob. Aziz might have screwed up her story, might have already sold her out. But he was the only one she could turn to now. "Aziz," she gasped. "Help!"

25

"You're crazy!" Masaki shouted into the telecom unit. "The spirit is dangerous. It's just as likely to kill Carla as to save her!"

A three-dimensional image of Aziz glared at the reporter from the projection unit of the telecom. "You're wasting valuable time, Masaki. Bring the girl to the address I gave you. Now. Every minute counts."

Pita rubbed the sleep from her eyes and sat up. She'd been sleeping on the couch in Masaki's apartment and had only heard fragments of the conversation. Something about Carla, the spirit—and herself. She leaned forward, listening avidly.

Masaki shook his head at the telecom. "No," he said firmly. "I'll get in touch with the building's security guards. They'll call the guard dog off."

"It's a hell hound, not a guard dog," Aziz spat back. "And what do you think its handlers will do when they find an intruder who's compromised the security of a top-secret research facility? The security guards aren't just going to politely ask who she is and then let her go. Any questioning they will do will be brutal. And if they don't get the answers they want . . ."

"Carla's a reporter covering a story," Masaki countered. "The station will back her up." His voice, however, held a hint of uncertainty. Aziz pounced upon it.

"She's also someone who illegally broke into a restricted area of a powerful corporation, and that makes her no better than a shadowrunner," he said. "Do you honestly think Mitsuhama cares about adverse publicity when it can downplay the incident as security guards who were 'just doing their jobs'? And what's to stop them from coming after anyone else connected with the story? You could be next, Masaki. Your byline was on the original report, too. You even did a stand-up for it, as I recall."

The reporter wet his lips nervously. "I still don't think that using the spirit is the right thing to—"

"What's happening?" Pita asked.

Masaki turned, surprised to see her. He'd obviously forgotten she was there.

"Carla's been trapped in the Mitsuhama complex by a hell hound. Aziz wants to use the spirit against it. He seems to think that if he can attract its attention again, you can control it. But that's crazy. I don't see how you could possibly help. Control a spirit that's already killed one mage? Impossible! You're just a kid with no formal magical training. I won't allow it."

Pita narrowed her eyes. Just a kid, huh? Yeah, just a dumb ork kid who could be shoved around by the police and shunted off to a group home when she became inconvenient. She pushed the blankets to the floor and stood up. Her eyes bored into Masaki's. "I can so control it," she told him in a level voice. She turned to the telecom unit. "What do you want me to do, Aziz?"

The mage spoke rapidly. "Remember the boarded-up Stuffer Shack you came to in astral form when the spirit was attacking me?"

Pita nodded.

"I want you to go there—in person—as quickly as you can. I'll give you the address. I'll meet you there and explain what we have to do. I've ordered a taxi for you. Tell the driver to hurry."

Pita started to answer, but Masaki cut her off. "Never mind the taxi," he told Aziz. "I'll drive her."

Pita stared at him. "I thought you forbade me to do this."

Masaki said goodbye to Aziz, and tapped off the telecom. Then he sighed. "You're obviously going to go through with this crazy idea, no matter what I say. You think I want to sit here, worrying about you and wondering if you're all right? I intend to be there. In case anything goes wrong."

Pita blinked, surprised. If the spirit refused her commands and attacked, there would be nothing Masaki could do. Except, maybe, get fried alongside her and Aziz. Perhaps the reporter really did care about her, after all. But there wasn't any time for speculation. Aziz had told her to hurry. She scooped up her jacket from the floor and shoved her feet into her sneakers.

The drive to the shop was a quick one—traffic was relatively light for a Saturday night, and for once Masaki seemed more than willing to break the speed limit. He didn't say a word to Pita, but instead sat in a tense silence, drumming the fingers of one hand nervously against the steering wheel. It wasn't until they reached the boarded-up Stuffer Shack and parked in front of it that he at last spoke.

"Aziz asked me to bring this," he said, reaching into the back seat and lifting out a portable trideo camera. "He wants to document this. I guess something rubbed off when he was living with Carla; there's a little reporter in him, too." He gave Pita a forced smile. She supposed he was trying to be funny.

Pita clambered out of the car and made her way into the boarded-up building. The convenience store looked much as it had during her astral visit to it. The counters and display racks were still covered with dust but the floor was swept clean. On it, a hermetic circle enclosing a pentagram was marked in faintly luminescent paint. Aziz knelt beside it, laying out earth, water, and a lighted candle in the angles of the pentagram. He looked up at Pita, then smiled as he saw the reporter.

"Thanks for coming, Masaki. Set your camera up over there, and then stay put. Whatever happens to us, don't try to cross the hermetic circle. You'll only make things worse if you do manage to break it—not to mention putting yourself in danger. And keep your camera rolling. If the spell fails, the trid may help me learn what I did wrong."

He waved Pita over. "You, Pita, will sit here, at the apex of the pentagram. Once you're in position, it's vital that you don't interrupt the protective spell I'll be casting or try to leave the circle. It's best if you don't try to move at all. Just close your eyes and concentrate on the spot on your arm where the spirit wrote its name. When you feel its presence, use the visualization techniques we talked about earlier, and form a clear image of Carla in your mind. Then picture the hell hound—a big black dog—and order the spirit to attack it. If it helps, you can speak the command out loud as well as in your mind. The spirit will be forced to obey you once it's under your mental control."

"What if I can't control the spirit?" Pita chewed on her lip, feeling nervous. She was just starting to realize the danger she was placing herself in. Her earlier bravado and pride had evaporated, leaving her with second thoughts. She looked at Aziz's heat-blistered skin, and scratched the itchy spot on her arm, remembering the sharp sting when the spirit had burned her.

"If you feel the spirit getting the better of you—if you find you can't control it—then raise your arm and wave it away," Aziz answered. "You've already banished it once. This time, you'll be inside the hermetic circle. The simple act of raising your fist against it should be enough to drive the spirit away, as long as the force of your will is behind the action."

The force of her will. Now Pita was really nervous. Her magical powers weren't, strictly speaking, under her direct control. She couldn't be certain they would manifest themselves here tonight. She eyed the door, tempted to back out. As if sensing her fear, Aziz moved to close it, then secured the door with a chain and padlock. "We don't need any interruptions," he said.

He crossed to the hermetic circle and motioned impatiently for Pita to sit down. "Come on," he said. "Carla's life depends upon this. You don't want the hell hound to kill her or the security guards to catch her, do you? We're the only chance she's got."

Pita hesitated. She couldn't tell if that was genuine concern for Carla in Aziz's voice. From what Carla had said, she and the mage had been pretty close, once. But

that had been years ago. Aziz's story about Carla and
the hell hound might be nothing more than an elaborate
hoax, dreamed up by the mage to trick Pita into helping him to control the spirit. Carla might not be in
any danger at all. But then Pita shook her head. That
didn't make sense. The spirit had nearly killed Aziz
the last time he'd messed with it. He wouldn't be willing to risk his own life again without a good reason.
Would he?

If Carla's life were really in danger, Pita was obligat-
ed to do what she could. The reporter might have lied
about doing a story on how Lone Star killed Chen, but
she'd saved Pita's ass when the yakuza came gunning
for her and Yao. Pita owed her one for that. Besides,
Pita was curious. Could she really do it? Control a spirit
that corp mages and other experts like Aziz couldn't get
a handle on? The thought of having so much power at
her fingertips was tempting. Just let anyone try to call
her "porkie" again with a spirit backing her up. She'd
show them.

"Show me where to sit," she told Aziz.

Masaki watched her from a corner of the room. "You
don't have to go through with this, Pita," he said. The
wheeze was back in his voice. "It's not too late to
call—"

"Keep quiet!" Aziz snapped. "If you call attention to
yourself, the spirit might choose you as a target."

Masaki swallowed, then moved so that a dusty
counter was between himself and the hermetic circle.
He adjusted his trideo camera nervously. A tiny red
light came on. "We're rolling," he said.

Pita sat where Aziz told her to, cross-legged at the
apex of the pentagram. She toyed with the laces of her
sneakers as the mage positioned himself within the hermetic circle. He lay on his back, clutching a broken
chunk of window glass and staring up at the store's
grimy skylight, his head beside Pita's feet. He cau-
tioned Pita and Masaki once more about interruptions,
then took a deep breath and began to chant.

Pita couldn't understand a word Aziz said. She
glanced at Masaki, moving only her eyes. Her arm

itched, but she didn't dare scratch it. Instead she worried the tip of her shoelace between blunt fingers, afraid to shift position.

Masaki gave her a nervous smile from the shadows. His face was seamed with worry lines, and his gray moustache was twitching as a tic tugged at his lip. Was it only Pita's imagination, or could she see the reporter more clearly now? Something was shining in through the skylight.

Aziz just kept chanting, his voice droning a series of weird, harsh sounding words.

Panic began to claw at Pita's gut as the interior of the Stuffer Shack grew steadily brighter. What was she doing here? Masaki was right. Despite any natural shamanic talents she might have, she was untrained. Just a kid, and way out of her depth. It took everything she had to fight back the urge to jump up and run.

Out of the corner of her eye, Pita saw movement. Not overhead, where the spirit would materialize any moment, but down low, in a corner by the floor. Was that moving shadow cat-shaped? Was the whirring of Masaki's trideo camera really starting to sound like a purring cat? Or was Pita just going crazy?

Then she felt the brush of soft fur against her hand. Cat! The touch calmed her, gave her the courage she needed to resist getting up and running from the room. She flexed mental claws, preparing for what was to come.

Suddenly a bright spiral of light flashed overhead, throwing the room into stark relief. Masaki let out a horrified cry and threw up his arms, then ducked down below the counter, leaving his camera running. Aziz raised the jagged sheet of glass he held, chanting louder, stronger. He twisted his head away from the light, staring back at Pita and raising a finger to point at the ceiling. Then he squeezed his eyes shut.

The light that filled the room was painfully bright. Taking her cue from the mage, Pita closed her own eyes. She didn't want to look up, to see the spirit looming above her. She could feel its heat on her body. At the same time, shivers ran through her, making the hair on her arms rise. Instinctively, she clutched at her forearm, squeezing the spot where the spirit had burned her, trying desperately to concentrate.

"Carla," she croaked fearfully, visualizing the reporter's face in her mind. She concentrated, adding the image of a huge black dog menacing the reporter. "Kill it," she whispered fiercely. "Save her."

The light strobed around Pita, dazzling her eyes with red spots, even through her closed eyelids. She could feel the heat beating against the top of her head and shoulders. Sweat trickled down one cheek. The spirit was pressing closer. It was coming for her, trying to suck her up into its spinning vortex. She couldn't control it. She'd never control it. The thing would tear her body to atoms . . .

"Go!" Pita leaped to her feet, raising her burned arm. She pointed to the skylight, focusing her will in an arrow-straight line. "Go!"

At that same moment, Masaki began to scream her name. "Pi—"

Suddenly the convenience store lay far below her. She was a flash of light, streaking through the star-speckled heavens. Arcing up, then swooping down and skipping across the lake below. Flashing in a jagged ladder toward a series of six silver towers with black-tinted windows. Rushing in through one of those squares. Zig-zagging impossibly fast along a corridor that was more a boxy blur than a hallway. Coming suddenly upon a dark-haired woman, sprawled on the floor on her back, a huge black dog atop her, fangs a few centimeters from her throat. Arcing down, plunging in through the animal's burning red eyes, sizzling them in an instant and piercing its brain. Then out again through its nostrils in twin white beams, so quickly that the animal had no time even to collapse, so quickly that the woman below it had not yet even blinked. Back through the hallway, back up into the heavens. Expanding into a flash that spread paper-thin over hundreds of kilometers, stretching ever outward into a sheet of lightning, waiting, waiting, while the nanoseconds ticked by with impossible slowness . . .

Pita's mind sluggishly formed a thought. *Control. Command?*

She could sense the spirit's impatience—its desire to flow, be free. And its anger. Somewhere below were fiber-optic cables, humming hardware, and knots of computer nodes that together spread an invisible mesh across the globe. The Matrix. A sticky spider web into which the spirit was forced to throw itself, compulsively returning over and over again. *Break,* it hissed at her. *Tear.*

Pita felt the creature's anger blaze through her mind. There, it joined with her own. An image formed in her consciousness. A cop's face, leering at her, twisted with hatred. A chromed hand. A patrol car, hissing through the night.

The spirit coalesced into a point, then shot down toward the city in a jagged streak of lightning. Pita watched from an impossible height as it zoomed down into the street where the beams of headlights crisscrossed, frozen like rays of ice. In through the tinted windshield of a police patrol car.

Through the glass she saw two frightened faces, washed with brilliant light. Their eyes were squinted tight, their hands thrown up as if to ward off a blow. One of those hands was chromed. The patrol car was just starting to spin in response to the driver's panicked reaction. *Kill?* a voice whispered in Pita's mind.

In the same instant, Pita heard an echo. A second voice had overlaid the first. It somehow seemed more in tune with Pita's own thoughts. *No,* it whispered with a soft purr. *Play.*

Recognizing the voice of Cat, Pita tried to smile. She felt her brain start to send the command to her lips. The world she was occupying was moving much too quickly for it to get there. *Yes,* the first voice echoed, long before Pita could either agree or disagree with the suggestion. *Play.*

Fingers of light licked out at the two cops in the patrol car, searing their faces, crisping their hair, blinding them instantly. A part of Pita exulted, enjoying the fear and pain the spirit was causing. These

were the two cops who had killed Chen, Shaz, and
Mohan. She had them now, right between her paws.
She could bat them about or rend them with her claws.
She would draw their blood a little at a time and savor
the taste of their scurrying panic.

At the same time, another part of her was repulsed.
What was she doing? She'd ordered the spirit to kill the
hell hound without a second thought. But this was torture. And it was ugly. Suddenly horrified at what she
had become, she drew back violently from the scene
that was unfolding . . .

Something snapped. A light blinked out in her mind.
At the same moment, her muscles twitched her lips into
a smile, at last obeying the command that her brain had
seemingly sent hours ago. She opened her eyes on a
dark room, her mouth curled in a foolish grin.

"Pita? Are you all right, Pita?"

Masaki peered at her from behind the counter, eyes
wide with fear. He clambered to his feet, then edged
around the corner of the counter, one eye on the skylight. Beside him, the trideo camera was still whirring
softly.

Aziz rolled over, groaning and rubbing his eyes.
Then he jerked around to look up at the ceiling.
"Where is it?" he asked suddenly. "Where'd it go?"

Pita sighed as relief made her body rubbery. "It's
gone. I let it go."

Aziz clasped her knee. "Were you able to control—"

"Yes," Pita answered. Her arm was itching fiercely.
And she was dead tired. The spell seemed to have
taken a lot out of her. "Can I get up now?"

"Of course." Aziz helped Pita to her feet and guided
her out of the hermetic circle. "We did it!" he chortled,
slapping her on the back. "We controlled the spirit!"

"You mean Pita controlled it," Masaki interjected.
He moved closer to Pita, then wrapped an arm protectively around her shoulders. Pita slumped against him,
too tired to protest at him taking the liberty of hugging
her. Actually, it felt kind of nice.

"Pita didn't do it on her own," Aziz said. "She's not
a trained—"

An electronic beeping in a corner of the room cut him off. Aziz ran over to it and picked up a cel phone. "Yes?"

After listening for a second or two he flipped the phone shut. "That was Carla," he said with a broad smile. "The hell hound is dead. Carla's a little shaken up, a little bloody, but she's on her way out of the MCT building now."

26

Carla twisted a scanning stylus between her fingers, trying to contain her anger as she stared down Greer. The scratches from her close call with the hell hound stood out as red welts on her hands. "What do you mean, the story is spiked? I got what you wanted—proof that Mitsuhama Computer Technologies was behind the spirit. I've even got a hardcopy document addressed to the director of their research lab, outlining the uses the corporation planned to put this tech to. I risked my drekking life to get it and nearly got mauled by a hell hound in the process. I spent all day yesterday—my day off—putting the piece together. I have footage of a hermetic circle in the Mitsuhama lab that matches the diagram on the datachip, and I obtained a collaborating quote from a Renraku source who admits that their corporation is also experimenting with Farazad's spell. And all you can say is, 'The story is spiked'? I can't believe it!"

Greer leaned back in his padded chair, rocking uneasily back and forth. He seemed distinctly uncomfortable. Usually, when he called a reporter in for one of his infamous "private conferences" he would bluster and roar like an angry bear. The whole newsroom would hear the dressing down, regardless of whether the door was shut or not. Normally, he and Carla would have gone at it tooth and nail, shouting at each other across the desk, and eventually—maybe—Carla would win and the story would air. But today Greer refused to be provoked. Instead he picked up his mug and took a sip of soykaf that had long since gone cold.

"You heard what I said," he said gruffly. "The story's not going to air. Drop it."

"That's insane!" Carla protested. "This story is huge. Not only does it imply that magic might be used to access the Matrix, but it foretells a possible repeat of the Crash of 2029. It's a groundbreaking story—and ironic, too. Imagine a corporation secretly developing a magical spirit that could single-handedly destroy the entire information and telecommunications industry! You can't bury a story like that! If KKRU doesn't run it, somebody else will."

"No they won't," Greer said quietly, staring at his soykaf as he swirled it gently around in its cup. Beside him, a wall-mounted monitor broadcast a super-heavyweight boxing match. The sound had been muted; the trolls on the monitor traded silent blows. Greer kept glancing at it. "Nobody's going to—"

Carla was too wound up to listen. She rose to her feet, pointing her scanning stylus at her producer. "If KKRU won't run the story, I know a station that will. NABS has promised me a reporter's slot if I can prove my worth to them. I'll jump ship this minute—and take the Mitsuhama story with me—if you won't air it."

That made Greer look up. He set his cup down as Carla stormed toward the door, and half-stood behind his desk. "Carla. Wait!"

Carla paused, one hand on the doorknob. "Well?"

Greer moved around the desk and laid a meaty hand on her shoulder. "I agree with you, Carla. One hundred per cent. It's an excellent story—the best you've ever done. And Wayne's done a brilliant job of editing. It really has punch. But I can't run it, much as I'd like to, because—"

Carla didn't wait to hear his excuse. "They got to you, didn't they?" she whispered. She searched Greer's eyes. "I don't understand it, Greer. What could Mitsuhama possibly threaten you with? It's not as though you have a family to worry about, or that you scare easily. You didn't back down on doing that piece on organized crime in Puyallup, even though Jimmy Chin threatened to firebomb your car if it aired. What could Mitsuhama possibly have done to frighten you off?"

Greer's hand fell away from Carla's shoulder. His attention strayed once more to the monitor that was showing the boxing match. On the screen, one of the fighters fell heavily to the mat. Greer swore softly as the other boxer was declared the winner. Then he walked back to his desk and sat down heavily.

"They bought the station," he answered at last. "The deal was closed this morning before you came in to work. Mitsuhama owns KKRU. They're calling the shots now. And they don't want the story to air."

Carla frowned, a hot wave of anger rising inside her. "And you're going to obey their orders?" she spat. "What have you turned into, some sort of corporate lap dog?"

Greer sighed heavily. "I know it stinks, Carla. But I can't afford to lose my job. I'm due to retire in five years, and I'll be relying upon the company pension when I do."

"But you're a trideo producer," Carla said, unable to comprehend what she was hearing. "You make a good salary. Surely you don't need the nuyen that badly."

"Yes I do." Greer's wide cheeks flushed with embarrassment. "I . . ." He pursed his lips, unwilling to finish the sentence.

All at once, the pieces came together for Carla—Greer's obsession with sports, his constant bumming of drinks from other staffers at the press lounge, the tiny dump of an apartment that he lived in. She glanced at the monitor, then back at Greer.

"You gamble, don't you?" Carla asked softly. "What did Mitsuhama do, offer to wipe your debts? How much do you owe?"

"A lot," Greer muttered. He looked up with a sad, self-deprecating smile. "I guess I never should have taken that first job as a sports reporter. That's when it started—with bets of just a few nuyen between friends. I've been throwing my money down the toilet ever since."

"Oh, Gil." Carla sank down into the chair in front

of the producer's desk. Her anger had suddenly evaporated into pity. "No wonder you work so much overtime."

"Yes." Greer had returned his attention to his cold soykaf.

Carla had been taken aback by the bearish man's confession. She was saddened by the fact that Mitsuhama had found his weak spot and forced him to dance to their tune. Giving in would be galling for any newscaster. It was especially so for Greer, who cherished his reputation as a tough, no-nonsense newshound. She wanted to reach out, to comfort him. But now was not the time.

"I'm sorry about what happened, Gil," she said, rising to her feet. "But it leaves me no other option. I'm taking my story to NABS."

He looked up. "I tried to tell you already, Carla. NABS won't touch it. No one will. Not if your byline is on it."

Carla had a sudden premonition of impending doom. Slowly, she sat down again. "Why not?"

Greer looked even more embarrassed as he opened a drawer in his desk. "Given our modern technology, when digitalized images can be edited with a few strokes of a stylus, a news station has only its reputation to fall back upon. The public has to have utter faith that the images they're watching on their trideo sets are the pure, unaltered truth.

"Ultimately, it comes down to the credibility of the station's reporters. If the reporters are perceived to be honest, the station is believed to be credible. But if the reporters are perceived to have compromised themselves in any way, to have lied about their stories—or to have questionable personal lives . . ."

He paused, and shut the drawer. He focused his attention on the unlabeled optical memory chip he'd pulled from it, refusing to meet Carla's eyes.

Carla was afraid to ask what was on that chip. The ice water in her gut meant that her subconscious mind already knew.

"Our new boss gave this to me this morning," Greer

said, punching a button on his desk that wiped the
boxing match and switched the wall monitor over to a
closed-circuit playback mode. Then he got up and
closed the blinds in his office window, shutting out the
curious faces of the other reporters who were peering
up from their work stations, trying to catch a glimpse
of Carla's dressing down.

"I know it's a lie, Carla, and you know it's a lie. But
when the public sees the images on this chip and hears
about your 'shadow career as a porn star' and how you
kept it in the closet all these years, your credibility will
be zero. Nobody will ever take you seriously again."

Sitting down, he put the chip in the editing unit that
was built into his desk and hit the playback icon. He
deliberately turned his back to the images that blazed
across the monitor. He hadn't bothered to deactivate
the mute, and for this Carla was thankful. She watched
in horrified fascination as trideo footage of herself,
locked in a naked embrace with Enzo—Mr. November
of the Men of Lone Star calendar—filled the flatscreen
monitor. After a few moments, she buried her face in
her hands. Not only had Mitsuhama found Greer's
weak spot, they'd found hers, too. In spades. She
refused to feel guilt for having made the recordings of
her romantic liaisons. But she couldn't help feeling
regret—and anguished rage—while watching the trid
that could spell the end of her career.

Greer reached over and thumbed the editing unit off.
He popped the memory chip and slid it across the desk
to Carla. "Here," he said. "Take it. Wipe it clean. I'm
sorry I had to see that. I'm not even going to ask if it's
real or not."

Numbly, Carla took the chip. She recognized it
immediately as the original recording by the scuffs on
its yellow plastic case. Wipe it? What good would that
do? This was only one chip. The shadowrunners who
broke into her apartment had taken dozens of her "personal recordings." Mitsuhama could have made as
many duplicates as they liked of the chip, could be
holding back a copy, ready to torpedo her career whenever they wanted to. And she'd never . . .

"Wait a minute," Carla said, her reporter's instincts taking over. "Who, exactly, gave you this chip?"

"Our new boss. John Chang. Head of Mitsuhama Seattle."

"But the shadowrunners who stole this were working for Renraku," she said, leaning forward. "That means the two computer corporations are working together to bury this story. But why? They ought to be at each other's throats, in fierce competition to be the first to develop this new form of magic. If they're working together . . ."

"It doesn't really matter now, does it?" Greer said, looking pointedly at the memory chip in Carla's hand. "The story is spiked."

"I realize that," Carla answered. "But I can't help but wonder what the sudden cooperation between rivals means. Even if the story never airs, I'd like to satisfy my own curiosity . . ."

The telecom built into Greer's desk pinged softly, interrupting her thoughts. He answered it, activating its handset and holding up a hand for silence. After a moment, he handed the handset to Carla.

"It's for you."

"Who is it?" Carla mouthed, then put the speaker to her ear when Greer did not reply.

The voice at the other end of the line was polite but firm, with a hint of a Chinese accent.

"Ms. Harris?"

Carla didn't recognize the voice. "Yes?"

"This is John Chang, vice president of Mitsuhama Computer Technologies' UCAS division, and the new director of KKRU News. I'd like to see you in my office, in the Chrysanthemum Tower. I believe you know where that is. Please report to me here. At once."

27

Pita was hiding inside a large box, her fur on end. She peered out through a slit in the cardboard at the grimy window that led outside. Humans stared in through its broken glass, their eyes coldly scanning the room. One of them looked like Aziz; he was pointing. The others were Asian men who were only vaguely familiar. Their faces were soft, dream-fuzzed blurs.

Suddenly Pita's world tilted as the box was upended. She sprawled out onto the dusty floor, her clawed feet scrabbling for purchase on the cement. But it was too late. Hands reached down to pick her up, clamping her tiny body firmly in their grip.

Pita bared her teeth in a hiss and twisted her body, drawing her rear feet up to scratch. Her tail lashed back and forth. She flexed her hands, revealing wickedly hooked claws. But although she could raise one paw, she was unable to move it, unable to slash. She should have been able to wriggle out of the grip of the man who held her, but she felt as if her body was moving through thick syrup.

Then a trideo set in the corner of the room flickered to life. The static shaped itself into the face of an ork. One of his huge hands held a microphone. "Hey!" he yelled into it, in a voice like amplified electronic thunder.

It startled the man who was holding Pita. At last she was able to launch herself out of his hands. She scurried for the door, which was open just a crack. But the distraction had been only a temporary one, and now the humans were closing in. In another moment the hands would close around her again. And then . . .

"Cat!" Pita jerked awake, her heart thudding in her chest. It took a moment or two before she remembered where she was. She looked wildly around the room at the dusty journalism diploma on the wall and the jumble of clothes in the corner. She was in Masaki's apartment. And the time—she craned her neck to look at the digital display on the telecom—was five a.m.

She got up from the couch, crossed to the window, and stared out at the Seattle skyline. Somewhere down there, in those blocks of buildings framed by glowing streetlights, was the store whose basement she had claimed as a place of refuge. And the white cat that had led her to it.

Pita hadn't been to the basement in—how long? Nearly three days. She leaned her head against the cool window glass, staring down into the city and trying to collect her racing thoughts. Had the dream been a plea for help? Was the cat in trouble? Pita gnawed her lip. She hadn't even given the animal a name—she thought of it only as Aziz's cat. But she had to know if it was all right.

She briefly considered waking up Masaki and asking him to drive her downtown. But his bedroom door was closed, and his boyfriend had spent the night. Pita didn't want to just walk in on them. Besides, she didn't need the reporter's help.

Her mind made up, she picked up her jacket from the floor. She reached into its pocket, then grinned as she pulled out a certified credstick. She hadn't trusted Aziz—not entirely—and so she'd made Masaki take her to the Salish Credit Union yesterday. She'd closed the bank account he set up for her there and transferred all the nuyen into this credit stick. Just let Aziz try and take his money back now.

Slipping the credstick back in her pocket, she went to the kitchen and took a couple of Chickstix from the fridge. The processed chicken sausages were frozen, but would thaw by the time she was downtown. Even if Aziz's cat weren't in trouble, it would be hungry.

Pita called for a cab, then went to the lobby to wait for it. When the vehicle pulled up to the front of the building, she cast a wary eye about before leaving the apartment complex. She also took a good look inside the cab before getting in. There was no one but the driver, a bored-looking ork woman who seemed harmless enough. When she saw Pita, the cabbie gave her a toothy grin, then turned up the Meta Madness tape she was listening to.

"Hoi, kid! You goin' to the concert tomorrow night?" she asked. She drummed her fingers on the wheel as she drove, keeping time with the screamrock's frantic beat.

"Maybe," Pita shrugged. "I don't know." With all that had happened to her in the past two weeks, it was difficult to think about such mundane affairs as rock concerts.

"Yeah, I know how it is," the cabbie replied. "It's bad enough that the tickets are fifty nuyen a pop, but then you have to add the service fee of thirty nuyen. And you know why? It's 'cause humans control both the ticketing agencies and the clubs. You don't find that kind of fee tacked on to a concert given by a human rock band. Those fraggers are trying to make out like us orks do more damage to a venue. No way. Why, it's the humans who cause the most trouble. I had two humie kids in my cab last night who . . ."

Pita glanced out the window, not really listening to the cab driver's harangue. But at the same time, she smiled. The driver had accepted her unconditionally as a fellow ork. Just as Masaki's boyfriend Blake had.

Pita had watched the sports network with the two over a beer last night, and Blake had avidly debated Masaki about Japan's decision to ban metahumans from the Olympic games in 2056. When Masaki carefully pointed out that orks and trolls had an obvious physical advantage over the weaker elf and human races, and that short-statured dwarfs could hardly compete in the same track and field events as longerlimbed opponents, Blake had nudged Pita with an elbow. "Back me up, kid," he said. "We orks have got to stick together on this one."

Pita liked the way Blake and Masaki bantered back

and forth. They obviously disagreed on the topic, but didn't let it get in the way of their relationship. It was certainly a contrast with her own parents, who, even though they were both human, had spent most of their time screaming at each other.

At last the cab pulled up around the corner from Aziz's burned-out shop, near the alley that the cat had led Pita to. Pita slotted her credstick and keyed in a tip for the driver, then scanned the street. It was light out now, although the sun hadn't fully risen. But the streets were still empty of pedestrians, and only the occasional car drove by. It seemed safe enough.

"I'm just going to look for my cat," she told the driver. "I lost it here a few days ago."

"You want me to wait?" the cabbie asked.

Pita toyed with the credstick. What the hey; she was rich. "Sure," she said. "If I can't find the cat I'll come back and let you know. I'll be going back to the address where you picked me up."

Cracking the door, Pita stepped from the cab and hurried to the mouth of the alley. She paused at the broken window that led to the basement, and inspected it closely. It didn't look as though anyone had touched it—the mesh was still propped up the way she'd left it. And the basement room beyond it looked the same.

She reached inside and opened the window, then slithered in through the opening. As soon as her feet hit the dusty floor, she heard a friendly *mrrow?* A wave of relief swept over her as the white cat emerged from behind a box, jumped to the floor, and wove a figure-eight pattern around her legs.

Pita scooped it up in her arms, nuzzling its fur. The cat was dusty—and skinny—but otherwise seemed all right. Pita placed it on the floor, pulled the now-soggy Chickstix from her pocket, and fed them to the cat. She scratched it behind the ears while it ate, and was rewarded with a loud purr.

"You like that, hey, cat? Bet you were hungry, huh? Well you're coming with me, back to a place where there's plenty more of those. No more scrounging on the streets for you. This place is okay, but we've got something better now. At least, for a while, until Masaki decides to heave us out. Aziz might have left you on the streets, but not me. You can trust me. Nothing bad is going to happen to you now."

When the cat had finished eating, Pita picked it up and put it outside the window. Then she climbed back into the alley. She bent down to pick up the cat . . .

And found that she couldn't move. Then she was straightening, her body jerking suddenly into an upright position. One of her legs shot forward, then the other. They moved stiffly, one foot following the other in a jerking walk. Her arms were bent at the elbow, frozen in the position they'd been in when she was about to pick up the cat. She couldn't even move her fingers—could barely blink. It felt as though she were a cartoon character in a trideo arcade, controlled by unseen hands on a clumsy keyboard console. Her mind raced as she fought to control her limbs, but they were no longer obeying her commands.

What was happening to her? Panic swirled in Pita's mind as she realized that her body was taking her further into the alley, away from the spot where the cabbie waited. The white cat trotted along beside her, *mrrowing* with concern. When it stepped into Pita's path, one of her feet knocked it aside as her body moved relentlessly forward. The cat howled in anger and ran away, a white streak that disappeared somewhere behind Pita.

Then Pita saw the man who waited for her at the end of the alley—a dreadlocked elf in a baggy jumpsuit. One hand was balled into a fist, except for two fingers. He walked these through the air, and each time a finger took a step, Pita's legs moved. The glow sticks woven into his dreadlocks haloed his sly smile.

Pita fought even harder as she recognized the mage—and the burly yakuza sitting behind the wheel of the car toward which the mage was forcing her to walk. But even though sweat trickled down her temples and her mind ached from the strain, she was unable to pull free of the spell. As the yakuza hit a button on the dash that opened the rear door of the vehicle, Pita felt her body fold. Against her will it got into the back of the car. She winced inwardly as her head bumped against the door frame, and heard the yakuza's rumbling growl through the perforated plexiglass sheet that separated the front and back seats of the vehicle.

"Watch out, R.T. We're not to damage her."

The elf made a face at the yak, then slammed the door shut behind Pita.

Immediately, she was back in control of her own body. It spasmed in reaction to the adrenaline that was suddenly pumping through it. She scrabbled at the door, but there was no inside handle. Driven by fear, she pounded at the plexiglass that caged her in with one large fist. The yakuza ignored her, instead starting the engine as the elf climbed into the front seat beside him.

"Where are you taking me?" Pita screamed. "Let me out! I don't have your fragging chip any more!"

The mage stared at her and his dark eyes flared. "Be quiet," he hissed. "I may not be permitted to damage you, but I can still hurt you." He raised a hand menacingly, his fingers curled to cast a spell.

Pita fell silent and tried to blink back tears as the car sped away into the morning.

28

Carla stepped into the plush office and automatically panned the room with her cybereye, lining up an establishing the shot. Then she caught herself. There was no point. Mitsuhama's security had forced her to remove the image-storage chip from the camera implanted in her cybereye. The eye still functioned, but the data it captured was not being recorded anywhere. Security had also removed the datachip from the recorder in her ear. They didn't want Carla to make any record of this meeting.

Trying to hide her discomfort, she made her way to a chair that had been placed in front of a massive hardwood desk and sank into it. On the other side of the desk sat John Chang. His fingers rested lightly on the desk's polished surface, and he looked completely composed and serene. He was a lean man, with jet black hair, manicured fingernails, and a clean-shaven jaw. He looked as if he worked out, but perhaps that was just the cut of his expensive Volachi suit. His right index finger was decorated with a heavy gold ring that featured a large diamond set into the Mitsuhama logo, and his sleek wristcom was gold-plated. The smell of his aftershave hung in the air.

He regarded Carla coolly, with rock-steady eyes. As she settled herself more comfortably in the chair, he flicked a finger toward the secretary who had ushered Carla in. The woman returned with two cups of tea, bobbed her head in an abbreviated bow as she served them, and left the room.

Carla picked up the tea and sipped at it. Jasmine. Chang was playing a waiting game, trying to set her on edge. Instead Carla half-turned, looking past the holographic models of Mitsuhama's latest robotics line and through the windows that framed a spectacular view of Lake Washington. The sky was a patchwork of clouds; the sun slanted through the blue spaces between them, painting the lake below with light. Carla stared at the unusual effect, wondering where the spirit was now.

John Chang cleared his throat. He was obviously ready to talk.

"Your producer has informed you of MCT's most recent acquisition."

It was a statement rather than a question. Carla nodded slowly, watching Chang's face. He still hadn't touched his tea. A wild, irrational thought flew through her mind—maybe the stuff was drugged. But she shook it off. She had already entered the lion's den and Chang had her at his mercy. There was no need for him to get heavy-handed. Not now that he had those optical chips.

"MCT Seattle will be issuing a brief press release about the purchase of KKRU shortly. Mitsuhama is pleased to get into the local communications industry. It will give our company an opportunity to test some of the new trideo technologies we've been developing. It's a move we've been planning to make for some time."

"Sure," Carla said. "If you say so." Her reporter's training screamed at her to directly challenge this bald lie, but she held her tongue, wanting to see what would come next. She found herself framing Chang, zooming in and out, even though the effort would prove fruitless without her datachips.

"There is a second press release we want to issue," he said, at last picking up his tea cup and sipping from it. "We'd like to use our latest acquisition—KKRU News—to turn it into a news story. I've seen your work; it's excellent. I'll be asking Gil Greer to assign you to handle it."

Carla wrinkled her nose. "I don't write puff pieces," she said. "If all you want is a press release, why call on me? Any data hack could do it. What do you really want?"

John Chang's smile vanished. Clearly he was not used to being spoken to so abruptly. He sat forward slightly.

"Since this is an off-the-record conversation," he said, raising a finger to tap one closed eye, "I will be blunt. I am aware of the story that you recently put together—the one alleging connections between our research facility and the spirit causing system crashes in the Matrix."

Carla snorted. Alleged indeed! Even with her cyber-eye chip removed, Chang was still being cautious. "The story that you ordered Greer to spike?"

Chang ignored her barb. "We'd like you to put a slight spin on the story," he continued. "We're willing to concede that the spirit was developed by a mage who was formerly in our employ. But his research was not sanctioned by MCT. You will re-edit the story so that it stresses this fact."

"You and I both know otherwise," Carla said. "I saw the hermetic circle in your research lab. And the memo that—"

"Both could have been fabricated," Chang said smoothly. He cocked an eyebrow at her. "It all comes down to your personal credibility, doesn't it? And we've both *seen* how fragile that credibility can be."

Carla felt her cheeks start to burn. The bastard had probably enjoyed watching her personal recordings. But she wasn't going to lose her cool. Not yet.

"You do want to continue working as a trid reporter, don't you?" Chang asked.

Carla decided to use the only edge she had. "I have information from a well-placed source that Renraku—your competitor—has stolen your spell and is experimenting with it." She watched for a reaction, but wasn't really surprised when she didn't get one. She pressed on. "You can keep a lid on your own researchers, but not on the competition. Sooner or later—especially if Renraku's experiments also start chewing up the Matrix—the Crash of 2029 will repeat itself.

When it does, nothing can stop the story from getting out. If I don't cover it, some other reporter will. And when they do, they'll trace the original spirit that started it all right back to Mitsuhama."

"Back to Farazad Samji, you mean," John Chang said in a soft voice. "Thanks to the story you're going to do."

He pulled a datachip out of a drawer and slid it across the desk toward Carla. "On this chip you will find a joint statement by myself and Dr. Vanessa Cliber, director of computer operations for the Renraku Arcology. In it, we announce that we have at last discovered the cause of the virus that is currently infecting certain nodes of the Matrix: a spirit, conjured up, regrettably enough, by one of Mitsuhama's former employees."

Carla picked up the disk and turned it over in her fingers.

"The mage was working on a private research project during a leave of absence," Chang continued. "A project that MCT Seattle did not officially sanction. Only when the spirit became free and killed him—and then began attacking the Matrix—did our corporation begin examining the spell that Dr. Samji had created. Because this was a task of such grave public importance, we brought in experts from around the world to work on the project—even those employed by our chief rival, Renraku Computer Systems. It was simply imperative that we find a way to bring the spirit back under control and force it to stay out of the Matrix. And so the two corporations have pooled their personnel and resources in an unprecedented effort to eliminate this threat to the world's computer and telecommunications systems by banishing the spirit."

"So that's what you want me to do," Carla cut him off. "Paint Farazad Samji as the bad guy, and MCT and Renraku as the crusading knights, riding in to clean up the 'unsanctioned' mess he made. Well, it's not going to fly. You're going to wind up looking foolish."

She knew Chang was lying to her. Mitsuhama might try to tell Renraku that they were banishing the spirit, but she was certain the corporation would try to control it instead. If not as a magical means of accessing the Matrix, then as a parabiological weapon. She tried a lie of her own: "Nobody can control that free spirit. You'll be making false promises to the public—and they'll be angry when it turns out you aren't able to keep those promises."

"That's where you're wrong," Chang answered. His leather chair creaked as he sat back in it. "We now have someone on staff who knows the free spirit's true name—and that's all we need to control it. By the time that press release airs on the evening newscast, the spirit will be out of the Matrix. We've found a mage who can do the job."

Things were starting to click into place. "Aziz Fader?" Carla asked. It made sense. The mage had obviously gotten the true name from Pita and used it to bind the spirit. He'd used it to kill the hell hound in a blaze of light. Now, presumably, he was going to hand over the true name in return for whatever goodies MCT Director Ambrose Wilks had promised him. Aziz had probably gotten in touch with the corporation as soon as his efforts had proven successful—and been kept busy in their lab ever since. That would explain why he hadn't returned her calls.

Was that a hint of amusement in Chang's eyes? He shook his head. "No. Not Mr. Fader," he answered. "An . . . associate of his. She will be working with our own researchers. And those from Renraku, of course."

Carla felt a growing sense of dread. "She"? Chang could only be referring to one person. But that was impossible. Carla had spoken to Masaki less than two hours ago, when he phoned in sick, and he'd said the ork girl was safely tucked away in his apartment. Was Masaki in on the deal, too? Carla swallowed her anger and forced herself to think logically. No. It was more likely that Mitsuhama had forced Masaki to lie. She couldn't even imagine what they'd used to blackmail him. Maybe the threat of violence. Once again, her imagination started to churn out unpleasant images.

Was Masaki face-down on the floor of his apartment, even now, a bullet in his brain?

"The girl is safe," Chang said, obviously reading Carla's expression. "She's much too valuable an asset to damage, although your co-worker doesn't realize that. He, too, is unharmed."

Carla felt a rush of relief. That was one worry down. Masaki was safe. She was surprised at how much she cared about the timid old fragger. And about the girl.

She shook her head. Caring what happened to Pita was logical—the girl was, after all, still Carla's only chance at a big story. Not on Mitsuhama, but on the racist elements within Lone Star. It was one story that Carla's new masters—especially with Chang's yakuza connections—wouldn't try to spike. It was also a story that would make NABS take notice of Carla—and get her out from under the thumb of this smooth-talking fragger.

But Carla wasn't thinking about that now. Or at least, it wasn't the only thing she was thinking about. Pita might be "safe," but she was probably also terrified. Especially if Mitsuhama was holding her. She was probably every bit as frightened as Carla had been when the hell hound stood on top of her, teeth bared and ready to strike. Carla felt a twinge of sympathy and wished there was something she could do for the girl.

Perhaps there was.

"I'll wrap a news story around your press release," she told Chang. "I'll make it the best you've ever seen, and will vilify Farazad Samji as much as you like. On one . . . no, on two conditions. First, that you remove that foul little spirit from Mrs. Samji's home and agree not to persecute her further—by withholding her husband's pension, for example."

"It's already done," Chang answered. "We at MCT Seattle are not entirely heartless, after all. The Samjis will be provided for, despite the harm that Farazad has caused. It's simply good corporate public relations."

"And second, that I be allowed to talk with Pita."

"I do not think that will be possible," Chang began.

"Listen," Carla said, leaning forward and using her

firmest voice. "You need me. You own KKRU now, and could hire any of the reporters there to put together your news story. But I'm the station's top investigative reporter, and the public knows it. If I commit to this piece, I can't go back on it later and say it was all a lie. It would ruin my credibility—just as surely as the recordings on those chips would.

"Let me see Pita, or I won't do your dirty work for you."

Chang sighed, exchanging his polite mask for a weary frown. "We really do wish to bring the spirit to heel, Ms. Harris. It has the potential to become an enormous economic liability to us. It is completely unsuited for the task for which it was originally conjured. If Wilks had listened to his researchers, all of this unpleasantness might have been avoided. He's just lucky that he came up with that trideo footage in time, proving that the spirit could be controlled. Otherwise . . ."

"What trideo footage?" Carla asked.

"The shots that Mr. Fader took of himself, calling the spirit. He tried to pretend that he had bound the spirit to himself, and that his little demonstration in the Chrysanthemum Tower had been entirely his own work. But he did a clumsy job of editing the girl—Pita—out of the footage he shot as 'proof' of his power over the spirit. Our deckers were able to salvage pictures of her from an unwiped memory sector, and we determined that she was the one we really wanted. It was then just a matter of using the right lure and picking her up. And once again, I assure you that she is unharmed."

Carla blinked. Pita was the one who'd sent the spirit to kill the hell hound? But Aziz had said . . . No. Aziz had lied to her, all along. He'd sold the kid out—and now he'd been cut out of the loop. Mitsuhama had probably paid him a small finder's fee for the girl, then sent him on his way.

"I still insist upon seeing Pita," she said. She forced a smile. "What harm could it do? If she really is safe."

Chang sighed. He considered for a moment before

answering. "Very well," he said at last. "It might prove useful, after all. She's somewhat . . . reluctant . . . to assist us. Perhaps you can talk her into it."

He gave Carla a stern look. "If you try any tricks, it will be your credibility on the line—and on the air. Just keep that in mind when you talk to her."

29

Pita sat on a padded chair, gripping its cushioned arms. She could smell the plastic hood that was wrapped tightly around her head and face, and the lingering perfume of one of the people who had come in to the room earlier. And she could feel the warm stream of air from a heat vent overhead. But otherwise, her senses were completely blocked. The hood covered her eyes, and soft pads over her ears delivered a steady white-noise hiss. The sound made it impossible to think, let alone hear anything.

This must be the magemask that the other prisoners had warned her about, back when Pita had been in jail. She could see now why the cops used it. She felt completely disoriented, cut off. There was no way she could call to Cat, or hear Cat's comforting purr. Her world had shrunk to a few tactile sensations and a dark, static hiss.

They hadn't tied her up this time. They'd simply hustled her into this office, put the hood on her head, and shut the door. She'd explored the room by feel, gradually navigating her way around its table, chair, and couch, and trying the locked door. She'd even tried to remove the hood—only to find that each time she tugged on it, the static in her ears cranked up suddenly, making her dizzy and weak. If she let it alone, the sound returned to a bearable level. And so she sat in the empty room, trying to calm her breathing and slow her racing heart.

She didn't know where she was, but she could guess. They'd driven across the Intercity 90 bridge to Bellevue, then to a two-story building whose walls were completely covered in ivy. She'd been hustled in past some heavy-duty security at the front door, through a series of hallways, and past a large room whose floor and walls were covered in strange symbols. This had to be a magical research laboratory of some sort. One owned by Mitsuhama, the corporation whose goons had been on her case since the beginning of this thing.

From time to time, people came into the room. They would turn down the noise generated by the hood and fire questions at Pita. They seemed to know everything that had happened the night before last. About how Aziz had attracted the attention of the spirit, and how Pita had directed its actions. They were even able to describe the motions the two had gone through and the hermetic circle in the abandoned convenience store. They'd found the burned hell hound in the Mitsuhama office tower, and had figured out that Pita had ordered the spirit to do the job. Odd, how they kept referring to this as a "demonstration" rather than the rescue mission it had actually been.

But the people questioning Pita didn't seem to understand exactly how she had used the spirit's true name—despite the fact that they knew it was burned into her arm. Hell, that was something Pita herself didn't understand. Somehow, she had watched as the spirit flashed its way across the city, and had directed it against the cops who had killed her friends. But she certainly wasn't going to volunteer that information. Not to the mages who kept questioning her. She was in a tight enough spot as it was, without admitting to assaulting two cops.

The mages wanted her to summon the spirit and give it a different command this time. She was to order it to stay away from the Matrix. But even if Pita had the guts to face the spirit again, she wasn't sure she would be able to do what the corporate suits wanted. The Matrix was a complicated thing for someone like her— a high school drop-out—to describe. All she knew was that it was a bunch of computers that were somehow linked to one another; she'd flunked out of Basic Tech and didn't even really understand how a telecom worked. But no matter how many times she tried to tell them this, they weren't willing to listen. They wanted her to do it right now, today, as soon as possible. And they promised her that if she tried to turn the spirit against them, she'd be dead. No matter how many of its employees she fried, Mitsuhama would get her in the end. The corporation was huge, with connections in every city and plenty of magic and money to back it up. Cross Mitsuhama, and she'd be dead meat. She could count on it.

Pita lifted her head as the door opened. She knew better than to charge toward the doorway; the last time she'd tried, a pair of thick arms had wrapped around her, forcing her back into the chair. Then her nose caught a whiff of perfume. Where had she smelled that fragrance before?

Hands fumbled at the plastic hood that covered her face. The white noise died away, and then the hood was tugged free. Pita blinked, unable to focus in the brightly lit room. Footsteps receded, and the door clicked shut. But someone was still in the room with her.

"Pita? Are you all right?"

Pita gasped as she recognized the person. "Carla!" she croaked. "What are you doing here? Did they capture you too?"

The reporter crossed the room and sat down in the chair next to Pita's. She didn't look as though anyone had roughed her up. Her tailored jacket and skirt were unwrinkled, and her dark hair was held back in a neat braid. Her makeup hadn't even smudged, and her face held a composed smile. But that was hardly unusual. The only time Pita had seen Carla looking even slightly flustered was after the yaks had gunned Yao down and were chasing after Masaki's car. And even then her clothes hadn't been mussed. At least, not much.

"I'm here because I asked to see you, Pita," Carla said. "I wanted to talk to you."

Pita squinted at the reporter. The glare of light from the white walls still hurt her eyes. She was finding it difficult to concentrate, but the reporter didn't resist

her and she was able to insert a catlike claw and tease
out what was uppermost in Carla's thoughts. What she
found there startled and angered her. "So you're
working for Mitsuhama now, huh? Then why the frag
should I talk to you?"

Carla caught her breath. "How did you—?" Then the
corners of her mouth turned down. "It's true I'm
working for them," she answered. "But not willingly.
And I really did come here to make sure you're all
right."

She was telling the truth. Pita retracted her mental
claw from Carla's mind. "But you can't do anything
for me." She scuffed the toe of her running shoe
against the floor. "No one can. I'm stuck here until I do
what they want—until I talk to that fragging spirit
again. They don't care drek about me—just about what
I can do for them. And if I agree, they'll only kill me
when I'm done. When they don't need me any more."

Pita could see from Carla's expression that the
reporter didn't need to be convinced that Mitsuhama
saw people as disposable. The corporation's goons had
killed Yao, and his only crime was being in the wrong
place at the wrong time—standing in the way of something the corporation wanted back. And they'd burned
down Aziz's shop without a second thought. The only
reason they were keeping Pita alive was because she
was valuable to them. Or at least her arm was, anyway.

She stifled the urge to scratch the burn. The mages
who had talked to her seemed to be convinced that only
she could "read" the true name that had been seared into
her flesh. But if she stalled too long and they figured
out how to decipher that code themselves, they might
decide that everything but her arm was expandable . . .

"Pita, listen to me."

Pita returned her attention to the reporter.

"Mitsuhama doesn't just want the spirit kept out of the
Matrix," Carla said. "They'll want to do more research
on it. And that means they have to keep you alive. You're
the only one who can control the thing. You're the one in
charge of it. And Mitsuhama knows that.

"Listen," she said, leaning closer. "I know they've

treated you badly—I saw the magemask you were
wearing when I came in. They've tried the stick
approach so far, but I've persuaded them that the carrot
is more effective. They're willing to pay you thirty
thousand nuyen if you cooperate. And to release you
afterward."

Pita looked up. Thirty-K nuyen? That was as much as
her father made in a year. She'd be rich! She'd have her
own apartment, nice clothes, maybe buy a car . . . But
then reality set in. The corporation had done nothing but
manhandle and bully her so far. Why the frag should
they actually pay her, once they got what they wanted?
And what else would they make her do with the spirit?
Probably force her to use it to kill. The one taste Pita had
of that power had been enough. She hadn't been able to
smell the cops' skin crisping as the spirit licked across
their bodies, but she'd seen the terror in their eyes. It
was hard enough to do that to someone she hated, never
mind geeking some innocent person. She didn't want
any part of that deal. At any price.

"Do you really believe they'll give me the money
and then just let me go?" she asked Carla.

"Of course," the reporter answered. But her head
moved a fraction of a centimeter to the left and right.
The body language in the head shake was clear. The
real answer was no. "And in the meantime, I'll be
working on your behalf, keeping tabs on you. We still
have that story on Lone Star to do, after all."

Pita sat for a moment, thinking. Was there no way
out? She stared at the reporter, watching as the pupil of
Carla's cybereye dilated and contracted independently
of her real eye. At first she was angry at the thought of
the reporter shooting trideo of her without her permission. Even though they were pirate broadcasters, the
guys at *Orks First!* had been up-front about the fact
that they were shooting trid. Anwar's bulky, antiquated
camera had been especially hard to miss. Pita wondered where he was now. And then, all at once, she saw
a way out.

"Tell Mitsuhama that I'll do it," she said carefully.

"I'll control the spirit and give it new commands. But only if it's covered—live—by *Orks First!* trideo."

A grin was growing on Carla's face. "A live trideo broadcast? That's good. Now you're thinking like a reporter, kid. They won't dare continue to hold you here against your will—not while the cameras are rolling. And we'll keep the live broadcast going until you're out of here and have reached somewhere safe."

Safe. Pita mulled the word over. Would she ever really be safe? She was just one kid up against a huge corporation. But at least she could buy herself some breathing time. And some temporary freedom. All she had to do was confront an immensely powerful magical creature and explain a concept to it that she herself didn't really understand. Piece of cake.

"Is there anything you want?" Carla asked. "Anything I can get you?"

"Yeah," Pita answered. "Tell those yak fraggers not to put that hood back on me. And tell them I'm hungry. I want a sushi burger, some deep-fried noodles, a Growlie bar, a can of Fizz, a medium Wide Wedge pizza with everything, some . . ."

"Slow down!" Carla said. "I'm sure they'll bring you whatever you like, once you've agreed to cooperate. But first you'd better tell me how to get in touch with *Orks First!*"

30

The *Orks First!* pirate adjusted his tripod-mounted portacam and peered through the range finder. Anwar was
wearing jeans and a fringed Tribal Wear shirt, and had
a red scarf knotted around his head. He even had an eye
patch. It was a dull silver, rather than the traditional
black pirate patch, and full of electronics. While his
portacam was rolling, it would provide him with a
direct feed, showing exactly what the camera was cap-
turing. Pita couldn't image how he could watch both it
and the real world at the same time and not be disoriented and stumble about. But the double vision didn't
seem to bother him in the least, even though the equipment was brand new and he must still be getting used
to it.

Anwar stepped in front of the camera and touched
the audio feed in his ear. "Hoi Alfonz! You gettin' a
feed? Give me a code-blue signal if it's comin'
through."

After listening for a moment, he waved a hand to
catch the attention of those who had gathered in the
room. "Okay," he told them. "I'm set. We can start
any time you like." He turned to address the Mitsuhama and Renraku executives directly. "Just one
warning. I'll know if you break the patch to the
KKRU transmitter. If I don't get a steady feed of
codes from my ah . . . associates . . . I'll know the
broadcast has gone off the air or has been tampered
with. So no funny stuff, huh? We want this livecast to
go smoothly."

Pita stood between two suits, shuffling her feet
uncomfortably. A cluster of executives had been

assembled in the research lab where the spellcasting would take place. Behind them, mages put the finishing touches on the hermetic circle, placing the elements in their positions and making sure the lines were intact.

One of the executives—a slender Asian fellow with a gold ring and wristcom—nodded at the ork reporter. "We too will have associates watching the broadcast. If the voice masking slips and reveals any copyrightable spell material, we'll pull the plug."

"Agreed," the ork rumbled. Then he turned to the mages. "Ready?"

They nodded, and he raised his microphone. It looked slender as a twig in the ork's massive hand. He turned to face the camera as a red light winked on.

"This is Anwar Ingram, comin' at you live from the Mitsuhama Computer Technologies secondary research laboratory in Bellevue. We're here today with an exclusive *Orks First!* interview with a young ork by the name of Patti Dewar. This previously unknown magical talent has been chosen to head up a joint magical experiment by MCT Seattle and Renraku Computer Technologies.

"You've probably already seen the story that KKRU's Carla Harris aired earlier today, about the plans by these two corporations to stop a renegade spirit that has used its energies to cause damage to the Matrix by shutting down systems and wiping data left and right. Now *Orks First!* brings you the dramatic fruits of this labor—live! For the first time ever on trideo, you'll see the spirit that has been wreaking havoc all over the city. Not only that, but at the conclusion of the spellcasting we'll follow Patti to the Street Savers shelter for street kids, where she will be turning over to the charity the 30,000 nuyen fee she is being paid for today's magical services, and where she'll be working over the next few months to ensure that this credit is properly spent."

Yeah, Pita thought. *Spent on me.* The "donation" to the shelter was just a means of ensuring that the corp actually paid out what it had promised. Mitsuhama would look bad, if they stiffed a charity. Once the nuyen was transferred to Street Savers, a friend of Anwar's who worked at the shelter would place it in an account that Pita could draw upon. The five thousand nuyen she'd have to leave untouched in the account would be a small price to pay for his help.

The pirate newscaster paused to listen to his audio feed, then stepped behind Pita and the suits. He laid a hand on the shoulder of one of the executives, an Asian man with an air of strained dignity—which strained even further as Anwar's grimy hand crinkled his expensively tailored jacket.

"This is John Chang, vice president of MCT UCAS and president of MCT Seattle. He's agreed to accompany Patti to the shelter and help her make the presentation."

Pita nodded to herself. That was good. With the suit coming along for the ride, nobody would dare try to kill her on her way to the shelter.

"I have?" Chang's eyes widened. But he recovered quickly and smiled broadly at the portacam. "Yes. That's right. I'll be pleased to make the donation on behalf of Mitsuhama Computer Technologies."

The pirate shifted his hand to an equally uncomfortable-looking executive who stood on the other side of Pita, a man with thinning gray hair and a pompous expression. "And this is Donald Acres, project manager of the Renraku Arcology. Like Mr. Chang, he's agreed to join Patti in making the presentation at Street Savers. Renraku has pledged to meet Mitsuhama's donation with one of its own, and will also be contributing thirty thousand nuyen to the shelter."

Pita looked up. This was something new. She didn't know who had thought of doubling the payout—but it was brilliant.

Acres' eyes narrowed in what was almost a wince. But he recovered as quickly as Chang had. "I'd be pleased to," he said, albeit a little stiffly.

Anwar squatted in front of Pita and held the microphone up for her to speak. "I'm sure Patti would like to thank both corporations for their generosity. Isn't that right, Patti?"

Pita stammered a little, then smiled widely, for once not ashamed of her oversized canines. "I'm very happy to have this opportunity to help Street Savers, Anwar," she said, playing along. "And to work for a charity that really helps kids like me. You can come and interview me at the shelter. To see how I'm doing."

"That I will, Patti," the pirate chuckled. "I'm sure everybody in the Underground will watch your progress avidly. You're a celebrity, as of tonight."

Anwar motioned the executives to one side, then did a voice-over while the mages put the finishing touches on the hermetic circle that would form a protective barrier around them while they helped her to summon the spirit. While the executives and other observers scurried into another room to watch through a thick, warded glass window, the mages showed Pita where to sit. Anwar continued his monologue, reiterating Carla's earlier story about how the spirit was using its energy to tear gaping holes in the programming of the Matrix. But instead of dwelling on how wonderful it was that the two corps were pooling their resources to fight the thing, he focused on Pita's role in what was about to unfold.

It was embarrassing, really. And a little hard to believe. Pita would be a celebrity once this was over. Assuming it worked. The corporations were taking a big gamble. What if she couldn't do it? She licked dry lips and tried to calm the fluttering in her stomach as technicians attached bio monitors to her temples, upper left chest, and wrists. Additional sensors were attached to her arm beside the burn mark, and then all was ready.

Three of the mages positioned themselves at the center of the circle. They sat cross-legged, holding hands in a ring around Pita. One was a young Asian elf with a crew cut and a suit that hung sloppily on his lank frame, as if he had dressed up in his father's clothes. The other two were a blonde

human woman in a white lab coat with a bright red
Mitsuhama logo over the pocket, and a Native American in a beaded leather jacket with the words "Renraku: Interface With the Best" emblazoned across the
back.

The Amerind smiled at Pita reassuringly. "Null perspiration, kid," he whispered. "Nothing to worry
about." Then he, like the other two mages, snuggled
welder's goggles over his eyes.

Pita glanced at Anwar, who was using a remote to
lower his auto-adjust tripod. The round glass eye of the
lens seemed to be staring at Pita, boring into her
thoughts. She closed her eyes, shutting it out and concentrating. The three mages had spent the afternoon
with her, running over the steps of the spell, discussing
the wording of the command Pita would give the spirit
when it arrived. She toyed with the idea of probing
their thoughts, to make sure they hadn't left anything
out. But she was afraid that she would find that they
were as nervous as she was.

As the mages began their chant, something soft and
warm settled on Pita's lap. She opened her eyes,
startled, and saw that her lap was empty. Yet if she
reached down, brushed lightly with her fingertips
against the air, she could feel the soft fur of a cat.
Closing her eyes again, she stroked the air—and was
rewarded with a vibration that set her fingertips tin-
gling. In her mind's eye she saw a rainbow-colored
cat sitting in her lap, gazing up at her with glittering
eyes of gold.

Pita concentrated on the feel of the radiant fur
beneath her fingers, and focused on Cat's throbbing
purr. It flowed up from her fingertips and along
her arm, then into her chest. From there it radiated outward until her entire body was softly vibrating.

"I'm ready," she said.

"Begin," a voice beside her urged.

Pita raised her arm, concentrating on the patch of red
where the spirit had burned its true name. She felt the
hairs there rise, and the skin begin to warm. She pic-

tured her arm as a cyberdeck screen, flashing a single word over and over again: "Come. Come. Come." At the same time, her lips parted. A word was on her tongue—a word she could neither pronounce nor understand. A name.

Slowly, the room began to brighten, and Pita felt a warmth on her head and arms. She turned her closed eyes toward it, savoring the spirit's presence like summer sunlight. Even Anwar's whispered, "Oh my God!" didn't faze her.

Now she could feel the heat intensifying, could see a bright whirl of light through her closed eyelids. The welder's goggles they'd given her hung about her neck, untouched. She didn't need to wear them, didn't need to open her eyes to see the spirit. Not when she and it were . . .

One.

This time, she felt no fear. Cat was close by, a warm presence in her lap. And the spirit was a familiar echo in her sluggish mortal mind. *Play?* it whispered in a voice as quick as a flash of sunlight on metal. It tugged at her, seeking direction.

Pita looked around her, saw only a vortex of spinning fragments of light. They spread in an infinitely wide rainbow, shading from a deep violet that she felt more as a hum than a color, to an intense crimson that blazed with heat. Individual photons spun crazy spirals around her, cutting the air like brilliant dervishes. She was captivated by their beauty, swept up in their dance. The spirit seemed to be trying to tell her something, trying to communicate. Its words rushed past at a frantic pace that no mortal mind could comprehend. If only she could understand its message, Pita knew that she would be conveyed to the source of all light, the source of all . . .

Her brain sluggishly sent out a signal that—had nanoseconds not been crawling along like seconds—would have caused her to shake her head.

She struggled to form a word-thought. Not the convoluted command that the mages had instructed her to give, but a single message: *Go.*

The spirit paused for a nanosecond, then blazed brightly with anger. *No. Stay. Play.*

Pita felt a wash of horror as she realized what she'd done. When she'd controlled the spirit before, she'd been responding to the call of her totem. Like a cat playing with its prey, she'd directed the spirit to use its destructive energies against the cops. It had enjoyed the experience, and now wanted to repeat it. And it didn't care who the target was. Pita had unleashed a monster—one that would strike out at the innocent, as well as the guilty.

She tried again. *Leave.*

The burn on her arm began to throb in time with the light that strobed overhead. The sensation drew Pita back toward her body, back toward herself. The spirit flared with laughter, tilted and spun . . .

The purring. Concentrate on the purring. Centering herself, wrapping her will around the calm place that Cat had created for her, Pita lashed out. She raked the spirit with claws, tore at it with her teeth. Her hair was on end, was on fire, but she didn't care. She used the throbbing in her arm, blending anger with calm, blending hot fire with icy determination. Summoning every ounce of her will, she screamed at the thing one last time: *GO HOME!*

Something snapped.

Pita fell into her body from an impossible height. Down, down into darkness. When she opened her eyes, the laboratory was in utter darkness, except for a tiny red eye that stared at her. Then the portacam's autolight came on, washing Pita with a beam of light. She threw up her arm to shield her eyes—and saw that her skin was whole. Healed. The pale pink scar of the spirit's burn had utterly vanished.

The room's lights came on then, and everyone started talking at once. Dimly, Pita was aware of the three mages leaping to their feet, of executives rushing into the room and congratulating them with slaps on the back and hearty handshakes. Anwar was standing somewhere beside her, talking excitedly into his microphone and helping Pita to her feet.

"It's too soon to tell yet, folks, if the spellcasting was successful," he touched the audio pickup in his ear, listening to it. "The reports are only just starting to come in from the deckers who are monitoring the Matrix. But you saw what happened here today, live on *Orks First!* trideo. The spirit is under control. And it took an ork to do it."

Pita murmured something in response to Anwar's questions, then staggered. She was bone weary; wrestling with the spirit had utterly drained her. When someone else reached out to steady her, she clasped the proffered arm. And looked up into the face of John Chang.

"Well?" he whispered, pulling her off to the side and out of camera range. "We saw you control the spirit. It responded beautifully. How did it react to the new commands?"

"I didn't give it those commands," Pita whispered back.

"What?" Donald Acres had also crowded close, and now was sputtering with rage.

"What do you mean you didn't—" He broke off as Anwar homed in, thrusting his microphone up to Pita's mouth.

"I banished it," Pita answered. "I sent the spirit home—wherever that might be. It's never coming back."

Chang's face went pale. "But that was the only . . . We weren't able to bind any of the other . . ." His hand clenched Pita's shirt. "You were supposed to—"

"Yes?" Anwar asked, shifting the microphone. "Is there anything you'd like to add, Mr. Chang?"

The executive shook his head, hid his discomfort with a smooth smile, then abruptly turned away.

The pirate broadcaster wrapped a heavy arm around Pita's shoulders and walked her toward the camera. Technicians scurried along after Pita, peeling off the sensors that had been attached to her skin.

"And now we'll take you to the Street Savers shelter," Anwar announced as he lifted the camera from its tripod and held it at arm's length. "I'll be broadcasting live all the way there as Patti tells us the story of how she came to learn the magical skills that enabled her to banish rogue spirits." He turned. "Mr. Acres? Mr. Chang? This way please."

He walked Pita toward the exit. Chang and Acres fumed as they followed the two orks out of the lab and into the street, occasionally turning their grimaces into a smile for the camera that Anwar was carrying. Surrounded by bodyguards, they climbed into sleek corporate vehicles.

Anwar helped Pita into the taxi that was waiting outside the research lab's door.

"Your friends have told me, Patti, that your talents are entirely self-taught. I understand that you're a cat shaman?"

Pita rubbed her throbbing temples, then noticed the driver of the taxi. It was the ork woman who had chatted with her—when? only this morning?—about the Meta Madness concert. The woman turned around and gave Pita a toothy grin.

"Hoi kid," she said. "I found your cat."

A white bundle of fur launched itself over the seat and into Pita's arms. Purring loudly, the cat nuzzled against Pita's chin, then sniffed at the shirt pocket where the Chickstix had been. One yellow and one blue eye peered up at her as the cat let out a questioning *mrrow?*

Pita stroked the animal, dumbfounded by the turn of events. What a coincidence that the taxi that had come to take her to Street Savers just happened to be driven by the woman she had met this morning! But then she started to mull it through. Even if the cabbie had found Aziz's cat, she wouldn't have driven around all day with the animal in her car. She'd have returned it to Masaki's address, and he would have contacted Carla, who would have . . .

She smiled at Anwar, who confirmed her suspicions with a wink. The lens of the portacam whirred as he shifted the camera to take in both Pita and the cat. "So," he said into the microphone. "Tell us about your cat. Do you use it to work your magic?"

Pita laughed. She was starting to understand how the news business worked.

31

Carla watched as Wayne put the finishing touches on the Lone Star story. Despite the fact that everyone she'd interviewed had been busy covering their own asses, the story drove one point home. Pita wasn't just some street-trash ork kid any more—she was the brilliant young shaman who had single-handedly driven the spirit from the Matrix. It didn't take a genius to realize that, had the cops gunned her down with the rest of her friends that night, the Crash of 2029 would have repeated itself, with devastating results to the world economy.

As a result of Pita's fame, offers were pouring in from Seattle ork families who wanted to offer her a home. There was even a handful of telecom messages from handsome young orks who saw Pita as their means of escaping the Underground, either as her personal bodyguard—or as her spouse. For now, however, Pita was still living at Masaki's. She said she liked it there—that she especially enjoyed talking with Blake, Masaki's burly oak partner. Carla snorted. She wouldn't be surprised if the two adopted Pita. It would do Masaki good—give him someone else to fuss and worry over.

Carla leaned over Wayne's shoulder and drew an imaginary box with her finger on the monitor. "Put the image of Pita describing what happened to her that night into a crop box here, and superimpose it over a slow pan of the street where the shootings occurred," she instructed. "Then we'll dissolve to the leaked ballistics report that matches of caliber of the slugs found in the bodies with the weapons inside the patrol car. Superimpose the graphics of the squad car's weaponry over it, and roll the lethality stats beside it."

Wayne nodded and went to work, cutting and pasting images with a digital stylus and manual commands entered via keyboard and palette-paste mouse. Carla watched as he cut to her interview with the two cops: Corporal Larry Torno, and Private Renny "Reno" Mellor. They looked pathetic, lying in hospital beds with their faces and hands bandaged and intravenous tubes feeding liquids into their arms. Their burns were officially caused by the crash of their patrol car, and the resulting fire. But that didn't explain the regular pattern of burn marks across their faces and hands, or how the burns had gone to third degree even though the vehicle's automatic extinguishing system had cut in immediately after the vehicle caught fire.

Carla didn't for one moment believe their claim that the accident had been caused by extremely bright headlights shining at point-blank range in through the squad car's tinted and glare-proof windshield. She knew what the real cause had been. But she hadn't used it in her story.

Both cops claimed to have been nowhere near the spot where the ork kids were gunned down, despite the fact that their on-board computer nav-log for that evening showed clear signs of tampering. Chief of Lone Star Police William Louden was denying any sort of Lone Star coverup, and was claiming that Torno and Mellor were the only "bad apples" on the force. When Carla asked whether any other Lone Star officers were involved in the murders of street kids he shut the interview down entirely. She had hoped that her story would prompt a full-scale investigation into racist elements within the police corporation. But that had obviously been a pipe dream.

Carla instructed Wayne to cut the officer's denials short with a dissolve to the gruesome file pictures of the kids who had been murdered that night. They deserved the air time. Not those lying Lone Star fraggers.

She followed the file footage with the interview she had done with the leader of Seattle's Humanis Policlub. At least she'd gotten him to admit that the cops were former members of the organization. But then he insisted that they had been tossed out of the group months ago for being "too radical," and that they had been acting on their own initiative. More ass covering.

Carla sighed. "Wrap the story with the comment by the Ork Rights Committee member who lost an eye in Friday's confrontation in front of Metroplex Hall," she instructed. "That should give Chief Louden something to answer for, at least."

As Wayne finished the piece by tagging on Carla's sign-off, Pita entered the editing booth. She hopped up on a table and watched as the completed story was replayed, swinging her feet. The white cat poked its head out of her jacket, where it had been hiding. The kid seemed to take the mangy little creature with her everywhere these days. The cat stared at the screen as if assessing the story, its mismatched eyes darting back and forth as images moved across the monitor.

"Well?" Carla asked, turning to the girl. "What do you think?"

The ork girl tilted her head to rub a cheek across the top of the cat's head. A contented purring filled the editing booth. Carla couldn't tell if it was coming from the cat—or the girl.

"We like it," Pita said softly. "It won't bring Chen and the others back, but maybe it'll stop some other kid from getting geeked."

Carla forced a smile. In the larger scheme of things, it seemed as if nothing had changed. Lone Star still had its quota of bad cops, the corporations were denying all responsibility for the spirit and instead reaping the rewards for having saved the Matrix from a repeat of the Crash of 2029, and Carla was stuck under Mitsuhama's thumb for the rest of her career.

But at least Pita had come out of this all right. One day, the kid would realize that the world was still just as tarnished as it ever had been. But for now—for today at the very least—the future looked shiny and new.

"Yeah, kid," Carla answered. "I hope so."

ABOUT THE AUTHOR

Lisa Smedman makes her living as a freelance game designer and fiction writer. She has designed numerous adventures for the Advanced Dungeons & Dragons game, primarily for the Ravenloft campaign world, and has done design work for several other game companies. Her short fiction has appeared in various magazines and anthologies. She previously worked as a magazine editor and newspaper reporter, and has fond memories of working a hard-news beat that included stories on train wrecks, murders, political scandals, and floods.

Smedman lives in Vancouver, B.C. with a small menagerie of felines. She has been an active member of that city's science fiction community for a number of years. She is also president of Bootstrap Press Inc., publishers of Adventures Unlimited gaming magazine.

The sound brushes her ears like a feather, like the haunting whisper of a breeze on a forlorn winter's night. Slipping through the mists of her sleeping mind like a phantom . . . a specter . . .

A single footfall, near-silent.

Very close.

Coming from just beyond the rice paper walls of her room. So subtle a sound it nearly eludes her notice. Yet, for one who has trained mind and body and spirit to remain alert, though she sleeps, this subtle sound is just clear enough, distinct enough.

She realizes what it portents even as she awakens. She has heard sounds like this before. She has spent whole months of her life listening for such sounds, learning their subtle codes and the Way of the people who make them. For even the smallest, most trifling of sounds might reveal the tread of an enemy, an assassin.

And tonight the sound she perceives, this faint, faint touch of a soft-soled shoe to *tatami* flooring, is the sound of one who does not belong.

Coming for her. Coming now.

As she opens her eyes she sees the intruder's seething heat signature through the veil of the rice paper wall beyond her feet.

The radiance shed by his flesh paints him clearly against the shadowed canvas of the night. He seems almost to smolder in a flickering aura of flames, like a demon, a fiery monstrosity of muscle and steel, bulky and broad and heavily cybered, now pausing just a step beyond the rice paper doors to her room.

She sees the impending assault in his posture. Her duty is clear, and she has only a moment to prepare.

She shifts her right hand across the lacquered *honoki*-wood that sheaths the katana lying over her stomach, the twining serpents of the steel *tsuba,* the sword's guard, and the fine-grained *same,* shark skin, wrapping the grip.

Then she breathes.

She settles her spirit.

And the killer comes.

He smashes the doors into fragments, bursting through paper panels, splintering wooden supports. The weapon encasing his right forearm erupts with a deafening roar. Bullets tear at bedsheets and bedding. Mere flesh would be ripped to tatters. But she is no longer there. She is a bedsheet flung into the air, twitching and twisting like a tortured ghost. She is a specter darting from shadow to shadow, tumbling, rolling away.

The killer snarls as if enraged by her deceit. He ducks as a lacquered *honoki*-wood sheath flies at his face like an arrow. He winces and jerks as the disk of a small hand mirror glances off his brow. The thunderous stammering roar of the gun skips a beat, then another, but the murderous barrage erupts anew.

The killer tracks her with computer-assisted precision.

Bullets rip at the lacquered floor and pastel-paneled walls so near her feet and back she feels splinters of wood raining against her skin. She is barely an instant ahead of the assassin's onslaught when abruptly she turns, her long, lustrous black hair swirling around her like a cape, the gleaming blade of her *katana* rising before her face, ready to meet the enemy head-on.

It is no ordinary blade. This blade, this sword comes from four *masume* steel bars, hammered, folded and welded into four million layers, then forged, shaped, ground and polished to a diamond dikote-tempered hardness by a master of the ancient Masamune technique. One blade may take months to fabricate, smith and mage working ever in concert. The result is as

strong a steel as the hand of metahumanity can forge—
strong and hard, yet pliant.

For rigidness is death, a dead hand. Brittle and weak.
The living hand must be pliant, like a leaf in springtime.

Poised, prepared, she pauses, motionless, an easy
target. The stammering autofire weapon zeros in at
once. A torrent of metal-jacketed shells stamped out by
spiritless machines clashes against her steel. The bullets blaze like fire, tracking toward her belly, her
breast, her throat. Always the sword is there, guarding,
defending, swaying like willows in a breeze, supple,
unhurried, deflecting the ruthless stream like so many
burning drops of rain.

Yadome-jutsu, it is called. Arrow cutting.

The killer roars as if possessed by outrage and disbelief, as if witnessing the impossible.

It is neither possible nor impossible. It goes beyond
luck or instinct, beyond talent and skill and rigorous
training. Beyond even magic. It is the Way and the
Way is the Void. Without thought, without feeling,
without intention or design. It is all and it is nothing
and it comes to her now as naturally as she breathes. It
is, the ancient masters would say, above all a matter of
timing.

In everything, there is timing. Even in the Void. And
the timing of the enemy is the essential element in all
battle.

And now, abruptly, the gun goes silent.

The killer grunts. His movements lay bare his mind.
He rushes to reload. No time. He snatches at a second
weapon. Too late. For she is already moving, flowing
forward like a wraith, breezing through clouds of harsh
gun-aroma, rising tall and large of spirit before the
killer's face.

The killer lifts one massive armored fist and out
snaps a gleaming steel spike, but this is irrelevant. It is
useless now.

For she sees the Way with perfect crystalline clarity
as never before in all her experience. And the Way is
death. The resolute acceptance of death. The warrior's
death. In this moment she may choose either life

or death and so she instantly chooses death, merciless death, reckless and uncompromising.

Death. Inevitable death.

The killer thrusts with his spike, but her *katana* rises, glaring like the summer moon on a rain-swept night.

The sword is her spirit, the spirit her sword, striking strongly, thrusting inexorably upward, piercing armor, metal, and bone, slicing through sternum and larynx, till finally the tip of the blade slides inside the killer's cranial vault.

The hands of the killer reach toward her—snapping, grasping, clenching—but she is already drifting away, an autumn leaf buoyed on a silken zephyr of wind . . .

With a flick—*chiburi*—she clears the blade of blood and gore.

Honoring the blade. Restoring its sheen. A young blade, no older than she who wields it. Bearing a polished pattern like the icy rains of the fall, a shower of silvery teardrops. The swordmaker's silent lament.

And the assassin falls, like a boneless husk.

A gentle, swift end.

MORE EXCITING ADVENTURES FROM
SHADWORUN®

YOUR OPINION CAN
MAKE A DIFFERENCE!
LET US KNOW WHAT *YOU* THINK.

Send this completed survey to us and enter a weekly drawing to win a special prize!

1.) Do you play any of the following role-playing games?
Shadowrun _____ Earthdawn _____ BattleTech _____

2.) Did you play any of the games before you read the novels?
Yes _____ No _____

3.) How many novels have you read in each of the following series?
Shadowrun _____ Earthdawn _____ BattleTech _____

4.) What other game novel lines do you read?
TSR _____ White Wolf _____ Other (Specify) _____

5.) Who is your favorite FASA author?
_____

6.) Which book did you take this survey from?
_____

7.) Where did you buy this book?
Bookstore _____ Game Store _____ Comic Store _____
FASA Mail Order _____ Other (Specify) _____

8.) Your opinion of the book (please print)
_____
_____
_____

Name _____ Age _____ Gender _____
Address _____
City _____ State _____ Country _____ Zip _____

Send this page or a photocopy of it to:
FASA Corporation
Editorial/Novels
1100 W. Cermak Suite B-305
Chicago, IL 60608